BLUE
WINDOW

BLUE WINDOW

Adina Rishe Gewirtz

CANDLEWICK PRESS

Copyright © 2018 by Adina Rishe Gewirtz

First edition 2018

Library of Congress Catalog Card Number 2014934185
ISBN 978-0-7636-6036-9

18 19 20 21 22 23 BVG 10 9 8 7 6 5 4 3 2 1

Printed in Berryville, VA, U.S.A.

This book was typeset in Adobe Jenson Pro.

Candlewick Press
99 Dover Street
Somerville, Massachusetts 02144

visit us at www.candlewick.com

In memory of my father,
who showed me how to look for windows.
And for the five who first went through.

Out of the longest night,

Into the age of wolves,

The five

Will come.

Strangers

Bringing hope of light.

Watch for them

When the time ripens

And the danger grows.

Wait then

For the opening

Of the window.

—Orchard Vision, Age of Anam, Ganbihar

✦ PROLOGUE ✦

If Max were to begin this story, he would tell you that one day science will discover the seams of the universe, the edges where things lie side by side, unnoticed until they bump together in the strangest ways. He would say that one day, someone brilliant, maybe even he, would know the reason for what unfolded that long winter's eve.

If Nell were to begin it, she would start, of course, with Mrs. Grady, the cheerful lady next door, who liked to tell her neighbors that if her kitchen light ever went out, she'd be gagged, bound, or possibly dead. This was, after all, why Nell was watching Mrs. Grady's window that night. Part of her hoped the light would go out, just to see what would happen.

If Kate or Jean were to begin, they'd say it started with an accident. So many things seem accidental when you're eight and seven, hours of the day pieced together like a patchwork quilt, one square fastened to the next because someone once discarded something colorful and someone else picked it up with needle in hand.

But it's Susan who begins this story, because Susan is the one who names things. She finds words for the summer wind that blows through before an afternoon storm or the awkward pause when you've forgotten what you wanted to say after beginning to say it. It's Susan who marks the texture of moments and wonders why they might mean what they do.

Though she loved the word *dusk*, which felt like smoke, and *evening*, which spoke of romance, Susan called the span between day and night *blue window time*. Somehow she knew the blue that filled the window was the essence of the hour, turning clouds into filigree and trees into lines, obscuring some things and revealing others. And perhaps it was the blue, after all, that last, stubborn hue clinging to the sky, that opened the door — or, in this case, the window.

◦ BOOK ONE ◦

SUSAN

Chapter 1

On the day before it all began, Susan found herself wishing mightily that she could melt into light-gray paint, which by no coincidence was the color of Ms. Clives's classroom wall. Lucy Driscoll was making a scene, and Susan stood at the center of it.

"But, Ms. Clives, you promised!" Lucy sobbed. "Don't you remember? You said I could be Juliet!"

Criminations! Susan thought. *Exactly what I deserve for opening my mouth.*

She stared out the window at the December sky, where the clouds had swallowed the sun. It winked feebly from beneath a smear of gray, looking half suffocated. Which was exactly how Susan felt, trapped up there in front of everyone as Lucy moved from sobs to conniptions. Five full minutes of it left Ms. Clives looking fatigued. She turned a pained and apologetic face to Susan.

"Susan? You don't mind, do you? And you can have a turn next time?"

Susan had only been waiting to get a word in edgewise anyway. Her cheeks were on fire, and she thought she'd combust if she had to stand near Lucy for another second.

"Of, of course not! That's okay!"

She darted to her seat, thinking that wild horses couldn't drag her back to the front of that room for another tryout. It was a phrase of her grandmother's she particularly liked. Wild horses and an eight-hundred-pound gorilla seemed to be the two things that could drag a person anywhere, at least according to Grandma. Susan was certain she could withstand both of them more easily than further drama from Lucy, along with the humiliating, gossipy glee the rest of the class took in watching the whole thing.

Unfortunately, thanks to Max, the scene wasn't over. The entire time Susan had been at the front of the room, her twin brother had been mouthing, "Stand up for yourself! Say something!" and she'd answered with the tiniest shake of her head. Now that she'd taken her seat, he began lecturing her in a low, insistent whisper. "You could at least say you worked for it! You don't have to act like you don't care! It's not just about you, anyway; it's about what's fair. . . ."

She turned and shot him a look hot enough to singe his eyebrows. Apparently, he was flameproof.

"I don't want to talk about it!" she hissed. "So stop already!"

Flameproof and deaf.

Max leaned forward, gripping the edges of his desk. "How long did you practice? All this week, remember? Lucy doesn't know the first thing about —"

"Max, do you have something to share with the class?"

It was Ms. Clives, glowering from the front of the room, tapping a purple manicured nail on her desk. Ms. Clives had started the year as one of those aggressively cheerful, pretty teachers the class tended to love — the kind that arranged the desks, including her own, into a circle so everyone could be friends. The kind that made Susan nervous, because in her experience, the Ms. Cliveses of the world generally lost their patience by about December. By winter break, all the cheerful good humor would have drained away, replaced by the temperament and patience of Godzilla. The worst of it would be the whiny, peeved reminders of the good old days back in September, when the kids had supposedly known how to behave.

Lucy Driscoll had moved the teacher perilously close to that point now, in Susan's estimation, and the look on Ms. Clives's face said it would be Max who pushed her over.

Max did not see the warning in the teacher's stiff posture and tapping fingers. He just shrugged and repeated what he'd said, along with a few other things of interest, while Susan withered in her seat and Lucy gulped air and shuddered. Susan sometimes thought that she and Max must be about the two least alike people in the world, especially for a set of twins. Make that the universe, since that was the scale on which Max tended to put things. He liked to argue over principles like Justice, and Rights, and Progress. Max's principles were always introduced in capital letters. At home, Susan argued right back. But despite the fact that her favorite books were all about spunky, outspoken girls who played as hard as the boys did, Susan abhorred having everyone look at her. The only trouble she ever got into was for reading under her desk, and that, along with slightly exasperated notes home — "If Susan only applied herself, she could be a real star in school. . . ." — was enough to manage. Max, on the other hand, had a habit of making a splash. He'd been doing it since they were both little: breaking things, playing too rough, having trouble sitting still. Lately, his splashes had to do with being taken seriously, a difficult thing for a bulky thirteen-year-old boy with a soft face, hair that sat like a dark, rumpled mountain range on top of his head, and theories that came out of reading *The Giant Book of Why.*

Susan wasn't interested in making other people see what they didn't want to, or couldn't. She only wanted to do her work and go home. She'd try, often, to make this point to Max after one school disaster or another, but he refused to get it. And he wasn't getting it now, despite the expression on Ms. Clives's face and the fact that Susan repeated his name three times in a low, urgent, you-will-pay-for-this-later-if-you-don't-stop-right-now type of voice.

Finally she had no choice but to speak up.

"Max, it's *okay!*" she said firmly. "I don't mind. Really, I don't!"

Ms. Clives's purple nails had been doing a drum solo on the desk.

"Max, your sister doesn't mind, and Lucy will do a wonderful job, too. The discussion is *over.*"

This time there was steel in her voice, and he subsided, grumbling. Lucy, tears all gone, made her way shakily to her seat. When she got there, she beamed at the teacher. "Thank you, Ms. C. I'll work really hard — I promise." She turned Susan's way and flashed a sudden, wicked grin. "And thank *you,* Susan."

"There, that's nice," Ms. Clives said, her voice tight with irritation. "I'm proud of both of you."

Susan closed her eyes. When she'd been little, younger even than Jean, she'd thought that if you closed your eyes, no one could see you. She wished it were true now. Either way, she wanted to block out the sight of Lucy's smug face, and Max's outraged one, too.

But she couldn't settle. She had the strangest feeling someone was waiting to ask her a question.

She opened her eyes and frowned at her brother.

"What?"

He frowned right back. "*Now* you talk? I didn't say anything."

"Well, stop looking at me, then."

"I wasn't looking. And you're not in charge of my eyes, now, are you?"

Ms. Clives shot a warning look their way, and Susan didn't answer.

Susan was still smarting as she and Max got off at the bus stop and started walking home. She trudged along the street in a coat that had once fallen to her knees but now was at least two inches short. It would swallow Nell, though, so she'd kept it for one more year. Beneath it, her skirt blew against her legs, which had gone red with the cold. She was on her way to getting tall, and lately her body had begun to stretch into unfamiliar angles and lines. She wasn't used to it and so preferred to focus on what was the same: same slightly messy, loose brown curls; same pointy chin; same blue eyes. They were her secret favorite, sky blue and just the shade of her grandfather's. Her eyes made her feel like she belonged somewhere, and she liked that.

Right now she felt like she belonged nowhere at all. Even the street seemed unfamiliar, changed with the first snowfall.

The remains of it had begun to turn brown at the curb, and when the wind blew, a grimy mist rose from it before settling back across her boots. Overhead, an oak tree full of stubborn, dead leaves chafed in the wind.

Susan glanced at Max, who usually had something meteorological to say as they walked home. This time, he only shook his head at her.

"You should have said something."

She rolled her eyes. "Like *you* always stand up for yourself? I saw Ivan and Mo in the hall after class. I heard what they called you."

He wouldn't meet her eye.

"That's different. Ms. Clives doesn't threaten to kick the smart out of you if you stand up for yourself. She can be reasonable, not like those two idiots."

Susan shook her head. "You could tell someone. You don't have to put up with it all the time."

Max sighed. "I'm not a *girl*, Susan."

She was about to say that no, girls were more reasonable, when Nell rounded the corner to prove her wrong. Max and Nell swore up and down that the two of them were opposites, and it was true they looked nothing alike. Nell was small for eleven years old, with intense blue eyes a shade darker than Susan's and the round, freckled face of a pixie, though only the stupidest people had the nerve to tell her that. But looks were deceiving, because inside, Nell was just as full of big ideas as Max was, and just as certain she knew how to make them happen.

Their particular sameness usually meant that Nell and Max sat on each other's very last nerve, a pattern that only changed when they turned their mutual energy to analyzing what had gone wrong with Susan. Susan wondered now if the two of them had radar communication set up on the subject, because as soon as Nell jogged up, she looked from one to the next and raised an eyebrow.

"What's wrong?"

"Susan," Max shot back.

"Nothing," Susan snapped.

Nell zigzagged up the road, pouncing on every half-decent snow pile that remained in the street as Max replayed the afternoon for her. When he was done, Nell nodded sagely.

"You let people push you around too much," she informed Susan.

"She's the *teacher*," Susan protested. "I couldn't say anything. Why would I even want to?"

"I said something!" Max cut in.

A chilly wind whistled past Susan's ears and set them tingling.

"I should have clobbered you before you did," she grumbled, rubbing the feeling back into her ears with a gloved hand. "I still should."

Nell ambushed another lump of dirty snow, splattering Susan's exposed leg.

"Bad temper in all the wrong places," she said. "That's you. If anyone deserves a clobbering, it's Lucy Driscoll."

She frowned suddenly and turned around. "Hey!"

"Hey what?" Max asked.

Nell tilted her head. "That's juvenile, Max."

"What is?"

"Tapping me from behind and pretending you didn't."

"I didn't."

Nell's frown deepened. "Susan, did you?"

"No!"

"Well, somebody did. And whichever of you it was, just stop it."

Max hitched his backpack higher onto his shoulder. His puffy coat sighed under the weight of it.

"Maybe it was some of that snow you keep flattening, hitting back," he suggested.

"Yeah, right." Nell looked over her shoulder again, brow furrowed.

Susan felt suddenly antsy, as if she'd forgotten something she'd been supposed to remember. But then it had been a strange day, full of wishing she could fly out the classroom window, or at least turn invisible. She tried to shrug it off and set her mind to getting home and finding her book, the only proven way, so far, of disappearing.

She did just that for most of the evening and went to bed early, hoping sleep would wash away the mortification of the day.

"Susan? I had a funny dream again."

Susan squinted in the sudden light from the hall and glanced at the clock. Past midnight, and Kate stood there in her nightgown, waiting.

At eight, Kate was too old to be waking her parents but apparently not too old to be waking her big sister. This big sister, anyway, who had a soft spot for pensive eight-year-olds with bad dreams. *Pensive.* That word had been a find, and one Susan had immediately applied to Kate. It seemed to fit them both, and maybe that's why they got along so well. Being pensive, at eight or thirteen, always kept you a half step out of the main. For Susan, who would rather read than talk, and Kate, who seemed to hear things differently than other people did, *pensive* was just the right word. Susan rolled over and nodded to the small figure standing in the doorway, Kate's unruly curls lit by the light of the hall. They were sandy brown, a shade lighter than her eyes, and gave the impression of being lighter still, the color of amber or honey.

"Funny how? Scary? Were there monsters?"

A long pause from Kate, until Susan waved her in, permission to climb into bed beside her. The mattress bounced and Kate slipped under the covers. Susan could feel her sister's bony little body, warm against her.

"Not monsters. And I don't think I was scared. But I was someplace different. And there were other people there. I could hear them."

Susan yawned. Sleep was tugging at her.

"And? What did they look like?"

Kate sighed in the darkness. She rolled over and threw an arm across Susan. "They were gone when I turned around. I think the splashing scared them off."

"Splashing?"

"My feet were in the water."

"Oh."

Susan waited, but Kate didn't elaborate. She was that kind of kid, always dreaming of strange places and people calling from out of thick trees. Susan wondered if she ought to tell Mom.

Kate lifted her head slightly, and her hair brushed the

bottom of Susan's jaw. "I wasn't scared," she said. Kate had a knack for reading her intention even in the dark, and somehow, with Kate, Susan didn't mind. "You don't have to worry about it." Kate waited, head up, for Susan to answer.

"But you wanted to come in here anyway, I guess?"

Kate rested her head back on Susan's arm.

"Just for a little," she said drowsily. "And besides, Jean was talking in her sleep."

Susan smiled. Sleep, warm and comfortingly heavy, crept over her again, and she closed her eyes. "Maybe she was having funny dreams, too."

She fell back to sleep thinking what an odd twenty-four hours it had been. She swore to herself tomorrow would be different.

She was usually very good at keeping her word.

*T*he exile found company only in dreams. Beneath tall, unfamiliar trees, others would appear: a sunny-haired girl who sat on the edge of a shining pool, her bare feet in the water. Another, darker, older, who stood in the dappled shade, eyes on the blazing sky.

The ancients had spoken of a place outside time, a whispering orchard, a sparkling wood, a dream that lived. And yet if they had spent nights walking its paths of wisdom, the exile was given just moments, flashes that drifted away with the dawn.

What was to be found on waking? Only the hard sky over the mountain, the cottage, the trees, the garden, and the ever-present muttering of the valley, with its undertone of warning, its reminder of punishment. Few came through it, and those only reinforced the solitude — watchers, radiating judgment harsh as summer heat, and the broken ones, who screamed their agony into the wind before disappearing through the trees, beyond help or hope.

The sounds of exile were few. No voices, no words.

Speech now was folded into books, the aging pages polished by the turning of many hands. In the silence, the exile clung to these pages, with their smell of years, their prophecies of doom and of promise.

Doom had come. The exile waited now for the promise.

Chapter 2

Do you know how much electricity gets used on the shortest day of the year?" Max asked Susan as he mixed his instant oatmeal at the kitchen counter the next morning.

Susan raised an eyebrow at him. This was Max's peace offering, she knew, a useful bit of information that he thought would cheer her up.

"Don't you mean longest night of the year?"

"Same thing."

"Not exactly."

"Well, fine. Longest night, then."

She decided to accept his apology.

"No, how much?"

She scooted over on the kitchen bench to make room for him. Their house was old, and the kitchen seemed older than the rest of it. The short Formica-topped table jutted out from the window, and two benches sat on either side of it, a setup that Dad said was like a diner at a truck stop. To get in or out of the seats closest to the window required climbing over one or two siblings or the high back of the bench, which sat only about half a foot from the side of the fridge. And yet Susan favored it. She loved to sit by the window and rest her head against the cool glass.

Max grinned as he sat down. "Five thousand megawatts. But of course that's an estimate. But guess when people use even more? In summer. Guess why? Air-conditioning. *Much* more wasteful than lights. Or at least it was last time I checked."

Outside, the snow was melting. December never seemed sure it was really winter, no matter what the calendar said, and the day had dawned unexpectedly sunny. Susan pressed her forehead into the glass. Still cold enough to ease the ache there from having an interrupted night's sleep.

"You okay, Susan?" Mom asked her. She had come into the kitchen with Kate's backpack, which always managed to get left behind when it was time to go to school.

"Just tired," Susan said. She didn't mention why.

"Me, too," Max said. "I feel like last night lasted longer than normal."

"Ha-ha," Susan said.

"No, I mean it. Like it was full of dreams. And not my usual ones."

"What, no spaceships involved?" Mom asked. She plopped a carton of orange juice down on the table, followed by two small glasses. "Drink up — you'll feel better."

"More like a lot of trees," Max said, pouring himself some juice. "No idea why. Maybe it's because I'm taking earth science."

The word *dreams* pinged like a small bell in Susan's mind. She paused, thinking of Kate, then for a moment had the hazy feeling that she'd seen . . . she didn't know what. It evaporated as soon as she focused her attention on it. She shook her head. She almost never remembered dreams, anyway. Probably it was only her imagination, filling things in for her. She poured herself some juice.

Jean came in then, climbing up to sit across from Susan at the table. She set her Barbie doll next to her cereal bowl.

"Kate!" she called. "Barbie's ready for breakfast! See?" She showed Max. "She's a birthday Barbie."

He looked distinctly uninterested.

"She was born in a factory," Max said. "I doubt she has a birthday."

Jean wrinkled her nose. "It's for pretend, Max," she said. "And so she can have a pretty dress."

She admired the dress for another minute before standing up to pour herself some cereal, giving Barbie a shower of cornflakes at the same time.

"You'll get her dirty!" Kate said from the doorway. She carried her own matching doll, which she held against her chest. "And you said you'd keep her nice!"

"We'll give them baths tonight," Jean told her. "And maybe a haircut. That's part of getting ready for the party."

"No haircuts," Kate said, looking alarmed.

Susan grinned into her orange juice. Jean had recently restyled one of her skirts (it needed to be shorter), a pair of new shoes (she didn't like the straps), and her own hair. Where she'd once had longish dark waves, she now had a short bob and bangs that fell half an inch above her winged eyebrows. She'd been on her way to convincing Kate to let her give her a trim when Mom confiscated the scissors.

"Well, a bath, anyway," Jean conceded.

Susan watched Max roll his eyes, and Jean grinned across the table at him.

"Max, write me a letter."

Max gave Susan a sidelong glance that begged sympathy for his long suffering.

"Not now."

"Please? A short one."

"I don't have a piece of paper."

"Letters" was a favorite game of Jean's, which she'd devised after having received one from Grandpa the year he'd been on a trip and missed her fifth birthday. She'd heartily agreed with him that messages on paper lasted longer than a phone call. She'd then gone on a campaign to get everyone to write her letters, and in a fit of generosity, Max had made the mistake of complying.

"Say one, then. Like, pretend you're reading it."

Max grunted, but Susan knew that for all his bluster, he wouldn't refuse her. He rarely did.

"Dear Jean, Enjoy your breakfast. Your brother, Max."

Jean beamed at him, and Max drained his juice and finished his oatmeal in silence.

Nell joined them last of all. She, too, looked like she'd had a long night. She glanced moodily out the window. "I wish it would snow again," she said. "Then I could sleep late."

"It's a short day," Susan told her. "It'll be night before you know it."

And it was. Before the afternoon was half over, the sky had turned a deep, evening blue. Susan went into the family room and stood by the big window, looking out at Mrs. Grady's house next door. It had been another peculiar day. Standing near her locker at lunchtime, she'd been sure someone was looking over her shoulder, waiting for her to turn. When she did, nobody was there. It had made her feel funny again, off-kilter.

They all seemed to feel it. On the way home, Max and Nell had kept silent. They were so quiet at supper that Dad put his hand on everybody's foreheads, but no one had a fever.

"Winter blahs," he concluded. "And it's only the first day."

Susan did what she always did when she felt unsettled. She found a book. But before she opened it, she stood at the family-room window and watched Mrs. Grady's ever-present kitchen light filter through the colored figurines in the window across the way.

Mrs. Grady did not believe in curtains, a fact Susan knew well because Mrs. Grady was a woman who liked to announce her likes and dislikes as if she were carrying a bullhorn. Collecting the Gradys' garbage cans one day, Susan had been stopped by the pronouncement that horizontal stripes would never again be a part of Mrs. Grady's wardrobe; apparently they made her behind look like a beach ball. Curtains had been the subject of at least three separate bulletins, because according to Mrs. Grady, despite her disapproval of them, *Mr.* Grady insisted on them. Susan doubted this. She'd barely ever heard the man say a word, let alone voice an opinion. Insisting on something seemed a stretch.

But it was true that all the Gradys' windows were covered except this one, in the kitchen, the one filled with colored glass. For a second more, Susan stood looking into the blue, at the hazy rainbow that glimmered in the space between the houses.

Then she opened her book.

Because she was reading, she didn't much note when the others came in. She was only half aware of Max sitting down at the table to do his homework. She did look up when Nell came in, wrapped in a blanket cocoon. But that was only because Nell plopped down beside her on the old maroon sofa, letting her blanket fall across the pages of Susan's book.

"Hey!" Susan said.

Nell shot her a look. Susan huffed and retreated to the table, her back to the window. Kate and Jean trooped in then, their matching Barbies fresh from the promised bath and once again dressed for a party. They sat down on the floor and began to play.

And this was the moment the curious feeling that had nudged Susan for two days blossomed into something more.

On the couch, Nell bolted upright, letting her blanket cocoon fall open.

"It's out! Mrs. Grady's light's gone!"

Max didn't turn.

"She's probably blown a fuse," he said. He shot a wry half grin at Susan. "But let's call the police anyway. I'd love to see her face when they come."

Susan twisted around in her chair to look and blinked in surprise. It wasn't just the light.

The whole square of Mrs. Grady's lit kitchen had disappeared, and their own window now glowed a brilliant cobalt that drew the last of the light into it and pushed it back again. The glass seemed to curve outward, a dark mirror casting their faces back in shimmering curves.

In reflection, the room looked oddly out of shape. Susan swiveled back to see it and found everything in place — family pictures on the wall, the old couch, the overstuffed recliner, the long oval table. She glanced at Max, who was still bent over his homework, his back to the window. Kate and Jean had noticed, though. Gripping their Barbies, they had gotten up to gape at the glass.

Susan could almost feel the pulse of the glowing light behind her. She turned back to it.

"Max," she said quietly. "Look."

Her tone must have caught him, because he didn't argue. He turned, drew in a sharp breath, and stood up.

"What in the world?"

Susan took a step toward the window and tried to peer through the reflection. On the other side of the glass, Mrs. Grady was indeed gone. Her window, her kitchen, the old grill, the stairs — the neighborhood itself seemed to have winked out of existence. In its place stood a wide old tree, black as a charcoal drawing against blue glass.

"That can't be," Susan said.

"What happened to it? Did something explode?" Nell asked. Cautiously, she crept from the couch to stand beside the twins, clutching her blanket around her neck.

"I didn't hear anything," Kate said.

"Explosions leave a pile of house," Max told them. "This is more like an optical illusion. Maybe somebody's playing a practical joke on us. You know, beaming something at the glass."

Susan thought for a minute, then ran to the bathroom, with its small window that faced Mrs. Grady's kitchen. Outside, the colored glass still glowed from the other house as the neighborhood settled placidly into the night. She squinted into the evening light, looking for Max's practical joker, but there was no one. Puzzled, she walked back into the family room. The others hadn't moved. They all stood staring at the window. It smoldered like a blue coal.

"It's normal out there when I look from the bathroom."

"And did you see who's doing it?" Max asked her.

"No one is. No one's outside."

"Makes no sense. It's got to be an optical illusion."

"Why does it bend out like that?" Jean asked. She came around the table and past them, her hand extended toward the window.

"Don't!" Nell said. "It could burn you!"

Max shook his head. "Do you feel any heat coming off it? Optical illusions don't burn." He followed Jean to the window.

Jean leaned up on the sill and poked at the blue curve with her Barbie. The doll's blond hair sank into the glass like a waffle dipped in syrup.

"Wow!" Max said. "That's some trick." He poked the glass, too, and his finger disappeared in blue up to the knuckle.

They all had to try it then. They climbed onto the wide sill, probing the window with hands, resting cheeks on it. On the other side, the sky was the same deep blue they'd seen over Mrs. Grady's house, but where her house should have been, the lone tree now stirred in a faint wind.

As she had in the morning, Susan pressed her forehead to the glass. This time it was warm — soft as wax left in the sun.

She pulled back, startled, then cautiously leaned in again.

The window dissolved.

Susan pitched forward with a gasp. The others toppled on either side of her, Max hiccupping with surprise, Nell grabbing her blanket as it unrolled and released her into open air, Kate and Jean letting the sleek pink Barbies fly from their hands into the dusky sky.

Susan landed on all fours in the grass beneath the tree,

and it was summer grass, thick with the smell of growing and damp with the settling night. Across a wide expanse, she could see the dark edge of a forest.

Her brain seemed to stutter in her head, and for a moment it was emptied of words.

Nell didn't have that problem.

"*This* is an optical illusion?" she gasped, sitting up and brushing grass from her hands. "Remind me what *optical* means again?"

Max didn't answer. He just gawked.

"Wow," Kate said, looking around. "How did we do *that?*"

Just in front of Susan, Jean rolled to her feet and stood up.

"Our window's still there!"

Susan turned to look as Jean scooted over to collect her Barbie. Soon they were all standing, squinting upward.

Above them, Nell's blanket hung from a rectangle of light, a cloth waterfall tumbling from a boxy sun.

"Come on!" Nell said. "We can climb!"

Words flooded back into Susan's head, the primary one being *home*. By the light of the window, she saw Max look with interest at the strange landscape around them, and a fresh surge of panic brought her voice back.

"Come on, Max! We've got to get back up there!"

He hesitated, then glanced at the little girls and nodded. Nell had already grabbed the bottom of the blanket, and now Max did, too, putting out a foot to brace himself against the wall that must be there. But there was no wall, and after a moment, no window, either, because with a sharp *pop*, the blanket came loose, fluttering down upon them. The light blinked out.

The window was gone.

Chapter 3

Nell might look something like an elf, but nobody could accuse her of sounding like one. Susan often complained that standing next to Nell when she yelled felt like being blasted by a train whistle, or a rocket launch. She was grateful for it now, though, when Nell opened her mouth and started hollering for Mom and Dad. Nobody within a block's distance could fail to hear Nell when she really tried.

"MOM! DAD! COME TO THE WINDOW!"

Nell paused, and they all waited. No response.

Everyone joined in for the second round, screaming themselves hoarse. Susan thought that if Mrs. Grady hadn't had apoplexy when her kitchen disappeared, she'd definitely be calling the police now.

But not even an echo answered them. Their calls died on the wind of the strange, empty field, lost in the border of the distant wood.

Finally, they collapsed beneath the tree, stunned into silence.

Darkness had truly fallen by then. It was not the darkness Susan knew, pocked with streetlights and friendly, bright-eyed houses, sliced through with the headlights of moving cars and the occasional taillights of an airplane overhead. This was a tar-black curtain, mottled by the blotted shapes of the far-off wood.

Above, stars glittered like crushed glass.

"There are so many of them!" Kate said. "Are there always so many?"

Susan had never seen such a sky. She searched for the Three Sisters, the line of stars that sat in Orion's Belt, but she could not make out a single familiar constellation.

"They look different because there aren't any city lights. Those hide most stars," Max said. "It's called light pollution." This last he added only faintly. His voice dribbled to nothing beneath the shock of that strange sky. In the tree, crickets chirped sleepily.

"It's so different," Susan said. "Maybe you're right — maybe we can't see the ones we know because there are too many."

Max was breathing at least twice his normal speed. "No," he murmured back. "That's not it. The sky's all wrong. Just like the ground is. Where *are* we?"

A small hand prodded Susan's. She squeezed it. Kate.

Susan's eyes began to adjust, and she could see the shape of Nell, a foot or so away. It looked strangely humped and bulky until she realized that Nell had retrieved her blanket from the ground and wrapped it around her shoulders despite the warmth of the night.

"This has to be a dream," Nell said. "But it doesn't feel like one. Does it?"

"Is it usually this dark in dreams?" Jean asked. Her voice came from next to Max.

"Maybe we're drugged, or sprayed with some gas that makes you see things. They can do that, you know," Max said.

"They?" Susan asked. She could feel the damp in the grass soaking through her sneakers. "Who's they?"

Max sighed. "I don't know. But if this is real, we just fell out of our house into summer."

None of them said anything for a long minute.

"Ouch!" Max yelped. "Jean! Did you just pinch me?"

"Maybe."

"You did! You pinched me!"

Jean's voice was a little smaller than usual. "I thought you can't get hurt in dreams."

"Where do you get this stuff, Jean? Of course you can get hurt in dreams! You might be lying on the corner of a book or something. Your brain would make up a story where you got pinched, when really you've got a hardback jabbing you!"

"So maybe you're just lying on a book, then."

Max growled in exasperation, and Susan saw him lean over in the dark and pull a strand of grass, then put it to his mouth.

"I don't know. Can you taste in dreams? I can't remember."

Susan knew she'd never had a dream as vivid as this. She could smell the dusty aroma of tree bark and hear the faint hum of crickets.

"What should we do?" Kate wanted to know. "If we're dreaming, I want to wake up and go home."

She squeezed Susan's hand, and Susan squeezed back.

"Me, too," Nell said. She slapped her own face. "Wake up!" She paused, then grunted in dissatisfaction. "I'm still here. And for your information, Jean, you *can* get hurt in dreams."

"So you're saying this is a dream," Max said.

"Yes," Nell answered. "Maybe. I don't know!"

Susan touched the rough trunk of the tree. The smell of

grass and heat and wood hung in the air. In the distance, an owl hooted, low and long. No, she thought again, dreams couldn't possibly feel like this. Kate pressed herself close, and Susan tried to think what to say. She was the oldest by a few minutes, but in emergencies, she never forgot it. Now she could only think to try to keep the younger ones calm while she and Max figured out what had happened.

"We need to go to sleep, and *then* we'll wake up," she told them, using her most sensible tone of voice. Sometimes, she knew, when all else failed, it was best to return to routine. Maybe if they acted as if things were normal, the world would take the hint.

She released Kate's hand. "Nell, give us your blanket," she said.

Nell hesitated, then unwrapped the coverlet from around her neck and handed it over.

Susan spread it beneath the tree.

"If we all lie down together, close our eyes, and forget all this, we'll wake up in the morning and be back home."

Max, still staring up at the star-drenched sky, didn't answer. But the little girls lay down, and Susan tucked their dolls beside them. Even Nell, after folding her arms long enough to show she didn't take orders, especially concerning bedtime, finally joined them, and Susan found a spot next to her. As the others' breathing slowly deepened in sleep, Susan held still, wide awake and watching. In the tree, the whistling of the crickets dwindled. The moon rose, and at last Max crouched beside her.

"It's only half," he whispered. "And at home it was full. Do *you* think it's a dream?"

"I don't know," she whispered back. "I don't think I've ever dreamed the moon before. But maybe morning will tell."

At last, with nothing left to do, Max stretched out on the other side of the blanket. Together they lay there, staring at the vast, strange sky, as overhead, the too-narrow moon climbed to its distant midnight perch.

*D*eprived of the comfort of human voices, the exile had learned to hear the sounds of the mountain. Not merely the mumbling danger of the valley, but the melody of birds and wind, buzzing insects and small animals. And the steadiness of these sounds as they rose and fell, chittered and hummed and sighed in their unconscious conversation, offered a comfort of its own, its steady backdrop a reminder that life went on.

And then, one night, the sounds stopped.

From within the cottage, the exile rose and sought the darkness outside. Beneath the stars, the world had gone silent. Even the valley, far below, seemed mute in the pause. And then something stirred. A strange breeze, a new wind. A moment more, and the world let out its breath — as if all the small animate members of the night's chorus had sensed the new and made it welcome.

Chapter 4

Susan opened her eyes to a haze of dew rising toward a pink sky. It would have been beautiful if she'd seen it through a car window or from inside her own house. But she was lying on a clammy blanket in a strange field on a summer morning, when it should have been winter and had been, just last night. Despite what she'd said, they'd slept, and woken, and if this were a dream, it was real enough to leave the blanket damp and smelling of grass. She closed her eyes again and wished herself fiercely into a different morning, but the sound of birds twittering in the tree told her this place was immune to wishes.

On the other side of Nell, Kate sat up and looked around. "We're not home," she said. "You said we'd be home!"

Pretending to be asleep struck Susan as her best option, but her heart betrayed her. It was pounding so hard, she could feel her shirt move.

On the other side of the blanket, Max groaned and sat up. "Kate," he said. "Calm down."

"But we're supposed to be home!"

"I didn't say that. Susan did."

Criminations! It was the last little push Susan needed to force herself into the day. She sat up.

"I said *maybe*, is all. *Maybe* we'd wake up home. But we haven't. So we're going to need to figure something else out."

"You did not say maybe," Kate said. "You said we *would*."

Her tight curls had gone frizzy in the humid morning, and they stood out in several directions. She pushed them out of her eyes and frowned deeply.

"That's true," Max said. "You did."

Susan glared at him. "Fine, maybe I did. But we're not home. Sue me."

Kate looked around at the steaming grass, the dark border of woods that ringed the field, the hard knot of the rising sun swimming up into a candy-colored sky, and began to cry.

"Kate! Kate, it's okay!" Susan leaned on Nell and grabbed Kate's hand. "We're going to figure this out! We will!"

Nell woke with a grunt and shoved Susan off her. Meanwhile, Kate nodded, trying to swallow the tears as her curls bounced crazily on her head. Jean sat up, looking groggy.

"We're still here," she said.

Max sighed loudly and rubbed the back of his neck. "We've noticed. But don't worry, we're working on it."

He nodded to Susan, who attempted a half-hearted nod back.

The little girls looked from one to the other of them expectantly, and even Nell tilted her head, waiting.

"Let's think about this scientifically," Max said.

There were days when Susan hated having a twin brother. Today wasn't one of them. Just hearing Max talk in his usual Max-like way made Susan breathe better. Max's scientific ideas were sometimes harebrained, but he never ran out of them.

"What would we do if we got lost at home?" he asked.

"Find help," Susan said.

"Right. So let's go find it. We're somewhere. Let's find out where."

Trees ringed the field on all sides. To the west, where a sheen of purple still glossed the sky, a herd of deer meandered from the wood and began to graze. Jean tapped Kate and pointed, and Susan raised an eyebrow. At least twenty soon ambled out, including several speckled fawns.

Just then a hawk screeched from the western wood, and Susan looked up to see it dive over the deer and yank a rabbit from the grass. Kate yelped as the herd bolted back into the trees.

"Well, not that way," Max said, frowning. "Doesn't seem like that many deer would be wandering around civilization."

"Civilization?" Jean asked him. "That's what we're looking for?"

"Yup," he said. "It's got to be around here somewhere."

He nodded eastward, as Jean and Kate retrieved their Barbies and Nell shouldered her blanket. "That way, then."

They set out in the direction of the rising sun, scattering butterflies feeding on flowers and sending a surviving rabbit hurtling from a thicket of onion grass. Near the place where the clearing met the wood, the land dipped and they found a brook bubbling along through stones and moss. Overjoyed, Max said that water led to civilization—people, and commerce, and cities. Jean stooped to drink, but Susan pointed out that water could lead to typhoid, too, so Jean let it be and they walked along the bank, following the water as it flowed glibly over rocks and through small cracks, beneath a split tree, and on as the wood grew tangled and the heat rose.

Having read countless fairy tales, Susan looked for a forest trail, good for walking. But there were no mossy paths here, no faint track left by kind hunters or red-hooded girls who brought fresh bread to their grandmothers. There was no path at all. Nets of slim green vines, narrow as string, obscured rocks underfoot; tall stalks coated in sharp, translucent hairs grew knee- and waist-high; and bristling shrubs the dusty color of evergreens grew so wide and dense, they could not be pushed aside and had to be circumvented.

"This isn't that much different from a hike I took with the Boy Scouts," Max said reassuringly. "We're okay."

Susan rolled her eyes.

Nell pushed back her moist bangs. "Didn't you come home with a concussion from one of those?" she asked him. "And poison ivy?"

Susan flicked her sister's arm, trying to get her to be quiet, but like Max, Nell was immune to suggestion.

Instead, she told Susan not to be so annoying, and they stomped along in silence for a while as Susan counted the ways they irritated one another.

As far as annoyances went, from Susan's point of view the long walk was full of them. Four times they had to stop when Jean or Kate lost her Barbie in the weeds. The fifth time Susan found herself fishing a doll out of a knot of prickly, looping vines, she jammed both Barbies into the backs of the girls' waistbands and yanked their shirts over the offending dolls so their plastic hands and hair would stop catching in the undergrowth. Nell, meanwhile, had tied her blanket round her like a belt and kept snagging on broken twigs and low-hanging branches. Jean refused to use a tree for a bathroom until she was so desperate she was hopping, and Kate remembered suddenly that Nell had once told her your teeth fall out if you don't brush them, which made her frantic until Susan explained hyperbole to her. Nell then marched ahead in a huff—"I *never* exaggerate!" And despite his Boy Scout comment, Max kept mentioning how strange some of the fauna was and surmising that this must be some kind of winter heat wave, because who falls out of a window into a new season?

And then, every once in a while, the underbrush would rustle as if something bigger than a rabbit was pushing through it and Susan would catch sight of a hulking dark shape streaking through the trees.

"You don't think there are any dangerous animals around here, do you?" Nell whispered to her.

Susan shook her head. "Probably more deer. They're fast like that, right?"

She said it as much to convince herself as Nell. She'd had only the briefest glimpses of the thing, but it had seemed far taller than a deer. Susan picked her way through a thorny patch, her winter shirt clinging to her damp skin, and tried to think what she'd read about being lost in the woods. Stay put—that was the rule. Make a lot of noise. That last she knew couldn't apply here. Not with that flicker of darkness in the trees.

"I think there are bears here," Jean said. "And bears eat people, right?"

Nell fanned herself with one hand.

"There aren't any bears here."

"But I think I saw one."

"Shut up, Jean."

"Max! Nell said shut up!"

"Shut up, Nell."

The day wore on, and there seemed no end to the thick woods. Eventually the brook they were tracking branched in several directions, and then the trickle they followed dwindled until it was no more than a small gush of water over stones. Finally the earth took it, leaving only a shallow depression in the ground where rain might find its way. Still they walked on, keeping east, until Susan began to feel that she was full of holes — a gaping emptiness in her stomach and a hollow, fear-chewed spot in her chest. Every so often Kate took her hand, until their palms were so grubby they lost their grip on each other.

"We're almost there, right, Susan? We're going to find someone soon?" Kate asked her.

"Right," Susan said, trying to make herself sound sure.

"Right really, or right, you think so?"

"Right really."

"You're sure?"

"I'm sure."

But how could she be sure? She could only try to sound it, because as usual Kate heard every microsecond of hesitation in conversation, took note of the smallest wrinkle between her eyes, and caught that almost frown she was about to make in annoyance before she stopped herself. Kate's watchfulness drove Nell absolutely batty, and to be honest, that was one of the things Susan liked best about it, usually. But not here, not now. Now Susan needed to be unafraid and sure.

She was neither.

Chapter 5

The stone wall was so overgrown, they nearly smacked into it before they saw it. Long ropy vines crisscrossed the stones and bloomed in the crevices, but it was a wall, man-made and very old by the look of it.

"Civilization!" Max said. "I told you!"

They moved around it, trying to find a way in. The wall stood at least eight feet tall and cut through the woods in a wide, unbroken curve.

"Let's climb it," Nell said. "Look at these vines! They'll hold us!"

She grabbed one and hoisted herself up, jabbing the tip of her shoe into the stonework.

The rest of them followed her, groaning and nearly losing their grip, but the growth was so thick, it held.

"Wow!" Nell called when she reached the top. "Max, wait until you see this!"

On the other side, an orchard of peach and plum trees spread out in genteel rows.

Susan swung over the wall, eased herself down to the other side, and dropped to the ground. It was covered in moss and clover studded with round-headed white blossoms. The trees in the nearest row were full of peaches.

She grabbed one and tugged. It dropped into her hand, red and orange and perfect.

"Here!" She tossed a fruit to Kate, then another to Jean. Soon the juice was slipping down their chins and making their hands sticky.

"Civilization." Max sighed. "Finally."

"Civilization tastes great," Jean said. "I never knew."

Susan picked several extra peaches and shoved them into her skirt pocket.

"We'd better look for the owners," she said. "I'm sure we'll find some people now."

The aroma of hot peaches clung to the air beneath the trees. They walked along, and Max peered up at the branches. He shook his head.

"I don't think peach trees are this big at home," he said. "Fruit trees are usually shorter."

Susan tried to ignore him. She didn't want this place to be odd or puzzling. It was an orchard, and that meant people, and help, and getting home soon.

And yet the place was strange. Whoever had done the planting had definitely neglected the harvest. Flies lit on mounds of rotting fruit. Wormy peaches littered the space between the trees.

She reached the end of the row and saw why. Past a short clearing full of white clover and moss stood the ruins of what must have been a huge stone house. Only the outer wall remained, and only the lower half of that. It framed a square full of charred gray stones half covered by climbing weeds. The children stepped through a space that might have once been a back door and walked among the jumbled remains.

"Guess they had a fire," Nell said. "And left it."

Susan bent and ran a finger across a mossy stone.

Max examined the ground.

"But how long ago?" he asked. "There's nothing but stone left. No wood, even. A house would have probably had some wood in it."

Kate and Jean had climbed to sit on the half wall and rest their legs. Nell slouched to a seat beside it, her head against the stones.

"How old can it be if the trees are still so full?" she asked. "Wouldn't some of them have died or something?"

None of them had an answer for that. Susan sank to her knees and tried to fold her arms across the wall. She only wanted to rest a minute, but the stones were too hot against her bare skin. She sighed and leaned back onto her heels.

"Hey," Kate said suddenly. "Is that singing?"

Susan raised her head. "Where?"

Her sister pointed at a line of plum trees on the far side of the orchard. "That way. Can't you hear it?"

For a moment, Susan heard nothing but a chorus of enthusiastic cicadas. Then she caught the sound of a girl's voice.

Swiftly, she climbed over the short wall and headed back into the trees. The others followed. The voice petered out, but Jean and Kate ran ahead in its general direction, and the rest of them were right behind. Halfway down the row, they heard the girl take up her song again from somewhere up among the plums.

"*Genius has but one command:*
Useful hands, useful hands.
Work the day long, work the land,
With your two good useful hands."

Susan looked for her. The plums hung in great clusters of red and purple, obscuring the view, but after a moment, she caught a flash of red trim, the stained hem of a long-hanging dress. The girl had perched a basket on one of the lower branches, and from above it, fruit rained down, hitting the wicker in a rhythm that punctuated the song.

"With useful hands come bang the drum!
With useful hands does progress come!"

She had a funny accent. For a second, Susan wondered if she was singing in a different language. But she couldn't have been, since the words were perfectly plain:

"Clear the old, the worn, the low.
The new day dawns! The past must go.
The bounty waits for the brave and sure,
A prize for the useful and the pure."

Susan circled the base of the tree, trying to get a look at the singer.

"Excuse me?" she called into the leaves. "Hello?"

The girl stopped singing abruptly. In the sudden hush, the cicadas trilled a small chorus of alarm.

The silence stretched for a long minute.

"Hey, there!" Nell called suddenly, smacking the trunk with her hand. "We can see you up there! Could we ask you a question?"

This time the girl did answer. Her voice came nervously from the green shadows. "Who's that?" she asked. "Purity?"

Susan guessed that must be some friend of hers. "No," she said. "Sorry, we're lost. You don't live around here, do you?"

There was a small release of breath from above, and when she spoke this time, the girl sounded confident and a little surly.

"Who's asking?"

She began to climb down. "And just so you know, this place is spoken for. I've got friends in the Domain that . . ."

Her words died away as she neared the bottom. "By all that's new!" she gasped. "You're beautiful! Look at you!"

Susan flushed and took a step backward. "Well, thanks," she said awkwardly, not sure how to respond. "I mean, that's very nice of you." The girl's tone had changed so suddenly that Susan didn't know what to make of it, or of the fact that she gave compliments like an old aunt serving tea.

But the girl hadn't finished. She tossed her basket into the grass, rattling the plums, and then leaped down beside it, landing half a foot from Jean. She wore a coarse red jumper with a large pocket across the front. When she stood up straight, she was Susan's height. She gawked at Jean, then looked from face to face.

Something was wrong with her.

Susan tried to focus. The girl's face put her in mind of those lenticular pictures that shifted between two things depending on which way you held them. For a flicker of an instant, she was a mild-faced girl with small almond eyes, light hair, and a narrow chin. The next second her features slid out of place, jaw wider than it should have been, nose and mouth jutting slightly forward so that her already narrow chin tapered to a point, and her eyes receded into deep sockets. Susan blinked, feeling cross-eyed and slightly dizzy, and the girl's features settled.

The mild-faced version was gone.

Chapter 6

Sunlight glazed the plums and leaves and grass. Squirrels chattered in voices that sounded like small gears winding. Susan took it all in and all she could think was — why doesn't this feel more like a dream? She thought it must be a dream, after all, despite how wide awake she felt, because of the girl's teeth. The bones of her face, too.

They were all wrong. Her chin and nose protruded, and her lips stretched over a set of sharp teeth that crowded her pointy mouth. Her wrong-shaped face was flecked with what looked like pencil marks.

No, Susan corrected herself. That was hair. A light coat of it dusted her cheeks, forehead, and nose.

For a moment, they all stared at her, struck dumb. Then Jean yelped and scooted behind Max.

"Jean!" Susan whispered. "That's not nice!"

If the girl noticed, she didn't show it. She was too busy looking from one face to the next, astonished.

"How'd they do it?" she asked. "Was it bad? Did they have to cut you?"

Susan had been rehearsing her mother's *people look different sometimes* speech, for later, but that question stopped her.

"Cut us? What do you mean?"

"I mean you're smooth as plums; look at you!"

Oh. Susan tried to be diplomatic. "Well . . . people are different," she began.

The girl snorted. "Not that different, they're not!"

She leaned in, squinting at Susan's forehead. "I can't see the seams of it! Are they under your hair?"

She raised a hand to check, and despite herself, Susan jerked backward. The girl's fingers were knobby as a troll's.

Max edged up beside Susan, and the girl turned to look at him, too. The small hairs on her face glinted where they caught the sun.

"What do you mean, seams?" Max asked her.

She tilted her head and began examining Susan's neck so closely her hot breath lifted Susan's hair. For her part, Susan stared at the light coat of hair that continued from the girl's jaw onto her neck and shoulders. The red straps of her jumper were dark with sweat, and Susan guessed she must wear it every day, because the straps had rubbed a strip of each shoulder bald.

"Scars!" the girl was telling Max. "There ought to be scars when they do that kind of job on you. It's not just a regular wax and file."

As Susan stood half frozen, letting the girl look her up and down and thinking that people with awful illnesses like this one needed patience and an extra dose of politeness, Max flinched suddenly beside her.

"Ow!" He slapped Jean's hand away.

"Will you quit that? We're awake!"

Jean's head poked from beneath his arm and she shook it — no. Max pushed her face back with the palm of his hand.

"We are! Now, quit it!"

The girl looked at them curiously. Her eyes tilted strangely toward her sloping nose.

"So they're near here, are they?" She still leaned into Susan's face. Her breath smelled of plums.

"Who's near?" Susan asked, taking a step back. She'd meant it to be discreet, and it would have been if she hadn't bumped into Nell, who was crowding her, trying to get a closer look.

"Not who — what. The workshops, I mean."

A slight breeze lifted the plum leaves, and Susan took a gulp of humid air. It was strange, but she could no longer hear the girl's accent. Susan wondered if she'd ever had one, or if that had only been a trick her mind played.

Nell looked from the girl to Susan. "Workshops?"

"Uh-huh." She didn't explain further. The girl wiped her hands down the front of her jumper, the large pocket in it lumpy with coins that clinked when she moved. "How'd you get loose, anyway?" she asked. "They must be near here, right? People say they're in the center of the Domain, but maybe the Genius is even cleverer than that. Maybe, after all, they're out here in the ruins."

She said the word *Domain* like it meant something.

"Well? I'm right, aren't I?"

While Max and Nell had moved in to look, Susan had been steadily inching away, and now she'd stepped completely out of the shade of the plum tree. She could feel the sun baking the top of her head. The girl noticed the grassy space between them and frowned.

"Well?" she said. "Go on and tell me. I figured it out, didn't I? Ma always says I'm clever."

Susan sighed. "I have no idea what you're talking about."

The strange girl got instantly stranger. She thrust her head forward and drew back her lips, showing them her teeth.

"If it's a secret," she snarled, "you could just say so."

This time, Max and Nell stepped back, too. Jean and Kate had retreated as far as the next orchard row and were clinging to the trunk of a plum tree.

Just outside the girl's line of sight, Max put a finger to his head and tapped it. Crazy. That was it. Not just different on the outside, then.

"Nothing's a secret," Susan said carefully. "We just haven't been to any workshops."

Max and Nell shook their heads to back this statement up. The girl looked from one to the next of them, and as quickly as she'd gotten angry, she softened.

"Oh, my lambs," she said. "You really don't remember, do you?"

A squirrel leaped from the plum tree into the grass and edged toward the full basket. The girl stomped at it, growled, then turned back to them, chewing this thought over, as Susan wondered whether it might be better to run now and find some other kind of help that didn't involve teeth.

"I think I have it," the girl said, unaware of the looks they were giving one another on her account. "That's part of it, too. They emptied you like an old boot!" She shook her head sorrowfully. "Bet you couldn't even tell me your own names, could you?"

Susan's eyebrows shot up, and a wave of irritation threatened to swamp the pity she'd been feeling for this strange girl. "Well, we're not quite idiots," she said, landing somewhere in between the two.

The girl did not look prepared to take her word for it. She pointed at Jean, still clinging to the plum tree. "You, what do they call you?"

Startled, Jean looked up at her. "Jean," she said.

The girl mouthed the name as if tasting it and wrinkled her nose.

"That's a strange one. What about you?" She jabbed a finger at Susan, like a little kid pretending to be the teacher in a game of school.

"I'm Susan," Susan told her, feeling impatient. "Nice to meet you. And what do they call you?"

The girl sniffed. "Liyla. And that's a city name, for your information. Not like . . . what did you say yours was?"

"Susan."

"Like Susan." She shook her head. "What kind of useless name is that?"

Susan's face burned. There was politeness, and charitable thoughts and there-but-for-the-grace-of-God-go-I and all that, and then there was letting some lunatic insult you.

"Excuse me?" Susan said to her. "What did you say?"

The girl drew her lips back and looked at Nell. "How about you? You have a useless name, too?"

"It's Nell," she said. "And who are you calling useless?"

Liyla slouched back against the plum tree and reached over her head to pull a fruit from a low branch.

"Well, there's use for you now, of course," she conceded,

taking a bite of plum with her sharp teeth. "Just look at those faces! I only meant how you were before. You know, Ma always said they only take discards for the workshops. She'll be glad to know she was right."

She extracted the pit from her plum and flicked it away. It arced up a few feet and landed in a pile of moldering fruit beneath the next tree in the row. They all watched her. If the girl's face had been a shock, her talk was worse. She didn't seem to have the faintest self-consciousness about it, though, which struck Susan as a sure sign of insanity. She remembered reading once that the truly crazy lived in a state of absolute certainty they were right.

Liyla jabbed her finger at Max and then at Kate, insisting they repeat their names for her once, then a second time, as she finished the fruit and licked plum juice from her fingers with a startlingly long tongue.

Then she stopped, her brow furrowing.

"You said you're lost, right?"

They nodded.

"Is that the kind of lost that's got the red cloaks after you?"

Susan thought of the dark shape in the woods.

"What are red cloaks?" she asked.

The girl shot her a look. "Now, that *is* an emptying, isn't it?" She brushed her shoulder, miming a cloak. "Soldiers, remember?"

Susan shook her head, and the girl sighed. "Well, can you at least recall how you all met up?"

"Met up?" Max said. "These are my sisters!"

It took a second for Susan to recognize the strangled snort that followed as laughter.

"Not only emptied, but filled back with fluff! Sisters! That's rich." She laughed some more. "No, you're discards; that's a fact. At least you girls are. Don't know why anyone would put *you* out," she said to Max. "But maybe you were sleepy."

She reached up and picked another plum, then sliced off half of it with her sharp teeth and chewed vigorously.

"Riiiight," Max said in his I-sometimes-have-to-suffer-fools voice. "Sleepy. So they threw me out."

"So you do remember!" the girl crowed. She tossed the half-eaten plum in the air and caught it in a rough hand. "Thought so!"

Susan had had about enough.

"Look," she said. "You mentioned a city, and that's where we need to go. Could you take us there?"

The girl cocked her head and grinned.

"I can, pretty-picture girl!" she said. "Just as soon as I know this place is safe from prying eyes." She went to the outer wall, hooked a foot into the network of vines, and hoisted herself to the top. They watched her scan the forest before she dropped softly back into the mossy ground of the orchard.

"Looks clear. You sure you weren't followed?"

They shook their heads, and she smiled.

"Well, then you are lost, and I've found you. Isn't that right?"

She raised her eyebrows with the look of someone who expected applause. Susan only shrugged.

"Sure," she said.

"Good!" Liyla gave a great clap with her gnarled, thick-nailed hands. "Very good. You'll all come home with me, then, and my ma will fix you up. You'll be back where you belong in no time."

Adult intervention. Exactly what Susan had been hoping for. Finally, Liyla was making sense.

"Great," Susan said. "How far is it? We really need to get home."

"Not far," the girl said, settling her basket of plums in the crook of her arm. "Not too far at all. You just stick with me, and I'll take good care of you."

◇ ◇ ◇

*F*or pity's sake, when the cry came from the valley, the exile
set a bundle of food wrapped in a bright-blue cloth beyond
the garden wall, hoping the broken would stumble upon it on their
wretched journey. Who else would leave a gift for the lost, the vile,
the twice discarded?

But none had ever come. Too bewildered they were, after paying their terrible price. Unknowing, they fled past the last living
thing that offered anything with open hands.

On this day, the heat thickened and the afternoon sun glared
through the trees. Another shattered soul moaned and screamed
through the wood, and the exile listened as it crashed toward the
garden. The horror of the thing sent the deer and fox scrambling,
until the underbrush snapped with their flight.

When silence descended again, the exile went to the garden
wall. This time the gift, at least, was gone. Would it help the
wretched one? It had been left hungry for more than food. The
thought settled bleakly on the silent wood. To banish it, the exile
sought the old words, and found among them an orchard vision.

Let the dark be done.
Have I not kindled the light?
Where stands the dawn?
Why keeps the night?
In an age of madness
Such are the questions of one
Who casts a shroud across the day
And blots the sun.

The exile sat over the verse as the day dwindled and the sun slanted through windows and slipped beneath the door, stirring the glittering dust. The age of madness. A blind year. Eyes long closed had yet seen.

Chapter 7

The hot air was full of peaches and plums and the sound of bees as the children followed Liyla out of the orchard. A bumblebee made its drunken way past her, and she bared her teeth at it, then knocked it to the ground with a sharp *thwack*. For a moment, Susan hesitated, wondering again if it was altogether smart to head into the woods with this girl.

But there were five of them and one of her, and they needed to find the city and somebody who could help them. So they trooped along behind her, past the ruined house and through a break in the vine-smothered wall. The forest had taken whatever road had once been there, and they were instantly enfolded in the deep shade of it again, skipping over thick roots and thorny vines as they tried to keep up. Susan glanced back and couldn't see the wall at all. The greeny dark had swallowed it so completely she wondered how Liyla had ever found the place.

Max sped up to walk beside the girl, and Susan watched Nell quickly follow.

"So what city is this we're going to?" Max asked.

Liyla grinned widely. "Oh, you're in for a treat. It's the Domain itself you've come to. Exciting, right?"

Max stared at her blankly, and her smile dissolved.

"Domain of the Genius! Don't tell me you can't remember that!"

He shook his head and she barked a laugh.

"Well, if you really don't remember the capital, then I'd wager your flat new eyes will pop from your head when you see it, you being a savage from the ruins."

Both Max and Nell looked like they were going to say something extremely unfriendly. Susan quickly cleared her throat.

"What's it the capital of?"

Liyla swung around.

"They'll have to work the kinks out before I get my face turned back, that's certain. I'd hate to be as empty as you! What a thing that is!" She leaped a humped root and dispersed a cloud of gnats hovering in a sunny spot as she trotted along ahead. "Where do you think you're standing? Ganbihar!"

Susan blinked at her, trying to be sure she'd heard right. Liyla only shook her head and mumbled to herself.

"That's savages for you. Greatest city on the face of Loam, and all they do is blink."

She walked on, and Kate looked up at Susan. "Who's she talking to?"

"Herself, I guess," Susan told her. "Seems like she's alone a lot."

They kept a little distance from her after that, as Susan silently reviewed all the stories she knew about lunatic kidnappers, mad ax murderers, and phantoms who hid in opera houses or the woods. None of them had been Liyla's age. At least there was that.

Ahead, Liyla began singing a marching song, using one hairy fist to punctuate the beats:

"Gem of the ea-east, home of the pure,
Our great Domai-ain, it will endure.
The past is dea-ed, see future's rise,
In progress clai-aim the victor's prize.
O Ganbiha-ar, where darkness reigned,
All hail the Genius and his Domain."

A squirrel scuttled across a flat patch of weeds and disappeared under a mound of vines that had overtaken some low bushes. Insects chirped beneath the undergrowth, sounding like they were shaking a can of dry beans.

Even Max and Nell had drawn back once Liyla began to sing. They motioned to the others to hurry up, and Susan jogged toward them.

"Well, she's cracked," Max told them. "It's confirmed."

"Thank you, Doctor Obvious," Susan said. "Can you try to keep your voice down at least?"

Nell waved a hand. "She's singing too loud to hear. Don't worry."

A few paces up the nonexistent path, Liyla launched into another verse:

"Scour the ci-ty and clear the farms.
The pure will con-quer with force of arms.
O Ganbiha-ar, your day is here.
The change is go-ing, never fear."

Max shook his head. "What a creepy song! She gets weirder by the second."

Kate wiped a sweaty hand across her forehead. "What's wrong with her face?" she asked.

She was flushed, and Susan could see how tired she and Jean were. She hoped they were near the city; the little girls needed to rest. The forest steamed around them, the air so heavy she could feel the weight of it on her skin.

"She's a mutant," Max said. "That's my theory."

Jean scratched at a mosquito bite on her arm, and Susan watched her dig her nail into it, trying to get the itching to stop.

"A mutant?" she asked.

"Something got changed around in her genes. Make sure you don't stare at her. It's not nice."

Jean gave her arm one final, vigorous scratch and looked up at him.

"I wasn't staring. She was."

"Yeah, well, either way. She's crazy. Just wanted to warn you."

Kate looked dismayed.

"So how come we're following her?"

Good question, Susan thought. But she said, "Well, even crazy people can know where the city is, can't they?"

"I guess."

"So we'll get there, and find a phone, and call home. That's the plan, okay?"

"Okay," Kate said.

"And in the meanwhile, try to be nice to her. Think what it would be to have a face like that. You wouldn't like it, would you?"

Kate shook her head vehemently and Jean sighed. "No."

"Right. Neither would I. So just keep that in mind."

Susan would have liked that to be the last word, but of course it wasn't.

"Is she crazy enough to have made up a whole geography of crazy? You know, a city no one's ever heard of, and songs?" Nell asked. "That's a lot of crazy for one person."

Max sighed. "It's called a delusion," he told Nell. "They can be very elaborate."

The forest was leveling out now, and a faint footpath appeared among the weeds. Susan thought that a good sign. Civilization, she told herself. Roads, telephones, and air-conditioning. She was looking forward to it.

Jean had been pondering Max's explanation. "Delusion," she said. "So she's singing it right now?"

Max nodded. "Exactly."

Ahead, the singing stopped. "Hey! Plums!" Liyla called back. "Hurry now — we're almost there!"

They hurried. A few minutes later, the trees thinned, and the children emerged into view of what Liyla proudly announced was the city, the Domain of the Genius, marvelous capital of all Ganbihar, greatest city on the face of Loam. Max opened his mouth to say something, then promptly shut it.

"Interesting delusion," Nell whispered beside Susan. "Who's having it — us or her?"

And Susan thought: *Criminations.*

Chapter 8

The greatest city in the world was made of sticks and mud. The greatest city in Ganbihar, actually, Susan reminded herself, or maybe Loam, whatever that was. Five minutes ago, she'd been telling herself Liyla had just made that up. But the city was real enough, or at least the collection of dirty, badly made houses on the edge of it was. They'd come out of the woods into a weedy field, where the forest path gradually widened into a road. The houses here were less lined up than thrown down, as if some giant child had tossed his toys in a fit. They sat at all angles, squatting in bald yards, their brown walls sweating in the humid afternoon. Some seemed to sag in the heat, straw roofs dipping toward mucky patches that had dried to dust where the sun hit them. Goats tugged at the weeds here and there, and a couple of mean-looking cats fought in the shade of a parched tree, but Susan couldn't see a single person.

"Laundry day," Liyla said, in answer to her unspoken question. "They're all down by the smoke blowers. But that's the better for us, isn't it?"

Susan didn't see why it would be, until they came to a forlorn market square, several blocks in. Flat stones marked it off, and dusty stalls sat around it. All but one was empty.

Liyla jogged over to that booth, and reluctantly, the children followed.

The fruit seller sat hunched between two piles of browning apples, snoring with gusto.

"Hey, Pull!" Liyla yelled. "Got wares for you!" She slapped a hand against the side of the stall. An apple rolled off and broke softly in the dirt. The man lifted his head blearily.

Susan stopped. She heard Max draw a sharp breath, and Nell nearly tripped.

The man had the same ferocious features as Liyla.

"I thought you said she was different," Jean whispered to Max.

"I thought she was," he said.

The words *waxed and filed* became suddenly clear as Susan stared at the man. His face had the look of a skinned knee. All but his eyebrows seemed to have been ripped out by the roots, and as he yawned mightily, she could see that his long teeth had been blunted at the ends, filed artificially flat, like his nails.

He caught sight of the children and stood up so fast his head hit the dirty canopy and his chair hit the ground.

"What's this?" he asked. "Is it rally day, then?"

Liyla waved the kids closer. "Every day will be soon," she said. "Found these out in the wilds, and they stick this way."

The man came out from behind his stall to look at them. Despite the sharp lines of his face, the rest of him was all soft dough. The tattered woolen undershirt he wore was patterned with what looked like fruit stains. They definitely were, Susan decided as he closed in on them. The man smelled of sweat and the sick-sweet perfume of rotten apples. Beneath the unraveling hem of his shirt, one strip of stomach peeked out, a hairy belt.

"Workshops," he said. He reached for Max's face, but Max ducked out of the way.

"Oh, let him touch," Liyla said. "So he knows it's real."

Reluctantly, Max let the man reach for him. Susan shuddered in sympathy as the merchant ran a blunted finger down the side of her brother's face.

"By all that's new," he said. "He's done it, hasn't he?"

Liyla puffed up like a rooster.

"Yes, he has. And I'm the one found them, aren't I? Next you'll see me standing beside the Genius on rally day."

The fruit seller looked at her swiftly and frowned.

"You watch that, girl. Clever enough to find me plums doesn't make you clever enough to keep out of the workshops yourself."

Liyla deflated slightly. "I'm an only," she said. "You know it."

He shook his head, and a few drops of sweat went flying. "That's a bed tale of your mama's," he said, tugging his shirt down over his stomach. "And you'd be wise not to trust it with your skin, not now you've got wares like these."

Liyla only tossed her head, but the word *wares* made Susan go cold. She looked at Max, who seemed to be having trouble recovering from the sight of the fruit seller. He kept rubbing his face and blinking his eyes, as if he were testing his eyesight. But Nell had heard the word.

"What's that supposed to mean?" she demanded.

One of the browning apples might have spoken, given the way the man jumped at the sound of her voice. He shot Liyla a look, but she only shrugged.

"Nothing," he said after taking a minute to collect himself. "Only wondering how you got lost, is all. And who might be looking for you."

Susan found herself liking this conversation less and less. She scuffed her shoe against the dusty ground, scattering some hay that had been pressed into the dirt. "We need to get in touch with our parents," she said firmly. "Could you tell us how to do that?"

Even on the man's malformed face, she knew a look of profound pity when she saw one. He shook his head.

"Such a pretty thing," he said. "It's a shame. I don't like to think the stories are true, but it seems they are."

"What stories? What are you talking about?" she asked him.

He ignored her. From his back pocket he pulled a stained handkerchief, spread it over his hand as if he were going to do a magic trick, then used it to wipe his face from forehead to chin. He repeated the procedure on his neck. When he was finished, he stuffed the sodden cloth back into his pants and looked over at Liyla. "Listen, lamb," he said. "I like you, you know it, so take my advice. Get these to your mama fast as you can, and by the side streets. Red cloaks are busy with the crowds today, so you'll have a little space from them. Just don't go through the main market like you do. You'll do well to hear me."

The girl bit her lip but nodded. "Thought of that myself, anyway," she said. "Just came here to get my due."

Pull smiled at her. "Of course you did."

He reached behind the stall and brought out a deep wicker hamper with a hinged top. It smelled strongly of mold, and Susan wrinkled her nose as Liyla poured out half the bright plums. They thudded dully to the bottom.

The man inspected the fruit and then, with a certain amount of huffing effort, extracted a leather pouch from the belt he wore, half hidden by the great ledge of his stomach.

It took him a moment, searching, to find it. From its smooth mouth he produced what looked like two small iron rings and several coins that might have been brass. Liyla squinted at them.

"You shorting me? It's supposed to be a full ven I get!"

The man shrugged. "Had to pay extra to keep the reds out of this space today, and me to get an early slot for the wash. We split that, don't we?"

The girl frowned but scooped the coins from the counter, pulled a pouch from her dress pocket, and put them inside.

"Seems to me I ought not to split it when I do all the climbing and scrounging," she grumbled, dropping the pouch back into her pocket.

The man only shrugged. "There are plenty who'd pay me to know where you get fruits without being dunned by the Purity, wouldn't they? I think fair's fair, isn't it?"

A look of mild alarm crossed the girl's face, and she hitched up one shoulder. "I guess so," she said. "Fair's fair." She seemed to think of something then, and looked swiftly at the children.

"But this lot, this isn't something you heard about, right?"

He folded his arms and shook his head. "Oh, no, Liyla. Like I said, I like you, and there's no sense in me getting mixed up in all that. You see what your mama says, why don't you? That'll be her think, not mine. I'm just a fruit seller, and happy to stay that way."

She gave him a curt nod. "Right. Good, then. We'll take the side streets. Thanks."

She led them from the square, and Susan looked back to see the man watching them as they went. He didn't stop looking until they'd turned the corner.

Chapter 9

A line of mournful rectangle-faced houses with close-set window eyes and awful complexions of peeling paint sat on this side of the square. Porches hung off the front of them, drooling trash into the street.

The roads were paved here, but whoever did it might as well have left the dirt. So many of the flat stones were broken or missing that the children had to hop over the gaps as they walked.

Occasionally, what ought to have been a block of houses turned out to be only the remains of them, a clearing full of splintered wood, iron tubs, wagons missing wheels, and dented worktables.

Almost no one was outside, but once or twice they spotted someone sitting on a porch, and to Susan's dismay, these people looked no different from Liyla and the fruit seller.

"Getting crowded," the girl grumbled after a man fiddling with a broken wheelbarrow stood up to get a second look at them. "Keep your heads down."

She led them into the back alleys after that. If anything, it was worse there. Every few steps they'd pass through a pocket of rancid humid air. Susan gagged.

"Outhouses," Max said, pointing to the wooden huts behind the houses. "They must not have indoor plumbing!"

The marvelous city kept getting less marvelous, Susan thought bitterly.

"What happened to the people here?" she asked Max. "They can't *all* be mutants, can they?"

He shrugged. "Shouldn't be possible, I don't think." He looked over quickly at Jean and lowered his voice. "But if this isn't a dream, then *something* happened. It would be nice to know what."

Nice wouldn't have been Susan's choice of words. As they moved along, the houses grew slightly bigger, and some were made of brick, but they were still pocked and soot stained. The smell of burning drifted over from several blocks ahead. She squinted between the houses and caught sight of what looked like smoke.

"Something's on fire," she said.

Liyla barely turned her head.

"It's wash day — I told you," she said. "The machines are out. That's where everyone's gathered."

They could hear activity in the distance, the occasional shout or bark of a dog. They had come from the back alleys into the street again, and here the road was wider. A series of empty sheds, gray collections of boards with doors hanging half off hinges, peppered the side of the road. Susan thought they probably held more garbage, but when she peeked inside one, she discovered it was full of huddled shapes. The air in the shed was worse than the outhouses. For a second she thought this must be where people dumped the waste out, along with old clothes and the rest of what they didn't need. Then something moved.

She jumped. The shapes were men and women.

The others had seen it, too. As Liyla marched on ahead, the children stood staring into the shadowy space. An emaciated woman lay on her back, arms flung over her head. A man with a patchy beard coughed and snorted, curled into a ball nearby. Three, four, five people lay there, limp on the hard ground. Susan peered in and saw more mounds in the corners. How many were in there?

"I don't think they're conscious," Max said. "But they're definitely breathing."

Something moved again in the shadows, and a child crawled over the pile and out into the light. He might have been Nell's age, by the size of him. Like Liyla's, his nose sloped out low in his face, and his cheeks were wide and dusted with a film of hair. But he was dirty, so filthy, that his hair, slicked back from his forehead, looked streaked with gray. And despite the unnatural width of his face, his cheeks sank inward; his eyes sat in hollow sockets. He gawked at them.

"You real?" he asked in a surprisingly clear voice.

Susan nodded.

He accepted that without comment.

After a second he said, "Got any food?"

She reached inside a pocket and handed him a peach.

"Here."

Liyla came jogging back to them.

"What are you stopping for? Shoo, you!" she said to the boy. He retreated into the shed.

"Hey!" Max said. "Don't be like that!"

Nell looked stricken. "He wasn't doing anything."

Inside the shed, the boy dug among the unconscious

figures until he retrieved a ragged sack. He untied it, dropped the peach inside, then buried it behind a woman's head. He glanced back at them warily.

"Sleeper's boy," Liyla spat, watching him.

The children stared at her.

"Sleeper? You mean those people in there?" Jean asked. Inside the shed, one of the women groaned and turned. The boy laid a hand on her arm and bent to whisper something in her ear. He kept his eyes on Liyla, though.

She curled her lip at him. "I'd hardly call them people," Liyla said. "They're useless, all of them. Leeching change-bringers, that's what they are. It's against the law to feed them."

The boy receded farther into the shed.

"Against the law?" Susan echoed. "How can it be?"

"I said they're useless, didn't I?" Liyla stuck her tongue out and licked her lips, then flashed her teeth again, as if the thought of people sleeping touched some nerve in her.

The boy watched them from the shadows. With Liyla's mention of the law, he had gotten halfway up again, unburied his sack, and clutched it in one fist. He looked ready to run.

"Change-bringers?" Max said. "What's that?"

Liyla waved toward her own face distractedly. "Change-bringers! They're the reason you had to go to the workshops to begin with, or don't you remember *that*? Seems like if there's one thing the lot of you would keep in mind, it'd be what you're here for. How do you expect those faces to stay if you feed the useless?"

She leaned in toward the boy, grimacing at the stench of the shed. "Or maybe you'd like to give yourself over, huh? Look what the workshops did for these discards. Makes you think, doesn't it?"

The boy said nothing, but he curled in on himself and blinked rapidly in the shadows.

"Leave him alone," Susan said. "Like Nell said, he's not doing anything."

Liyla gave a triumphant laugh. "Exactly! Nothing but spreading his filth and dragging the rest of us down." She shook her head in disgust. "Come on. Farther from him we get, the better."

She turned to begin walking again, motioning for them to follow. But Susan didn't go. She looked back at the boy, crouched there between the sleepers, still watching them. After a second, she slipped the second peach from her pocket and tossed it his way. He pounced on it, and Susan heard Liyla suck air sharply through her teeth. The girl looked up and down the block, shook her head, and blew out.

"Don't you know what they say about feeding the useless?" she scolded, shaking her head at Susan. "What were you thinking?"

At the moment, Susan was thinking that she'd get a certain amount of pleasure from giving Liyla a swift kick. She pressed her lips shut and tried to think good thoughts.

"What?" Nell asked the girl. "What do they say?"

"Give them a gift, they'll pay you double, in the only coin they know — that's trouble."

Susan stared at her sourly, wondering if Liyla's entire education consisted of memorizing ugly rhymes. It seemed like it.

For a moment, Liyla looked as if she expected them to clap for her. When they didn't, she sagged a little.

"Well," she said, "I guess I can't expect you to know it. Probably don't teach you much in the ruins, do they?"

She shook her head and turned, heading back up the street. "Let's go," she said. "Before the red cloaks come and think we're useless, too."

With a last guilty glance back at the boy in the shed, they followed.

Chapter 10

Susan had once heard a friend's grandmother say that no matter what the calendar told her, when she closed her eyes, she was still a young mother, with a small daughter. It didn't matter that the daughter now had a daughter of her own. The picture hung there inside her head, unchanging. Susan had thought about that, wondering whether she had her own picture, hanging behind her eyes. Now she knew she did. While Nell toted around her blanket, and Kate and Jean carried their Barbies in their waistbands, Susan held on to the picture of a girl who was good at the *supposed to*s in life. She went to school and did her work and helped at home. She liked checking things off lists and knowing she'd done them right. *Supposed to*s. *Ought to*s. *Should*s. She had those covered.

The picture had suddenly become clear because all the *supposed to*s had gone wrong. The Susan in the picture was not meant to be walking down a foul-smelling street, following a petulant girl who could use a shave, or — she corrected the thought — a wax and file.

"Maybe we should get away from her," she said to Max. She kept her voice low, not wanting Kate to hear. Her sister clung to her hand, round eyes taking in all the sights, none of them good ones.

He shook his head. "You want to get lost here? At least she knows something about the place. Somebody's got to help us make sense of it."

Susan wondered if anybody could. The farther they walked, the less sense it made. On the other side of a short alley, they caught a glimpse of laundry day. Bunches of people milled in a large square, arms full of clothing. The machine Liyla was so excited about turned out to be nothing but a spinning black barrel, powered by steam.

"You see those in museums," Max said, astonished. "They're like a hundred years old! And what is that? A musket?"

A red-cloaked man, gun slung over his shoulder, stood checking off names on a list as people jostled one another in line. A couple of red-sashed children moved up and down the row, keeping people in order.

"What are those kids doing?" Susan asked the girl. "They're not soldiers, too, are they?"

Liyla laughed. "Purity Patrol. Even girls get to do it. Now, that's really being useful."

Susan cringed, watching the patrol members prod people twice and three times their age. The square looked crowded and hot.

"You'd think they'd spread it out a little," Nell said. "Who says everybody has to do the wash on the same day?"

Liyla made a face that said she was long-suffering, having to answer such questions. "Only the law — that's all," she said. In a little singsong, she recited another one of her strange rhymes:

"Wash day's here, don't you forget it.
Be in the square or you'll regret it!"

She caught sight of their dumbfounded looks. "Well, everybody's got to keep clean, don't they?"

"That boy didn't look too clean," Kate said to Susan. "The one you gave the peaches to."

Liyla snorted.

"Well, not discards," she said. "'Course not them."

It occurred to Susan that she'd been walking along teetering between panic and outrage, and she really did have a choice. She decided on outrage.

"That's ugly," she said. "Stop it."

Liyla looked at her in genuine surprise.

"It's only the truth," she said. "What am I supposed to say?"

Supposed to. Here, Susan didn't really know.

"Well, not that. That boy deserved food as much as anybody."

"Deserved? What in the name of progress does that mean?" Liyla asked. "Where do you get such ideas? Reject's a reject, and useful are useful. What else matters?"

"Don't you feel sorry for them?" Jean asked Liyla. "Even a little?"

Liyla considered this as if it had honestly never occurred to her. After a minute, she shrugged.

"Might as well be sorry for one of our chickens when she won't lay and turns into supper. Doesn't change anything."

She started back down the street, unfazed by the looks they gave her.

Susan thought that maybe Max was right about following her. Nothing seemed to bother Liyla, and maybe not too many other people could lead them through these strange streets, unruffled by everything. She did seem to have a firm idea of where she was headed, too.

Only once during the walk did the girl falter. She had taken them deep into the city, where squat buildings took the place of squat houses, their outer walls plastered with decaying flyers and newer notices pasted over old until the bricks were no longer red or even brown, but a mash of gray, the color of leftover paste. The occasional hot breeze set the wall aflutter and sent the grimy, torn bits swirling into the street.

They had weathered one of these small blizzards and turned into the next alley when Liyla stopped short and let out a yelp. Someone had been leaning against one of the grimy walls halfway through the passage and bolted upright at sight of them, nearly as frozen as the girl.

He — by the height of the figure it seemed a he — wore a hood, and every inch of his body was covered in mottled-green cloth. Despite the heat, gloves encased his hands and thick mesh hid his face.

"What is that?" Jean whispered.

Liyla didn't answer. Her breathing had quickened, and she lost her grip on her basket. It fell onto the broken paving stones, spilling plums into the path.

The figure seemed to study them a moment. Hesitating, it took a step forward.

Liyla's hands flew up, and Susan was stunned to see a knife in one of them. "You get back, you! There are six of us! We won't go easy!"

Again, the silent figure paused. Liyla stood breathing hard. The knife trembled in her hand. The figure only regarded her another minute, then turned and walked away.

The girl refused to move until he was out of sight.

"Fanatic," she breathed, slipping the knife back into the pocket of her jumper. "Never seen one that close before. We'll take a different way home."

They helped her collect her spilled plums, blowing dirt off them and rubbing them against their clothes, before she led them from the alley. As she moved quickly back across the street into the harsh sun, Susan regarded her with new respect.

"Do you always carry that knife?" she asked.

"Have to," the girl said, patting her pocket.

This time, she didn't need to elaborate.

Chapter 11

Liyla's house looked like it had been on the losing end of a beating. An unstable fence of wooden planks leaned crazily round it, gaps like missing teeth strung closed with chicken wire. The house's outer walls had once been white-washed, but they'd yellowed in the sun and were bruised now with patches of red-brown clay that wept in the heat. Off-center windows peered blackly out at the children from its smeary face. Still, a jaunty red sash hung over the front door, which Liyla proudly pointed out as "the sign of the Genius."

"You wait here," she said, directing them to the chicken yard around back. "I'll go talk to Ma."

A small pen housed the chickens on one side of the yard, just paces from an outhouse of weathered boards with a slop-ing roof that had buckled with age. Near the back fence, the ground had been dug up and the hole trimmed with rocks. Susan looked into it and saw a fire pit, a nest of ash and coals like small gray eggs. In the muggy air, the aroma of burnt wood coming from the pit proved the only relief from the unfortu-nate mixture of chickens and outhouse. Worst of all was the chopping block, a stained old stump that sat in the center of the dusty yard in full view of the chickens. Several sawhorses, some upright and some on their sides, littered the rest of the yard.

Max wrinkled his nose and inspected the chickens, which slept fitfully, bunched together in the shade.

"Have you noticed," he said, "that the animals look okay? How come they're not different, like the people?"

Susan jumped the fire pit, squinted into the sparse grass to make sure she wouldn't be sitting in chicken leavings, then slid down to sit with her back against the fence post.

"I'm too tired for science questions now," she said. "And hot." She pulled her sticky collar away from her neck and blew into it, trying to make a breeze.

Max squatted beside the chickens. "We've got to figure it out, though."

The splintered fence jabbed at her back, and Susan jerked away from it in annoyance.

"What are you going to figure out? The whole world?"

"Maybe."

Kate and Jean had pulled their Barbies from their waistbands, and now Jean stood by the fence, running her doll along the boards. *Bump. Bump. Bump.*

"You said we'd wake up at home," she said dejectedly. "You said somebody would help us."

Susan rolled her eyes. "We're working on it," she sighed. "Will you give us a second?"

"It's been all day," Jean reminded her.

Kate, meanwhile, sat smoothing her Barbie's hair. She kept her eyes locked on the doll, as if ignoring the ugly yard would make it go away.

"Do you think she'll be able to help us?" she asked. "Liyla's mother, I mean."

"If she's anything like Liyla, I doubt it," Nell said gloomily.

She had taken one corner of her blanket and thrown it over her head to keep the sun off. "I don't know why we're trusting her at all, not after that man called us wares."

"Yeah, what did he mean by that?" Kate wanted to know.

Max shrugged. "Nothing, probably. Anybody who talks as much as Liyla can't be too crafty. Don't worry."

At the moment, *don't worry* sounded to Susan like the most frightening words in the English language. Worry seemed the only sensible course of action in a place like this. But all she said was "I hope you're right."

She noticed that her arms were sunburned and poked at them with a finger.

"Anyway," she said, "I don't see that we have much choice. Somebody around here's got to know something. Liyla's mother's as good a place to start as any."

She heaved herself off the scratchy fence, got up, and surveyed the area. The next nearest house stood far enough from Liyla's that a shout wouldn't rouse the neighbors. An old-fashioned well, complete with chain and bucket, marked the boundary between the houses, and a lean cow grazed on weeds just past it.

"Hey, Jean," she said. Her little sister still ran her Barbie mercilessly across the fence. "Look at that old cow."

Something flickered in the corner of her eye. Susan turned and saw a hooded figure, swathed in green, standing beside the well.

She grabbed Jean.

"Into the house! Quick!"

In half a second, they were scrambling for the back door, yanking it open, and barreling through. Nell slammed it behind them.

Susan blinked, blinded after the glare of the yard. When her eyes adjusted, she saw Liyla and her mother, on their feet on either side of a rough table, gaping at her.

"What's wrong?" Liyla asked.

"Fanatic outside," Susan breathed. "Near the well."

Liyla's mother jumped from her chair and ran to the back door. Susan looked over the woman's shoulder as she opened it an inch and peered outside. The hooded figure had gone.

"They're fast," the woman said. "Faster than anything. Soldiers hunt them all over the city and never have caught one."

She closed the door, bolted it, and turned back to the children. If she'd been surprised at the sight of them, she didn't show any of that now.

The woman wore her hair pulled into a knot so tight on the top of her head that it dragged her forehead up. She wore a jumper much like Liyla's, except hers was covered with an apron that might once have been white, maybe when Susan's grandmother was a little girl. But what drew Susan's eye was her face. She was pinched and stubbled, a dried-up version of Liyla. Her expression brought to mind the man who guessed people's weight and height at the county fair. Susan had seen him once on a break, and even when eating his corn dog and funnel cake, he couldn't seem to look at people without taking measurements.

Liyla's mother studied the five of them in the same way. Her eyes moved from Susan to Max to Nell, and she wore the smile of someone who had just won the lottery.

"Oh, my, what wonders," she said, resting her gaze on Jean. She leaned over and pulled Jean's chin up so she could look into her face. "You're as exquisite as an old painting! And *this*, how amazing!" She reached for Jean's Barbie.

Jean pulled it to her chest and shot a pleading look Max's way.

Max bit his lip. "It's all right," he whispered. "She'll give it back."

Jean reluctantly released it.

"So this is the model, then?" The woman looked from Max to Susan.

With the heel of her hand, Jean pushed a sweaty lock of dark hair out of her eyes.

"It's just my doll," she said.

The woman smiled giddily and handed it back to her.

"Of course, of course it is!" she said. "But who gave it to you? Hmm?"

"My father," Jean said. A stubborn edge had crept into her voice. "For an unbirthday present."

At this, the woman raised an eyebrow, but Liyla said, "I told you, Ma: they don't remember."

For a long moment, the woman considered them again, taking in faces, hands, clothing, dolls. Kate squirmed and Nell squeezed her wadded-up blanket, her fists clenched.

"We do know we need help, though," Susan said, unable to stand the inspection any longer. "Can you tell us who around here might know about — strange things?"

At that, the woman abandoned her calculations and grinned widely. "Strange things? Well, you leave that to me. I'll find the right one to help you first thing in the morning."

She was peering into Nell's hair when she said it.

Chapter 12

W e are *not* staying here," Nell said when Liyla and her mother had gone out to the yard to make dinner. They heard the squawk of chickens and then the hollow snap of ax against chopping block. "Please tell me we're not."

Susan turned away from the back door and looked around the room. The house was little more than a large open space outfitted with a fireplace and table, a rag rug, and several chairs, rough ones beside the table, better ones near the cold fireplace. The only bedroom she could see was through an open door on the right side of the room, and on the far side of the back door, a curtained alcove half hid an unmade bed beneath a good-size window.

"It's not that bad," she said, raising her voice over the sound of panicked chickens. "It's okay."

The others disagreed. It *was* that bad. They insisted on searching the place, sure they were going to find the skeletons of a few of Liyla's playmates somewhere. Under the rug, Jean uncovered a trapdoor.

"See!" Nell shouted when they'd pulled the rug away. "Close your eyes, girls! I don't think you're going to want to see this!"

Kate drew back, but Jean got down on her knees beside Nell. Max, who'd been rolling his eyes a minute before Jean yanked the rug back, now bent over Nell's shoulder, his mouth pressed into a thin line.

A hinged handle lay in a shallow dip in the wood, so it left no bump in the floorboards. Nell pried it up and heaved the door open. A puff of cold air issued from the dark under-floor. Susan shivered. Dimly, about four feet down, she could make out a square of dirt. Nell lowered herself to it. Shoulders jammed together, they leaned over to peer in after her.

"Move out of the light! I can't see a thing down here!" she said. "My gosh, it's cold!"

"Maybe it's a crypt," Max muttered. Susan hushed him.

They tilted back to give her some light, and Nell gasped. Susan's stomach dropped.

"What? What is it? What has she got down there?"

Susan stuck her head into the hole, but Nell shoved it back.

"Bones!" Nell said. "Oh, gross! There's a whole lumpy row of them! And then — ugh! What's that? Underneath she's got a basket of something dark and bloody looking."

Jean had begun to make a gagging noise, and Kate's face had turned the color of chalk. But Susan paused a second.

"Hold on, did you say a basket?" she asked Nell.

"A basket. Definitely a basket!"

Susan looked around the room. She didn't see Liyla's basket anywhere.

"Hey, Nell, take a closer look in the basket. You sure those aren't plums?"

There was a long pause from below.

Then Nell, sounding sheepish: "Oh, yeah. Actually, you're right about that."

Max grunted.

"How about the bones?" Susan asked her.

Another pause, longer this time.

"Uh . . . yeah, I think these are eggs. Yeah, they are. Hard-boiled."

Max sat back on his heels and blew out a long breath.

"Good work, Nell, you just found the family fridge."

They hoisted her out and put the door and rug back in place. Nell rubbed her arms. She glanced at Susan, then quickly away.

"Well, who puts their fridge underground, anyway? Isn't that suspicious?"

Susan shook her head. "People who don't have refrigeration — that's who. Why it's under the rug is anybody's guess. But that settles it, anyway. We're staying, at least for now. Right?"

Nobody said a word this time. Jean sat down on one of the chairs by the empty fireplace and kicked moodily at the rungs, while outside, the chickens continued their screaming. Susan glanced at the window and wrinkled her nose. Stained feathers drifted by.

"People have different ways about them," she said half-heartedly. "Maybe Liyla's mother is nicer the more you get to know her."

Not even Kate looked like she believed that. They waited in glum silence as the chickens were plucked and bled, and finally roasted.

At last, Liyla and her mother came back in, brushing feathers and bits of fat from their clothes and carrying two roast chickens on a stick.

Susan tried to find her voice.

"Would you like some help with the table?" she asked faintly.

She might have suggested diving headfirst into the well for the look Liyla's mother gave her. Liyla wagged a finger.

"Nobody touches the food before supper," she told Susan.

A short time later, Liyla's father came home. He was a stringy, stoop-shouldered man with a face that looked sunburned with a recent waxing. On either side of his nose, his jaw and cheekbones jutted out as if some invisible hand had grabbed hold of his face and pulled. Liyla's mother met him outside and must have explained the situation, because he only stared at the children as he took his place at the table.

Liyla ran and dragged in some of the dusty sawhorses from the yard.

"You all sit here," she said.

She grinned as they perched themselves on the planks.

"Oh, me! What a party this is, right?"

No one set out any plates. Or forks or knives or napkins. The children were given a tin cup of water to share. They teetered uncomfortably on their makeshift seats as Liyla's mother laid a wooden platter before her husband. It was piled with a large loaf of bread and the unfortunate chickens. The man sniffed at it and nodded, pleased.

As they all watched, Liyla's father yanked the platter close to him, snatched a chicken, and thrust it into his mouth. Next to Susan, Jean's jaw dropped. The man chewed the way the neighborhood dogs did, snapping chicken breasts in two with his teeth and tossing his head back to send the food down his throat. Crumbs of meat and marrow sprayed from the corners of his mouth. Susan slid her eyes over to Liyla's mother, but the woman only watched with appreciation. Or maybe she was watching the chicken. After a minute, she reached for a piece that had fallen back to the platter. Her husband's head came up. "Hey!" he snapped, flashing his teeth. "Wait your turn!"

She pulled back her hand as if slapped, raised her lip for a moment, then settled down, saying nothing. Susan stared at them, aghast. She caught sight of Max, who looked faintly green, and Nell, eyebrows so high on her face they disappeared beneath her bangs. Beside Liyla, Kate looked ready to crawl under the table, and Jean's mouth was a perfect round O. Liyla herself only watched her father, licking her lips.

After another minute of tearing choice pieces from the chicken, loudly breaking bones, and swallowing, Liyla's father nodded at his wife. She grabbed a chicken by one leg and plunged her face into it, ripping handfuls of bread with her free hand. Susan glanced at Liyla as the snap of chicken bones and the grunts of the diners filled the room. The girl only waited, leaning forward like a spectator at a race, eyes on her parents and the food.

Eventually, the woman gave a curt nod, and Liyla jumped at the serving dish. Susan watched her, at a loss.

"Well, go on! It's your turn now!" Liyla said, chewing vigorously.

"Sss!" Liyla's mother hissed. "No talking at the table!"

Looking at her siblings, Susan saw them frozen, waiting for her to tell them what to do next. Even Max looked dumbfounded. Gingerly, she reached for the bread. The loaf looked like it had been through an explosion. She pulled off a piece, then passed the loaf to Nell. Her sister did the same. It was lucky none of them wanted any chicken. Nothing was left of those two unfortunate birds but skin and some nasty-looking innards. The bread tasted like cotton in Susan's mouth.

At last, Liyla's father sat back, gave a table-shaking belch, and sighed happily.

"Good meal," he said. "Issi, you've outdone yourself."

The woman sniffed. "Genius doesn't eat any better, I wager."

"Sign of the future," Liyla chimed in. "Useful is as useful does!"

The girl turned to Susan as if it were her turn to say something.

"Uh, the bread was very soft," Susan stammered.

They looked at her, and Susan felt a flush creep up her neck. "Well, maybe we ought to get some sleep," she said hastily. "It's been a long day."

No one said anything for a minute. Max was still staring at the table as if he'd just witnessed a natural disaster or a five-car pileup. She kneed him and he jumped.

"And the little girls are tired," he said. "Really tired."

Kate, who at home treated bedtime like a personal affront, immediately nodded. *Second night in a row,* Susan thought grimly.

Liyla's mother jumped on the suggestion and hustled them behind the curtain. The girl's unmade bed waited there, sheets half on the floor.

"Useful girl I've got, to give you her bed tonight," she said.

"Useful?" Susan asked her.

The woman only nodded.

"Well . . . we're very grateful," Susan said.

She nudged Nell, who stood next to her.

"Yes," her sister said. "Very."

With a curt nod, the woman left them. Susan peeked around the curtain and saw Liyla's father reach into a pile of broken chicken bones and miraculously produce an intact wishbone. He handed it to his daughter.

"Make it a good one now," he said. "There's never been a night better for wishing."

Liyla grinned and snapped it in two, then stuck the larger half in her mouth, for sucking. Beside Susan, Nell grunted at the sight.

"Wonder what she's wishing for," she whispered.

Thinking of nothing good, Susan made no answer. Nell sighed and turned away, untying the blanket from her waist. She shook it out and spread it across Liyla's mattress.

"Well, come on," she said to the little girls.

They slipped off their shoes and climbed up onto it. The rest of them did the same until they were all bunched together on the bed.

"We're closer than the chickens," Max complained in a whisper.

"Yeah," Nell said. "And look what happened to them."

◇ ◇ ◇

*T*his time, the cry came in the night. From the window, the exile saw a crescent moon. It glimmered overhead, its grin ghastly in the dark, as if it took joy in the miserable sound.

Such punishments came at all hours now, a vicious pattern that ravaged sleep.

Moaning, wailing, roaring, the outcast climbed the mountain, rousing the wood, a wild thing lost amid the wild.

The small bundle of food waited by the garden wall.

Closer the sound of thrashing through leaves, the crack and pop of splintered wood.

It reached the garden and stopped.

Hesitating, the wretched one leaned to lift the bundle. Could it know? Did the lost remember? Was there yet hope of return?

The exile waited, watching the shadow of the thing in the moonlight, its silvered outline hunched and trembling.

It lifted its head and sobbed. A human sound. The exile took a step toward the door. Could such a thing be?

The sob roughened to a shriek, then bled to a howl, a lament jagged as broken glass.

The lost one raised the gift and dashed it to earth. It threw itself upon the garden, smashing the fencing and ripping plants from the dirt, tossing the new growth from the torn soil.

Then it ran, keening, from the garden.

The exile turned from the door and returned to bed, listening for a long time as the ragged voice echoed through the trees.

The Feared, they had been called in times past. It was a fitting name. For a thing full of fear is the most dangerous of all.

Sighing, the exile stared into the darkness, thinking that in the morning, the garden could be planted anew. If there was little else in exile, there was at least always time.

Chapter 13

A rustling of the curtain woke Susan. The five of them had fallen asleep from sheer exhaustion, but now she jerked awake and blinked to see Liyla's mother outlined in the flickering light of a lamp. She stepped into the alcove and toward the bed.

Susan held her breath and half closed her eyes as the woman leaned over them, smelling of chicken and sweat, searching for something. After a minute, she gave a satisfied little exhale and her hand came down on Kate. With a tug, she pried the Barbie from Kate's sleeping hand and retreated to the main room, letting the curtain fall closed behind her.

Susan nudged Max, putting a finger over his lips as he woke. She jerked her head in the direction of the curtain. Together, they crept out of bed and prodded it aside. A small oil lamp sat on the wooden table, its flame casting rusty shadows on the walls. Liyla's father sat beside it, fingering the doll.

"So this is what they're supposed to look like, hmm?" he asked his wife. He examined the doll with a perplexed expression. "A little different from the old paintings, these."

The woman snatched it from him. "The model's the *face*, Toper, and the hands." Susan watched her run her own gnarled hand along the plastic arms.

"Who do you say is best to seek out, for the reward?" she asked him.

Susan stiffened.

"You know those types in the center, always ready to gain off the hardworking," Liyla's mother continued. "They might just claim them themselves if we don't speak to the right one."

She tipped the doll upside down over the lamp. Its stiff dress opened into a frilly cone, and its hair hung above the flame, splayed in the light. Both the adults stared at it, and Liyla's father nodded.

"That's why we send this in, ahead. I'd go to Elot, but he'd know me and come back here looking."

The woman frowned. "He's good for a pass on the tax for Liyla but not something big as this. This isn't an egg bribe, is it? No, we've got to find someone right at the center. And wouldn't hurt to disguise yourself a bit, would it? Last thing I'd like is cloaks storming in here. They'd take them and more." She looked uncomfortably toward her room. "You'll have to be careful, Toper."

He nodded. The flickering lamp threw the doll's shadow across the wall, turning it into a curving giant with spidery legs.

"It's a risk, yes, but well worth the prize," he told her.

For a moment, they sat in silence, then he cocked his head and looked toward the curtain. Max and Susan ducked back. "Only thing I can't figure is how they got loose. Someone's head rolled on that mistake, you can be sure. Especially the boy. He doesn't even look a discard. You sure both of his legs were the same length? No missing fingers or a bad eye? Maybe he's a half-wit."

Susan glanced at Max, whose shoulders had come up at that last.

"If he did have a bad eye, he doesn't anymore," Liyla's mother said.

"That's so. But perhaps they fixed that, too, yeah?"

He flicked the doll's leg with a finger and pulled one of its small feet this way and that.

"Wonders," his wife said. "That's progress, isn't it?"

"It is," he agreed. "And we're going to ride its back. They'll pay more for those five than I could make in a lifetime selling eggs. You'll be living in the center soon, Issi. You'll wear one of those gems they get out of the mines, like the Genius himself."

She chuckled. "And maybe a dress like this one!" she said.

She rubbed the sparkly fabric between her fingers, and he watched her, looking pleased.

"So tomorrow, you keep a sharp eye on those five," he said. "Bolt the door and don't open it for anyone but me. I'll go first light."

She agreed that would be the best thing, and they sat up a while longer, talking about the bounty the children would bring them. At last, they snuffed the lamp, took the doll, and went to bed.

Neither Susan nor Max moved until they heard the click of the bedroom door. Then Susan let out a long breath.

"Liyla might babble on too much to be dangerous, but her parents mean business," she whispered. "They're going to sell us! We've got to get out of here!"

He shifted uneasily beside her. He'd been on his knees, and now Max got to his feet with a stifled groan. "We do," he said, nudging the girls over a little so he could sit on the edge of the bed. "But should we try to go in the dark? You saw that thing yesterday. What about that? We won't even see it coming!"

"Maybe it's gone now," Susan said. She made a place for herself between Kate's feet and Jean's. From the window over Liyla's bed, the moon filtered in, just enough so she could make out Max's worried face.

"How lucky do you feel?" he asked her.

She frowned at him. Max usually didn't believe in luck.

"Not lucky at all," she said to him. "Not even a little."

"Me neither."

Chapter 14

A lone mockingbird whistled in the dark, and the chickens dreamed in the yard as Susan and Max woke the others. It didn't take much to convince their sisters to leave. They pulled their shoes on wearily, and Jean shoved her Barbie back into her waistband.

"Where's mine?" Kate asked, rummaging in the bed.

They told her. She raised her head unhappily.

"She's a burglar?" She looked from Max to Susan.

Standing next to Kate, Jean puffed up with indignation.

"A monster burglar," she said. "A witch burglar." For half an hour before they had fallen asleep last night, Jean had argued with Kate over which nightmare figure Liyla's mother fit best. Apparently, Susan thought, she had decided on both.

"Hush up, you," Nell told Jean as she collected her blanket. "Can't you see we're in trouble?"

Susan peeked into the main room. All was quiet, and the bedroom door remained closed. Behind her, she heard whispering.

"I said hush!" Nell snapped at the girls.

"We weren't talking!"

Susan turned to separate them and saw a shadow flick past the window. She climbed onto the bed to look out. Nothing.

The chickens glowed whitely in the moonlight, and the mockingbird sighed somewhere near the well.

"Ready?" Max asked.

She nodded. One more check of the window, just in case. Maybe the shadow had only been a cloud rolling across the moon.

Inches from her face, two hooded figures peered through the glass.

"Ahh!" She flung herself backward, landing on Nell, who elbowed her reflexively.

"Hey!"

"Shush!" Susan sputtered, pointing. There was nothing there anymore, but now they could hear a rattling at the back door. Kate clutched at her.

"Fanatics!" Susan hissed. "They're getting in!"

Max and Nell ran to put their shoulders to the door. It shook against them a second before stopping. Susan looked out the window. The figures stood conferring in the yard.

"Can they open it?" Jean asked her, quivering.

"No, no, they can't," Susan told her. "Everything's locked."

She watched as one of the hooded figures leaned toward the other, shaking its head. They paused another second and turned their hooded faces her way. The first tugged at the second. A minute later, they disappeared into darkness.

"How do they do that?" Kate asked. "Disappear like that?"

"They're fast," Susan said. "That's what Liyla's mother said."

"What do they want?" Nell asked. She and Max had returned from the door.

"What everybody seems to want," Max said shakily. "Us."

Unable to go and afraid to stay, they sat and argued as the night waned.

"Wish we had a knife," Max said. "I wouldn't mind one like Liyla's."

Nell suggested he take it, in trade for the Barbie.

"And what are you going to do with it?" Susan asked him. "Stick Liyla's mother?"

He shrugged. "Maybe her father. This is kind of like a war, isn't it?"

Susan looked at Kate and Jean. She sighed. "Yeah, and we're your army. I don't think a straight-on attack's going to work."

"Besides," Kate said, "that's yuck."

"Yuck will be what happens if they send us to whatever those workshops are," Max told her. "Don't you remember Liyla asking if they had to cut us?"

Kate looked dismayed. She picked at the sagging edge of the mattress and sniffed. Outside, the window had begun to lighten, and gray, unhappy light seeped into the room.

"Can't we push her into the oven or something?" Jean asked.

Nell snorted. "She's not a witch! How many times do we have to tell you?"

Max ignored them both and began explaining how he planned to slip into the bedroom, steal the knife, and get them out of there.

But Susan had another idea.

"She's not a witch," she agreed. "But you know what she is? A crocodile."

Even Max stopped when she said this. They all looked at her like she'd lost her marbles.

So she told them the story of the monkey and the crocodile,

in which the crocodile, hungry for monkey's heart, tempts the monkey onto her back and tries to drown him in the river. The monkey saves himself by convincing the crocodile he's left his heart in a tree back home.

"Don't you see? We're the monkey. They don't want us; they want whatever makes us look this way. You heard Liyla, didn't you, when she called those people sleeping in the shed change-bringers? And her mother said Jean looked like an old painting! They think they used to look like us! And that *we* used to look like *them* until whatever happens in those workshops. So what if they thought we were changing back? What would they do then?"

Nell turned on her in horror.

"What do you mean, 'back'?" she asked her. "We can't look like them, can we?"

Susan prayed it was true when she said, "No, we can't. But they don't know that, do they?"

By the time the light turned from gray to pink, they had it settled. Susan got up, stretched, and peered outside. She shuddered. The strangers were gone, but their footprints still covered the chicken yard. Kate sat on the bed, legs pulled tight to her chest, her chin resting on her knees. There were dark circles under her eyes. Lack of sleep would be better than makeup, Susan thought.

"Now, don't overdo it, right?" she said, mostly to Nell but a little to Max, too. He had just returned from the fireplace with two fistfuls of ash. "Just enough to convince them to leave."

Neither of them said anything. Nell put her hand out, and Max dumped a small mound of ash there. He gave the same to Susan, Kate, and Jean.

Susan took a pinch from her own hand and rubbed an ashy line down the side of Kate's jaw.

"You ready?" she asked.

Kate nodded queasily. She looked at the curtain.

"Where will we go when we get out?" she asked hoarsely.

That, too, had been decided in the night.

"Same place we started," Susan said. "Who knows? Maybe the window will just come back for us."

It wasn't a good answer, but Kate accepted it anyway. She sighed. "Okay, me first?"

"You first," Max told her.

Kate seemed to be counting to herself. After a beat, she took a deep breath, looked swiftly at Susan, and screamed.

"Ah! Ahhhh!"

Susan winced and covered her ears as Kate flung herself across the bed.

A crash sounded on the other side of the house. One, possibly two people had fallen out of bed. A second later, the bedroom door slammed open and Liyla's parents thundered across the floor and ripped the curtain back.

"What is it? What's happening?" Liyla's mother shouted.

Kate writhed on the mattress, wailing in a voice so piercing that the woman drew back and goggled at her. Liyla's mother's hair was askew, and the faint bristle that had grown back on her forehead overnight stood on end. Her husband hung over her shoulder, blinking frantically, as Liyla, wearing a yellowed nightshirt, bounced behind them, trying to get a look. She caught sight of Kate and her jaw went slack.

"It's the change!" Susan yelled at them. "It's coming back!"

Liyla's mother wheeled on her. "You said you didn't remember!"

"It's coming back to us!" Max shouted. He slapped a hand to his head. "This has happened before! Yes! Yes, it has! If we don't stop it, she's going to lose it all!"

Criminations! Susan bit her tongue and shot Max a warning look, but Liyla and her parents were captivated by the drama unfolding in the curtained alcove. Jean chose that moment to throw herself on the floor, raising a cloud of dust and startling a mouse, which shot from under the bed and zipped past them to escape under the curtain. Jean rolled over and passed a hand near her face, leaving a dark line there.

"Ayeeee!" she shrieked. She hugged herself and kicked her feet, rolling across the dirty boards. Liyla's father jumped back and uttered a couple of unfamiliar curses.

"Look at that one's face! We've got to stop it! How do we stop it?!"

Susan didn't answer him. She only looked at Nell, who had begun to vibrate. From head to toe, she shook as if she were standing at the epicenter of her own private earthquake. Max knocked her onto the bed beside Kate, where she continued to shake and kick her legs. She threw an arm out and it, too, was streaked with what looked like a coat of grayish hair.

Liyla's mother seized Susan by the arm and jerked her around.

"He said it's happened before! But you must have stopped it! *How do you stop it?*"

Max moaned loudly and bent double, slamming conveniently into Liyla's father's knee as he did it. When he looked up, he had a smudge across his eyebrows.

"Two days! That's what we've got!" Susan shouted at them.

"Two days and without the procedure, we turn! It's awful! Please help us stop it!"

She ground her teeth and let her knees buckle. Liyla's mother, who still had hold of her arm, caught her as she sank to the floor.

"The procedure," Susan choked out. "That's what stops it. Only that!"

Procedure had been Max's suggestion. Susan agreed it sounded appropriately complicated and forbidding. Over the next few minutes, between gasps, strangled cries, and a few well-placed shrieks, Susan got Liyla's family to understand that the procedure for keeping the change at bay required eye of newt, toe of frog, and wool of bat, plus two large bathtubs, soap, and a good amount of warm water.

Leaving them thrashing, moaning, and blooming gray, Liyla's parents ran to get the supplies. Liyla bolted the doors behind them. When they'd safely gone, Nell hacked up what sounded like half a lung and begged the girl for water.

"But I can't leave! Ma says I need to watch you!" she cried.

Max assured her there'd be nothing but a hair ball left of them if she didn't get some water from the well, and at last she sprinted out the back door, still in her nightshirt.

Chapter 15

They didn't stop running until the dirt road had turned to pavement again and they could move in the shadows of buildings.

Panting, they walked along the sloping curbs, too hot and wishing they'd had breakfast. Already the streets were filling with people, men pushing wagons and occasionally a mule pulling one, its harness clinking along and the carter casually slapping the animal with a thin stick when it paused in the road. There were women, too, hauling baskets or children, hurrying on to wherever people went along these dirty, crowded streets. The five of them kept their heads down, and few people looked their way. Still, following Liyla's example, they walked in the alleys when they could, despite the stench. Here, the narrow roads were full of the people Liyla had called sleepers, figures sprawled in doorways or against blackened walls, cats and even the occasional rat nosing at them. As they walked past one man, he stirred and groaned, and the children jumped and hurried on. At the end of the alley, Max dug into his pocket and pulled out Liyla's knife. He ran his hand along the flat side of the blade.

"You actually took it?" Susan asked him, shocked.

He tilted his head to indicate the alley. "How else are we going to get back across this city?" He held the knife up to catch the sun, and it threw a brilliant shaft of light their way. "She needed it for the same thing, didn't she?"

Susan felt a strange pang of guilt, looking at it. Liyla hadn't meant them any harm. . . . Well, maybe she had, but Susan felt that she hadn't meant to mean it. She said so to Nell.

"Are you crazy?" her sister asked her. "She was planning to turn us in for a reward at the lost and found!"

Still, Susan couldn't shake the bad feeling it gave her.

"Put it away, anyway," she said to Max. "We don't need to ask for trouble, do we?"

"Our faces are asking for trouble," Nell said. "You don't think that, out here in the sunlight, anybody's going to be fooled by a little bit of dirt from the fireplace, do you? Besides, it's only good planning to be prepared."

Max grinned at her.

Susan thought that if the two of them were so keen on being Boy Scouts, they ought to at least work on the important things, like marking direction by the sun and finding running water now that the daylight glared down through the buildings in long, searing lines. By midmorning, the dawn cool had burned away, and even the patches of mud along the curbstones sizzled where the light hit them. The streaks of ash on Susan's face itched, and the outhouse stench of the city rose with the heat. Worse, all the blocks had begun to look the same, full of squat, small-windowed buildings of pebbled concrete or wooden slats, flat roofed, with overhangs of cloth or rippled lengths of tin. Some had been painted, but the paint had chipped and faded, and occasionally Susan would catch sight of a flake of it underfoot, pressed into the dried mud in the road.

"Max, do you remember this street from yesterday?" she asked him as they rounded a corner where an oily table displaying broken bits of machinery sat in the sun, advertising the wares of the dark shop inside. Past it stood another reeking shed, a single sleeper curled inside.

"Sure I do. We go this way."

A few blocks later and Susan knew that they'd taken a wrong turn. They stood facing a tall building much older than the rest, though just as dirty. Sleepers lay thick along one of its walls, propped against one another or sprawling into the roadway. There was little traffic here. A stray cat snarled at the five of them, then went on hunting rats. Yet despite the ruin of the street, this building was better made than the others they'd seen. It sported an ornate front portico through which Susan spied a wide, high-ceilinged hall littered with shards of old crockery, legless chairs, and so much trash it looked impassable.

"Now, this I know we didn't see before."

Max frowned. "We just took one wrong turn. Let's go that way."

They slid along the road, trying to keep their heads down and making their way back to the crowded avenues, which had grown more crowded as the lunch hour drew near. The five of them bunched together, moving as quickly as they could manage without drawing attention.

Another turn and they found themselves facing a second grand old building, as empty of life as the first. It seemed to Susan a ghost city had sprung up in the midst of the living one.

"We didn't see this, either," she said.

They went on, but nothing seemed familiar. After a while, a bullhorn sounded in the distance.

"What's it saying?" Kate asked. "I can't understand it."

None of them could, but at the sound of it, people started streaming into the streets, making for the source of the noise.

"Is it laundry day again?" Jean wanted to know.

Nobody was carrying any clothes. A few of them carried babies, though, and one had a picnic basket under his arm. They were in a jolly mood, too, talking and waving to friends. The few who glanced at the children only grinned widely.

"That's strange," Max said.

"We should go the other way," Nell whispered to Susan as a man jostled them in his rush to get ahead. "Everyone's going this way."

"Good point," Susan said.

But when they tried to turn around, the crowd was too thick. A woman knocked into Kate, ripping her from Susan.

"Let's at least get to a side street," Susan said, grabbing Kate's hand again. "Then we'll get out of the crowd."

The bullhorn continued its squawking.

And now Susan could make out the words.

"Citizens, gather! Citizens, rejoice!" it screeched. "Come all, come all! It's rally day!"

Chapter 16

Susan tried to backpedal, but the crowd swept her forward into a wide square dominated by a large open-topped bandstand. The platform was draped in scarlet bunting, and soldiers moved across it busily, their ruddy cloaks glossy in the sun.

They were unrolling a long banner, and, watching them work, the people around Susan vibrated with anticipation. After a moment, the soldiers straightened and hoisted the banner in a sudden triumphant gesture of raised arms. The crowd cheered.

Susan looked up and froze.

A man's face, fifteen times life-size, smiled down from the painted sign. But he wasn't like Liyla. He had none of the stretched features, neither the hair nor the raw skin. He was just a reasonably good-looking middle-aged man beaming above a slogan that read "Our past, your future — all hail the Genius!"

"He's normal!" Jean gasped. "Look at him!"

Hope rushed at Susan so fast it made her knees weak.

"He's normal," she repeated.

Around them, the square buzzed with excitement. People glanced their way and sang out "rally day!" as if the children themselves had brought it. They clapped Max on the shoulder and winked at the girls, laughing.

At first the five of them shied away. Susan felt as if she had stumbled into a carnival to which she hadn't bought tickets. But after a while, it didn't seem to matter. Good feeling abounded. Soldiers moved through, shouting "rally day!" through megaphones. Children zigzagged, laughing, between the adults, and nobody scolded them. A woman handed out sweets, and a boy made a point of pressing one into Susan's hand, then her siblings'. When she tried to give it back, he shook his head, laughing.

"Rally day!" he said, as if that were an answer. Soon it felt like one. Joy radiated from every face, and so many people smiled at them that at last the children found themselves smiling back.

"Rally day is fun," Kate said.

Susan watched people take their places against the walls of buildings, as if a parade were on its way.

"It is fun," she said.

All the laughter and cheer loosened the knot in Susan's chest. Nearby, a man whooped, and the group around him laughed. Someone else yodeled into the sky, and Susan saw it was a grown woman, her mother's age, doing a little jig.

People applauded, and the crowd whistled in appreciation. Couples turned to look at each other, beaming.

"He's on his way!" a boy next to Susan said. "He's coming!"

A woman clapped her hands, and the crowd hummed eagerly. Susan laughed. Her heart rapped giddily in her chest — *pop, pop, pop* — and she smiled back at the people in the square. This was exciting! Everything was going to be okay!

The creases that had gouged their way into Kate's forehead for nearly two days had finally been ironed out. Jean hopped on the balls of her feet. Behind her, Nell let out a cheer, and instead of shushing her, Max nodded.

"Rally day!" the red cloaks shouted through bullhorns.

The crowd took up the chant. "Rally day! Rally day!"

The sound of it beat in the courtyard until Susan could feel it in the soles of her feet. The rhythm of it felt irresistible, music demanding a dance.

"Rally day," she tried.

"Rally day!" Kate said beside her.

They were all saying it now, chanting it, shouting it. Around her, the same words issued from everyone's lips, all of them thrumming with the same feeling of excitement, expectation.

Susan saw heads turn, and the adults craned their necks. A man lifted a small boy onto his shoulders.

"The Purity Patrol!" a girl said, waving. With a blast of horns, a group of red-sashed children marched into the square as the people whistled and called. Soldiers followed with drums and trumpets, making way for a wagon swathed in crimson and flanked by red cloaks. On it stood a man, waving, a large black dog at his side. At the sight of him, the crowd roared.

"Is it him? Is that the Genius?" Jean asked.

Susan squinted. Though the dog beside him stood out sharp and glossy in the sunlight, there was something fuzzy about the man, something that wouldn't quite hold still to be looked at. He jumped from the wagon and mounted the platform.

"It is!" Kate said. "It's the man on the sign!"

Susan's heart beat faster. Now she saw him. Yes! Yes, he was so beautiful!

Jean bounced beside her. "Let's go to him! Let's get up there!"

The crowd was too thick for that. A moment later, the Genius raised his hands, the music stopped, and for a second, there was no sound but the breaths and sighs of the people in the square, the murmurs of small children and the piping the babies made as their parents shushed them.

Hemmed in on all sides, the children beamed up at the wonderful man on the platform.

"I can't see!" Jean whispered. "Max! I want to see!"

He boosted her onto his shoulders, and Kate nudged Susan. "Could I get up, too?"

Susan hoisted her. She herself could just see the man on the bandstand between the heads of those in front of her, and now she adjusted Kate on her shoulders as the Genius began to speak.

"My friends," he said, and the smooth richness of his voice enveloped the square, blanketing all of it, the breaths and the sighs and the murmurs. "We meet again in a fateful hour." He paused and looked soberly down into the upturned faces.

"Fateful, for you must sense, as I do, that we stand at the edge of greatness."

His voice was more stirring than the music had been. He smiled, and Susan felt he was sharing a secret with her, a gift that was splendid and precious. She only needed to reach for it. She smiled back.

"Already, I see cause for celebration. There's victory — a hundred victories, a thousand! — in your strong, useful faces. Celebrate that! Celebrate your victories!"

Celebrate! The crowd cheered and the word filled Susan like an expanding balloon. Exuberant, she jiggled Kate on her shoulders, hugging her sister's legs. How terrific it was! They were strong! All of them!

"Yes!" the man purred. "Congratulate yourselves. Be proud of your city, of this marvelous Domain. Be proud of your broad avenues and the beauty of your buildings! Every one of you is a soldier, marching to battle the change with your busy hands! Each day of usefulness is a skirmish won! Each tall building is your triumph, your victory!"

From Susan's shoulders, Kate laughed giddily, and Susan looked around, swelling with the pleasure of it all. How had she missed this before? The buildings were so much taller than she'd thought! The crowd cheered and whistled. Why had she thought the city dirty? It sparkled in the sunlight. Even the people were smoother than she'd imagined. What had caused her so much grief? She'd been exaggerating — that's what. Worrying for nothing. She turned to tell Max and found him squinting, openmouthed, at the polished bricks. She grinned and saw Nell blinking in confusion, her eyes darting from the buildings to the people to the Genius.

Susan had never been in love, but she had read about it, and the thought struck her that this must be the way of it. She had been wrong, all wrong, about the man on the platform, about the city, about everything here, and now she could really see it for the first time. What was it about him? She couldn't put her finger on it. And after a minute, she couldn't puzzle it out anymore, because there was nothing, really, but that voice, those words, that powerful rightness that she could feel so strongly it made her want to shout.

Her whole mind went to that voice. The man was beautiful. She wondered why she hadn't seen it before. Everything was beautiful here.

"You," he was saying, "my useful ones. You can sense the change withering. You know it! You can feel the nearness of the final victory."

Victory! A sigh of eagerness wafted through the crowd, and like an electrical current, it snapped through Susan, connecting her to all the people in the square, all the wonderful, wonderful people and the glorious man on the platform. The crowd was a living thing now, a single mass, and she was part of it, and glad — so glad to be useful! The word glowed vibrantly. It was the best of words, the best she'd ever heard. What was anything compared to usefulness? Nothing at all. Susan looked up at the man and saw him pause, beaming down at them. Then he grew somber.

"Yes, we're close to victory. And because we are, because we stand upon our victories, we forget. We forget! We don't see the danger lurking so close."

He shook his head, disappointed, and Susan's heart sank. What was wrong? What danger? She would fix it!

"You've let them lull you," the Genius chided. "You've relaxed your guard. The forces that would destroy you are here! At your doors!"

Susan looked around, appalled. Here! How could it be? Who would dare?

"Susan, I want to come down now," Kate said. The giddiness was gone from her voice, and Susan eased her to the ground.

Heads were nodding in the crowd. Murmurs and shouts of "Tell us!" rang out. Kate took hold of Susan's shirt.

"They live to drag you down," the Genius went on. "But you tolerate the sickness in your midst. You ignore the sleeping, the insane! The wasteful and the useless! Are they like you? Are they?"

"No!" came a shout from the crowd. "No! Never!"

When had it gotten so hot? There were too many people in the square. *There shouldn't be this many people.* Susan couldn't move.

"Do you think you're kind to let infection fester?" the Genius called.

"No! No!"

The square stank of sweat and dirt and sour breath. Susan wrinkled her nose.

"But you do," the Genius continued. "You must! Why else would you allow them to litter your streets as they do? You invite it! You offer your necks so they may suck the life from you!"

The crowd shifted, nodding, murmuring. At the end of the square, Susan saw the people draw back. There, slumped in the gutter, were three sleepers. Two filthy children crouched beside them, trying to drag the prone figures into the shelter of doorways.

At the sudden attention, the two increased their efforts, tugging at one limp-bodied woman until they'd pulled her over the curb and beneath the overhang of a building. The sleeper children looked out at the crowd, eyes wide in the shadows.

The people rumbled with discontent. The last of the good feeling drained away.

"Wait, what's happening?" Nell asked.

"Shh!" Susan barked. Why did everything always go wrong? She'd thought —

"A nest of rats!" the Genius called. "And you spare them! You coddle them! You feed them!"

Everything grated now. Susan shrugged Kate's hand off her.

"He's no different," Jean said from Max's shoulders. "I thought he was different."

Susan turned back to the man on the platform. He was red. There was an animal sharpness to him she hadn't seen before.

"The useless devour!" the Genius called.

The heat from all the bodies pressed against her. Susan choked on the smell of them.

"The useless devour!" someone shouted from the crowd. Others took up the chant. "The useless devour! The useless devour!"

There was so much noise! The people pounded their feet to the words, and the rhythm of it shook the ground. *The useless devour!* The call squeezed Susan's lungs and jolted her bones.

Shrill in her ears, the boy to her right screamed, "The useless devour! The useless devour!" his voice like a bee swarm. She shoved him away, repulsed.

"Hey!" he snarled. A second ago, he'd been smooth. Now fine hairs sprouted across his forehead. He drew back his lips in a wild grin like a hyena's. Then he spat "The useless devour" into her face.

Fury splashed through Susan so suddenly, she was lunging at him before she could think. She'd rip the hairs from his head! She'd squeeze the shout from his throat!

Midleap, someone yanked her back. Bellowing, she swung around and knocked her attacker to the ground. She pulled back, eager to let fly again, but someone else had her arm now, and she struggled, enraged.

"Get off! Get off me!"

Blood throbbed in her ears.

"Susan! Susan, stop it!"

She heard her name as if from far away and fought another second before it came to her that it was Nell calling, beneath the still-pounding chant of the crowd. Abruptly she stopped and saw Kate on the ground beside her, a red mark vivid on her cheek.

Hot shame rushed into her throat.

"Kate! I —"

But the crowd took the words. It had begun to move as those near the edges turned to spring on the sleepers. A small group reached one prone figure and set upon him, kicking his limp body until one of the soldiers came to drag him to the waiting cart. When the red cloaks threw him into it, the people cheered. The crowd broke wide open then, rushing the sleepers and chasing their children, who scattered.

Susan stood alone in the midst of it, staring at the mark on Kate's face. Bewildered, she looked at her hand as if it belonged to someone else.

"It was an accident! Kate! I'm sorry!"

Her hand was shaking. Kate took it.

"It's okay," Kate said. "It's okay."

But nobody was okay. Susan looked over at Max, who stared at her, openmouthed, and then at Jean, sitting thunderstruck on his shoulders. She couldn't meet their eyes. She looked past them through the moving crowd to the man on the platform. She could see him plainly now.

He had stopped chanting. Beneath him, the crowd seethed, and he stood smiling, his hand on the black dog's head, nodding at the cries of triumph as another sleeper was thrown onto the cart. How had she not seen it before? He was as craggy and blotch faced as the rest of them, scrubbed and plucked and misshapen, despite his embroidered red cloak and his rich voice.

She was so struck by the change that it took a moment to realize he was looking their way in surprise, staring directly at Jean, who sat on Max's shoulders, bobbing above the sea of heads.

Susan's breath caught.

"Get down! Jean! Get down! He's seen us!"

Jean slid to the ground, but it was too late. The man had snapped his fingers, pointing, and red cloaks were leaping from the bandstand into the square, muskets up, breaking a path through the crush of bodies.

"Come on!" Max shouted, yanking Jean by the arm. "Now!"

"Susan!" Nell yelled. "Snap out of it! Run!"

Kate's hand was still in hers, and together they dashed after the others, smashing through knots of people, burrowing under adults' waving arms, and ducking around frenzied chanters as the soldiers plunged after them.

They sprinted for the side streets. The crowd screamed and cheered, and now they could hear soldiers shouting "Make way!" as they charged through the mob in pursuit.

"Stop them!" someone shrieked, and Susan snatched Kate from beneath a grasping hand and kicked at the pursuer as they lurched free of the crowd and leaped for the curb. "Get them! Stop them!"

A man stepped into their path, and Max mowed him down, hauling Jean behind him. They veered round a corner, past a shuttered store where the windows had been smashed. Glass crunched beneath their feet, and they turned again only to find themselves rushing headlong toward another part of the mob, which had now surged into the side streets, hunting sleepers.

"This way!" Nell yelled. She turned and they ran deeper into the city, searching for an empty path. But the soldiers had reached the streets, too, and in the gaps between buildings, Susan could see them fanning out along the main roadways on either side. One block, two, and there seemed no place to go. Her chest was bursting when she passed one of the dirty old buildings that loomed above the rest. She darted into the alley beside it, yelling for the others. They ran down the long passage, past clouded windows and heavy doors, as the shouts from the streets bounced muffled against the walls. Jean tripped and fell, sprawling. Kate slowed, panting.

"Don't stop!" Susan cried. "They're coming!"

But they had stopped. Max had his hands on his knees, and Nell stumbled.

"Search that way!" someone yelled.

Desperate, Susan scooped Jean from the ground and yanked her into one of the deep, recessed doorways in the side of the old building. She beckoned to the others. Kate scurried in and Max and Nell squeezed beside them, pressing their backs to the splintering wooden door.

Susan heard the clatter of boots in the alley.

"Oh, please," she whispered. "Please."

And then she tumbled backward as the door opened. Someone grabbed them from behind, dragged them inside, and shut it, quickly, again.

Chapter 17

Susan stifled a shriek, jerked herself loose, and turned to find three sharp-faced sleepers' children, two of whom still had her siblings by the collars.

"Quiet!" one of them said, putting a finger to his lips. He had a chipped front tooth and blond hair clumpy with grime. With him stood a girl who'd wound her light hair in knots on top of her head and a small dark-eyed boy with protruding ears. None of them could have been more than ten years old, and the smallest looked like he might be younger than Jean.

With a jerk of his head, the blond boy took off down the hall, moving silently through the once grand hallway, where the remains of a mosaic, pitted with missing stones, showed smooth-faced women harvesting apples on a green hill. Susan glanced at it as she followed the sleepers' children down a corridor, through a set of double doors, and into a large room with a high ceiling and wide windows. A fat iron stove took up the center of the floor; garbage littered the rest — rags, half a broomstick, part of a rusty chain. Even the stone fireplace between the windows was stuffed with lengths of broken pipe. Three narrow closets lined the right wall. One of them, doorless, gaped like a lost tooth.

Susan could hear the soldiers in the alley now, boots pounding on the paving stones.

The smallest of the street children, the hollow-faced boy with dark eyes, shot a frightened glance toward the door. He ran to the stove, wrenched it open, and folded himself inside, pulling the door shut. The other two hustled the children toward the doorless closet.

"In here," the blond boy said, pointing to Susan. "You!"

He reached down, pulled at an uneven edge in the wooden flooring, and lifted it to reveal a square pit like the one in Liyla's house. He gave Susan a little shove toward it. "Get in," he said. "And take these with you."

He meant Jean and Kate.

Susan turned back for Max and Nell. "What about them?" she whispered.

"We got other places!" the girl assured her. Nodding, the boy nudged her toward the pit again. Susan jumped into it. Unlike the cellar at Liyla's, this place was warm and shallow. If she stood straight, her chest and shoulders cleared the floor-boards and stuck up into the closet. But when she squatted in the darkness, Susan could stretch both arms and only touch the crumbling edge of the wall. She put her hands down and realized it was not dirt but wood she was touching, a floor beneath the floor. Kate and Jean hopped in beside her, and she pulled them to her, their bodies so close she could feel their hearts making frantic moth-wing flutters against her chest. The light-haired girl pressed the board into place, and a mil-dewy darkness descended, the floorboards overhead framed in pencil lines of light. Susan wrapped her arms around the younger girls and tried to master her shuddering lungs.

The soldiers were pounding on the outer door. Above her, Susan could hear footsteps as the two remaining children hustled Max and Nell across the floor toward the wall full of windows.

A moment later, the far door gave way, and soldiers clattered into the hall, then stomped overhead as they rushed into the empty room. The doors of the two intact closets slammed open. Boots moved to the outer wall, and Susan felt dizzy. But then one of them muttered, "Trash!" and moved across the floorboards. She heard a ringing, metallic kick — the stove — and a muffled, quickly suppressed yelp.

"Here!" a man's voice called. Susan could hear the small boy squeak in protest as they pulled him out.

"Useless!" she heard a soldier say. "Take him!"

But a second voice intervened. "No time for that now," he said. "We're looking for those others. Leave him."

And then the boots were gone.

Susan waited, crouching in the damp cotton darkness, her legs slowly cramping. She listened, but there was nothing to hear but her sisters' shallow, quivering breaths.

Paralyzed, she waited for what seemed like hours, staring into the black. Spots formed and disappeared before her eyes, and she could feel her shirt slowly grow wet where the girls pressed against her. She tried not to flinch when something small scuttled over her foot. Jean felt it and squeaked.

"Shh," Susan breathed in her ear.

They held still, frozen, until Susan's legs screamed in protest and the thick heat of the place felt like it had crawled down her throat and turned her stomach.

At last she heard a scrape, followed by light footsteps. The square over her head creaked open, and her sisters flinched. Susan threw her hands up, dazzled by the light.

The girl stared down at her, offering a hand.

"Sorry," she said, pulling the younger ones up. "Have to wait awhile before we know they're really gone. Gets tight down there — I know."

Susan groaned to her feet and climbed up and out of the closet. Max and Nell, blinking and dusty, stood behind the girl. The boy from the stove sat hunched against the wall, head in hands. As they emerged, he looked up and sighed shakily. Ash clung to the fine coating of hair on his skinny face, and when he shook his head, soot sprayed from it like so much snow. It settled in small gray drifts along the gritty floorboards.

"You guys okay?" Max asked Susan. She nodded.

Her neck prickled, and she turned to find the older boy and girl staring at them intently. She met the girl's eye.

"Thank you," she said. "I'm Susan. You saved us back there."

The girl continued to stare at her for a second, then blinked and turned to the small boy who sat by the stove.

"Get Omet," she said.

Chapter 18

The boy scurried from the room, and the other two continued to stare at the five of them with the same sober expression Susan had seen on Mrs. Grady's dog when he sat by the table at suppertime. It seemed to her that the silence gained a pound or so as it sat there between them, the other children gaping like that, and the five of them unsure which way to look or what to do with their hands.

At last, Nell said, "What do they call you two?"

One of the girl's blond knots dipped toward her forehead, and she pushed it now with the heel of her hand. "Yali," she said, and tilted toward the boy. "This is Modo." All the time, she kept her eyes on Susan's face.

Not another word after that, but plenty of looking. A minute later, the sound of running feet broke the silence. Yali and Modo didn't flinch, but to Susan it sounded like another rally, or maybe a riot approaching. Her heart, which had only now steadied after the terror of the soldiers, sped up again. She glanced sideways and saw Max slip his hand into the pocket that held the knife.

Before she'd had a chance to decide what to do, a small crowd of maybe fifteen children burst through the door, followed by a tall, lean girl with straight black hair and equally dark eyes. She had jagged bangs that looked like they'd been cut with a knife, and the hair on her face cast a dull shadow over her gaunt cheeks. One vivid clear spot stood out on her jaw, and after a moment, Susan saw why. Every few minutes, the girl swiped at it with the back of her hand, as if there were still something to rub away.

The other children made way for her as she came toward the five of them. She elbowed Yali and Modo aside, went for the side of her chin again, and nodded.

"So it's true, then. Espin was right. You're not just rally real."

She had a surprisingly soft voice. The children crowded behind her, eyes fixed on the siblings.

"Rally real?" Susan said. She thought suddenly of the fruit seller, asking Liyla if it was rally day.

Omet shrugged. "When he told us what he'd seen yesterday, that's what we thought. Get hungry enough, you see things even on a regular day. But of course, he did have those peaches. They were real enough." She tipped her head. "Thanks for that. Takes something, to feed the useless."

"Useless?" Susan repeated, surprised.

The girl nodded. "Of course. Espin, this is the one, isn't it?"

She'd indicated a boy near the back of the group. Susan saw him now. It was the boy from the shed. He pushed forward, grinning.

"Yes, Omet," he said. "That's the one."

Susan was suddenly ashamed that she hadn't asked his name yesterday.

Behind the dark-haired girl, the group had gotten restless. A slim girl with red curls that extended faintly onto her cheeks slipped past Espin.

"So how did you get out? How many others did you see?"

It was like someone had rung the bell at recess time. The others surged forward.

"Do you know Asto? Is she still there?"

"What about Elta? Short? And with brown hair? Scar over her eyes?"

"Oto, he's got a limp — right foot's twisted."

"Yand! You'd know him 'cause he squints, like this!"

They smelled of sweat and dirt, and the noise of their questions bounced off the high ceilings and echoed across the room. Names and more names, too many to make out.

Omet gave a great clap.

"*Ssst!* Give them a minute! Not all at once!" She shoved a few kids back, and Susan took a good breath of humid air. Kate clung to her shirt, and Jean had practically climbed onto Max's shoulders. Nell stood elbows out, trying to keep a small perimeter of space around her.

Near Susan, two little boys danced on the balls of their feet, straining to hold back the questions.

Omet nodded. "Now," she said. "Slow like. Of course you're all impatient to know who they've seen. They must have been there a long time, to look the way they do."

Susan glanced, half desperate, at Max and Nell, but they looked bewildered. Omet turned back to them.

"So, slow like, if you don't mind." She bent her head, waiting.

None of them said anything for a minute. Finally Max cleared his throat.

"You're talking about the workshops?"

The girl looked up. "What else?"

The children had begun inching in again, and Susan could feel the heat radiating from their small bodies.

"They take you from a village?" a boy whispered.

"Mines?"

"Ruins?"

"Do you know my sister? She's got brown hair, like me!"

Again, they were shouting. She tried to follow the rush — sisters, brothers, friends —

Another clap from Omet.

"Forgive us," she said, shaking her head. "But we've lost a few, and they're missed."

Susan looked at the ragged little group, thin faces dusted with hair and hollowed out by hunger.

"I'm so sorry," she said. "We don't know anything. We don't . . ." She tried to find the right word, but there were no right words, and to her dismay she blurted the ones Liyla had supplied: "We don't remember."

Nell shot her a look and she cringed. The younger kids didn't seem to register what she'd said. But some of the older ones frowned and bit their lips.

Omet's expression darkened. "Don't remember? How can you go through the workshop and not remember?" Even she stepped closer now.

"We're not from here. We come from a different place altogether."

Like a balloon leaking air, the children slumped.

"Different place?" a boy said. "What different place is there?"

Yali shoved her way through. "You sure you didn't see Daleli? She's my sister. Looks a lot like me. She was only took this month."

Omet frowned and tugged Yali back. "All right, you all heard them. They don't remember. So leave them be. We oughta eat, anyway. Isn't it rally day?"

A few of the children nodded half-heartedly. They stepped back, and suddenly the open space around the five of them felt to Susan like a slap. She watched Omet knock Modo in the shoulder. "Come on, Modo! Is that all I get? A grunt? Don't tell me you're not hungry?"

The boy only hung his head. A dark-skinned girl rubbed his arm.

"His brother got took today," she said. "The sleepy one."

"Oh." Omet said. She patted the boy on the shoulder. "Hey, Modo, we'll save you some."

The boy nodded, and Omet sighed. She swiped at her jaw and looked around at all the dour faces. "Being hungry won't make it better, will it? Go fetch the grub, Sefi. You, too, Espin."

Sefi was the redheaded girl who'd started the rush of questions. She and Espin ducked out of the room and returned carrying a dirty sack. When they saw it, the children brightened.

"What'd you get?"

"Good haul?"

"Any cheese today? I like cheese!"

Omet had taken charge of the food, but before she could answer, a girl rushed into the room, breathless.

"Omet! A slasher! He nearly had me! I couldn't shut the door in time!"

Omet dropped the sack.

"Where is he? In the hall?"

She needn't have asked. They heard the thing, whatever

it was, slamming and roaring in the hallway. A door smacked against a wall, and Omet's head came up.

"Second room!" she shouted. From the corner, she snatched a thick stick. The older children did the same, plucking weapons from the pile Susan had taken for garbage. Modo hefted a rusty chain; Sefi grabbed a piece of broken pipe.

Omet shoved an old fence post into Susan's hands.

"You little ones stay put!" she directed. "The rest of you, come!"

They ran toward the sound, and Susan saw Max heft Liyla's knife. Nell had armed herself with the jagged remains of a broomstick. Down the hall, whatever had gotten in was smashing itself against the walls, but the howling had stopped.

Ahead, Omet stepped lightly into a stuffy, shadowy room. What had once been tall windows were boarded, and a few broken gaps leaked sunlight onto the floor. Beside one of these, a broad animal, its head down and its back humped, stood panting, its shoulder to the wall.

"Ay! Slasher!" Omet shouted.

The thing lifted its head and turned. It had the shape of a man, but it didn't look like one. While the sleepers' children had the faintest coat of hair on their faces, this thing peered from a thicket of it. The heavy growth spread all over its body, and its teeth, long and yellow, curved to sharp points over its blackened lips. When it saw them, it stopped panting and growled softly. Omet lifted her stick, jerking her head to the right.

"That way," she said to Susan. "And keep your stick up."

Susan raised the slab of splintering wood and moved to

the right to join the others in a half circle around the beast. From the corner of her eye, she saw Nell, white-knuckled and clutching the broomstick. Max held the knife in front of him, point out.

A low rumble from the creature; its eyes darted from child to child. Modo shook the chain, and with a snarl, the creature's head swiveled his way. Omet and Espin edged around to the side of it.

"Cut off all paths but the one out," Omet said in a low voice. Yali and Sefi stepped into the hall and blocked the way.

The thing half crouched, its arms brushing the floor, and growled softly.

"Careful now," Modo said. "Keep your eyes on him. He's nearly ready."

"For what?" Max whispered.

"To slash. Arms up, and try to look bigger than you are."

Susan squared her shoulders and raised her head. All the time, she watched the thing as it bobbed there on its matted feet.

Suddenly, Nell gasped, and for a split second, Susan turned her head.

"No!" Omet yelled.

Too late, Susan realized her mistake. She wheeled back, but the creature had launched itself at her. A monster the size of a grown man, it snatched at her as she tried to jump aside, and she fell with a thud. The blow knocked the breath from her, and she struggled, gasping, as the thing lunged. A sharp pain in her shoulder! She cried out and clawed at the creature, half suffocating from the foul stench. Her fingers closed on a stiff bristle of hair, and she yanked backward. She pulled her other arm free of the monster's weight and shoved at its putrid face, slick with spittle.

The others were on it by then, pounding at it with sticks and yanking at its head. They shouted and the beast screamed, losing its grip on her and scrabbling at her neck, trying to regain it. Gasping for air, Susan squirmed beneath it. Over the din, she heard Max and Nell shouting. Spots swam before her eyes and she thought her ribs would snap when suddenly the beast was off her. She looked up to see Max dragging the thing by its ears. He hauled it backward, and Modo slapped the chain around its neck. He tugged sharply and the creature flailed, falling onto its back. Susan panted and coughed, rolling onto her knees to try to find air.

She gulped, her shoulder on fire, as Nell dropped beside her.

"Susan! Susan! You okay?"

She could only cough and nod and look up in time to see Omet and Modo dragging the thing across the floor as it clawed at the chain around its neck.

Max helped her to her feet.

"It bit you!" he cried.

For another moment, Susan watched as the others dragged the thing to the door. Its feet scraped against the tiles, but every time it gained purchase, Omet and Modo jerked the chain and it fell back, gurgling, until they heaved it into the hall. Susan heard the thud of the outer door. She could finally breathe.

Nell took her arm. With shaking fingers, Max touched the small hole in her shirt.

"It's not too bad," she told him. "I'm okay."

Her brother's face looked ashen. He didn't say anything.

"Really, it's fine. Not too deep." She tugged at her shirt and saw a vivid bruise forming there. "See? It didn't even break the skin."

Max sighed shakily and stepped back. "I dropped the knife. I didn't even stab it when I should have."

Susan took another long, welcome breath. "Well, that's good. Sometimes a wounded animal's even worse than an angry one, right?"

Nell's grip tightened on her arm.

"That was no animal," she said.

"What? What do you mean?"

Nell's round face looked pasty. She eyed the small hole in Susan's shirt.

"I saw it. A second before it jumped you. That thing had on pieces of clothes. Whatever it is now, it used to be a man."

Chapter 19

She's right," the redheaded girl said. Outside, Susan could hear the slasher howling and pounding the wall. "They're people, or something like." She tilted her head at them. "Didn't you see them back in the workshop? Some say they get made there."

Susan put a hand to her bruised shoulder and shuddered.

"Sefi, what story are you telling now?"

Omet had returned with the others, who now collected weapons that had been tossed aside when they wrestled the beast away.

"Only asking," Sefi said. She kicked at a crack in one of the floor tiles. "That's what I heard, anyway."

Max ran a hand through his sweaty hair, making it stand on end.

"Is that true?" he asked, sounding a little sick. "Somebody made that thing on purpose?"

Omet only shrugged. She hefted the rusty chain and slung it over her shoulder. Modo collected Susan's fence post.

"Nobody knows," Omet said. "That's one story, but there are others. Sleeper lost to a nightmare, I once heard; only that's no sleeper I ever saw. Take your best guess which one's right."

The slasher gave a final scrape and howl, then subsided. Omet let out a grateful breath. "Off to go after someone else's supper," she said. She turned and led them down the corridor, back to the room where Kate and Jean waited, huddled beside the black stove with three of the smaller children. Susan tugged at her shirt, trying to hide the torn part.

Modo took his chain from Omet and threw it into the corner with a loud clank.

"Guess I'm ready to eat now," he said.

Omet smiled faintly and retrieved the sack. The sweaty, exhausted children promptly sat down on the floor and watched as she emptied it.

"What a haul!" Modo said. "Omet, you're the best!"

The half smile widened into a grin. Susan took a quick inventory to find out what a haul meant for children of sleepers: a loaf of bread, a slab of cheese, an apple, and two plums of fairly good size.

"Somebody left a door open," Omet said. "Almost."

Having eaten at Liyla's house, Susan steeled herself for what was coming, but to her surprise, Omet broke the cheese and bread into pieces and handed the fruits to Sefi, who produced a small knife from her pocket, carved chunks of apple and plum, and passed them around.

"We don't wait here," the girl said when she saw Susan looking. "Too hungry for it."

Gratefully, Susan accepted her share. If she'd supposed having a bite taken out of her would damp her appetite, she discovered she was wrong. Two days of nothing but peaches and bread had carved a crater inside her.

They ate, and Max being Max, he didn't wait long to pursue

the latest topic of interest: slashers. Susan listened to him go at the subject as if he were doing field research for *National Geographic*: Was anyone born a slasher? What did they eat? Where did they go when they weren't in the city?

To his obvious disappointment, the children didn't really know. They traded stories of slashers who'd been grabbed by soldiers, slashers who'd gone after sleepers, slashers who kept to the ruins, eating small game.

"We used to have one that howled all night outside our village," Yali said. "My da finally went after it with a pitchfork. He didn't catch it, but it never came back, either."

Susan raised an eyebrow. This was more interesting than what slashers ate. "You used to live in a village?"

The girl tugged at one of the knots in her hair. "Uh-huh. Till my ma went sick and died, and my da started sleeping in the square. Purity burnt our house, so we had to come." She eyed Susan. "Anything like that happen where you come from?"

"We're not from here," Nell said firmly. "We told you that."

Yali opened her mouth to protest when Sefi leaned over and whispered to her. Susan caught only the words "fiddled with" and "brains rearranged." She saw Nell flush. Yali said nothing more, but after a while, she moved next to Kate, staring so long that Kate turned to look back at her.

"What?" she asked.

Yali flushed. "Only, I just wondered if I could touch it."

Kate frowned. "Touch it?"

"Your skin. It looks so nice."

Beneath the dirt and ash on her face, Kate flushed scarlet. She nodded.

Susan watched the girl put a gentle finger to Kate's cheek, then open her whole knobby hand to run it down the side of Kate's jaw. She sighed.

"It is soft," she said. "I thought it would be."

Susan thought of the mark she'd left on Kate's face earlier and looked down at her hands, her own cheeks burning. She glanced back at Kate and saw that her sister had closed her eyes, her lips trembling. Yali noticed.

"It's all right," she said, withdrawing her hand. "I don't have to touch if you don't like it."

Kate sniffled. "No, it's okay," she said. "You can."

Again, Yali brushed her hand down Kate's cheek.

"Before my da went sleepy, he told me stories of a girl like you," she said.

Kate turned to look at her. "Me?"

"Well, he said she'd be me, one day, when the change went back. Showed me the painting of her in the village market. It hung there, rally days, you know."

"Rally days? In the village?" Jean asked. "Like today?"

Yali's bumpy hair bounced as she nodded. "Only it was a red cloak who spoke. We were too far out for the Genius to come."

"Not as good," Espin said. "My ma grew up in the city, and she said the village rallies were so dull they could put the Purity to sleep."

Sefi snorted. "No! They were good! They even brought a dog out, though he wasn't as big as Spark."

"Spark?" Nell asked her.

"The Genius's dog. You saw him, didn't you?"

Sefi sighed. "I used to love rally days!"

Susan's face grew hot as she remembered her own excitement at the rally. Her mind suddenly seemed like a foreign country.

"What happens there, during the rally?" she asked. "I thought . . ." She didn't know what she thought, really. "Things seemed like they looked different," she finished lamely.

Max lifted his head. "They did! I thought so!"

Omet only shrugged. "Rally change, that's all." She shook her head and clucked sympathetically. "You've lost some, no doubt about that. But maybe you'll get it back, if you try to think real hard."

Nell caught Susan's eye and shook her head.

The late-afternoon light had begun to soften, and the sounds outside the ground-floor windows were quieter now. Susan rubbed once more at the lump in her shoulder and stood up.

"Thank you so much," she said to the children. "For everything you did for us. They would have taken us without you. But now we've got to head out. The farther we get from the city, the better we'll be, I think."

Omet frowned at her. "That might be so, but you'd be a fool to go now," she said. "Night's coming on. Red cloaks and their dogs check the borders, and that's not to mention the slashers looking for dinner."

"And the green hoods," Modo said. "Fanatics. Don't forget them."

Sefi and Yali were nodding. Omet waited. Reluctantly, Susan sank back down.

"I guess we'll stay the night," she said.

*T*ime, *the ancients had written, is a vast house. In this room a man lives, in another he dies, in this one a child is born, and in this one, he holds his grandchild. Yesterday and tomorrow are mere illusions. All thens are now.*

The exile read these things over and over, trying to believe them. If all thens were now, there was no aloneness, no banishment, no loss. If all were now, the promise of redemption had come, the five stood nearby, and the age of empty silence was no more than a single room in the vast house, a thousand others alive with joy and union. One could leave the small room and close the door.

But the ancients had also written of a man whose house holds a treasure in its walls. If he knows it not, he owns nothing. If he cannot find his wealth, though it surrounds him, he is poor.

And so the exile stood at the center of the small room in the great house of time and had not the eyes to find the door.

Chapter 20

Three nights, Susan thought. Three nights away from home, and not a clue as to how to get back. She shuddered. The sleepers' children were layering the floor with rags, and Yali motioned to her, showing Susan she'd cleared a corner near the window. She blew a small mountain of dust from it and swept a spiderweb away with her stick.

"Spiders, you know, they can bite," she explained. Sefi and Espin brought two battered old coats and half a tablecloth over for padding, and Nell spread her blanket over the pile. The five of them took their spots on it, sagged between the lumps, and sweated as night fell.

Yali stretched out on the other side of Susan.

"I won't touch your face in the night," she assured her. "I just like to look at it. You don't mind, do you?"

Susan flushed, but she shook her head and tried to find something to look at besides the girl's wide eyes, inches from her face.

Above her, the long windows deepened from blue to black. Outside, the sounds of steam engines and people in the streets dwindled.

"Sefi, will you sing?" It was the little boy who'd hidden in the stove; Susan tried to remember his name and couldn't. "Like you did last rally day?"

Beside Espin, Sefi yawned. "I'm tired."

"Just one. I don't like to sleep after slashers. Please, Sefi?"

A long pause, and finally Sefi sighed. "Just one. You choose."

The little boy thought a minute. Then Susan heard him say, "I don't know. A rally song, how 'bout?"

"Yes," someone else said. "Those are always the best."

Sefi cleared her throat and sang:

"The useless brought the change and still
They suck you dry — they always will.
No better than a plague are these
So treat them as you would disease."

Susan gave a start. The song went on, ending with the words she had heard from Liyla:

"Give them a gift, they'll pay you double,
In the only coin they know — that's trouble."

"How could you sing that?" Nell asked in the darkness. "That's awful!"

An uncomfortable silence followed.

"It's just a song." There was an edge to Sefi's voice when she said it. "And they're all like that, aren't they?"

Omet's voice came from across the room.

"It's a nice tune, Sefi," she said soothingly. "No harm in it."

But Nell wouldn't let it go. "But there is!" she said, propping herself up on her elbow. "How could you say there isn't?"

For another long moment, the silence stretched. Susan rolled over and tried to see Omet, but the room was only full of dark mounds.

"I don't know," the girl said after a while. "It's just a story they tell, like all the others. Discards brought the change, sleepers turn to slashers, you know. I couldn't tell you what's true. Once heard a story that it was dark magics brought the change, and wicked magicians with books of evil. It's all just village tales."

Espin laughed softly in the dark. "Wicked magics," he said. "I heard that one. But my ma told me that's just what the useless say. She said that before she was useless herself, of course."

Susan thought of the woman she'd seen in the shed. She wondered if that was Espin's mother.

Modo, who'd bedded down near Omet, laughed at this. "What books, anyway? Where are they, then?"

"Maybe in the ruins," Yali said from beside Susan. "I heard they were burned to ash there in the first wars."

"Village tales," Omet said again. "Only way books bring the change is by being useless, and the only books I ever saw were the red cloak law book and the farming rules given out by the Purity. Those aren't dark magics."

"I had one of those!" someone else said delightedly. "I almost made the patrol, too, before my da went sleepy. Always wanted to."

"I was in it," Modo said. "And it was nice. I liked the fruit picking. Weekly harvest. It helped at home. But then, you know, my sister came, and they pushed me out. Still love the songs, though."

Omet laughed again, softer this time. "See that, Sefi? Modo loves the songs, too."

But Sefi was already asleep, snoring softly on her pile of rags.

Chapter 21

Outside, the moon had risen, and through the windows, the dark shimmered with the ghost of it, strands of silky light that caught the dust. It was too quiet for a city, Susan decided. There was no hum of machinery, no distant honking cars, only the occasional shout or bark of a dog far away.

Red cloaks, she reminded herself. Patrolling. Her mind began to play tricks on her, and though she knew it couldn't be, the city stretched out all around her, swallowing the world, swallowing even her own home, everything familiar and normal and known. It was impossibly big, so big she wanted to fold herself into a small space and hide from it. *It's not that big*, she told herself. *It's not even as big as a city back home. I bet it's not.*

And yet the world suddenly did feel bigger. Too big. Not in miles or meters or acres or any of the other familiar measurements, but in strangeness. She knew that even her own world was bigger in that way than she typically liked to believe. She reflected now that the place she called home was really very small. It was comforting that way. The bigness of it existed only in books, where the ugliness could be put away when you were done. She looked around at the sleeping children: dirty, bruised, hungry. Their world was so big, it had eaten them up.

So big, they couldn't put it away, ever. Susan thought about what it would be like to be them, to be trapped here forever. She shuddered.

Across in the dark, Jean stirred. "Max," she whispered, "write me a letter about going home."

Max groaned sleepily, and there was such a long pause that Susan thought he must be dozing, but after another second, he murmured, "Dear Jean, We're going home in the morning. Now, try to sleep. Your brother, Max."

Jean exhaled softly, satisfied, and Susan thought, *We're going home in the morning, and the world will be right sized again.*

In the morning Omet pressed a sack on them before they went. Susan peered into it and found a bit of the remaining bread and part of an iron chain.

"Just to be safe," Omet said.

The children thanked her.

"Wish you'd stay," she said as they walked out together. "Gives us a bit of hope, looking at you." She rubbed at her face, and Susan winced at the rawness of the bald little sandblasted circle she'd made there. "But you couldn't beg, not with faces like those. And I expect as soon as the sun gets high, they'll be looking for you again." She sighed. "If you need us, you know where we'll be."

They watched her head down the street, several of the smaller children behind her. Yali turned and waved cheerily at them before they turned the corner.

Max squinted at the sun. "This time let's follow the sky instead of the streets. We walked east before, so we should head west now." They set off, moving away from the rising sun.

Despite the early hour, the air was already thick and smelling of garbage. A torn strip of red bunting rolled past on a muggy breeze, looking more brown than scarlet. Nell kicked it as they passed. Susan rolled her shoulder, which throbbed where the slasher had bitten her.

After a while, the blocks began to look familiar. They passed the series of sleepers' sheds where they'd first seen Espin, but though they looked, none of the children were inside. They made their way along the line of thin-faced houses they'd seen with Liyla.

Ahead, they heard the sounds of an outdoor market. A merchant shouted; a steam engine chugged in the distance and then closer. They walked several blocks before they reached it and then finally turned a corner into a square full of booths and hawkers, flooded with summer light.

Susan looked for the fruit merchant but couldn't see him among the other stalls. Relieved, she motioned to the edge of the square, and the others followed, picking their way around the market, trying to make themselves as inconspicuous as possible.

"Just a little farther now," she said. "Once we get past these blocks, we'll head straight to the woods."

Then, from behind, a familiar voice hailed them.

"Hallo! You five! Where'd you run to yesterday? Ma was a sight when I told her I'd lost you! She threatened to put me out!"

Criminations! Susan thought as Liyla ran toward them.

"Only joking, of course," the girl continued. "But she *was* mad. Ranting and raving! I told her I'd bring you back. Useful; that's me, right?" She squinted at them. "And look! You stopped it, didn't you? Still smooth as plums!"

Susan pulled herself as much as possible into the shadow of the nearest house and favored Liyla with a tepid smile.

"We — we couldn't wait," she said. "Max remembered where we could get ..."

"An antidote!" Max supplied helpfully. "Antidote to stop the change. So of course we had to run and get it."

Liyla nodded in sage agreement. "Wait until I explain it to Ma. She'll give me breakfast *then*, I wager!" She grinned at them, and Susan almost felt sorry for her.

"Unfortunately," Susan said, "we're not going to be able to come back just now. Maybe later. There are some people we need to see."

She liked the sound of that. People to see seemed business-like and forbidding at the same time.

Liyla frowned. "But Ma said —"

Susan glowered at her and decided she needed to ratchet up the forbidding.

"This is official business," she said severely. "And you don't want to be getting in the way of that kind of thing."

This statement had a completely unexpected effect on Liyla. She stopped short and the color drained from her face. Then Susan noticed where she was looking. She followed Liyla's gaze and felt herself go pale, too.

A red-cloaked soldier, standing beside a market stall, had seen them. He released his dog, and it galloped over, snarling. Kate whirled around and yelped, and the dog crouched down in front of her, a low growl vibrating in its throat. The soldier hurried over, musket up.

"He'll rip your throat out if I snap my fingers!" the red cloak shouted at them. "All of you! Stay where you are!" They stood as still as they could. When he reached them, he surveyed the group, eyes glinting from their deep sockets. They lit on Liyla, and he gave a curt lift of his head, dismissing her.

Liyla surprised Susan by holding her ground. "They weren't doing anything wrong, sir," she said. "I mean, I found them, and they're not useless. My ma's taken charge of the whole thing. She's —"

"Girl," he cut in, "your mother's not in charge of anything. You go home and tell her children shouldn't wander the streets alone. Someone might think they were useless."

Liyla cringed, and the light hairs on her face seemed to rise. She took a step back, looking uneasily at the soldier and his dog. But the red cloak had turned his full attention to the children.

"You're wanted in the center of the Domain," he said.

Max's hand had been inching toward his back pocket, but the soldier noticed and clicked his tongue at the dog. It pounced, knocking Max to the ground. The soldier leaned over, extracted the knife, and took Omet's sack from Susan. He pocketed the blade and tossed the food into the road.

"Let's go," he said.

The dog growled, spurring Jean and Kate forward. It rounded next on Nell, who jumped to follow them. The soldier prodded Max, and then Susan, with his gun, shoving them toward his wagon.

Turning back as they hurried along, Susan caught one last glimpse of Liyla before she was out of sight. She stood where they'd left her, big eyed and afraid, and, for once, silent.

Chapter 22

The wagon sputtered and blew steam on the street across the market square, waiting for them. The soldier shoved Susan and Max into the back of it, then turned and tossed the three others up behind them. The dog bounded up to block the opening, and the soldier climbed into the driver's seat. The wagon lurched, hot steam pouring from it, and they set off, bouncing over the ill-paved roads.

Susan crept toward Kate, and the dog growled a threat. Kate lifted a hand to reach for her, and the animal snapped. So they sat there, hugging their own knees, as the wagon chugged through the market square and into the side streets, winding back past the taller buildings the children had seen before, then through the large rally square. It was littered with red paper and the spoiled remains of smashed picnics. Oily crows picked at the leftovers and flew off, screeching, as the wagon rolled by.

There were no more tall buildings on the far side of the rally square. Here the bricks were gray and the streets full of soldiers. Under a leather canopy, Susan spied a long table, where red-shirted officials ate with a gusto that reminded her of Liyla's father. One block farther, and a line of fidgeting people stood outside a low stone building, waiting in the heat to be called forward by an official who sat fanning himself with the edge of his red cloak.

Susan's legs were shaking. She gripped them tighter and tried to reason with herself. *It can't be as bad as they say*, she told herself. *People exaggerate in rumors.* But her heart wouldn't listen to reason and kept knocking stubbornly against her chest.

Too soon, they sputtered to a stop before what seemed to be the main building, a blocky structure only about three stories high, but the tallest one in sight. A scarlet flag flew from its roof.

The soldier dismounted and gave a whistle. Several guards jogged over.

"These are the ones wanted," he told them. "Take them to Ker."

They were hustled down from the wagon and shoved through the door. If the building had seemed small on the outside, the opulence of the furnishings inside made up for it. Great slabs of marble gleamed in the floor, and oil lamps flickered in sconces, casting shadows that danced along the red banners on the walls. The lobby ended in tall red doors, their greasy finish glistening in the yellow light.

The soldiers propelled them down a wide lamplit hall so warm Susan felt the sweat trace lines on her face. There were no windows, and beneath her feet the polished stone felt slippery, as if it, too, perspired.

"Here," one of the soldiers said, stopping them at another red door. He rapped sharply on it, and it was opened by a woman dressed in a deep-ruby gown.

"Ker," the soldier said, dipping his head to her.

The woman had covered her raw face, recently waxed, with a slick layer of skin-toned makeup, and Susan realized that the smooth, almost-normal complexion made her ferocious, angular features even more unnatural.

Ker's eyes widened when she saw them, and she smiled, showing her long teeth, the ends shaved to a flat line.

"Thank you, soldier, for accompanying our guests," she said. Her voice was nasal and breathy. "I'd like one or two more of your men to come along with us. We're going to the back room."

The back room had a chilly sound. Even the soldier flinched, almost imperceptibly, when she said it.

He nodded and turned to two men standing at attention in the hall. Ker looked over his shoulder, then back at the children.

"Two more, I think."

Susan's throat tightened. *Rumors,* she told herself. *Exaggerations.* But her heart continued galloping behind her ribs, and her mouth went dry. Two more soldiers approached from the hall and came to stand, one each, behind the children. Ker smiled again, baring her teeth.

"Excellent. Come along, then." She closed the door to her room and walked up the hall, her long dress snaking behind her. Susan flinched as a soldier put a hand on her bruised shoulder and pressed her forward. She glanced at her siblings in the flickering light. Sweat stood out on Max's forehead; his face looked dull and yellow in the shadow of the lamps. He blinked over and over, wiping perspiration from his eyes. Beside him Jean had her hand wrapped around her shirt, clutching the unseen Barbie.

Ahead of them, Ker stopped at another red door, produced a ring of keys, opened it, and stepped inside. Kate, thrust forward by the soldier behind her, was first to reach the threshold. Susan saw her stop suddenly and try to step backward. She met the soldier's stomach and ducked sideways. He grabbed her arm.

"No! I don't want to go in there!"

He shoved her through.

Susan flinched and tried to reach her, but before she could move, the soldier behind her had her arms.

From the right, Jean made a break for it, jumping away so suddenly that she managed a few steps before a red cloak snatched her back, dragging her through the door. The soldiers propelled Nell and Susan through together. Beside her, Susan felt Nell go rigid.

A grimy tiled floor spread out from the doorway of the windowless room. Tile walls glimmered slickly beneath kerosene lights; the scent of warm metal clung to them.

A series of straight-backed iron chairs stood on clawed metal feet along the walls, and on each hung leather straps for arms and legs. At the other end of the room, a wide door stood half open, and through it Susan could see a row of iron tables. They, too, had straps. She turned her head and saw a glass case full of syringes, tubes, and long thin knives.

Instinctively, Susan arched backward, but the soldier drove her forward. She found herself shoved into a chair, her back clanging against the hard metal.

She yelled and thrashed, kicking and slapping, but the man was too strong. He bound first one arm, then the other; the hot leather gouged deep into her wrists and elbows, then her ankles. Her shoulder throbbed. She couldn't move.

She heard Max shouting. The soldier holding Nell cursed,

and Susan saw him grab at a red spot on his arm; Nell had taken a bite out of him. Furious, he slammed her down into the chair. Kate whimpered unevenly, too terrified to draw breath, and Jean shrieked, one long extended scream that strangely did not echo in the smothering room.

"Enough!" Ker shouted. "Be silent or you'll have what to cry about!"

Still, Jean whimpered.

"I'm cold," she said. "I'm cold."

Susan saw her shivering. *It's fear,* she thought. *She's freezing from fear.*

But Susan was hot. The still air stopped up her throat and threatened to stifle her. She watched the soldiers step backward to the wall. One whispered something to Ker, and she nodded. He pushed the back door open farther and gave a low bow. A large black dog came through, followed by a man.

The Genius.

Chapter 23

This close, he looked different. Coarser. His features jutted outward, the carefully manicured eyebrows only lines of makeup in a waxed face. Beneath them, his eyes, pale in a way Susan had never seen before, seemed wet and thirsty at the same time.

And he was old. Much older than he'd seemed in the square. Ancient, withered.

He smiled.

"Beautiful," he said, and his velvet voice reached out to her. "At last."

He moved to the center of the room, the black dog a shadow at his side, and stood looking at them, turning to each child slowly. Sweat gathered at the edges of Susan's hair and slipped down toward her eyes. She blinked.

The Genius stepped to Jean. He squinted at her, leaning down, too close to her face. Jean whimpered.

"That face," he said. "I know it."

Jean squirmed in the chair, and Susan pulled against the straps.

"Please leave her alone! She's little!" Max yelled.

"Little," the man repeated. He put his hand out to Jean's face and touched one of the tears that rolled down her cheek. Again, that smile. "You remind me of my youth, child."

He stood looking at her a moment longer, then turned again to survey the rest of them.

"So many questions," the Genius said, half closing his eyes. His too-blunt teeth flashed behind moist lips. His hand strayed to the dog's head, and he stroked it.

"So much I want to know."

He lifted his hands and seemed to consider the thick nails. Then he looked up, and his eyes rested again on Jean.

"Girl," he said. "Answer me. Who gave you that face?"

Jean's lips shook as she tried to form an answer.

"I don't know what you mean."

"That face of yours. That unchanged face. Tell me where it came from."

Jean just shook her head. "I'm cold," she whispered. "Please let me out."

The Genius's face darkened. "It's impolite not to answer a direct question, child. I would have thought such a pretty face would come with better manners."

"Please! She doesn't know what you're talking about! None of us do!" It was Max, breathing heavily.

The dog growled, and the Genius patted its head. He gave the animal a gentle push, and it stepped back near Ker, watchful, as the man approached Max.

"He was savage when I found him," he said softly. "But you needn't worry. He's well trained now. So tell me. Tell me who did it. Who made those faces?"

Max looked up at the Genius, then across at Susan.

"I don't know what you're talking about," he said.

"Ah, but you do," the Genius said. "You must. A useful boy like you will tell me what made that face."

Max blinked sweat from his eyes. Susan watched as he struggled to answer. "No one made it. We were born this way. We've always been this way."

The Genius tensed, and Susan saw his eyes narrow.

"Do you mock me, boy?" he whispered. At his tone, the dog got to its feet again, but he motioned it back.

The room was so hot. It had no air. Susan tried to take some in, but there wasn't enough. Her chest felt tight; her shoulder burned.

"It's true!" she stammered, half gasping. "We're not from here! We don't know anything about this place! Please just let us go home!"

The Genius turned her way. Susan felt as if she were looking at a stretch of road on a hot day. The air rippled before her, and, as it had in the rally square, the Genius's face shifted. This time, she saw not the handsome man from the square but something feral, ravenous. A hunger, a wanting, throbbed from him.

"Such selfish children," he said, and now even his voice was frayed. "You can't hide it, you know. Do you think that if someone has discovered the answer, they'll be permitted to keep it from me? Do you think you can tell me lies and I will simply walk away?"

Susan didn't answer.

"I've waited," he said. "I've prepared. All these years. I will be satisfied."

He looked again at Jean, considering, then turned back to Susan, leaning so close she could smell the heat coming from him, musky and sour. Her heart stuttered in her chest.

For another moment, the Genius loomed over her, his

body coiled and tense. Then he pulled himself upright and smiled.

"Never mind," he said, and motioned to Ker. "I can see talk is useless here. But those faces hold secrets that my lady is expert at uncovering. She knows how much I treasure the right answers."

The Genius moved to a steel table across the room and rolled it toward them.

The heat seemed to stop up Susan's mouth and nose entirely.

He lifted a small scalpel from the table, then a long needle, and put them down again.

"Be thorough," he said to Ker.

He moved past the guards to the front door, the dog behind him. Once more, he turned, his eyes found Jean, and he smiled. Then he was gone.

Ker took hold of the table and rolled it forward. The humid air pushed against Susan's throat, and she watched the woman come. Beside the small scalpel, she could make out a long needle, a glass tube, and a knife with a thin blade. The woman approached Max. He pulled away from her, jerking and spitting, until a soldier stepped forward, gripped his head, and shoved it back against the metal. Ker leaned down with hooded eyes. She took the long needle and jabbed it into Max's hand. A drop of blood, nearly black in the lamplight, welled up on his skin. Max yelled, pulled, and once again the soldier knocked his head back roughly. Ker peered down at the wound, then pushed a glass tube against Max's hand. The blood slid into it, pooling in a dark puddle at the bottom.

She smiled at him. "Such a fuss," she said. "And for what? I just want to see what you're made of." She licked her thin lips and set the tube down. "You, it will be useful to preserve for now. After all, there is only one of you, isn't there?"

She lifted the scalpel from the table.

"Of course, there are four of these others."

Chapter 24

The heat and the woman and her tools, the long tables beyond the door, the knives in the case — all of it pressed on Susan, and the fear was like a physical thing in the room, pounding against her, crushing her chest, squeezing the sight from her eyes. The room tilted and grew dim for a moment. Words pulsed in her head. *I need to get out. Out. Out.*

Ker turned toward Susan.

"So pretty," she said as she moved forward. "So smooth."

Susan watched her come. All she could think of was running, flinging herself from the chair and hurling herself through the red door, out into the hallway, out, somewhere, into the air. And yet the leather straps trapped her, crushing her as the woman approached. *Out. Out. Out.*

Her heartbeat sliced jaggedly through her chest, and her breath came so fast it ached. Her throat burned. She closed her eyes and wished fiercely the straps would go. She saw them there in her mind's eye, dissolving, flying away, saw herself running, running. *Out. Out. Out.*

The woman's cold hand was on her arm now. She cringed. She could feel the edge of the blade. *Out. Out. Out!*

A pressure was building in her chest, pumping through her arms, her legs. She shivered, whether with cold or heat she couldn't tell, but the picture was a living thing now in front of her: the straps flung off, freedom, movement; all glared inside her head with a light much brighter than the one in the room. Pain in her arm. The bite of the knife.

A great force, heavy and swift at once, raced through her, rocketing down her legs, out her arms. *Out! Out! Out!*

In a sudden rush, Susan felt the great thing pushing inside her jump forward; the room shook. Her eyes flew open. The straps exploded, shooting across the room and hitting the opposite wall. Ker shrieked. Susan jumped to her feet.

The others! The fear leaped at her with such force that she staggered, and the same picture jumped into her mind. *Out!*

The pressure shot through her again, and she fell. Across the room, the chairs themselves broke open, straps gone, children dumped in heaps on the floor. They scrambled to their feet as Ker screamed and the soldiers, confused, stepped forward.

Out! Susan shouted it inside her head again, and a sudden gust of air slammed across the room, taking Ker and the soldiers with it. It whipped them back into the slick walls, toppling the metal table and the remains of the chairs. The tube of Max's blood arced through the air and hit the tile with a sharp *crack*.

"Out!" This time Susan screamed it aloud, and the others heard her and ran. Together they dashed into the hallway, down the corridor, toward the lobby. Soldiers approached, Susan heard distant shouting, but the one word roared in her mind like a wave. And as she repeated it, silently, with force, with terror, soldiers flew backward, doors ripped open, and the five of them were out, out in the sunlight and running down the long empty stretch of road that led away from the Domain.

✧ Book Two ✧

MAX

Chapter 25

Max had considered the subject from a variety of angles, and he had come to the conclusion that theoretically or hypothetically, if one were to fall into another universe, the best people to take along would be Sherlock Holmes, Albert Einstein, Nikola Tesla, and Daniel Boone. That was assuming you were allowed somebody fictional and/or dead. And that Einstein and Tesla could run fast. If not, he would have recruited an astronaut, a doctor, a samurai warrior, and a Green Beret. Unfortunately, nobody had asked him, and he'd landed here with Susan, Nell, Kate, and Jean.

Now he'd begun to wonder if any of that mattered at all. What calculations could help you decipher a world in which tornadoes attacked furniture, or the wind started inside and followed you down the street? He'd never read anything on *that* in *The Boy Scout Handbook*.

Running after Susan, he'd looked over his shoulder and seen the soldiers bracing against the gale, their dogs hunched beside them, noses to the ground and ears blown back. A moment later, up they all flew — cloaks and paws and arms and legs all waving as they somersaulted like toys. In the room, in the hall, and at the edge of the city, it had happened, until the five of them had crossed from the Domain into the dense woods that smudged the horizon, and lost the city in a mass of green.

They had run without stopping until they couldn't anymore, and then they had walked, their breath coming in hiccups as they pushed on into the hills, desperate to be as far away from that terrible room as they could get. At last, as the sky overhead began to shift, throwing up strands of vivid confetti clouds shredded through with high branches, Max had begun to breathe again. And so now, with his head aching and his hand stinging and his legs feeling like they had turned to wood or stone, or what was the heaviest metal — maybe uranium? — he set about trying to figure it out. Could he hurt this much in a dream? He didn't think so, unless he'd happened to fall asleep on a bed of electrified rocks. Or unless he was having some surprise surgery no one had mentioned.

But that seemed unlikely.

Nothing plausible had come to him by the time the shapes of trees and stones began to fade into the twilit haze. The only thought that did stand out was that if they kept walking, they were going to walk off a cliff in the dark, so when he spotted a small cave shouldering its way up from the forest floor, he pointed to it, and they crawled in. Nell untied the blanket she'd managed to keep wrapped around her waist and let it fall into a heap. Then the five of them collapsed against the cool walls and watched night take the forest.

Max rubbed his hand where the woman had pierced it. The back of his head throbbed, and he wondered if maybe all of this was just an elaborate hallucination. Maybe he was still in that chair, and she'd given him something to make him think . . . panic bubbled in his chest and he did a quick assessment of his surroundings. The rich green smell of the forest and the cool aroma of stone hung everywhere around him in the shallow cave. What was it he'd read about hallucinating smells? Oh, yeah, they were usually awful ones, like skunk and body odor. So he was probably safe.

It was dark before any of them said a word. Outside, clouds obscured the moon, and the faint outline of inky trees shimmered against deeper spaces the color of coal. It was the only way he could tell he wasn't blind. Inside the cave, it was pitch, but he could feel Jean, who had pushed up against him, feel the hard nub of her doll, the scratchy knottiness of its hair against his arm.

"I'm hungry," Jean said.

The sound of her voice seemed to wake the others out of their daze. In the black, he heard Nell shift and groan, and Kate sniffle. Susan kept silent.

"What happened?"

That was Nell. "What got us out of there?"

Her question bounced off the cave walls, a tiny echo.

"It felt like something exploded," Kate whispered after a minute. "Did something explode?"

Max pondered this. It *had* felt like an explosion. But where had the sound been? And the fire?

"I don't know," he said at last. "What could have exploded?"

From somewhere across the cave, Susan answered.

"Me."

His heart sank. The place had been too much for her. It stood to reason.

"Uh, Susan? People don't explode, remember?"

She sniffed.

"I'm not an idiot, Max."

Her voice sounded normal enough.

"I only meant —"

"I know what you meant."

Nell cleared her throat. "Susan, are you saying *you* sent that wind through the room?"

Max sat straighter. He hadn't hallucinated the wind!

"I don't know. Felt like it."

Felt like it? He squinted in Susan's direction. "What exactly does it feel like to make a tornado?"

Susan sighed. "I didn't *make a tornado*," she said. "I didn't make anything. I just wanted to get out. And then I just *was*."

Max fingered the bump on the back of his head and thought they weren't going to get very far with logic like that.

"Things don't happen just because you want them to," he said. He thought ruefully that if they did, he'd be talking to Nikola Tesla right now.

"Don't you think I know that?"

"Of course, but —"

"I don't know, Max. It just happened. I wasn't even sure it was real until about an hour ago."

Well, that made two of them.

"Still," he said. "We've got to figure it out. If you can do something like that —"

She cut him off. "Don't start going crazy. It's not like I did it on purpose."

Max sighed. Susan had one thing in common with Tesla, anyway. They could both be difficult.

Chapter 26

Max woke in the night to shrieking. Kate was screaming into the black, crying and slapping the wall. It took
them a while to find her, it was so dark, but at last he heard
Susan catch hold of her and wake her. She said she'd been
dreaming of the tiled room.

As if things couldn't get worse, at dawn they heard dogs.
Outside the cave, cicadas buzzed and birds whistled, but from
somewhere down the mountain, the urgent barking of a pack
sliced through the morning.

Max sat up with a stifled cry. He might as well have slept
on a bed of knives, the way his muscles screamed when he
moved. His head throbbed worse now from the inside than
from the knot on the back of his skull.

"Get up!" he yelled at the others. "Listen! Search dogs!
They're looking for us!"

Kate bolted up so fast, she might have been stung by a bee,
and Jean was on her feet before she'd opened her eyes.

"What do we do?" Kate cried. "They'll take us back there!"

"We run," Susan said. "And keep running."

They were too weak, though, to move quickly now. It had
been more than a day since they'd eaten, or even had a drink.
They limped from the cave into the forest, where a wet cotton
fog, smelling of old leaves, blurred the ground.

"Try to hurry," Max said. "We have to keep moving up this mountain. Eventually they'll give up."

Jean lost her footing and fell, disappearing into the cloudy ground cover. Max helped her up.

"The ground is strange," she said to him when he got her on her feet again. "Not like it was before. Look."

The fog was too thick to see anything below his knees, so he reached down and ran his hand over it. Bare dirt.

Again, the echo of distant dogs pierced the morning.

"Forget about it," he said. "We've got to keep moving."

His heart was ramming so hard behind his ribs, he thought he might keel over, but Max forced himself on, tugging Jean along, until the sound of the dogs disappeared and the fog melted. It was then he noticed the full strangeness of the wood.

The air smelled as if something green had curdled. Despite the thickness of trees all around, the forest floor stretched out empty as a vacant lot, dirt without a thing sprouting. A few withered weeds looked as if they'd started to grow at the base of a tree and thought better of it, shriveling nearly black before they sagged into the roots.

Nell looked around. "What is this?" she asked. "Looks like somebody poisoned it."

"All of it?" Susan asked, and pointed up the mountain. The sun was high in the sky now, and it sent stripes of light through the trees. Beneath them, the bald dirt stretched out to the horizon.

"I guess we took a wrong turn," Nell said.

Max had hoped to find the orchard again, behind the ruined house. Before they'd been taken, they'd meant to go west, back the way they'd come. Instead, they'd run eastward, into this strange wasteland. Overhead, the trees were full of chirping birds and the chipped-wood voices of squirrels, but below, nothing lived: no deer, no foxes, no rabbits, no green.

But that was a clue, wasn't it? Somebody had done something here, or how could trees grow when grass wouldn't? He wondered if that meant that as long as they were in this sprout-less wood, the dogs would be right behind them. Probably. Well, then job one was obviously to get out of this forest.

It was easier in theory than in practice. They walked all morning, and still the naked ground persisted. Worse, they hadn't found a single thing to eat or drink. Max tried climbing a tree to taste the leaves, but all that did was make him spit green.

"Can we eat acorns?" Jean asked him. "Like the squirrels?"

He'd have liked to test that out, but the few fallen acorns he'd spotted were shriveled husks in the strange dirt, and the ones in the branches were so high that even with Nell standing on his shoulders, they couldn't reach any.

Soon it was water they were most desperate for. The bitter-ness of the wood hung in the air, seeping into their pores and coating their tongues. Max thought his head couldn't get any heavier, but by the afternoon, he decided that it, too, was filled with uranium. And to his horror, when the birds quieted, he could still hear the faint sound of barking, far below.

Jean slapped at a mosquito and smeared a bright streak of blood across her sweaty cheek.

"Mosquitoes are about the only thing eating anything out here," Nell said, disgusted.

Ahead, another shallow cave yawned from the dead ground, and she dropped to her knees to crawl inside and collapse in the cool shadows.

"Nell, get up! They have dogs!" Kate said in alarm.

Nell pressed a hand to her forehead. "All they'll find is a dried-up raisin of me if I don't take a rest," she said. "I'm starting to see double. And my stomach doesn't feel too good, either."

Max felt the same way. Heat and exhaustion had ground down even the desperate fear that had rapped in his chest all day. His tongue was like a weight in his mouth. A weight covered in fur.

Susan sank to her knees, then dragged herself into the shade. "Later, we'll keep walking," she said, sounding as weak as he felt. "And we'll find something to eat, too. And drink."

"Is that a theory or a prediction based on facts?" he asked her.

"Oh, brother, Max!"

They piled into the tight space and dozed fitfully until afternoon, when a breeze sprang up, carrying with it the bitter half-burned smell that clung to the dirt. They struggled to their feet and continued walking. For the moment, the dogs were out of earshot, but Max wondered how long that would last.

His head was throbbing by the time a brief cloudburst gave them some relief. They tried to drink from the pools that formed at the base of tree roots, but the water burned their throats and made them retch.

"It's like drinking seawater!" Nell said, spitting.

They sampled the water that gathered in the crevices of rocks and clung to the few leaves they could reach. This, at least, was sweet, so they moved from tree to stone, searching out the moisture, until their heads cleared.

Unfortunately, quenching their thirst only seemed to sharpen the edge of the hunger.

"They salted the dirt," Max said to Susan. "That's my latest theory, anyway. What I don't get is how the trees survive it."

"Your latest theory?" Susan asked him. "There were others?"

He chose to ignore her doubting tone.

"Well . . . there will be." His eye roved the rising line of the wood. "There's got to be something to eat somewhere."

"Is that a theory or a prediction based on facts?"

He ignored that, too.

By dusk they'd found nothing. The woods stretched endlessly ahead of them. They had no choice but to rest again, and this time there was no cave, so as night fell, they sprawled around a pair of birches, listening fearfully for the dogs and staring up through bony branches at the waxing moon.

"We came when it was half," Susan said. "It's been days now. How did any of this happen?"

Max sniffed. A whiff of vinegar was in the air.

Nell wrinkled her nose at it. "Nothing's right here," she said. "This dirt's the least of it. I thought Liyla was strange, but she was nothing compared to the Genius, the wind . . ."

Her voice faded, and she sighed and lay down, trying to find a comfortable position.

Max didn't even try. He just sat there, his back against the tree, listening for the dogs. Would they keep searching at night? If he fell asleep, would he wake with teeth at his neck? He wished the five of them could keep running until the dogs were lost behind them, until they were so far away no one would ever find them, ever —

"Max?"

It was Jean, who'd crawled over from Nell's blanket.

"Go to sleep, Jean. It's okay. I'm watching."

"I can't sleep. I'm too hungry."

"I know."

"But you're going to figure it out, right? You'll find us food tomorrow?"

I can't wanted to come out of his mouth. *Don't ask me.* But he pressed the words back behind closed lips.

"Max?"

"Hmm?"

"You will, right?"

A theory would have been comforting, but he couldn't even make a realistic prediction. All he could offer was a promise, and what was that based on? Wishing.

He listened to her waiting.

"Yes," he said finally. "Yes, I will."

Chapter 27

For reasons that had always eluded Max, from the time Jean was Jean, she'd decided he was going to be her favorite. Max usually prized logic, but in this one thing, in Jean's dogged devotion, he was sheepishly grateful to accept serendipity. He'd always considered it a kind of miracle that this one little sister, who loved her ridiculous Barbies and who spent hours playing a game she'd devised called "dress for a party" with Kate, had in her own inscrutable way fashioned herself into the brother he'd always wanted. Here he was, the odd man out, the only boy in a family of girls and the one who, at least compared to Susan, made the most trouble, and behind him came Jean, climbing bookcases and deconstructing things just as he had, even if what she deconstructed — some of the time — were shoes and dresses. But she was as interested as he'd always been in the physics of flushing a toothbrush down the toilet, or whether a basketball could make it through the laundry chute. So they had an affinity for each other. One of Max's secret fears was that one day she'd wake up, turn pure girl, and leave him behind. But for now, to his private amazement and joy, she stuck to him like glue.

So he ignored the hammering in his chest and pushed away thoughts of dogs and the tiled room and that woman, Ker, rolling the metal table his way.

It shouldn't matter that I'm scared, he told himself. *I should be able to think.* He could do it at home. Even when guys like Ivan and Mo called him Einstein and egghead and waited in the hall to push him around, punishing him for offering his thoughts on experiments in science or suggesting that there was a faster way to do a problem in math, he kept on speaking up. Once, Ivan had slammed him into a bank of lockers while Mo asked him what the circumference of his head was compared to the toilet, and that hadn't stopped him from raising his hand half an hour later, back in math, as the two of them glared at him and muttered threats.

He told himself all this, trying to force his head into gear.

Only now, when everything depended on his finding the answers, his mind slid away from him, and there was nothing. It galled him.

Beside him Jean sighed in her sleep. He had promised he would figure it out. And yet all he had were the strange pieces Nell had listed: the tiled room, the rally, and Liyla. Had her face really changed, that first time they saw her? None of it made any sense. A lump rose in his throat.

He wouldn't sleep. He'd stay up until he figured it out. And if he couldn't figure it out, at least he'd keep watch. He'd keep one promise, anyway.

But even that, in the end, he couldn't do, and at last even worry, even sadness, fell away, and sleep settled over him. The ache in his bones slipped from him, the throbbing in his hand was forgotten, and he slid into the silent place where the mind wanders, lifting images and turning them over like bright pennies and autumn leaves. . . .

He saw the market square. The Genius stood waving and

shouting, making the buildings shimmer. A wind blew. It rose from the barren ground and tossed all the people away as their faces shifted from smooth to rough and back again.

Max jerked awake.

Jean lay curled against him like a baby; a foot away, Nell rested on a hump where the tree roots lifted from the earth. Kate had rolled herself so tightly in Nell's blanket that the only visible part of her was a gush of loopy hair. He looked for Susan and found her slumped against the other birch, the lines in its bark like a hundred small wounds, black in the moonlight. She dozed with her head tipped to one side.

"Susan!" he whispered.

Her head twitched. She blinked. "What?"

"Remember what Omet said, about rally change?"

"Rally change," she said sleepily.

He watched her head start to tip, and reached over to poke her, trying not to wake Jean.

"Remember the Genius? Remember how the buildings looked? That was what she meant! Rally change. People turning smooth. You saw it, right? Just like Liyla seemed so different when we first saw her!"

Until it clicked into place beside his memory of the rally, Max had nearly forgotten the moment when they'd first seen Liyla.

Susan didn't answer right away, but Nell lifted her head from the root. "Yeah!" she said. "She did look different for a minute — normal."

Susan straightened. She was awake now. "I thought I was going nuts. But we all saw it!"

"I didn't think it was real," Max said. "You know, maybe

a group hallucination or something. The rally, too. But that wind — that wind was real! And the busted straps! Do you think maybe all of it was real? Maybe you can do that here!"

Nell propped herself up on one elbow, and he could see her frown in the moonlight. "Susan, what exactly did you do?"

"Nothing!" Susan said. "Not on purpose, anyway. I just was so scared. I could see the straps, and I wanted to get out."

She pressed her head back against the tree trunk and studied the long ugly cut the woman had made on her inner arm. It had begun to scab, and Max saw her scratch carefully around the edges of it. In the pearly light, it looked as if someone had drawn a black line down her arm in marker or paint. He shuddered, thinking of the truth.

"I guess I imagined I *was* out, and then I was," Susan said.

Max's head throbbed again. So much of this place looked the same as home: same trees, same sky . . . No, not the same sky, exactly. But close. Maybe the sameness had misled him. This wasn't home. The rules were different here. . . .

"Do you think you can just imagine something and it happens?" he asked.

The word *imagine* sounded flimsy as daydreams. It had no relation to that awful tiled room. At least it didn't feel like it should. But then, he hadn't been the one who'd done it. Susan had.

"What were you thinking right when it happened?" he asked her. "Just that second? Do you know that? Can you remember that?"

She grimaced and wrapped both arms around her legs, hunching over to rest her chin on her knees.

"I was thinking the exact same thing you were! I wanted to get out of there. Who wouldn't?"

A cloud crossed the moon, and the wood darkened.

"But you yourself told us you did it," Max said. "So how? What did it feel like?"

He could see only the shape of her shoulders now, where they stood out from the silhouette of the tree. But he could see when she shrugged.

"The strangest pumping through my arms and legs, like something had to get out. Like I was going to burst into flame."

"And you couldn't have touched anything. . . ."

"No."

He shook his head. "We're going to have to go over it again, step-by-step. I know we can figure it out."

Nell rolled onto her stomach to face Susan. "Maybe you're more afraid of needles than the rest of us. Could that be it?"

Susan's voice was frosty. "She came at me with a *knife*, Nell!"

"I know, I know! I'm just saying . . ."

Susan sighed. "You just keep saying, I know. And now Kate and Jean are looking at me like I can just blow us home from here! Don't you think I would if I could? It's something that happened to me, Nell. I didn't do anything! I'm starting to wish I'd never said it was me. Maybe it wasn't."

Max knew that wasn't true. Susan had been out of her chair first.

"Just because something happened to you doesn't mean you can't figure it out," he told her. "You know what it felt like!"

For a moment, there was only silence. Then the moon drifted back into sight, and in the sudden illumination, he could see Susan shaking her head.

"Don't you hear how crazy you sound? That's like saying if someone gets sick, he ought to cure himself. That's what doctors are for!"

Nell huffed softly in annoyance. "And this place is so full of doctors," she said. "Besides that Frankenstein lady, I mean."

"Don't be so literal, Nell," Susan snapped.

"Don't be so stupid, then."

They were off after that, and when the sniping was over, Susan lay down and refused to say another word. Max felt like yelling at both of them, but especially at Susan. Why did she have to be so stubborn? She was so smart, except when it came to believing she could figure things out. Then it was all too big, too impossible, illogical, unrealistic. She reminded him of one of those roly-poly bugs back home that crawled along at a clip until somebody poked it. Then it would curl up into a little gray ball of nothing.

When Susan got like this, she didn't think anyone could figure anything out. As far as she was concerned, they were all little gray balls of nothing.

The next morning, she was no better. Jean made the mistake of wondering if Susan, who had made the wind blow, could make it rain, too.

"Of course not!" Susan snapped. "Can you?"

She blamed that on Max.

"You've got everybody thinking I can fix this," she

complained. "I can't!" She kicked at the dirt in disgust. "Even the ground hates me here. I can feel it."

Were there stages in losing it? Stage one, denial; stage two, anger; stage three, paranoia so bad you suspected the dirt.

"Maybe you're getting delirious," he said.

"Criminations! I'm not delirious!" she yelled. "I'm hungry! My head hurts! And I want to get out of here as much as anybody. I just don't think pretending we can figure this out is going to get us anywhere. We've got to find somebody who can help us!"

Back to anger, then. When Susan started hurling unusual curses, Max knew things were bad.

He sighed and watched her march up the mountain fuming. Jean, following her, turned and shot him a pleading look. But for that, too, he had no answer. He thought of the tiled room, and of Susan standing there, and the wind blowing from nowhere. Susan had done it; she'd said so herself. If he'd been the one, he would have figured it out by now. He wouldn't waste a second being mad. He would be *thinking*. But not Susan.

She preferred to turn gray and roll into a little ball.

The price of banishment was madness. So it had been, now, for years. If the exile's penalty had long been delayed, it had come due at last, for now the night swarmed with half glimpses of children — a nearly grown boy lost in shadow, a small dark-haired girl running beneath old trees. Perhaps madness approached this way, slowly, out of dreams that reawakened old yearnings. Flaunted each night was the future that might have been, the loss that had come with disobedience. With it came torment that clouded the mind and threatened to swamp it. For in dreams lived hope. And each morning came the dawn, to crush it anew.

Chapter 28

Gottfried Wilhelm Leibniz, mathematician, philosopher, moralist, and possible inventor of calculus, was, according to Max, solid proof that you didn't have to be old to know things. Leibniz had mastered Latin by the time he was twelve, finished college by sixteen, and written his first book of philosophy by age twenty.

Max had spent a night last fall telling the family about Leibniz's feats after trying to use the philosopher as his mystery person in a game of twenty questions. He'd stumped everybody, of course, but the girls had cried foul.

"Gottfried Leibniz?" Susan demanded. "Who ever heard of him?"

Max had said he didn't see what the problem was. Susan was always coming up with obscure people like Euripides or Charlotte Brontë when it was her turn.

"I'll take a turn," Kate had volunteered. Kate had the annoying habit of trying to be helpful when people got mad.

"Clara Barton," Nell snapped at her.

"How did you know?"

"You always choose Clara Barton."

Max didn't care. He liked Leibniz. If you don't know something, ask questions, why don't you? If nobody has the answer, then go invent one. That was Leibniz.

Max had been a little boy when he'd first realized that knowing things made all the difference. His ears had been clogged, and as a result the world was a garbled mess. Unable to understand what people wanted of him, not knowing any of the rules, he'd spent the months before they were cleared confused and getting into trouble. That feeling of not knowing had made him want to jump out of his skin.

Well, he was in bigger trouble now than he'd ever been. And that jumpy feeling had returned, worse than before.

That evening, they climbed a steep hump on the mountainside and found another cave perched atop it, larger than the first. Near the end of the day, the dogs had begun to bark again, far below, but no one had the strength to continue, and so the cave was the next best thing. It had a wide mouth that curved around, showing them the slope they'd climbed and the relatively flat piece of ground that rose gently upward from the hump on the mountain. They sprawled weakly across the dirt floor beneath the stone as night consumed the tall trees: ash, oak, and maple.

Kate's nightmare echoed through the cave an hour later, and when it was done, Max couldn't go back to sleep. His stomach felt like someone had caged a rabid cat inside it, all teeth and claws.

He felt emptied out, weak in a way he'd always thought old people were when they struggled just to get out of a chair. Hot acid washed up his throat. He wanted to cry out, like Kate did, like Jean did, when the emptiness burned that way. Stumbling, he crawled to the mouth of the cave. Above him, the broad face of the moon looked smugly down through the trees, gloating that it had never gone hungry.

He fell asleep looking at it. And woke a few hours later, ravenous. Powdery moonlight filtered through the cave opening, and he got up and immediately fell down, bruising his chin and tasting mud. He turned to look back at the girls, asleep.

There was Susan, head resting on her hands. She'd gotten them out. She could *do* things. More than he could, maybe. But she wouldn't, no matter how much she pretended she was trying. In the night, after Kate's nightmare, Susan had put her back to sleep telling stories. She'd had the nerve to talk of home, and soft beds, and big dinners.

Anger roused him. Who cared about stories? Stories didn't fill your stomach. If he'd been the one—if he'd done it—things would be different!

He rested his head against the cool stone at the threshold of the cave, trying to think. A problem was just a nut to be cracked. He'd heard someone say that once, and it was true. There were reasons for things; there were answers. You just had to believe you could find them.

He rose weakly to his feet and stumbled into the forest. There was food there; there had to be. He'd find it. Today, they'd eat.

He wandered up the slope, slow footed. The sun rose and the mist burned away and around him there was nothing but bright, hot green, trees perspiring in the heat. A trickle of sweat rolled down his face, and he caught it with his tongue, tasting salt. The heat made his head swim. He thought of Susan again and got angrier. Soon he was shaking, and tripped over the humped root of a birch tree. Above him, the sun glared through the plump leaves. He sat up, but the world spun, and he couldn't get to his feet. He leaned against the smooth bark and listened to his heart beat.

She could do it if she wanted.

Somehow, repeating it steadied him. Anger was the only thing that kept him sitting upright now. But then the hunger stabbed at him again, and he tried to swallow. His throat seemed to stick to itself. He wanted to cry.

If only they hadn't left the orchard. Why had they done that? There was fruit there. Peaches. He remembered the peaches. Plums, too. That was all he wanted. Just something wet, something juicy. A plum. A peach. His eyes burned and he blinked, then closed them. The image of the peach lingered behind his eyelids, bright and perfect. His wanting it was so strong his arm went out toward it. *Just a peach. One for each of us. Please. Please.*

The heat rose further and pressed against him. He tried to rise but found he couldn't. His head spun, and he collapsed backward against the tree, seeing flickering lights in front of his eyes. There was darkness now at the corners of his vision. He thought of the peach. Just one. Red and yellow, ripe. The kind so ready to eat that when you held it, your fingers left the slightest mark, a little valley in the soft skin. Orange inside, or almost. Just a peach.

The darkness moved in from the corners, obliterating the forest. In front of him, he could see only a small circle of light. *A peach*, he thought. *A peach*. It was there, waiting for him. He could smell it.

They were laughing. Coming to, Max heard them.

I must be dreaming, he thought. *I fainted, and I'm still dreaming.*

He breathed in the aroma of peaches. *Definitely dreaming,* he thought.

"Max! Max!"

It was Susan, somewhere to his right.

Nell laughed. "How'd you do it? Where'd you find them? Where's the tree?"

Max opened his eyes. He was lying amid a pile of peaches.

Chapter 29

Max sat among mounds of peaches, feeling as if a comet had dived into his open hands. He was certain nothing had ever tasted so good. The five of them ate until they couldn't anymore, and then they sucked the stones just to keep something in their mouths. The girls ran their hands over the soft skins, exclaiming. But for a moment, Max held perfectly still, spellbound.

I did this!

The thought came with such fervor that he wondered if this time he really was dreaming.

He breathed peaches, and touched peaches, and weighed them in his palm. The wind in the tiled room had swept through in a moment, but the peaches stayed, and the comforting weight in his stomach, the heavy reality of them, made him want to burst.

He glanced at Jean, still licking her fingers, and grinned.

"Jean," he said. "What's your favorite food?"

"Peaches," she said, and grinned back at him.

"Me, too," said Kate. "Peaches. Definitely."

Peaches. Definitely.

Of course, he couldn't enjoy it forever. The peaches were a miracle, but they were also a question, and Max knew better than to try to ignore the facts.

So when they'd finally gathered the remaining fruit into Nell's blanket, and he'd slung them over his shoulder, exulting in the weight against his back, he went to walk beside Susan.

"There weren't any peach trees," he said. "I didn't go out and find one, if that's what you were thinking."

Susan looked at him with surprise and relief.

"Then how?"

He could only shrug, feeling a prickly warmth in his cheeks. "I don't know."

Good old Susan. She didn't even say I told you so. In fact she didn't say anything at all.

"It wasn't the way you said, though," he continued after a while. "There wasn't any pushing or explosion or anything."

For the first time in two days, she didn't fidget or look away when he spoke to her.

"Tell me" was all she said.

The confused, awful feel of the morning washed over him.

"I was mad. I know it doesn't make sense, but I was mad at you. Just going crazy that you wouldn't do that thing again."

He frowned, a little embarrassed. But when he glanced at her, he saw she accepted this with nothing but a small nod.

"So I was wandering around, and then everything started to go black. I was passing out, from the heat and from starving, probably. And I thought of that orchard we first came to. I wished I was there. I could *smell* the peaches. And that was it. I woke up, and I saw."

The peaches, in their blanket sack, bounced against his spine. Even his shirt smelled like them now. He worried suddenly that it would call the dogs to them.

"You smelled them because they were there," Nell said. "I smelled them, too. They're wonderful."

"Yeah," Max said. "But they weren't there when I sat down. It was just so . . . strong. I wanted it so badly. I *needed* it."

"You needed it!" Susan nodded vigorously. "Just like I needed to get out. Maybe here, when you need something desperately, it just comes."

Max wondered. Jean had a peach in her hand; she'd been eating it as they walked. He watched her use her sleeve to wipe the juice from her chin. She caught his eye and smiled at him, holding it aloft like a prize.

Could Susan be right? They'd all needed to eat. Had he needed it more than the others? He shook his head.

"We were all hungry. We all needed to get out of that room — but *you* did it. That first morning, we needed to get home — we were desperate for it. But we're not home! It can't be just needing it, or thinking about it. If that were it, we'd all be doing it all the time. It's got to be more than that."

Nell kicked at a stray rock in the barren ground. "Then *what?*" she asked. "Tell me, and I'll do it, too. Because I'd like to have something better than just my blanket to lie on. And I'd like a drink of water. And a clean shirt."

She sighed, as if she'd run out of steam. Maybe she had. As grateful as Max was for the peaches, his back still ached.

They were all tired, exhausted from the hunger and then the food. They lapsed into silence and kept walking, tensing at the occasional lull in the wind, when distant barking rolled up the hill.

Max tried to ignore it. He needed to put the pieces together. The Genius. The wind. The peaches. What did they have in common? He thought of the marketplace. There'd been all that cheering, and everyone was excited. He remembered the thrill that had washed over him when it started. But it wasn't until the Genius began to speak that the buildings — even the people — had changed. Was it the excitement that had done that?

He thought about the tiled room. No thrill there. But there was fear. Lots of it. And with the peaches? He'd been angry. Angry at Susan.

He tried to take a mental step back, tried to see how it all fit. Could it be anger, then? Fear? Desperation? If it were, why hadn't they all made the wind in the room? Why hadn't they all made peaches?

*T*hough the sound of the mourning bell did not reach the mountain, the exile felt its toll. Too often, it rang now, singing its song of anger and regret. Wordless, soundless, it flowed up to the small cottage, grief alone reaching to press at the windows and push at the door. Grief, and the howls of the lost. If madness had invaded the exile's mind at last, it had reached into the valley, too, rage and retribution spreading like disease.

Each time, the exile followed that silent summons, the better to spy the faces of the sufferers, searching and hoping not to find a familiar one among them. And amid all this, or perhaps because of it, the dreams came and came again, children invading all the old places, children stepping from the whispering orchard into the day, climbing the wood and descending into the valley.

Children found and lost again; children welcomed, then discarded.

Chapter 30

Late that afternoon, the sky darkened and lightning flickered behind the clouds. Soon, fat raindrops slapped the tops of the leaves and churned the brown earth to mud. Max walked through it, getting chilled and wet as the five of them scrabbled up the muddy rise. The mountain changed here into a series of craggy steps, yawning with caves. They crawled into the first one that had enough space for all of them and turned to watch the storm, shivering with the sudden cold and flinching at the crack of thunder.

Max set the peaches down and sucked at his wet clothing, glad for the water, even if he was shivering. Outside, he could see the lower half of the mountain spread below him. Clouds foamed so thick over the wood a new mountain seemed to have risen from the roof of trees.

A fork of lightning split the sky.

"It can't get us, right?" Kate asked.

Max peered from beneath the stone rim and counted three before the thunder smashed above the trees.

"No, the cave's protecting us," he said.

"That's good."

Still, at the next burst she gripped his hand.

"I don't like it."

The trees bent and flailed in the wind, and Jean moved close, too.

"What if it hits a tree?" she asked. "Will it catch fire? Will it burn us?"

"We'll be fine," he said. "Don't worry."

But he could feel them jump beside him, and Jean dug her fingernails into his arm with each new clap overhead.

"Tell us a story," Kate said after a while. "Like Dad does when there's a storm."

The wind threw rain into the cave, and Max blinked it from his eyes. Despite the food and the rest, he was still tired, and his bones ached. "Ask Susan," he said. "Susan knows lots of stories."

But Susan had stretched out by the curve of the wall, and she only shook her head.

"You tell one," she said. "I'm too tired."

The sky flashed and the trees shivered and the rain drove into the earth.

"Okay," Max said. "I've got a story."

It was a story of thunder and lightning, and all the things people used to believe, before they knew anything.

"They knew things," Susan said. "Just not science."

"Right, before they knew any *science*," he amended. "And so they were afraid of things like storms. Some thought whole families of gods lived over the clouds, and thunder was the sound of one of their giant chariots rolling over the sky."

Jean leaned her head against his arm. "That's funny," she said.

He rubbed the rain out of his hair, and then out of hers, listening to the drops clatter in the dirt like small stones.

"Well, they didn't think so. Other people said thunder was a giant bird whose wings made the wind blow and the thunder come. There were lots more, but I don't know them all."

Nell had stretched out so that she lay parallel to the mouth of the cave, behind the three of them. "You're forgetting the one who threw thunderbolts," she said.

"Yes, there was that, too," he agreed. "And there's even a story about thunder being the sound of people bowling in the sky. But I'm not sure anyone ever believed that one."

There was a long pause when he'd finished, filled by the sound of the drumming rain and the rush of wind through leaves. After a while, Kate said, "So what's the end?"

Max looked down at her. In the gray-gold light of the storm, her curls seemed charged with electricity.

"What do you mean the end?"

"Well, a story's got to have an end, doesn't it?"

The trees bowed and hissed, and wet leaves slapped the stone above them as Max thought about it.

"I guess the end is that people learned to understand things. You know, lightning's just electricity in the air, looking for a place to go. And thunder's just the sound it makes. You hear it later because light travels faster than sound."

The little girls were quiet a minute.

"So people weren't scared anymore? Is that the end?" Kate asked him.

He gave her a half-hearted yes. There were plenty of things to be afraid of at home, even in a world framed by solid walls and rules he knew. Storms just hadn't been one of them. Here, even that certainty was gone. He wasn't sure he could say there was nothing to fear.

"Well, that's a good story, then," Kate said. "Thanks."

The storm did not calm until long after dark. As he watched it, Max thought about huge birds that brought the wind, and flashing thunderbolt weapons, and the truth of static electricity and polarization. Lightning and thunder made a lot of noise, he told himself, but it was all just physics. Explosions came from chemical reactions, and there was a reason for them, one plus one equaled two, no matter how big and loud two happened to be.

Emotions, they were chemical reactions, too, in a way. He thought about that awhile and wondered if the rules in Ganbihar meant that simple things like fear and excitement and anger could turn on the lightning.

The storm had long gone and the sky had turned from gold to black when Kate began to scream into the dark. Max had been waiting for it, and now he sprang up and grabbed her by the shoulders before the others could find her.

Strong emotion, he thought. Excitement, anger, fear. Chemicals. Maybe these were the rules in Ganbihar.

"Mom!" Kate wailed. "Mom!"

He leaned in and called into her ear. "Kate! Do you see her? Do you see Mom?"

She thrashed in his arms. "Mom! Mom!"

He could hear the others in the dark, groaning, patting at the ground to find their way. Still, he held on to Kate.

"Get her, Kate!" he shouted over her crying. "You can get her! Take us to her!"

Kate's voice rose an octave. "Mom!" she shrieked. "Mom!"

Susan had found him now. She located him with her hands and tugged.

"Max! What are you doing? Stop that!"

Max shoved her away.

"Aren't you scared, Kate? Don't you want her?"

"Kate!" Susan called over him. "Kate, it's okay, we're here!"

Kate sobbed. Max's throat tightened, but he thought of chemistry, and rules, and . . . then Susan yanked him sharply backward. Suddenly Kate's wails were muffled by Susan's shirt.

"Kate, it's okay," he heard Susan say softly. "It's okay. Wake up."

At last they quieted her. Max sat by the cave wall, silent, while Susan sang Kate back to sleep, and Nell told Jean, who had begun to cry, to come beside her and hold her hand. No one spoke to him, not even Jean, and he didn't have to see them all to feel the bite of their disapproval. He tried to shrug it off, but all the crying made him want to shrink inside himself.

Finally, he heard Susan rise and fumble along the cave wall until she reached him.

"That was mean," she whispered.

He cringed. "It was an experiment. I had to try."

Silence, then a long sigh from Susan.

"But it didn't work."

"No. Obviously not."

She moaned softly, a disappointed, hopeless little sound.

"What did you think was going to happen?"

He looked out of the cave into the forest, where cobwebby strands of mist clung now to the bases of the trees. The clouds had cleared away, and a full moon glared overhead, whitening mist and trees to bone. "I thought maybe it was chemistry."

"Chemistry?"

He nodded, even though she couldn't see him. "You know, like all those chemicals that work in your brain when you're upset or excited. I thought maybe it needed something more than just regular fear or being angry, something *really* strong, like a nightmare. So I decided to try it. But it's not just strong emotion. If it were, we'd be home right now."

Susan was quiet awhile. Then she said, "It couldn't have been, anyway, if you think about it. If it were, things would be changing here anytime someone lost his temper or fell in love."

"How do we know they aren't?"

"Did Liyla say a thing about it? Did Omet? No. They talked about rally real, but they didn't say it happened anytime they got angry or scared. Don't you think those sleeper kids are scared enough to make something happen? If it's like that, what happened to all those kids they took to the workshop?"

He couldn't escape her logic. Max bit his lip. Experiment failed.

Susan lay back down, and he waited in the dark, listening until her breathing deepened. Then he crawled over to Kate, her sleep interrupted every few breaths by small hiccups left over from the tears. He found her hand and leaned down close to her, keeping his voice low.

"Kate," he said. "I'm sorry."

She was only half asleep. At the sound of his voice, she rolled over and put her other hand on his. A lump rose in his throat. He knew what it was like to feel small, and helpless, and like nothing made sense. If this was hard for him, what must it be like for Kate, or Jean? He sat and thought about that, long after Kate's breath evened and he knew she was asleep.

To escape the dreams and the half-heard wail of the valley, the exile sought the sea. Four clearings from home, a cliff stretched to the end of land and looked to water. Below, the distant surf, blue and gray, reached endlessly for the sand. In ancient times, men had crossed the sea and seen the lands beyond. The world then had been busy with trade and invention.

Now the great cities were husks, and the last of the wise devoured their own. Ancient promises had turned to torment, and the song of the valley had become a lament.

Chapter 31

Nell emerged from the cave in time to catch a falling peach with her head.

"Hey!" she yelled at Max, snatching it from the dirt and rubbing furiously at her hair. "What do you think you're doing?!"

Max thought it was pretty obvious what he'd been doing. After a sleepless night, he'd come out at dawn and decided that he'd better try some experiments that didn't include sisters.

At least he thought they wouldn't include sisters, until Nell inconveniently decided to put her head in the way.

"Sir Isaac Newton," he said, by way of explanation. He retrieved the bruised peach from her hand and tossed it again. It shot up into the glare of the rising sun angling through the trees, performed a little somersault, then fell back into his hand, slightly stickier than when it had started.

All the while Nell stared at him blankly.

"You know? The guy who discovered gravity? It's an experiment. If the laws of physics are different here, I figure we should see it, and where would we see it better than with gravity? Sir Isaac Newton had an apple drop on his head. I'm just using a peach."

Nell rubbed her hair again. "Well, nobody asked you to use *my* head, did they? Besides, we've got to eat those! Why didn't you use a stone or something?"

Nell had little appreciation for the scientific process.

"That was an accident. And anyway, if I'd done that, you'd have just gotten hit in the head with a stone!"

She glowered at him, immune to logic, and nodded at the peach.

"That one's yours."

Gravity had flayed the peach, and the juice ran sticky through his fingers. Already an interested gnat had brought a couple of its friends over to see about it. Max remembered belatedly that there was no water to be had.

Nell waved, and the gnats dispersed and regrouped.

"It's not even full day yet, and it's hot," she said. "Now we're going to have a bug party. Great."

Max grimaced.

"You do better, then," he said disgustedly. He sat down to eat the peach. His hands itched.

"I will. And it won't be with crazy experiments, either; it'll be thinking."

He rolled his eyes. "Experiments seem crazy until they work," he said. "You'll see."

"Tell that to Kate."

Max flushed. Nell was a born expert at poking anthills with sticks. He tried to think of something to say, found he couldn't, and turned away, clutching the ruined fruit. By the time the others woke, he'd gotten so sick of the stickiness and the gnats that he'd rubbed his hands in the awful dirt until they stung.

The day didn't get much better as it went along. They trooped up the mountain, and if the gnats were having a party, by afternoon a gang of mosquitoes had joined in. Max looked guiltily at Kate, who had dark circles under her eyes, and then at Susan. He knew she had every right to call him a hypocrite. It wasn't as easy as he'd thought to have the others watch him as if he were hiding the window from them in his back pocket. At least that was one thing he could say for Nell. She wasn't waiting. She kept trying to crack the nut.

Unfortunately, her methods were exasperating. After having complained about his peach experiment, she'd gone on to ask the others if maybe they'd dreamed an answer.

Dreamed an answer. Now, that made sense. Max tried to stifle his irritation — and found he wasn't much good at that, either. It wasn't just Nell, it was the whole universe he felt miffed at, or parallel universe, or maybe the space-time continuum, if that's what had gone wonky and sent them through the window. It would have been nice to have been handed some kind of manual before you got pitched into things like this. As it was, he was sweaty and subdued, and every time he looked at Kate, he was both sorry for having scared her and full of regret that the experiment hadn't worked. Then there was the panic that jolted him regularly as he listened for dogs and thought about being dragged back to the city. Parallel universes stank, and that was a fact.

They trudged up the mountain as the sun burned a hole in the horizon, orange and white against the black stripes of the trees. It was Jean's turn to carry the peaches, but she and Kate said they were too heavy and had instead decided to share their turns, holding the edges of Nell's blanket like a sling. The peaches bounced inside it, and every so often, when the ground was level enough to permit easier walking, the girls would bend toward the little hammock they'd made, just to breathe the smell of the fruit.

Max watched them worriedly. He'd counted peaches that

morning, only to discover that Nell had been right about her fear of wasting them. Even if they were careful, the fruit would last another four days — no more.

To distract himself from that unpleasant thought, he added another item to the long list he'd been compiling of equipment he could have used in a place like this: a map. He wouldn't mind knowing where they were heading. For now, *away from the city* would have to do. But it wouldn't do forever.

"We've got to walk faster," he said to the others. "Fish could turn into fossils quicker than we're moving."

"But it's hotter than it was yesterday," Jean said. "And the peaches are heavy."

"I'll take your turn," he said, retrieving the blanket. "You guys just walk."

But he knew there was only so much anybody could do living on peaches. He needed to find another way.

The sunlight sizzled on the leaves and slicked the dirt with white puddles as he tugged silently at the knot of the problem. Nell was doing the same — minus the silent part.

"Maybe it was you guys being desperate," she was saying to Susan. She'd given up proposing theories to Max after his reaction to her dream idea.

Susan only shrugged. Nearby, falling pine needles sparked in the sun.

"Can't be just desperate. There were too many desperate people in that city. We'd have seen it more than once."

"Were we desperate in that rally?" Kate asked. "Is that what that's called?"

Nell shook her head. "Desperate! More like crazy. Everybody there was crazy."

An awkward silence followed that comment. Max knew exactly what she meant. For a second, he'd adored the Genius up there in his ugly red cloak.

"He changed the buildings, too," Jean said. "Remember?"

You could count on Jean. Thinking about the buildings changing was a hundred times better than having to remember the way the Genius's voice had gotten inside his head.

"I thought we were just seeing things," he said. "But now I'm not so sure. What if the buildings really did change? Just like the wind and the peaches? That means we're not the only ones who can do this. He can, too."

"But how?" Nell asked. "What exactly did he do at the rally?"

Susan looked away from them, into the trees. "It felt like a song," she said. "You know how it is when catchy music comes on? It's hard not to dance, right?"

"Yes, but what about the buildings?" Nell asked her. "Was that just a catchy song, too?"

Catchy song, Max thought scornfully. What did that even mean? He wondered if Gottfried Leibniz had had these kinds of conversations with *his* sister.

"I don't know," Susan said. "But I think I loved him so much for that second that whatever he said — I just wanted it to be true, so it was. Buildings included."

Max looked uncomfortably at his feet. Mention of the Genius was like a burr in his shirt, rubbing an already sore place. He didn't like to think that his own mind had betrayed him. It had seemed so right, what the Genius had said. Just for a second, but still . . .

"How did he make us forget like that?" Kate asked.

"Forget?" Nell said. "We weren't forgetting. He was washing our brains out."

"Brainwashing, you mean," Susan said.

"Whatever it was. He did it."

Max squinted into the trees. Was he still forgetting? It was midday already, and the heat pressed the whole wood down. Even the chirping of the birds in the trees had gotten drowsy and slow.

Susan sighed. "It did feel like a kind of forgetting," she said. "I forgot I hated it here. Is that what you meant, Kate?"

"Yeah. I forgot I wanted to go home. Just for a minute."

Susan drew her sleeve across her face. The heat had reddened her cheeks and damped the hair at her neck.

"That's just what it was like," she said. "He crowded me out of my own head."

How did Susan always manage to find the right words? Max felt crowded out right now, his brain full of random bits of information he couldn't add up.

"All that mattered was what he was saying," Susan went on. "How did he do that?"

"By telling lies," Nell said.

"Big, mean lies," Jean added.

"Maybe," Susan said. "But it didn't have to be a lie, did it? The point was it was his thought, not mine. I could only think of what he was saying, and like Kate said, I forgot all the rest. He made me think of just the one thing, and for a second, it was all that mattered."

Max nearly stopped walking.

One thing, he thought. *One thing.*

The words clanged in his head like a bell.

Chapter 32

It had often seemed to Max, when he was younger, that things were easier for Susan. She knew how to behave in school; she had always earned gold stars for sitting nicely and doing her homework. She didn't get sent out for roughhousing or for talking too much in class. She didn't get KICK ME signs stuck to her back for having too many brainiac ideas. It bothered him, made him think something was wrong with him, to always be the one getting into one kind of trouble or another.

But in the past year or so he'd realized that Susan didn't just behave; she made herself invisible. He didn't envy that. Even his encounters with Ivan and Mo hadn't made him want to shut up forever, never say what he thought or offer a new idea. He still envied one thing, though — her ability to blot out the world. Then *she* wasn't invisible — everybody else was. He'd always wanted to know how she did that. His thoughts seemed to jump around in his head excitedly, and Susan would just dive deep into a book and be gone, living somewhere else, so completely immersed that the rest of them could yell and throw pillows and she'd barely notice. Now all of a sudden he knew what that was, and he thought it just might get them home. He hurried up to walk beside her, the peaches thumping against his back.

"Susan!" he said. "You know how you're different from me? You know how?"

His unexpected enthusiasm made her jump. "How?"

"When you read a book, you don't hear anything. Isn't that right? We call you and call you, and you don't even know it!"

"Well, I —"

"No, I mean in a good way. You concentrate like nobody I ever saw! Dad says that all the time, doesn't he? And it's true. When you've got your mind on something, you don't even see where you are!"

"So?"

"So that's why you broke us out of that room! You were thinking one thing, *so hard*, that it happened. Don't you see? It's just what you said. All you could think of was getting out! And in that rally — nobody could think about a thing but what the Genius was saying. I wasn't even thinking about getting home anymore, and I bet you were the same! He crowded all the rest of it out with those words of his!"

Susan had been making her way around a ragged hemlock when he started talking, and now she stopped altogether, bewildered. The others caught up to them.

"Hey, what's going on?" Nell asked him. "Is Susan okay?"

"She's more than okay! She's going to get us out of here!"

Nell pressed her lips into a flat line.

"Max, I think you'd better give me a turn with the peaches. Are you sure you're feeling good?"

"I feel fine!" he said. "Susan, tell her!"

But Susan only shrugged, and Nell asked if maybe he'd hit his own head with a peach.

Max threw a hand up, sending the hemlock into shivers.

"Listen," he said, ignoring Nell. "And don't think about what makes sense at home, but about what might make sense here. When I was hungry, hungry wasn't enough — it was only when I started blacking out. All I could think of was peaches. I thought of peaches *really hard* — and they were there!"

"One thing?" Susan said. "Don't people do that all the time? If that's it, it should be common!"

Max nearly laughed. Of course Susan would think that — of course!

"People don't think that way nearly ever," he told her. "They're always thinking a million things at once." He pointed at Nell. "What are you thinking right now? Tell her."

"Uh — maybe you need more protein in your diet? Dad says your brain goes fuzzy without it."

"And?"

"And what?"

"And you're not thinking that your legs ache, and you're worried about the dogs, and wishing we could get out of here?"

"And thirsty," Jean said. "Don't forget thirsty."

"See?" he turned back to Susan. "It's never just one thing! We can pay attention to something, but it's hard to put all the rest away. Only you do that!"

Susan blinked a few times, looking dazed. "Just thinking?" she said. "Just that?"

"Just!" Max cried. "It's not *just* anything! Don't you know your brain makes electricity?"

"So?"

"So it does things! Back at home, they have machines that work on brain waves. What if it's like that here, only more?"

He could feel the others catching on. Nell was nodding.

"It's like I said before. Real here is different from what it is at home. Here you could make peaches out of the air!"

Sometimes having sisters wasn't half bad. He grinned at her. "Exactly. Maybe the rules here are as different as they are on the moon, only it's not gravity that's funny — it's some other thing we never heard of. Instead of being able to jump higher, you can do this!"

Susan bit her lip. "You're saying when I think, it's . . . louder here?"

He felt like shouting Eureka.

Jean had ducked under a hemlock branch, and now she peered at Susan from beneath a fringe of dusty green bangs.

"I don't hear her," she said.

Nell sniffed. "We sure heard the Genius at that rally, didn't we?"

Max shot her a surprised look. "I guess we did! I hadn't thought of it that way."

Nell beamed, and the electricity or whatever it was in the air must have been working right then, because Kate and Jean brightened, too.

"So Susan can make the window?" Kate asked. "We're going home?"

Susan practically jumped onto a hemlock branch. "Whoa! Hold on! Don't you think I would if I could? I don't know what Max is even talking about!"

Max held up a placating hand. "It's not just regular thinking," he told Susan. "You've been wishing to get home just like the rest of us, but this isn't like that! It's all about setting up the right conditions."

"You mean I need to be scared out of my wits again? Is that what you're saying?"

"No, not the fear, the focus! Just try it — will you? It's got to be right!"

Susan did try it. All the rest of that day, as they hiked upward with renewed energy, she muttered to herself. Once he had her stop and sit, and she closed her eyes for so long, she fell asleep, an unfortunate fact he discovered when she tipped into Kate's lap.

"Maybe part of the right conditions is not being so tired," Susan said. "What are we going to do about that?"

But now Max was full of plans. He sent Susan ahead with Kate and Jean while he and Nell and the peaches zigzagged right and left, leaving what he hoped would be a confusing trail for the dogs. They rubbed their sweaty hands onto lone trees, plucked their own hairs out and draped them on rocks, and even sacrificed a peach, smashing it against a hickory tree and leaving some of its pulp twined among the needles of another hemlock.

They caught up to the others in a copse studded with yellow birches, their bronze bark peeling in strips and smelling of wintergreen. Beneath them, Max could see the outline of fallen leaves the ground had withered. Susan emerged from a cave in the hillside.

"No snakes," she said to Kate. "I checked with a stick this time. Wish I could do *that* just by thinking," she said to Max.

"Maybe later," he told her. "Or better yet, think up that window, and we can sleep in beds tonight."

She wrinkled her nose at him. "I've been trying all day. Maybe I'm just not as loud as you think."

He resisted responding to that. Instead he said, "So we'll work together. And maybe windows are too big a start. Let's go with something simple, like water. My hands are full of peach."

They sat together beneath the birches, and soon Nell and Kate and Jean joined them.

"Think of water," he whispered. "Really hard."

"No problem," Nell said. "I've been thinking of that all day already."

At last they settled down, and Max closed his eyes.

Water, he thought. Despite how much he wanted it, it was surprisingly hard to think about just water without his mind skipping away — to the problem of the wood itself, and to the strange nature of Ganbihar, and then, much as he hated it, back again to the tiled room. He opened his eyes with a grunt of frustration. The others were doing the same. He saw Nell frown and squint before her eyes popped open. Kate gritted her teeth; Jean had already given up and was drawing lines in the dirt with the feet of her Barbie.

Only Susan continued to sit there, motionless, eyes closed.

He stifled the urge to say something that would help. *Water*, he thought at her as hard as he could. *Can you hear us, whatever you are in the air? Water!*

A faint crackle distracted him. Had the humidity thickened? And yet it was no hotter than it had been. Max sat motionless. If he hadn't been concentrating on it so severely, he'd have missed the low buzz in the air. And yet there it was. Susan hadn't moved, and he worried he'd imagined it.

Again that buzz, just at the edge of hearing. Max felt the hairs on his arm rise, despite the heat of the wood as it settled into evening. The light had softened, but the air felt sharp. Max held his breath to hear it better and kept his eyes on Susan.

Then came another sound, a gentle lapping. Max searched for it, sweeping his eyes across the ground until he found a slick spot.

Water, pumping out of nowhere.

*T*he dagger of madness was hidden in dreams, and though the exile knew it, still it cut deep. In the night a vision had come of the sea rising to land, and children drawing water from the dust.

How many had been undone this way in the years of wandering across the sea? Thwarted prophets aplenty there had been then, dreaming their false dreams of homecoming and return.

Thinking it fruitless, the fool cuts the frosted tree;
He calls the winter field dead and passes it by.
And the simple? He hacks at the sleeping earth,
Demanding spring replace the snow.

So the ancients had left their warning against both impatience and despair. And yet they had written, too: The years will turn, and even the barren wood will have its day.

How many in their madness had clung to that promise? How many blinded by longing and made foolish with desire? Yet another, the exile thought. Yet one more, alone in a silent house on a hill.

Chapter 33

A sleeping potion couldn't have made them sleep more soundly. After days of being parched, of running in the heat without end, they had drunk and drunk and then collapsed beneath the broad moon and slept like stones until the late-morning light turned the mouth of the cave into a bright circle.

They woke to barking.

Max opened his eyes and tried to place himself. He was lying on the edge of Nell's blanket. Peaches had rolled from it across the cave and glowed gold in the shadows.

Outside, the noise sounded too close. It was no longer a distant part of the din of the wood, sometimes lost amid the voices of squirrels and birds. This was sharp, insistent, and nearby.

"Susan! Nell! Get up! How long have we slept?"

They rolled over, sat up, listened. Susan leaned out of the cave and squinted at the sky.

"It's late! Nearly noon!" she gasped. "They've had all this time!"

Panicked, she looked wildly around the cave. "Can we still outrun them?"

They had to try. There was no time to collect the peaches, but Jean grabbed her doll. They fled the cave and scrambled up the rise, out of breath with the sudden exertion.

Below, a dog barked frantically, its pitch rising to an excited whine.

"Susan!" Max huffed. "Do you think you can make the wind blow? You know how now, don't you?"

He tried to do it himself, desperate to throw the dogs off their scent, but found he couldn't. He kept thinking of the pungent heat rising off his skin and signaling to the dogs, like a pointed finger, like a whistle. He shuddered and tried to focus. The sound of barking shattered his concentration.

Susan, too, was trying. As Max watched, a faint breeze swept the dirt. He looked up into the trees. The leaves had begun to lift.

"Send it up the mountain!" he said. "Throw them off!"

Susan's forehead creased, and she bit her lip, but they could hear the sound of the search getting closer. Someone shouted in the distance. She shook her head. "I can't keep it up!"

The effort made it hard to run. They'd fallen behind the others. Nell turned, bouncing on the balls of her feet. "Come on!" she begged. "Hurry!"

For another second, Susan and Max kept at it, but they could hear the dogs shuffling through the trees now, not far beneath the nearest ridge.

Susan let out a shuddering breath and shook her head.

"It's no use!" she said. "We can't do both!"

They ran. Nell bounded up the mountain with the younger girls, half dragging them over rocks and helping them scramble over sudden rises. Max sprinted to keep pace, but below him, he could hear individual dogs now, amid the frenzied baying and clamoring. He looked behind him. Six huge black-snouted beasts streaked through the trees, ears up and teeth flashing.

"Faster!" he shouted.

The girls charged ahead. Max's lungs ached, but he pushed himself to speed up. He came abreast of Kate, her arms pumping, face pink, curls flying.

He could hear the dogs panting, hear their feet hit the dirt. Their barks rose in pitch.

Faster!

The barks turned to growls, and then Kate shrieked and fell, a dog on her back. Before Max could do a thing, a second one lunged at him, snatching his sleeve. Teeth grazed his arm, and the dog yanked him sharply to his knees. He hit the ground so hard, his jaw rattled.

"Susan!" he panted. "The wind!"

Max squeezed his eyes shut, mind scrambling. He tried to see the wind swooping through the trees as it had swept across the tiled room, throwing off the dogs and toppling the men he could hear coming. But the dog's hot breath fired his wrist, and the animal shook him until his arm flailed and he fell onto his back, feet bent beneath him. He cried out.

At last the dog held still, pressing his arm painfully to the ground. He tried to find the others. Susan stood trembling, her back against a red oak. One of the dogs had leaped up and pinned her there, its paws on her shoulders. She stood with her eyes squeezed shut as it growled in her face. Another dog had Nell by the shirt, and still another had clamped its teeth around Jean's skirt and pinned her to the ground. Kate lay with a cheek pressed to the dirt, eyes wide, struggling for breath beneath the dog's weight. A sixth animal circled the others, snarling.

Think, Max told himself. *Focus!* But his thoughts ricocheted through his head. The dog shook him like a doll, wrenching his arm nearly out of its socket.

A zip of electricity, like a static shock, nipped at him, and dirt rose in a puff nearby. He looked to Susan and hope surged through him.

Then he heard the sound of running feet, and the breeze died. Two soldiers, muskets up, broke through the trees.

"Good dog!" one of them said. "You hold him!"

The dog wagged its tail and jerked Max's arm. He winced and twisted to look at the soldiers.

The first was a ruddy-faced, middle-aged man whose round knob of a nose looked out of place amid the rest of his strange, stretched, and stubbled features. His companion was a hard-eyed, thick-bodied young man with light hair. He glared at Max.

"Stand up, you! You'll be coming back with us now."

He snapped his fingers at the dog, and it bobbed its head, yanking Max's arm wrong way back. Max yelped and writhed, twisting until he was able to scramble painfully to his feet. The dog answered by tugging his arm so sharply that he stumbled, sleeve shredded, and fell back to his knees with a gasp. Growling, the dog snapped at him, and this time teeth found skin. Max winced. If only he could throw the thing off him!

Susan's eyes were open now. He saw her looking past him, fixed on something—a scattering of pebbles. With all the effort he could muster, Max focused on those stones. *Move them!* he told himself. *Use the wind the way Susan did!* The air whined thinly, and the dog bristled.

Think of the stones! He thought of wind hitting the smooth curves, finding the grooves, diving from the trees to lift them.

Was he imagining it or had the air sizzled? Now Nell and Jean, too, were looking at the stones.

Wind, he thought as loudly as he could. *Wind!*

The pebbles jumped in the breeze, and a gust lifted them and flung them at the dog holding Kate. *One, two, three.* The fourth was bigger than a pebble. A good-sized rock, it popped from the ground and hit the animal squarely in the ear. It yelped.

The soldiers jumped, and the knob-nosed man's jaw dropped. He gaped at Max.

"You — did you do that?"

The younger soldier glared at his companion. "Shut it, you!"

But Max seized the opportunity.

"Yes! And we'll do more if you don't leave us alone! I'm warning you!"

He wondered how menacing he could sound, still on his knees with a dog clamped to his arm, but the first soldier lowered his musket slightly. The second only tightened his grip.

"Quiet, discard!" he said to Max. "You'll be sorry for it soon enough. There's more coming to help us. The searchers are spread out all across the mountain. You've got nowhere to run!"

But Max thought he talked a little too much for someone completely sure of himself. He stared back at the man, trying to look confident.

"You'll need help," he said. "Didn't they tell you what happened in the city? Didn't you hear how we got out?"

His words hit the mark. The knob-nosed soldier blanched. The younger one glanced at his companion uneasily.

"You! Lift that weapon! It's like they told us, a harmless trick. You afraid of wind now?"

From the corner of his eye, Max saw Kate trying to squirm from under the dog's paws. It growled warningly.

"But there's stories," the first soldier was saying. "Old ones. There's worse they can do if what people say is true."

The second soldier's laugh sounded forced. "Does this one look like he could do worse? Those are nothing but village tales. You idiots from the edges all tell tales." He shook his head. "Who told you that one, your grandmother?"

"Grandfather," Knob-Nose said.

They argued some more, and as they did, Max looked around. A silvery beech stood a few feet from him. One of its branches hung strangely, and after a second, he spotted a crack running through it. *Damaged in the storm*, he thought. He caught Susan's eye, nodded toward the tree, and raised an eyebrow. She looked and answered with the faintest nod. Next she got Nell's attention, and showed her.

It was easier this time. Max called back the feeling of the wind against his cheek and thought of the storm he'd seen, the wind thrashing through the trees, flattening the leaves, making the branches bend . . .

Again, that tickle along his skin. Leaves fluttered, and the tree swayed. After a moment, he could hear the waterfall sound of air in branches, followed by a *crack*. The branch snapped and spun from the tree, whirling toward the light-haired soldier.

It clouted him sharply on the side of his head, and he fell like a stone.

At the sound of wood on bone, the older man jumped as if he'd been the one struck. He dropped his gun, and it went off with a bang, narrowly missing Max and the dog. The animal yelped and cowered, and Max rubbed his newly freed arm.

The soldier looked down at his colleague, stunned.

"It's true, then! The stories!"

He looked at Max, and all the color had gone from his face. After a moment's hesitation, he snapped his fingers, and the dogs came to him, leaving the children alone. He muttered a command, and the animals lay obediently at his feet. He bent down beside them, never taking his eyes off Max.

"You one of them, then?"

The tone of the question was so unexpected that Max stopped rubbing his arm and just looked at him.

"One of who?"

"The powerful. Heard talk of them when I was a boy, but I thought them all dead now."

Village tales, the other soldier had said. Max looked over and saw the blond man safely out for the moment.

"Well, we're not dead," he said firmly. "And you can see we're powerful. You'd better let us go if you don't want more trouble."

The man hesitated, and Max concentrated with all his might on the fallen limb. It stirred. The soldier jumped, then nodded.

From behind Max, Susan said, "Where are the other searchers?"

This time, when the soldier hesitated, Max felt the air buzz and saw one of the stones rise. He suppressed a smile at the look on the man's face. *Good for you, Susan!*

"All over these west woods," Knob-Nose said hastily. "From

here and down. We were ready to give up when we caught your scent again. Hard for the dogs with the bitter ground here. It fouls the air, too."

"Okay, then," Max said. "We'll go, and you can say you couldn't hold us."

Another hesitation, another nod. Max got to his feet, wincing at the ache in his knees. Kate had already managed to back herself up to where Jean stood, as far from the dogs as possible. They started to move back into the trees, eyes on the dogs and the unconscious man. The animals growled softly.

"Wait!" the soldier called.

Max's stomach dropped. He tried not to show it on his face. "What?"

The knob-nosed soldier looked red now. He whispered to the dogs and then let them go. Max froze, but they only turned and ran down the mountain, back the way they'd come.

The soldier twisted the end of his cloak.

"The stories," he said. "My granddad said . . ." He sounded sheepish but plowed on after a second. "He said that if the powerful ones blessed you, you'd stay blessed. Could you do that? Lay your hands on me?"

Max didn't know what he'd expected, but it wasn't that. His cheeks burned.

"It's not like that," he said. "I can't bless anybody."

"Please," the man said. "Else I'll be taken, for letting you go."

Max had never seen such fear in a grown man's face. He didn't know what to say.

"I wish I could," he said. "I — listen, why don't you run? Don't go back. That city's a terrible place. Just keep running until they can't find you anymore."

The man dropped his head.

"The dogs will lead them to me soon. Please," he said again.

Max was out of words. But Nell took a step toward the soldier.

"I'll bless you," she said.

He looked up at her. "What good would that do? I need him to do it."

Nell frowned, then glanced at Max.

"Okay, then, Max, you bless him."

He started to protest, but she continued: "Just you remember, now: it only works if you don't tell on us. Nobody can follow us or you'll regret it."

The soldier paled a little but nodded. "Please," he said. "Or it's the back room for me."

Max understood the desperation in his face now.

Awkwardly, he put his hands on the soldier's head. His ears were on fire, and he felt like a fool.

"Uh, consider yourself blessed," he said.

The man nodded.

"Better hit me, too," he said. "I can't be found without a mark on me. They'll know."

Max felt his stomach turn over. He didn't mind fighting back, but hitting a man who sat there waiting for it — that was another thing. The soldier saw him hesitate. When Max continued to say nothing, he looked frantic.

"You know what they'll do to me if you don't!"

Feeling queasy, Max retrieved the branch that had fallen. He closed his eyes and swung.

Chapter 34

They were never going to stop running. Soldiers might not come for a while, but Max understood now what he hadn't before. They would never be safe.

He sat on Nell's unfolded blanket beneath a stand of young aspens. They'd gone back to get it — and the last of the peaches — before climbing higher up the mountain. They had stopped near dusk here, in a clearing where the blackened trunks of a ruined poplar and several fallen oaks lay in the dirt. The aspens had sprouted in the space they made, white bark bright against the dark wood.

They'd been so many days beneath taller trees that Max hadn't seen the sky spread out this way. The sun was setting, and red and orange and gold colored the vast panorama overhead. It seemed bigger than he'd ever seen it — too big.

It's an optical illusion, Max told himself. *The sky's no bigger today than yesterday.* But he realized it had been big then, too. It stretched for miles, keeping pace with the ground. Black despair followed that thought. They kept walking, day by day, but where were they going, anyway? Only into more trouble. He'd been thinking about it since his encounter with the soldier. Max had never seen desperation like the kind in that man's eyes.

You know what they'll do to me, he'd said.

Max did know.

His mind came back again to the silky, dangerous voice of the Genius: *Do you think you can tell me lies and I will simply walk away?*

No, Max thought. *I don't.*

And that was the problem. He'd known it even before seeing the soldier's fear. The Genius would never walk away. The wood might be quiet for a while, but he was coming.

Max said nothing, but the unsettled feeling infected them all in one way or another. Susan came to sit beside him beneath the aspens.

"I know it was rotten, with that soldier," she said. "I know you didn't like hitting him."

That was true. Max had known his share of bullies. He remembered the first time he'd met Ivan, in the fourth grade. Already he was a foot taller than anyone else, and looking for someone to kick. He'd chosen Max because Max had brought a geode to class, and Ivan thought it funny to say that the kid with the strange hair thought a rock was show-and-tell. Mo had joined him a year later. He was a small wiry kid with a mean streak and a quick temper who thought the height of hilarity was someone falling down or getting knocked that way. He loved to make other people look like idiots. Even when he wasn't the butt of it, Max never thought that was funny.

Hitting the soldier — worse, fooling him — made Max feel like one of them. He hated it.

"He was ready to drag you back down to that tiled room

and that monster-faced lady," Nell said from her place at the other end of the blanket, where she'd been divvying up peaches for supper. "Now he thinks he's lucky. What's rotten about that?"

Max only shrugged. Susan knew.

"You didn't have to fool him like that," Max said. "That was uncalled-for."

Nell frowned at him. "You could say, Thank you, Nell, for making him tell the others not to follow."

He thought of telling her how useless that had been. Did one soldier's word mean anything against the Genius? Maybe it made her feel better to think so for a while. He didn't know. When he didn't answer, she glowered at him and turned her back.

A wind rushed through the wood and rustled the aspens until they clattered and whispered to one another. *Just like us,* Max thought. *Stuck in a cage and rattling the bars.*

"Let's try for the window again," he said suddenly.

Susan looked up at him.

"How?"

"What about it being too big?" Nell said.

He shrugged. "If you can make the wind blow, you can make a window," he said. "It's just understanding the rules, right? We need to picture what we want."

He started to tick off all the ingredients for making a window, and their window specifically.

Jean raised her hand eagerly. "Ooh! Me! I have something!"

Nell snorted. "It's not *school,* Jean."

Jean ignored her. "It was cold to touch it, but that night — it turned warm."

"Right!" he said. "Temperature. Good one, Jean!" She rewarded him with a grin.

Kate added the width of the sill, which she could climb on back home, and the way the shade was bent, having once been hit by an errant ball.

They talked about glass and wood, and the width and height of the window for so long that at last Max could really see it. And after a while, he thought about it so much, it was like a song in his head — glass and wood and height and width and cold-turned-warm — until the picture of the window hung behind his eyes.

And then the air hummed and thickened, and it was there.

The window hung in the sky just above Max's head, vivid with the colors of the setting sun. Jean squealed with joy, and Kate rushed to it, jumping up to try to reach the glass. Nell stretched to lay her hand flat on the clear surface.

"It doesn't give," she said.

Susan circled the glass, and Max hoisted Nell onto his shoulders so she could press her face against it. But it was no use. They'd produced a window at last, and it looked exactly like the window back home. But it was just a window, nothing more.

They tried again, then again, then a fourth time. It didn't matter. Windows hung, suspended from nothing, but they were only glass. They didn't open to anywhere.

At last they stood among the aspens, staring in disappointment at the strange hanging windows they'd made, glass fading with the sunlight and beading, eventually, with the heat.

Max wondered what there was left to hope for.

The watchers had long climbed the mountain in ones and twos, as lonely in their way as the lost, if only for a time. Was it easier to move into darkness clothed in anger? The exile thought it must be, for they pushed on in eagerness, seeking the roads and the cities of men. If they sensed the presence of another upon the rise, they gave no sign. Nor did the exile seek them. Eyes of the valley, they called themselves. The exile knew them better as its arm of judgment and its punishing hand. Still, life calls to life, and brothers carry with them the scent of home. So watching from a distance, the exile marked their coming and knew when they departed.

Thus it was that their increase told its story. At the height of summer, beneath a waning moon, they came steadily, a stream of them crossing beneath the trees, making their way to the dark place beyond. What was it that drew them there? In years past, the wisest had begged that they go. Open arms to the afflicted, welcome home the lost, he had said. Why let fear forever bind you? For such counsel they had called him poison, called him fool. Anger burned in the valley, and his coaxing talk of strength and welcome went unheeded. Had those below heard it at last? No. There was nothing of forgiveness in the whispers of the travelers as they moved through the trees.

If there had ever been forgiveness in the valley, it was long dead.

Chapter 35

The earliest story Max knew about himself was a story of struggle and surprise. He'd been born just minutes after Susan, and though she had come into the world mostly fine, it had been tougher for Max, whose lungs, at first, didn't work. As a small boy, he had liked to examine the pictures his parents kept of that beginning time, amazed that the scrawny, very un-Max-like baby in the glass box, covered in tubes and wires, could be him.

At age five or six, studying pictures of his newborn self, he'd come up with a list of questions about the entire incident, chief of which was why his chest was caved in as if he were starving. Didn't any of those tubes send food? His father had explained that he was trying to breathe, and though the doctors sent him oxygen through a tube, each day they'd send a little less, so he had to work at it, his lungs fighting to draw air.

"That's the only way to make lungs grow," his mother had told him. "If you didn't fight for air, you'd have been stuck in that box forever."

She said he'd fought so hard, he'd surprised them and come home early. Max had always been proud of that. He liked to think of his newborn self exceeding expectations.

Getting home again was now the focus of Max's day and night, but no amount of twisting his brain into knots seemed to help.

They had made glass, windows even, but they were useless things, hanging in the wood to mock them. Susan tried to make them disappear, but one fell, shattering in the dirt. The shards of it glared up at them, iced with afternoon sun.

"We should clean it up," she said. "It's littering."

Max sighed and told her they'd do it later. Watching the window fall had drained him, and he could see the others felt the same. Kate and Jean returned to a game they had devised with stones, Nell stretched out on the blanket and buried her head in her crossed arms. Max peeked to see if she was crying, but if she was, she made no sound, and after a while he could see by the way her back rose and fell that she was asleep. Susan collected bits of broken glass, but even she abandoned the project in the middle and sat looking at the way they caught the light.

"What are we doing wrong?" she asked him. "What's a window beyond glass and wood?"

Max squinted up into the slim branches of the aspens. They gave so little cover compared to the rest of the wood that heat prickled his skin, and he could feel the pressure of it on the top of his head.

"Maybe it wasn't our window that did it at all. Maybe something hit our window and took us through. Do you think that's it?"

Susan shrugged. "It didn't feel like that."

They jumped at the sound of an animal howling in the distance.

"What was that? A wolf?" Kate asked. "Are there wolves here?"

They hadn't seen any. Max had thought the barren ground responsible for keeping away the foxes and deer he'd seen on the way to the city. He hadn't considered wolves.

"There's nothing for them to hunt here," he said, as much to reassure himself as her.

"Maybe we should find a better place to camp," Susan said. "Maybe we should keep walking."

Nell looked sweaty and red faced when they woke her. The imprint of her arms had left a long pink stripe across her forehead.

"I didn't hear anything," she grumbled. "You sure you didn't imagine it?"

Max rolled his eyes. "Trust me," he said.

"I think wolves would have woken me," she said.

"Well, they didn't."

They returned the peaches to the blanket sack. Jean wrinkled her nose at it.

"Can't we make something else?" she asked. "I'm sick of peaches."

"Then think of something," Nell told her. "Complaining about it won't help."

"Grouch," Jean muttered.

They trudged along for a while, looking for a good cave or an outcropping that gave them a better view of their surroundings.

"Stop dragging your feet," Susan said to Jean.

Jean glared at her. "I can drag them if I want to."

She dragged them loudly for several minutes, driving Max

nearly insane. He swallowed the things he wanted to say and instead forced himself to fall back and walk beside her. He picked up a stick and handed it to her.

"If you're tired, this will help."

She took it and continued walking, still dragging her feet. But now she used the stick to stab at the ground, too, making a sharp *thwack* with each step. In her free hand, she held her Barbie by its ankles, swinging it beside her so its grubby hair came up as the stick came down. She glowered at him, daring him to complain.

Max sighed. He wasn't used to getting the worst of Jean's stubbornness. But he'd seen her slump when the windows failed to let them through, and now she bristled at everything. He missed the cheerful faith she usually had in him. He missed her in general. Jean didn't wake with nightmares the way Kate did, but she was growing silent and irritable, playing solitary games and brooding.

"Dear Jean," he said to her suddenly in his letter-writing voice. "When we find a good camp, we'll figure out how to make bread. Then you can have a peach sandwich. Your brother, Max."

Jean shrugged. He tried again.

"Dear Jean, Won't you like that? Bread and peaches? Peaches and bread?"

But she didn't even bother to play the game. "No. I'll hate it. I hate everything here. It stinks."

Dismayed, he watched her swing her doll, letting its dirty hair flap.

"Don't you like doing the things we can do here?"

Jean shook her head. "I can't do them. They're too hard."

"You can! It just takes a little practice!"

"I don't want to."

"Why not?"

"Because I don't. I hate this stinky forest with its stupid brown ground. I hated that bad city. I hate the people. I just want to go home."

He had no answer for that. She might be only seven years old, but Jean knew what was what. She was only saying what they all felt. Max looked around at the wood. The late-afternoon sun cast long shadows on the ground.

He felt a peculiar tightness in his chest. It seemed to him suddenly that all his life he'd been thinking about the day he'd leave home. There were so many things to do out there! Home was just the place you waited in between doing them. While Susan had to be coaxed outside, away from her books, he woke each morning thinking about where he'd go, what he'd do, the people he'd meet when he got there. If he thought about home at all, it was usually in terms of the day he'd be saying good-bye to it. He had big adventures planned — to the Arctic, maybe even the moon. It occurred to him that he hadn't wanted to get home so badly since before he could think, since he was a baby, stuck in that glass box.

But it was different now. The forest might stretch for miles; he could walk forever and every sight would be new. He was farther than the Arctic, than even the moon. And yet for all that, he was inside a box again. He trudged up the rising ground beside Jean and felt as if someone had taken everything away, erasing the bright glow of *tomorrow* and *maybe* and *what if?* There was nothing left.

It made it hard to breathe.

Chapter 36

They spotted the cave a little while later, when they'd wandered into a rocky section of the wood. Gray boulders flecked with white broke through the earth and jutted up among the trees, and where the ground rose steeply, a series of rock steps led to a wide-mouthed cave.

"Perfect!" Nell said. She slung the blanket sack over her shoulder. "From up there, we can see everything!"

They took the shortest way up, climbing the rocks to get to the cave. Nell reached it first and ducked inside.

"Does it look good?" Susan called after her. "How big is it?"

She didn't answer.

"Hey! Nell!" Max yelled.

He reached the opening next. The cave was tall enough to stand in, and once he'd ducked inside, he could see it was even wider than he'd thought. Nell stood in the center of it, her back to him, the blanket full of peaches still resting on her shoulder.

"Didn't you hear us calling you?" he asked her.

She was backing slowly toward him. He took a step her way, blinking, and caught a whiff of a heavy animal odor that made the hair on his neck stand up.

"What is it?" he whispered. "A bear?"

Nell kept backing toward him. She shook her head.

He could hear the others behind him as they reached the opening. Susan started to say something, and he held up a hand.

"Shh!"

He wasn't sure she saw him. She, Jean, and Kate stood blinking in the entrance.

Nell had almost backed up all the way.

"Get out," she whispered as she passed close to him. "Get out now!"

He saw it then. A foot from where she'd been standing, four filthy, matted bodies curled against the wall. Blue cloth littered the ground near them, torn to bits.

Slashers.

Max tensed and started to ease himself backward, too.

"Their hands!" Nell whispered to him. "Look at their hands!"

He squinted in the dim light. One of the figures lay sleeping with an arm flung out, and he saw the palm of its rough hand. It was covered in blood.

A slasher moaned and stirred in its sleep. Max tried to force himself to move slowly, to tread without a sound.

"What is it?" Susan whispered behind him. Her eyes would adjust in a second. If the others saw . . .

A slasher groaned and lifted its head.

Kate gasped.

The thing's head swiveled, and it took them in. It growled, then threw the others aside and jumped to its feet. Suddenly, they were all awake.

Before Max could even shout, it leaped for Nell. She

screamed and held up an arm, but it slammed her against the stone wall. Max grabbed its hair and yanked, but the others were up now, and he could feel their sharp nails on his back, their sharper teeth.

He flailed and kicked as they threw him to the ground and turned back to Nell. Overhead, the things shrieked and the girls yelled. Max struggled to his feet as the scuffling slashers kicked and clawed him. Susan charged in, swinging Jean's stick, and caught them with the end of it. He heard it smack sharply again and again.

He'd nearly reached Nell when a slasher threw him to the ground and rolled him over, tearing with rough nails at his shirt, his arm, his collar. He kneed it and it reared backward, yelping, when he caught a glimpse of its face in the shadows. Glazed eyes stared out of the mat of hair. For a moment, they sharpened, and the slasher opened its mouth.

"Hey!" Max yelled. "Listen! Can you understand me?"

But at the sound of his voice, it jerked its head as if slapped and the spark dimmed. Max looked again and saw only terror and desperation. The slasher growled.

Susan caught the thing from behind with the stick, and it howled and raised its hands, moaning with a nearly human voice. Max tried to shove it off him. The thing was so heavy! A second later, it growled again, then swiveled back to Nell, who rolled on the floor as the other slashers buffeted her, snatching at her shirt and hair, tugging at her hands as she clutched the ends of her makeshift sack.

"Nell!" Max yelled. "The food! They want the food! Throw the blanket!"

Three of the things were on her, and now he could see clearly that they were yanking at the blanket sack. She'd fallen on it, and they ripped and mauled her, trying to grab it.

He rolled over to get to her, but the fourth slasher seized him and tossed him down. He reached up to snatch at the hair on its chest, but this time his hand caught the remains of fabric.

Nell was yelling. One of the slashers had turned on Susan, and she kept at it with her stick. Jean darted to where Nell lay struggling beneath the other two and tugged at the blanket, cringing as the things swiveled her way. After a second, Kate joined her.

Reeking, mountainous beasts too big for the space of the cave, the slashers blocked the light and loomed above the girls, but Jean and Kate jumped out of reach, and Susan, who'd been caught for a second by a gnarled hand, wrenched free and smacked the attackers with her stick. Nell kicked and struggled, and Max reached for the slasher on his chest and grabbed its face, hand closing on a mass of hair, slick with spittle. He pulled as hard as he could, careful to keep out of reach of its teeth. It yowled sharply, like a cat.

"Here!" Kate screamed. Max saw her holding the blanket sack that she and Jean had extracted from beneath Nell. "Here! Take it!"

The slashers raised their heads. Their eyes locked on Kate.

She ran to the opening of the cave and turned again. "This way!"

The slashers leaped up, and Max, suddenly free, jumped to his feet. Behind Kate, he could see the stone ledge. She backed toward it.

"Kate! Watch it!"

Jean had flattened herself against the wall, and now she tugged Nell, who lay gasping in the dirt, out of the way. The slashers eyed Nell, then Kate.

Kate lifted the blanket. "You want this!" she said. "Come on!"

Then she flung the sack over the edge.

The four figures leaped, and Max yelled, but they were past Kate in an instant and bounding down the ridges after the food.

Gasping, Kate watched them go.

Max ran toward her, shaking. They were all shaking. He stepped out to the ledge and looked down. Below the series of stone outcroppings, the slashers scrambled over the blanket, ripping at it and fighting over the peaches.

"There's not enough for them," Nell said from behind him. "They'll be back up for us."

Jean stood hugging herself by the cave opening. Nearby, Susan leaned heavily on the walking stick.

"Why didn't you make the wind blow like you did before?" Jean asked her.

Susan only shook her head, trying to catch her breath.

"I didn't have time," she panted. "Couldn't."

The yelps and growls from below increased.

"They're almost done," Nell said. "We've got to go!"

Without another word, they started away, moving as fast as they could. The land continued to rise, and Max tried to steady his breathing. He looked down at his shirt. It was torn and stained red where the slasher had grabbed him.

He fingered the fabric.

"Max! Are you bleeding?" Susan asked him.

He wished his hands would stop shaking. He balled them into fists so the girls wouldn't see. "No, that was from them. I'm just scratched up."

They all were. They made their painful way up through the trees as the sound of the slashers diminished. Great gray rocks still pocked the ground here, jutting out like the teeth of some mythical beast. Between them, poplars with trunks like stone pillars rose toward the sky, their green foliage peppered with yellow leaves. The few that had fallen were black underfoot.

"What if they follow us?" Jean asked. Her voice sounded pinched tight.

Max looked over his shoulder, but nothing was coming. "I don't know if they can," he said. "They're not animals, exactly."

Nell looked at him sharply. "What do you mean?"

"They were wearing clothes," he said. "Like you saw before."

She nodded. "That doesn't mean they won't kill you," she said. "You saw their hands!"

He had. But there was something about the look in the thing's eyes. It had been like someone was there for a second and then gone. He didn't know how to explain it.

"I don't think they killed anything," Kate said.

They all looked at her. "What?" Nell asked. "How would you know?"

Kate bit her lip.

"I saw the walls," she said. "There was blood on them, and long scratch marks. It was like they'd been scratching at them until they bled. I think . . . I think they were trying to get out."

"Out!" Nell protested. "Why didn't they use the door?"

Kate only shrugged. "I don't know," she said. "But I think

maybe — maybe they were having a bad dream and couldn't figure out how to."

Max felt suddenly sick. He thought again of being locked in that glass box and not knowing the way out.

Nell shook her head. "Can't imagine a thing like that dreaming," she said.

But Kate, much to Max's surprise, seemed certain. "Not a dream," she said. "A nightmare."

*C*hange was coming. In dreams the exile felt it; on waking, it was a weight in the air.

The word, with its long history, its burden of good and evil, seemed everywhere now. Each day the exile woke to it, as if expectation were a thing breathed, a scent inhaled.

A new way. Once welcomed, now despised; once embraced, now shunned.

Like the exile, a contradiction.

And still, even in the valley, they spoke of change often, for it had been enshrined in the ancient books:

> With Eri came the dawn,
> And with Anam the day,
> For darkness shrouded all
> Before the light of understanding.

As was their way, the thinkers looked deep into the words and unwound the meaning woven there, telling tales of wise men who lit an everlasting flame to shine through the long night of years.

Oh, how the valley cherished the rebellion of its ancients and praised its own. We, the everlasting flame, are like the sun rising to color the sky in its glory, they said. We are the dawn.

And yet how like the dawn was the twilight. How like the coming of the light was its passing away.

Chapter 37

The terrain grew steadily stranger as Max searched for a new place to camp that evening. The earth bristled with boulders, and the knobby roots of trees rose from the dirt to overtake them, gripping the rocks like tentacles. Max couldn't help shuddering at the sight of them. He felt as if he were standing on the surface of a flat brown ocean and some creature from the depths had reached up to grab the stones.

Stop that, he told himself. But he couldn't help it. He felt battered and jittery, and every place the slasher had scratched or bitten him stood out as a separate hurt, stinging and aching and making him wince. Worst of all was the memory of the thing's nearly human face, the shattered expression of loss and terror that had flickered there a moment, then gone away.

He tried not to think of it as the five of them stumbled through the rocky wood, looking for a protected place to spend the night. At last, as blue shadows gathered in the trees and splashed across the rocks, they found a circle of clear ground, surrounded by stones. They collapsed inside it, shielded a little from the brooding trees, and struggled to concentrate enough to produce even peaches. Without any blanket to spread, they curled up in the dirt and tried to rest.

The rocks interrupted the pattern of the forest, so that overhead, the umbrella of leaves opened to let in the sky. Night fell and the moon rose, three quarters full, to float over the clouds. Max tried not to feel like he was slowly suffocating.

Next to him, Jean sniffled and rolled over.

"Max, write me a letter," she whispered. "About getting out of here."

He squinted up at the moon, wishing he could vault them to it, lie down in the Sea of Tranquility, even if it was just an empty crater, the name a mistake someone once made before space travel showed them the truth. But then he thought this probably wasn't even his moon, with its comforting, old-fashioned names: Sea of Tranquility, Sea of Serenity, Sea of Rains, Sea of Clouds.

"Dear Jean," he whispered back. "We're getting out of here. I promise. Soon. Your brother, Max."

At least tonight she seemed to believe him. Jean nodded and let her shoulders down a little. Kate wasn't as easily appeased.

"I wish we'd found another cave," she said, looking around. "It's scary out here."

She moved closer to Susan, who put an arm around her shoulder.

"I'm not walking into another cave for the rest of my life," Nell said. Max thought she looked a little forlorn, sitting there without her blanket. "At least out here you can see what's coming."

Neither option appealed to Max. The stones pressed in on him, and the trees moving in the wind sounded like a warning.

He looked up at the moon and tried to count time. The clouds drifted across it, blotting the light, and then uncovered it to reveal again the fierce shape of the land.

Was it two weeks now that they'd been here? Max spent a minute calculating. Almost. The thought dropped like a cold weight in his stomach. What if they never got home?

"Can this place get any worse?" Nell whispered. She pushed her back against one of the stones and hugged her knees. "Even the forest looks haunted. And that's not to mention this weird dirt."

"I told you it hated us," Susan said to Max. "I think I was right."

"Places don't hate people," he told her wearily. "We'll figure it out. Look how much we've figured out already! You'll see. I promise."

But he knew he said it now only out of habit. He was teetering on the edge of a cliff, ready to fall. The wind hissed in the trees.

If he didn't think they'd ever get home, what was there? What was there to solve, and where would they go? He closed his eyes and pushed the thought away. No. They would get out. They would get home. This place didn't hate them, because places didn't hate people, and the world, even strange worlds on the other sides of windows, made sense. If he was going to be sure of anything, he'd be sure of that. He had to be, or there was nothing left.

He closed his eyes and forced himself to sleep.

Things were supposed to look better in the morning, but they didn't. The hot wind had picked up, clattering through the branches and swooping down to raise tufts of dust from the dirt, so that the ground belched out a low, muddy fog.

When Max woke, the girls were already on the other side

of the stones, talking. All except Susan, who sat just feet away, staring fixedly at the ground inside the circle.

"Hey," he said. "You okay?"

She didn't look up.

"Susan!"

He had to practically shout at her to get her to look his way. Then she blinked at him, a little startled.

"Were you calling me?"

He nodded. "Twice. What's wrong?"

"Nothing," she said. "I'm concentrating. I was thinking that you're right. Places can't hate people. So if the ground's sour here, maybe we could do something about that. You know, like sweeten it up a little."

Max just stared at her. They couldn't manage a window, but she thought she could fix a whole forest. He turned away without saying another word. It was tiring, sometimes, being the only sensible one.

He found the others busy with a similarly ridiculous activity — teaching Nell to play the game Kate and Jean had made up, something called stones, or squish, he couldn't tell which, since they kept arguing about it.

"Susan done yet?" Nell asked him.

He shook his head.

"She told me she needs to have a talk with the dirt," Nell said. "I think she might be losing it."

Kate frowned at her. "She's not *losing it*," she said. "Don't say that."

Nell only shrugged, and Jean passed her a stone. "Ready?" she asked.

Max sat pondering all the places he'd rather be when he felt a slight buzz in the air. Maybe Susan had done something after all. He turned, and there she was, already emerging from the circle of rocks to join the game.

Again, the hair on Max's arms stood up, and he sensed a nearly inaudible hum.

"Do you feel that?" he asked Susan. "That zap in the air?"

She stopped for a second, listening for it.

"Maybe. What do you think it is?"

"I thought it was you."

She shrugged and shook her head.

The wind died, and they all sat, straining to hear something.

"All I hear is bugs," Jean said.

"Shh," he told her.

Again, that faint buzz, then a sound like a flag flapping.

Kate sucked in her breath and pointed.

Behind Susan, where no one had been a moment before, stood a figure wearing a hood.

Chapter 38

Max had never liked fairy tales — stories that made things easy, that kept the night at bay. What was wrong with the truth? The truth was layered and fantastic, full of quarks and quasars, microbes and galaxies. The truth didn't believe in bad guys who wore black hats and good guys who wore white ones. The truth was just the truth, and when you knew it — you could breathe.

But he stood looking at the hooded figure who had appeared from nowhere and wondered if in fact it didn't really matter what you believed in the end. If you were stuck in someone else's story — in the nightmare they'd created — who cared what you knew?

And then the figure did something unexpected. It reached up to pull back its hood.

Kate threw her hands over her eyes. Jean squeaked. Susan paled and Nell gaped. Max just stood there watching and thinking, *Whatever it is, I can stand it. Knowing is better than not knowing.*

The green mesh fell away.

It was a man. Just a man. No fur, no fangs, no strange, stretched features. The fanatic's hood had concealed nothing but a serious-eyed man on the early side of middle age, with light-brown skin and the beginnings of lines around his eyes.

Instinctively, Max took a step toward him. "You're normal!"

Susan caught his arm.

"Rally change!" she whispered. "Remember?"

Max stopped short. If this was a trick, if the soldiers had followed them this far, it was all over.

The man just stood there, waiting to see what Max would do. Could he be real? Max eyed him, trying to run through everything he remembered about the rally as fast as he could.

The stranger watched him consider. His eyes flicked from Max to Susan.

Just to his left, a dusty hemlock stood forlornly among the rocks, its jagged branches bobbing in the hot breeze. Every needle and cone hung crisp and sharp edged in the sunlight.

At the rally, the buildings had wavered. In the tiled room, the air had buzzed and gone hazy near the Genius as he changed.

"I think it's okay," he said to Susan. "Look."

She held on. "One of them tried to grab us in the city!"

Then the man spoke for the first time, and the sound of his voice startled them as much as the sight of his face. It was as if a monster or zombie had suddenly become human.

"Companions of mine," he said. "They were clumsy, but they meant you no harm."

Nell wasn't nearly as bowled over as Max by the sight and sound of the strange man.

"They could have said something," she said.

For a fraction of a second, the man frowned, but his face was placid an instant later, and Max wondered if he'd imagined it. When he answered, he spoke to Max as much as to Nell.

"That's forbidden. We're silent among the changed, and we never show our faces in the city."

"We're not changed," Nell said petulantly.

This time he did look at her, and the intensity of his stare made Max want to take a step back. "Not," he said, "anymore."

"Not ever!" Nell snapped back.

But the man only gave her a pitying look.

"So you've forgotten, then. It's not unusual for the past to be hazy after a return."

She opened her mouth to protest, but the man ignored her. He had a force that Max found both disconcerting and impressive.

"At any rate, they were there to help you, as I'm here now."

Max couldn't stop staring at him. He stood like a soldier and wore an expression Max wished he could manage and had sometimes practiced in the mirror.

"Creeping up on people in the night?" Nell said. "That's a strange way to —"

"What kind of help?" Max cut in.

The man shot him an approving look, and Max flushed.

"Rescue," he said. "Sanctuary."

Kate and Jean probably didn't even know the second word, but Max did. A safe place.

"You can keep us away from the Genius?"

The man smiled.

"Absolutely."

Nell had opened her mouth to keep going, but she shut it abruptly. And that made sense, Max thought, because there was nothing else worth talking about.

"Then let us get our things," he said. "We're ready."

Chapter 39

Someone's pretty full of himself," Nell griped as they walked back to the circle of stones. When, struggling to have the last word, she'd asked the man his name, he'd told them they could call him Master Watcher Lan. Nell's eyebrows shot up. To Max it sounded appropriately forbidding.

"What do you think somebody who goes around wearing a hood is going to want to be called?" he whispered to her. "Jim?"

She only rolled her eyes. But it seemed to Max that the Master Watcher was the beginning of something promising. He looked back over his shoulder and wondered what the man was thinking. What would he be thinking if he met five kids carrying nothing but some peaches and a birthday doll? It wasn't exactly an impressive sight.

"Keep that Barbie tucked away," he said to Jean as she ducked into the circle of stones to retrieve it. "Stick it back in your skirt, why don't you?"

Nell elbowed him.

"Of course *you* like him," she said. "He thinks you're *smart*."

Max half smiled. "So what?"

No use telling Nell that the Master Watcher unsettled him. He reminded Max of the kind of person he'd avoid back home, the kind who measured your worth by how hard you could hit a ball. But the man *had* acted like he thought Max was smart. That was different.

Jean stepped into the circle of stones and drew a sharp breath.

"Hey!" she whispered. "Susan, look!"

They followed her. The doll no longer rested on the dirt. Beneath it, a faint curl of green nudged its way out of the brown. Kate crouched and pushed at it with her finger. On one end, Max could see the beginning of a bud.

Susan had figured it out! He grinned at her.

"See?" he said. "I told you the dirt didn't hate you."

A wave of elation washed over him. For days, he'd been trying to understand how everything worked. He felt like he'd shouted *Show me!* at this place a hundred times. The answer had always been no. Now Susan had gotten her yes. He had a feeling he was about to get his, too.

"Dear Jean," he said. "You can cheer up. We're practically home already. Your brother, Max."

Jean beamed at him and Susan laughed. "Is that a promise?" she asked him.

"Better," he told her. "It's a prediction."

◇ BOOK THREE ◇

NELL

Chapter 40

Nell was not one to lose things. Unlike Kate, who regularly lost items of clothing, homework, and her backpack, or Jean, who walked out of the house and lost herself a couple of times, Nell kept track of things that mattered. She'd salvaged the old-but-still-good cushions off the living-room couch and installed them in her room to keep them from the trash, and held on to a stuffed dog her grandfather had given her long after the little girls had lost theirs.

But of course, losing stuffed dogs wasn't as bad as what Susan and Max did, which was to lose track of people.

Well, one person in particular.

At home, she was forced to remind them, regularly, that she existed. Here, it was worse. Listening to all those sleeper children saying the names of lost sisters and brothers, she'd wondered if the others would have said hers. And now, trudging behind Max and the Master Watcher, she wondered it again.

"Is the sanctuary on top of a hill?" she'd asked the man when the ground rose again sharply past the spiky clearing where they'd spent the night.

"No," he'd said.

"Then where is it?"

The Master Watcher hadn't even turned.

"You'll see it tomorrow. We won't be able to get there until morning."

Nell hated when people refused to answer questions.

"What kind of place is it?" she'd asked, trying again.

Max had shot her a "Cut it out!" look that time. The man only turned back briefly, barely looking at her. His eyes grazed the top of her head.

"All will become clear when we reach it," he'd said. "Save your strength for walking now."

Nell had been told to keep quiet in so many ways, by so many different people, that she understood perfectly what that meant.

She plodded through the humidity, thinking about the Master Watcher and about how, if she stopped walking right now, if she disappeared, he wouldn't care a bit. Would the others?

It was a panicky, rubber-ball kind of a thought that reminded her of a poem she'd learned in school, about a man who'd been swallowed by a sea creature.

And it swallowed him whole, body and name.

She'd thought about that line for a long time after reading it, wondering what it would be like to be erased like that, not just from the world, but from memory. Ms. Montgomery, her teacher, had said that a poet's job was to undo that kind of forgetting. Poets saw, and remembered.

Lying in caves at night, breathing in the chalky air and staring into stone-black darkness, Nell had found herself wondering if, after all, not just she herself but the whole world she'd known could be erased as easily and completely as the cave's cool walls blotted out the light. So in the long hike across the mountain, Nell taught herself to be a poet.

In her mind's eye, she'd taken herself back home a hundred times, toured her house, catalogued the pictures on the walls and the feel of the carpet, inhaled the earthy smell of wood and cloth that greeted her at the front door every day after school. She'd gone over her mother's face and then her father's, remembered the sound of laughter, the way her father's hands were shaped, and the songs her mother sang sometimes at night without knowing she was doing it.

She had learned to pack it all away for safekeeping, so nothing she saw could be erased. And doing it had become a comfort. Now, as she walked behind the silent Watcher, she did it again, taking in the flat light-green undersides of the beech leaves that waved just over her head and noting the shriveled husks of their nuts, where they'd fallen in the sour dirt. She memorized the shaggy bulk of a hemlock, the looming, dark triangle of a white pine, and the hawk that circled over them, the outline of its body black against the sky.

Other people might forget, but she never would.

Chapter 41

There once was a man with a hood
Who thought he was better than good.
Why a regular guy
Should act mighty and high
Is something Max won't ask
But should.

Nell was a poet in more ways than one. Rhymes ran around in her head, and she amused herself with them when she was bored, or tired, or annoyed, all of which she was now, as she continued to walk silently behind Susan, glumly following Max and the Master Watcher.

"What's so great about him?" she muttered to Susan as they fell back to keep an eye on Kate and Jean. "He hasn't even done what you and Max did."

"What, make peaches?" Susan said.

"Yeah! He acts like he's so all-powerful. You're powerful!"

Susan sighed. "Why, because we made lunch? How do you know that even means something here? Maybe those hooded guys can all do it! Making the window — now, *that* would be powerful."

Nell blew her sticky bangs from her eyes and swatted a cloud of gnats from the path. Max and Susan had not asked the man about windows or anything else, saying that if they wanted a real answer, an answer worth anything, they'd wait for the right moment.

Nell wondered what kind of moment that might be. It didn't seem like the kind of thing that came up in casual conversation. *Oh, and by the way, has anyone ever fallen in from another universe before? Just asking.*

Anyway, there was nothing casual about Master Watcher Lan. He wrapped himself in secrets so thick, she doubted he'd tell her what time it was without a fight. In principle, Nell liked having some secrets of her own. So she didn't mind keeping the man in the dark about what Susan had done in the city, or how they'd gotten the peaches, even if that meant that they had to wait a little longer for answers. But she would like to have been asked her opinion. And Max was getting altogether too friendly with the man, Nell thought. When the Master Watcher spoke, which was rarely, Max looked at him as if he'd suddenly become Albert Einstein.

She started on a second verse:

I'd ask him myself,
Since Max is so adoring,
But the man has a superpower;
He's a champion at ignoring.

Jean, who'd been trying to keep up with Max, now dropped back. "Can I have my peach?" she whispered. "I'm hungry."

Nell nodded. Having lost the blanket, she and Susan had been carrying the peaches in their pockets. She pulled one out and handed it to Jean, then took another for herself.

"Kate," she called. "Snack time!"

Ahead, the man turned to look at them. She watched his eyes fasten onto the peaches.

"Well done," he said to Max. "You prepared. The change may have dulled your memories, but that shows a sharp mind. Wanderers starve in these woods if they don't make ready."

Nell waited for Max to say something, but he only shrugged, coloring.

She nudged Susan from behind. "Lunch," she said, and grinned. Susan frowned over her shoulder. Way one million and eighty-seven of telling her to be quiet, Nell thought.

They went on. To Nell's surprise, on the edge of sunset, with the sky flame-lit overhead, they came to a place where the brown earth gave way to a green film of moss. It was so faint at first, it looked like a rash of mold on the bare ground, but soon it thickened, and after a while the forest floor came to life again, grass layering itself over the moss, and then, eventually, winding vines and low shrubs. She saw Susan grin at the thickness of it.

"It's done!" Susan said. "Will you look at that?!"

For once, the Master Watcher turned their way, smiling. "The barren wood is long," he said. "But it does end. And now we may eat."

Nell was about to point out that she hadn't asked his permission, when he pulled out a pouch of flat dried cakes and small fruits, and she thought better of it.

"Did the Genius make it?" Max asked the man, motioning back to the forest. "I had a theory that he salted the wood."

The Master Watcher smiled again. "A good thought," he

said, settling himself beneath a maple and passing Max his portion. "But the wood was afflicted long before the city was."

He handed Nell a cake next, and she was about to thank him profusely, when he said, "It's not our custom to eat in the barren wood more than we have to. It's a cursed place, that one. But from here on, you'll have plenty."

Her thank-you was a little limp after that, but she had to admit it was good, having something besides peaches and water.

They spent that night in the open, and Nell lay beside Susan and Kate, looking up into the trees and listening to the sound of crickets.

The Master Watcher sat, silent and awake, his back resting against a wide poplar several yards away. Max had stretched out halfway between him and the girls, with Jean scrunched against his side. For a while after everyone had fallen asleep, Nell lay thinking about the puzzle of the man, and the place he was taking them.

Then she heard Max fidget, roll over, and sit up with a sigh. The man called to him in a low voice.

"Can't sleep?"

"Not much."

"You should get some rest. We walk again in a few hours."

"How much farther?"

"That depends on the speed of your walkers there."

Listening, Nell suppressed a groan. Max's walkers. As though Max owned them. And did that man never answer a question straight?

But Max didn't pursue it. Instead he said, "What's the sanctuary like?"

There was silence. Then: "We don't talk of it outside. For everyone's protection."

Now it was Max's turn to be silent. Nell wondered what he was thinking. After a moment, the Master Watcher said, "But I can promise you one thing: It will offer you more than you can imagine."

That's a moment! Nell thought at Max. *Ask him about windows!* But in a mild voice Max only said, "I don't know what you mean."

Twigs crunched underfoot as the man moved closer, and Nell could feel Max nearby, waiting for the right answer.

"I mean that I've led my share into safety from the outside, but none like you. To change on your own, and bring four others with you! That's evidence of great strength."

Nell lay unmoving. *Bring four others with you?* She began to fume.

"So they can do things there, at the sanctuary?" Max asked him.

Again, the man wouldn't answer. "You'll see it all soon," he said. "Tomorrow. Best rest now, and save your strength."

When Max lay back down, Nell finally dropped off to sleep. It seemed only a moment later that Susan was shaking her awake. The others were sitting up, yawning, and the man waited, standing now, by the tree.

"The moon's risen," he said, as if that explained things.

They stumbled to their feet and followed. Overhead, the bright half circle of the waning moon frosted the wood, casting ivory shadows on the new growth of vines and tall grasses that covered the forest floor. Jean stumbled among them, and Susan caught her arm as Kate picked her way slowly over the dark knots of shrubs. Nell's eyes darted from the ground to the man and back again. Why didn't he just *tell* them something? she wondered. She didn't like silence, never had been good at letting it gather between people. She would have liked to talk to Max, but now the Master Watcher would not leave his side. So after a while she dropped back, trailing behind until Susan looked back in impatience and waited for her.

"Hurry up!" she whispered. "We're going to lose sight of them!"

Nell made sure the Master Watcher was out of earshot. "I heard him before, talking to Max," she said. "He thinks *Max* changed us."

Susan studied the moonlit outline of the man's back, thinking, but said nothing.

"Susan," Nell finally said.

"Hmm?"

"I think they're going to try and separate us when we get there."

"Separate us? How do you mean?"

"I think they're going to take Max away."

Susan looked at her. "Why?"

"Something in the way he was talking. You watch. They will."

Susan grimaced for a minute, then looked ahead at the Master Watcher and Max, moving on without them.

"No," she said. "They won't."

Chapter 42

Nell was numb with walking by the time she noticed that the woods had thinned. In the trees, the early birds were beginning to rustle and call out in their piccolo voices. She raised her head and saw the sky widen as the last of the branches receded. They clung like cobwebs to the edges of the gray expanse that had opened overhead. The moon had set and the sky was full of fading stars.

The clearing jutted sharply upward and Nell struggled through the wet grass as the pulsing rhythm of crickets, chirping from their hidden places, marked her footsteps. She was too tired to keep climbing. Just when she was about to say so, the ground flattened. She looked ahead, but there was nothing to see. The grass rolled into darkness. Had they climbed to the end of land? She squinted in the pale light, but a murky fog obscured the way, and Nell couldn't see more than a few feet ahead. The Master Watcher sat down.

"We wait here for dawn," he said.

She had grown warm on her way up the final hill, but the morning air had been cool against her skin. Now it took on the weight of a humid afternoon, without the heat. Was a storm coming? Nell wanted to ask about it, but the air seemed too heavy even for speech. So they all sat, silent, as the landscape took shape beneath the brightening sky. A milky light seeped from the horizon and showed Nell that the cliff had been an illusion. Though they sat on a peak, there was no sharp drop into open air. Instead, just below them, the ground began its slow descent, rolling smoothly into the smoky oblivion of a valley, shrouded in mist.

The man stared into it.

Nell looked around. The wood ringed three sides of the clearing in which they sat. The trees, dark against the rising light, seemed to nudge them toward the clouds below. And yet even as the outline of branch and mountaintop sharpened in the sunrise, the valley remained hazy, like something out of a dream.

It drew her eyes, but she couldn't seem to focus them. Light scattered in the mist; the sun rose overhead in an orange sky only to bounce away in a thousand directions below. The clouded valley glinted and twinkled, dazzling and deflecting her vision.

She dragged her eyes from it and sought the Master Watcher, but he seemed in no hurry. He just sat, gazing down into the blankness of the mist.

The weight in the air rubbed at her, and she fidgeted. She didn't like it. Suddenly everything irritated her: the strange fog, and the quiet, and most of all the man. She hated the way he sat, expecting their silence, not answering their questions, expecting their patience. Did *he* know how long they'd waited?

Nell was tired of waiting. She stood suddenly and marched down the slope toward the foggy, shrouded space. The others would follow, she decided. It was time to go.

In a moment, she faced the line of mist. She stepped

through and blinked. If the air had felt strange while she sat in the grass, here it was worse. Heavier than before, and not damp as she would have expected, but charged and vibrating with suppressed energy like the moment before a crack of thunder. Images swam before her eyes, half reflections she couldn't quite look straight at. And there was something else. She closed her eyes and tried to hear it. Nothing. Nothing at all. Sound had drained from the world. She could hear no birds, no wind, not even the faint comfort of her own breath.

Her eyes flew open and her stomach lurched. Nothing! White everywhere, a blank, terrible emptiness, pouring in on her. She'd fallen down a well and been lost, forgotten, swallowed. She was gone, nameless.

The emptiness reached inside her and erased her, bit by bit, until she felt as if she would scatter into shredded pieces, scraps of something that once had been. She stumbled, clutching at her own arms, her voice lost in the awful, hungry silence.

A reed of sound pushed its way through and brushed at her. Something familiar.

Her name.

"Nell? Nell!"

She steadied herself, tried to locate it.

"Nell!"

She took a step, trying to fix on it. As she did, it grew stronger.

"This way!"

In a few paces, she was out, and the world burst back into focus — colors, light, shapes, sounds, and the faces of Susan, Max, Kate, Jean. They were on their feet, frightened, calling. The man was standing, too, something like triumph on his face.

She turned back and saw the mist simmering behind her.

"It's not a regular cloud," she said breathlessly. "Not anything like — I couldn't find my way."

Susan was standing closest. Her face had lost its color; sweat stood in drops at her hairline.

"I went in after you," she said. Nell had to strain to hear her. A sudden tremor shook Susan, and she caught her breath. "I lost myself. I couldn't think."

"The quiet was terrible," Nell agreed. "Made me sick." She shuddered.

"Quiet?" Susan said. "No, it was the noise. All those voices, pounding at me. The sound could grind you into dust!" She shook her head with a motion like she had water in her ears. "If I'd stayed another second, I wouldn't have had anything left, wouldn't have remembered my own name. That's when I ran, and called you. I was afraid you wouldn't hear."

"I heard," Nell said. "Just barely."

Still the Master Watcher stood, silent, wearing that curious expression.

Max turned to him. "What is it?" he asked. "What makes it that way?"

The man smiled. "It's the sanctuary, protecting itself."

Nell would have thought Susan couldn't get any paler, but at that, she seemed to go white. "That's something *you* did?" she whispered.

"Not me," he said. "The sanctuary elders set it that way. It's to keep out the unwelcome. I was working on opening it. It takes patience." Nell saw his glance flicker in her direction.

Susan's eyes widened. "But it's not just a barrier. You — you lose yourself in that thing."

The man merely smiled. "Yes," he said. "It acts as a deterrent that way, for those who would try to come without being invited."

Nell felt the heat rise in her face, but even as she did, she watched Susan grow angry. Few people knew her sister well enough to know when she was furious. Nell was one of them. In anger, Susan grew very quiet — too quiet — before the explosion came. Then she would swoop down on you like a storm. Nell knew enough to get out of the way when she saw Susan's brows rise, her cheeks whiten.

The Master Watcher didn't.

And so he was startled when Susan turned from him to the mist, narrowed her eyes, then closed them.

He was stunned when a crack opened in it, and widened.

"Who's doing that?" he asked, breathless. "You?"

He was looking at Max, but Max shook his head.

"Of course not," he said. "It's Susan."

Anyone could tell it was. She stood, shoulders squared, facing the mist as if it were a living enemy, an opponent she had to wrestle to the ground. It shivered and fought, thickening at the edges and pushing out toward her in wispy defiance, but she glared back, and the crack widened until they could see a tunnel through the mist, a clear shot, straight into the valley.

Nell looked past Susan and gasped. Beneath them, at the very center of the valley, lay a great white fortress.

"A castle!" Kate breathed. "Is it a castle?"

The Master Watcher had gone rigid. He was staring at Susan, eyes round, unable to respond. Nell smiled grimly. For once, someone had made *him* keep quiet.

She looked gratefully at Susan, who still stood squinting

into the valley. After another second, Susan relaxed and took a step backward.

"Let's go in now," she said.

Nell glanced at the Master Watcher, who was trying to collect himself. A sheen of sweat glistened on his smooth forehead.

"Yes," he whispered. "Yes, let's go down."

He stepped into the path carved in the mist, and Nell saw him look back once at Susan, his face tense, before he turned and led them down into the valley.

*L*ike the rhythm of the distant sea, the dull undertone of the mist was ceaseless. It washed up the mountain and into the woods, ever present beneath the throb of crickets and the trill of birds. Even dreaming, the exile heard it.

The mist, taking.

The mist, erasing.

Again a dream. This time, there were only footsteps lost to the roar. Like a tidal wave, unstoppable, unbreakable, ever coming, ever there, the mist flowed across the valley, up to the highlands and back again, a great unthinking beast, always hungry.

And then the sound stuttered. For a moment, it broke.

The exile woke and thought, Dreams are wishes. Put them away or you will be undone with longing; you will go mad with hope.

But it was not the sound of the dream that echoed now through the dawn. It was a different sound.

More felt than heard, like a pressure in the air, but there. The mist, retreating.

Chapter 43

On a shelf in her grandmother's house back home sat a series of nesting boxes that Nell had loved to play with as a little girl. She would put one in the next and take them apart again, fascinated by boxes within boxes, space inside space.

As the group made its way down toward the sanctuary now, the white stone fortress reminded her of those boxes. Three concentric squares of huge snow-colored stones lay below them, separated by vibrant strips of green. At the center of the smallest, the squares gave way to a circle, a single dome resting within a bull's-eye.

"Is that someone's house?" she asked the Master Watcher.

His expression told her clearly to be silent. But Nell had had enough of that.

"Is it?"

His voice tight, he answered, "No. It's the heart of the sanctuary. The place our council meets."

"So where do people stay?"

"In the first band." He turned his face from her then, a door slamming shut.

They descended through a wide grassy slope. On either side of it, crops and orchards crisscrossed the hill. Something about them struck Nell as odd, and after a second she realized what it was: she'd never seen so many different kinds of food growing together. Lines of green corn waved beneath trees studded with plums. Knobby peach trees gave way to rows of oranges, apples, and pears. Yellow wheat fanned behind braided grapevines.

She saw Max looking, too.

"How do you get all this to grow together?" he asked the Master Watcher. "I never saw anything like it back home."

The man turned his head briefly in Max's direction.

"Patience" was all he said, but in a tone that showed he was pleased with the question. Nell suppressed a sigh. Why was it that "Be quiet" to Max really meant "Ask me later"?

She left the thought behind as they continued down into the valley. The sun rose behind the great fortress, and for a while it was black against the blazing light. But then they stepped into the building's shadow, and it was as if a curtain had lifted. The stones glowed white again. This close, Nell could begin to make out the details of the structure, and she saw that what she'd taken for a solid wall — the outer band — was much more. The man had said people lived in the band, and now she saw how: They were deep and hollow and marked by windows. Rooms and halls were built into the wall that surrounded the sanctuary so that it was one continuous building, a face with a thousand eyes. Nell searched for the doors beneath the many windows and found great archways cut into the white stone. From this angle, she could make out two.

The Master Watcher led them toward one of these, and walking into the clammy, shadowed tunnel, dim after the glare of the sunrise, Nell realized that she'd underestimated the size of the place. It must be nearly as thick as a city block back home, layer upon layer of stone that held the cold and the night and let them seep into the tunnel in bits of shadow and chilly breezes. Nell felt small, and suddenly lonely. She wondered how many rooms this wall held, as it wound around the first garden. Hundreds? More?

Ahead of her, Kate clung to Susan's hand, and Jean, usually tagging after Max like a puppy, seemed lost in the echo chamber of the tunnel.

"Jean!" Nell whispered. Her voice sounded harsh bouncing off the walls.

Jean looked back, and Nell offered her a hand. She was glad when her sister took it.

They emerged, blinking in the sudden brightness, into an interior garden, where a few people — as smooth faced as anyone back home — moved quietly along the walkways past beds of flowers and beneath shade trees. Seeing the Master Watcher, they nodded and stood back. Nell watched the man bob his head at them, wordless. *So stuck up*, she thought as he walked swiftly across the garden. She looked at Susan, wondering if she thought so, too, but her sister's head was down, her brow creased. Every so often, Susan would swat at her ear, as if batting away a fly.

"You okay, Susan?"

Susan looked up with a vague expression, then seemed to wake to the worry on Nell's face.

"What? Oh, yeah. I'm fine."

But Nell wondered.

She stole glances at Susan as they followed the Master Watcher across the first garden and toward the wall of the second band. Though smaller than the first, the second band towered over them as they approached it. Balconies hung over the lower half of the building, and here and there Nell could see an easel or a small table draped in colored cloth. Kate pointed to a woman several floors up embroidering a large hanging.

Unlike the outer wall of the first band, this one was full of doors, and Nell wondered what kinds of rooms lay behind them. But the Master Watcher didn't wait for questions. He moved briskly beneath the balconies to a passageway that cut through the second band, and they followed him into another garden. Here, empty booths festooned with twinkling fabrics sat near the wall, and past another set of walking paths, vegetable gardens in their neat green rows spread out beneath the windows of the third band.

"Why aren't there any doors in that wall?" Nell asked, pointing.

The Master Watcher squinted at her in the ruddy sunlight.

"Entrance to the third band is restricted to the third garden," he said. Ahead, another passageway, narrower than the first or second, cut through the third band. The man moved toward it, stepping over winding squash vines that spilled over the short fences around the vegetable gardens and pushing past a drooping tomato plant that had worked loose from its stake and swung into the path.

"A regular old tour guide, isn't he?" Nell grumbled to Susan. But if she heard, Susan gave no sign.

The third band was smallest of all, and they spent only a minute in the tunnel that cut through it before emerging into the last of the three gardens. If possible, this one was even greener than the others, crammed with bushes and flowers and leafy, looping vines that trimmed the paths. Thickets of shade trees clustered tightly in a few spots, and a dark, long-winged bird with red shoulders burst shrieking from one of these as they passed, sailing out of sight across the garden. Nell glanced that way and caught sight of an ornate metal gate. Beyond it she spied the tip of the dome she'd seen from the mountain.

The man quickened his pace along the path. On this side, there were many doors into the third band, but the Master Watcher moved past them, stopping finally at a narrow opening set off by a length of unbroken stones.

He turned to the children.

"Wait here," he said to Susan. "You and the younger ones. We'll be back soon."

He laid a hand on Max's shoulder, and Nell didn't like the way he stood there, as if suddenly he owned Max or had picked him for a team from which the rest of them were excluded. Luckily, Susan was paying attention at last. Her head came up, and she looked quickly at Nell, then Max.

"Where are you taking him?" she asked the man.

Max looked uncomfortable. He shifted his body so that the man released him, and took a step toward his sisters.

"Not far. Just inside, where he'll have the privilege of meeting our Guide. Few newcomers do." The man glanced uneasily at Max, who had edged closer to Susan.

"So you're separating us," Nell said, figuring it never hurt to make things crystal clear.

The man's eyebrows came down over his eyes. "For a moment, yes."

"No," Susan said in the voice she'd used last night. Her certain voice, her you'd-better-not-cross-me voice. Max squirmed.

"They can come, too, can't they? It's only for a minute, anyway. And they're my sisters. We like to stick together."

At the word *sisters*, the man's eyebrows shot back up.

"You've grown attached to them, I see," he said. He looked as if he were about to say more, but stopped himself.

"Wait here, all of you." He disappeared through the narrow door and left them standing in the sunlight.

"This place gives me the creeps," Nell said. She kicked at the white pebbles that lined the path and smiled grimly at the small mess they made coming down in the grass.

Jean had leaned into the wall, and now she slid to a seat in the dirt. "It's better than other places we've been," she said. "By a lot."

"Pretty isn't always better," Nell told her.

"How about pretty and nobody's trying to cut us up?" Jean said. "Is that better?"

Nell glowered at her. Little kids were annoying.

From behind, she felt Kate tap her soothingly. "It is pretty," she said. Nell shrugged her hand away. She looked worriedly at Susan, and then at Max. Susan wore that distant expression that had been on her face since they'd come into the valley, and Nell could tell she was only half hearing what was said. Max looked pained and embarrassed. He caught her eye.

"Just try not to make a fuss here, okay? They know things here. Don't you want to get home?"

She felt unreasonably angry at him. She knew it wasn't his fault the man favored him so much, and yet, Nell decided, maybe she could still be mad about his enjoying it. Of course, he didn't look like he was enjoying it at this exact moment.

"Who's making a fuss?" she snapped at him. "I've barely said a word yet!"

He harrumphed and slouched beside Jean on the wall.

"Yet," he said. "I hate that word."

Another minute and the Master Watcher was back, looking drawn.

"Come," he said sourly. "All of you."

Nell grinned and followed Max, who had slumped a little in relief, into the building. Max had said they knew things here. They were about to find out if that was true.

Chapter 44

The Master Watcher led them into a marble hallway adorned with weavings and the framed pages of old books. It ended in a thick mahogany door carved with a likeness of the sanctuary. The man pushed this open and ushered them into a round room where cushioned benches lined the walls. On them sat several men wearing loose trousers and light tunics, reading and talking in hushed voices. They looked up, startled, at the newcomers.

"Master Watcher!" one of them said.

The man hunched his shoulders, and Nell thought that the first privilege of having come into this place was seeing him scolded like a small boy caught at mischief.

But he only said, "I've just spoken with the Guide, and he's called for them," and waved the children on behind him.

Nell looked back to see one of the men on his feet, frowning in their direction as they followed the Master Watcher through another door to the foot of a flight of wide marble steps with brass banisters brighter in the places where hands had run along them. They climbed without a word and reached a landing where a tall window looked out over the second garden. Nell could see a group of young women emerging from the tunnel in the second band with buckets and trowels, moving toward the vegetable patches. A bumblebee pinged against the window, bounced back, and dived toward the greenery, and Kate put a finger to the glass where it had been. The Master Watcher twitched a shoulder and gave a short click of impatience before mounting the next set of stairs. Nell saw now that the staircase they were climbing ran the width of the third band, and at each landing a window showed the gardens below — second and third, vegetables and shade trees, a group of girls Susan's age harvesting tomatoes, boys not much older than Max emerging through the tunnel into the third garden and moving toward the doors, laden with books.

The last set of stairs ended in a wide room with a floor the color of slate and tall bookshelves that stood between the windows, casting shadows. Several small round tables sat around it, and at one of these, a lone figure bent over an open book. He was old, and at first Nell thought him very old, given his white hair and the curve of his back. He sat amid great puddles of sunlight. Nell looked up. The roof was all glass, and, strangely, a breeze riffled the pages of the book on the table and lifted Nell's hair off her neck.

"Tur Kaysh," the Master Watcher said. "This is the boy I mentioned."

The man had not raised his head at the sound of their entrance, but he did now. She had thought him very aged, but suddenly Nell wasn't sure. He sat up, his back straight and his shoulders squared, and turned bright eyes their way. His face looked grave, and Nell tensed, but then he spoke, and his voice, unexpectedly rich, filled the room.

"Welcome," he said. "To all of you."

Nell warmed to him. She grinned at the sound of that beautiful, gracious voice and shot the Master Watcher a look. *See?* she thought at him. *He's glad we came.*

The Guide looked from one to the next of them, and Nell was caught by those eyes. They were wide-awake eyes, searching eyes, understanding eyes. They made her want to talk to this man, stay near him. He smiled, and she felt happiness, feather light, floating inside her.

"Just as you said, Lan." The Guide nodded to the Master Watcher. "It's wonderful."

He raised a hand and beckoned to Max.

"Boy," he said. "Come here."

Nell could feel the others lean forward, wanting to move closer, too. Max, reddening, stepped toward the old man. With a flush of jealousy, Nell looked to the Master Watcher. Despite the warmth in the Guide's voice, the Master Watcher tensed, his shoulders rising.

"What do they call you?" the old man asked.

In a low voice, Max said his name.

"And where do you come from, Max?"

His voice was deep and musical, and Nell wished again that he was talking to her and looking her way.

Max hesitated only a second. "It's hard to explain," he said.

The Guide nodded as if Max had said something brilliant and wonderful. "The first step toward wisdom is admitting the difficulty," he said approvingly. "And of course beginning the search. So you've begun, by coming here." He grinned suddenly. "And what a mind you must have, to have helped your friends here." He swept his arm out to include the girls. "We were anxious to meet you once we'd had news from the city."

Nell wondered who "we" were.

"My sisters," Max corrected.

The Master Watcher flinched almost invisibly, but the Guide smiled widely at the word.

"Your sisters. How beautiful."

"No, I meant—" Max started, but the Master Watcher cut him off.

"There's more, Guide. As we waited on the mountain, the boy opened the mist."

Nell opened her mouth to say something, but Susan's hand closed on her wrist. Her sister gave a tiny shake of her head.

The smile that had been on the old man's face froze. It was as if a candle had been blown out behind his eyes. Nell watched him lose focus, regain it. He looked sharply at Max.

"You opened the barrier, boy? Lan, are you sure?"

The Master Watcher nodded, and Nell thought that if his shoulders went any higher, they'd be at his ears.

Max stammered, "I — it wasn't me, it was —"

Again the younger man interrupted him. "The boy was confused by what he'd done. It was almost instinct. But I saw it with my own eyes."

The old man raised a hand and pressed his palm to his mouth. He sat that way for a long silent moment, considering Max with those fiery, searching eyes.

"This changes things," he said. He looked away from them a second, and Nell had the uncomfortable feeling that his eyes were moist.

"Boy," he continued, "you come at a propitious moment. We have much to offer you, and you, in turn, have much to offer us." He leaned toward Max, who stood, suddenly still, staring back at him. "You have questions," he said. "You've come full of them."

Max nodded. "How did you know?"

The man sat back, and his smile was easy now, comfortable. "They brought you here," he said. "No one comes without them. I can answer them for you, if you'll let me."

Max grinned suddenly and looked back, trying to catch Susan's eye. But Susan again had gone somewhere inside her own head, and he saw that at the same time Nell did. So he looked at her instead and nodded, eyebrows raised.

Nell flushed. Was he asking her permission? Permission to do what he wanted, and what Susan had said they had to? She'd wanted to be asked, and now, for a fraction of an instant, Max was asking. Ever so slightly, she nodded back, feeling a warm pleasure spreading up her cheeks.

He had asked.

"Master Watcher," the old man said, "tell the council I have found my student."

Chapter 45

Nell had been asked, but she began to regret her answer on the spot when the Guide announced lessons would begin immediately. The Master Watcher took that as a cue to try to hustle the rest of them out the door, possibly by force, as necessary. The girls were saved the indignity of actually being shoved through only by Jean. Suddenly understanding that they were, in fact, being separated from Max, Jean got a familiar look on her face — the one that said she'd be getting painfully loud in under thirty seconds if somebody didn't do something quick. Max headed her off by begging for a minute to say good-bye to his sisters. So as the Master Watcher tapped his foot, looking like he'd just sucked a lemon, Max joined them in the hall.

He glanced down at his feet, and Nell saw in the polished tiles the faint reflection of the five of them, bulky, blurry shapes, one of which was fidgeting. That was Max. He leaned toward Jean and lowered his voice.

"It'll be all right, Jean. You'll see. I'm going to learn things here. Things that will get us home. Tell her, Susan."

Kate had taken Susan's hand and was hanging on for dear life. Nell watched her tug at it now, just to make sure Susan was listening, but she needn't have worried, because Susan's expression had sharpened. She looked from Max to the old man through the door, then back at Jean.

"He will," she said. "This is the place to do it, right? Look at all those books!"

"And I'll write you a letter!" Max added in a sudden fit of inspiration. "A real one this time. I'll tell you all about it — I promise."

"And he'll visit," Nell said, thinking she ought to get at least a word in. "A lot. Right, Max?"

Jean, who had perked up at the promise of a letter, nodded vigorously. "Letters," she said. "And visiting every day, right?"

Max glanced uneasily back at the Master Watcher, waiting none too patiently in the room with the old man. "As much as I can," he said. "It'll be great. I promise."

And so they left, but if Max's promise referred to general greatness, Nell thought, it was broken before they were halfway across the second garden, when the Master Watcher deposited them in the care of a florid-faced woman who smelled faintly of boiled carrots.

He called her Shepherdess, though she didn't look to Nell like she spent much time outside with the sheep. She wore her graying hair in a loose bun that bobbed at the back of her head when she spoke, and her spotless, sand-colored dress, which just brushed the tops of her shoes, billowed when she walked.

"You've brought me girls!" she said delightedly when she met them near the artisan booths. "And so changed already! Wonders!"

She was so enthusiastic that Nell took an instant dislike to her.

"Mistress Meva will show you your places," the Master

Watcher said by way of good-bye. Nell watched him go with rising impatience, wishing he were more like the old man, who seemed so delighted with questions.

Mistress Meva took Kate's hand and then Jean's, without asking.

"Such small things!" she said. "Wonders, really!"

Kate looked mildly scandalized, and Jean pulled her hand away, but the Shepherdess didn't seem affronted. She laughed and pinched Jean gently on the cheek.

"It's all right," she said. "We'll be friends soon. Now, come and I'll get you ready to start school."

Following as the woman hurried the girls along, Nell whispered bitterly to Susan that the Shepherdess was the kind of adult who treated little kids like puppies. Susan, distracted again, said nothing.

"You act like you're sleepwalking," Nell complained. "Will you pay attention at least?"

Susan looked up, frowning. "I am paying attention," she said. But her voice didn't sound right.

It was only when they reached the first band that Susan woke up. Following Mistress Meva, they crossed through the first garden, skirting fruit trees and jumping over flower beds in their haste to keep up. Unlike the Master Watcher, the Shepherdess, despite her speedy pace, said hello to everyone and waved at the ones too far to speak to. Nell wondered why she wasn't out of breath by the time they reached a wide set of double doors in the inner wall of the first band, but she never slowed as she beckoned them into a long passage that smelled invitingly like breakfast and hurried them toward a second set of doors.

"You're in for a treat now!" she said to them as she pushed through.

They came to a dead stop on the other side. Susan's head snapped up, and Nell grinned.

"It's a library," Susan whispered.

Nell breathed in the scent of old paper and warm dust and the lemony aroma of polished wood and thought that if it was, it was one that had swallowed a pill and become a giant. They stood beneath great cliffs of books, walls like mountainsides made of volume after volume without end. The books soared toward distant ceilings, where skylights poured sunlight onto the gleaming tiles, and stretched out of sight to right and left, following the great line of the first band into a dusty, sunlit haze.

Like clinging vines, ornately fenced walkways marked the levels, and Nell could see figures moving along them. Across the open space above, narrow bridges met like the spokes of a wheel, converging on twisting staircases.

She had the urge to shout, just to hear the echo of her voice in this huge place.

Mistress Meva beamed at them. "Impressive, isn't it?"

Susan nodded. "How many books do you have here? Where did they all come from?"

The woman raised a hand, indicating the shelves.

"Would you believe me if I told you this is only a fraction of what once was? These are the books saved from the study halls of Ganbihar, before the destruction."

"Destruction?" Nell asked her. "Are you talking about the change?"

She nodded. "You're a clever one! I'm going to have to tell Mistress Leeta to put you in the front seat in history."

Nell wanted to ask more, but the Shepherdess was already walking again. "The library's open at all hours," she was saying in answer to a question of Susan's. "You're free to come here day or night."

Susan looked like someone had just handed her a million dollars. And a pony.

"Do you see that?" she said to Nell as they followed the Shepherdess past oak tables piled with books. "There are at least six stories of books here! Maybe seven!"

The Shepherdess led them from the library to a hall on the third floor and into a large room with four beds, a wardrobe, and a desk. Unlit lanterns hung in brackets on the walls. Above the desk, a scene of a man emerging from a pool, glowing with light, had been rendered in fine needlework, with threads of gold and yellow and orange woven atop the green of a wood and the blue of the water. On the other side of the room, a wide window looked out on the valley. Nell went to it and peered up past the orchards and fields to see if she could make out the mist. She couldn't. In the distance, the tops of the trees on the edge of the wood stood etched into the skyline, deep greens and browns catching the sunlight as it inched westward.

Clothes had been laid out for them, clean light-colored dresses of the same long style the Shepherdess wore. To Nell's relief, there was a bathroom across the hall, complete with running water and something that looked wonderfully like a toilet.

"Now, that's civilization," she said, thinking of Max. She sighed. She'd have to tell him later.

When they'd washed and changed, the Shepherdess returned to tell them how wonderful they'd find their education. Nell was in too good a mood from finally being clean to resent her tone. Then the woman ruined it with her first question.

"Can you read, too?" she asked Nell.

Susan looked up at that, and she and Nell exchanged a glance.

"We all can," Susan said hastily.

Mistress Meva's eyebrows shot up. "Really! Even the little ones? How unusual!"

She clearly didn't believe them, though, until she'd had them each read something. The woman reached a new peak of excitement when she found that Jean could read a sentence.

"Now, don't show off too much," she grinned, when she'd summoned a younger woman to take Kate and Jean to join the primary classes.

"You two will be in the upper levels," she told Susan and Nell. "Expect to work hard. Even if you've been to school in the city, which it appears you have, you'll find things quite different here. We expect you to learn to use your mind. You'll need every bit of effort you can muster to keep the change at bay, especially in these first days."

Nell felt her spirits lift. She saw that Susan, too, seemed happier. They both knew what that meant. *Max isn't the only one who's going to learn something here,* Nell told herself with satisfaction. *The Shepherdess isn't half bad, even if she does smile too much.*

Anticipation shivered in her stomach. Susan had made the wind blow, and Max had made peaches. Now it would be her turn. She intended to be good at it.

◇ ◇ ◇

*F*our gates to the valley, four ways home.

It was an old saying. Wanderers and wise men, seekers and the bereft, carried the phrase with them, passing it, one to the next, as a cherished, free-given gift. And so for a century those who broke away, the unwanted or the far-seeing, were led to one of the gates or another, to find in the valley welcome, and shelter.

To these gates the exile returned now, to the clearings that overlooked the valley, to the place where the mist simmered, cold, beneath the heat of the day.

The first three, rarely traveled by any but watchers in these late years, lay undisturbed, the mist beneath them a dull, leaden cloud.

In the last, the grass was pressed to earth, and the mist rolled beneath the rise, angry. The exile searched the ground, counting signs: the broken stem of a wildflower, a trampled path, a second, a third. A curled hair, caught in a patch of onion grass and waving like a thin flag. More than one traveler had been here; more than two.

The mist crept toward the clearing, and the noise of it rose, a static, crackling sound of warning and hunger, of rage. Still the exile searched. Who had come? Who had waited upon this hill?

The cloud seeped upward, muttering and reaching, when at last the exile found a single clear footprint engraved in a bald circle of dirt, in a spot where the clearing began to slide toward the valley below. The perfect outline of a small shoe with a strange, lined sole. Too small, this, for a man or even a woman.

It was the print of a child.

Chapter 46

Nell had once been told, by a teacher whom she had undoubtedly annoyed, that her impatience would be the undoing of her. Perversely, she embraced the image, seeing herself wrapped in a snarl of thread, feverishly — because of her much-declared impatience — working her way to her own undoing.

The little motor of her impatience revved now as Nell surveyed the school that the Shepherdess had heralded with such enthusiasm. She took note of the ways it failed to live up to expectation. First and most important, it was not in the small upper room in the third band, where even now Max studied under the warm gaze of the honey-voiced old man. It was not in the third band at all, but mostly set in a series of rooms off the great library, two floors up from the dining halls and kitchens and overlooking the first garden. It did carry a pleasing whiff of the old books that permeated the entire first band, but then, so did her bedroom.

Second was the dismaying realization that the Shepherdess took frequent charge of Nell's level, and so accompanied her into the room, fairly bouncing, to introduce her to the ten other girls of her group. Third, and worst of all, was the lesson itself. Mistress Meva spent the hour or so before dinner telling them stories of mothers who made scholars of their sons when they were but infants, and tracing the routes of young men who said good-bye to their brides to travel to the great academies of Ganbihar from across the sea. The final moments of the day were spent reciting the chant of seeds aloud, a pretty but meaningless poem as far as Nell could see. By the time they were released to sit in the first garden beneath a wide willow, Nell felt frayed and edgy, wishing she could find the loose end of the thread that wound around her so tight she thought she'd burst.

The only thing of real interest in that first hour of school had been two girls her age — Wista and Zirri — who didn't look like the others. They seemed neither city nor sanctuary, for in their faces the ferocious profile of the Domain had softened — their jaws were narrower, their eyes wider set. But while parts of their skin were as smooth as her own, along the ridge of forehead and cheekbone, Nell could see a thin coat of hair, so light it was shadow.

She stared at the girls too long. Wista's light-brown hair lay in wisps that puffed out on either side of her round face, and her skin was freckling beneath the disappearing growth. Between her thick fingers, she twisted a copper pendant she wore around her neck, and she gazed at Nell longingly. Nell flushed in sympathy. The other girl, black-haired Zirri, regarded her out of dark-gray eyes with a look that made the hair on Nell's neck stand up.

On their way out to the garden, Minna, a vivid redhead whose nose was liberally peeling from a sunburn, explained quietly that Wista and Zirri were halfway through "the return"— the process by which newcomers shed the change after they'd come from the outside.

"Where'd you wait yours out?" Minna asked her, rubbing

her nose so vigorously a little snow shower of peeling skin flew from it. "Never seen anybody come like you. I heard the Master Watcher himself brought you in. Did he stay with you out there? Help you for a long time?"

Minna claimed a prime spot for her beneath the willow, pulled a sandwich left over from lunch out of her pocket, and offered to share. Wista accepted half gratefully. From where they sat, the group of them had a good view of the younger girls trooping along the paths behind their pretty teachers, or playing in the flower beds. The air was thick and smelled of roses, some of which climbed the wall of the first band and wound themselves around the edges of the white stones. Nell noticed that anyone over the age of ten was happy to sprawl lazily on benches or grass, breathing in the evening's perfume. She wished fleetingly that she felt like joining them, but at mention of the Master Watcher, the thread of impatience snagged inside Nell, and she shook her head.

"No, we just met him."

The others stared at her.

"But you're changed!" Wista said. "How else?"

Nell realized her mistake a moment too late. She shrugged. "Oh. We spent some time in the woods."

Zirri glanced at her out of the corner of her storm cloud eyes. "We all did that," she said. "But without the training, you don't start until you get here."

"The training?"

Wista motioned to the first band. "School."

Nell wondered how school could change anything. Besides, they had schools in the city, and that didn't seem to help.

"What does school have to do with it?" she asked.

Zirri snorted. "What do you think makes the change? I don't see how you look like you do without knowing *that*."

Nell caught the words before they were out of her mouth this time. In the silence that followed, two white moths fluttered down from the willow leaves, a handful of sparrows landed to gather the crumbs of Wista's sandwich, and some distance away, a group of girls that included Jean moved among the flowers, singing.

Wista said, "I think she means that it's different here, the way they teach us. I'm not sure how, exactly, but they say that the longer you're here, the more it sticks."

Nell wondered what other nonsense they taught in this school.

"That's nice," she said, trying to be diplomatic. "But when do we learn to *do* things?"

"Do things?" Wista asked.

"You know. Make things. Like the mist up there."

They stared at her, and Zirri broke out laughing, sending the sparrows into flight.

"Who do you think you are?" she laughed. "The Guide himself?"

Nell flushed. She wasn't sure what mistake she'd made now, but she could tell by the looks on their faces that it was a good-sized one.

"Is that very advanced?" she asked carefully.

Zirri laughed louder this time, and Nell narrowed her eyes, but Wista smiled sympathetically.

"Zirri, she's new, even if she doesn't look it!" She shook her head. "Be nice!"

"She's ungrateful, is what she is," Zirri said. "Looking like that already. You won't keep it, you know, if you're not properly grateful. They could send you back, and you'll be just the same as you were."

"Zirri!" Minna said, shocked.

The girl's open hostility caught Nell off guard. She'd expected Zirri to keep playing the game of pretending not to mean the snide things she said. But Zirri's anger had come into her face now and been spoken, and the other girls shifted in discomfort. The words hung there a moment, sharp and heavy, before Wista cleared her throat.

"Zirri," she said, "Nell doesn't know. There were plenty of things we didn't know when we came."

With a venomous look Nell's way, Zirri said, "I knew enough not to talk like the Genius."

Nell felt bewildered. "What do you think I'm doing? Making speeches?"

Zirri laughed and tossed her head. Clearly she felt she'd gotten in the last word. Nell squinted up at the willow tree. The branches moved in an early-evening breeze, throwing yellow bars of sunlight onto the grass. Each time the wind blew, it was as if the sun and the tree played a game of pickup sticks, full of shadows and light. She tried to adopt an air of carelessness, as if Zirri and her meanness were nothing, or less than nothing. As fleeting as the shadows beneath the tree, as unimportant as the moths that fluttered among the leaves. But it didn't feel like nothing.

Wista sighed. "Ingratitude's not rebellion," she said.

They let the subject drop after that, but Nell was full of questions. She wondered if these were the kind they answered at school.

Chapter 47

That night, as promised, Max's first letter arrived, addressed to Jean and delivered at dinner by a shaggy-haired boy who carried messages around to the various diners seated in the high-ceilinged room on the other side of the library. The windows here looked over the first garden, just like the ones in the schoolroom, and Nell had been sitting glumly watching a group of older men in vigorous conversation on a bench outside when she heard Jean squeal and rip open the envelope she'd been given.

"Let us all see!" Kate said, getting up to stand behind Jean's chair. But Jean held the letter up like a prize and then hugged it to her chest. "After me," she said. "If it's not private."

Nell wondered what secret Jean thought Max would share with a second-grader, but she didn't say it. She just drummed her fingers as Jean took her time unfolding the letter with ridiculous care. There was Max's familiar, cramped handwriting, flowing unevenly across the page. Nell had the urge to grab it. Had he found anything out or not? She stifled the impulse and watched her sister frown over the page.

"Susan, what are these words?" Jean pointed, and Susan, whose attention had been briefly recaptured by the letter, leaned over.

"Tur Kaysh," she said. "That's what they call the old man."

Jean nodded and bent back to her reading.

"How about this one?"

"Physicist."

Nell felt her ears heating up. She wondered if steam might actually pour out of them, like it did in cartoons, or if that was just pretend.

Jean pointed again.

"Interested," Susan said.

"No, I meant that one."

"Impatient," Susan told her.

Nell couldn't take it anymore.

"Why don't you just let Susan read it out loud?"

Jean gave her a supercilious look.

"I'm almost done," she said. "Just wait a minute."

Before Nell could decide whether knocking her over was a good strategy for getting her to share the letter, Jean handed it to Susan.

"Okay," she said. "It's not private."

Nell rolled her eyes.

"Maybe we ought to read it in our room anyway," Susan told her. "Just in case."

So they adjourned to their room, hurrying past the tapestried walls into the library and then across to the other side, and at last, Susan unfolded the letter.

"'Dear Jean,'" she began. Jean grinned widely at the mention of her name, as if she'd only just discovered the letter was hers.

Nell rolled her eyes again. "We know who it's addressed to. Just get into the letter, will you?"

Susan raised an eyebrow at her but continued:

"Remember I said we were going to be home soon? I really think soon is getting sooner now. The Master Watcher says Tur Kaysh knows everything, that is, he didn't say it in those words, but he did give that idea off. And I can tell that the man is very smart. He's not like the other people we've met here so far. That is to say, he knows a lot more of what's going on. I think he's kind of like a physicist, but here. You saw that room upstairs, with all its books! When he saw I was interested in them, he said I could ask any question, and he would try to answer. I have plenty of questions, and one of them is going to be the one that shows us how to get that window back. Try not to get too impatient waiting, but this is exciting, you'll see!

Your brother,

Max"

Jean was still beaming, but Nell suppressed a snort. So much for figuring things out! She wondered why Max didn't just ask the question straight out. *That's what I would do, if it were me*, she thought.

Max was definitively not her, however, and for a second she told herself that if the Guide was so smart, he would have known to invite the rest of them to stay up in that sunny room of his.

It was the kind of thing her father would have said, but somehow it didn't help. The old man did seem smart. Better than smart. And that room had looked wonderful. And Max was there, so he was the one who got to ask the questions. As many as he wanted. All she could do was grumble about it, which she did, while Jean carefully laid the letter on the nightstand for safekeeping, securing it with the weight of her Barbie.

Chapter 48

The ancients stood in full light
And we in shadow.
Late to the world we come,
Seeing little and hearing less,
The edges and ends and the echoes of song.

The words danced in Nell's head, shadows and light, edges and ends. This was the text Mistress Meva brought the next afternoon for lessons. The morning had been full of hours spent on calculations and with a curious talk on the makeup of plants and soil concentrations, followed by another long recitation of the chant of seeds, which Nell thought she'd never learn. But that had all been washed away by the words that hummed in Nell's head. She wondered what book they were from.

What did it mean, the edges and echoes? Nell was thinking a thousand things, not one of them having to do with purity, which was the Shepherdess's emphatic explanation. When Nell asked her if this was the same kind of purity they had in the city patrols, she scoffed and said that was an altogether false kind. "A twisted shadow" is what she called it, going on to say that true purity had gone from the world, lost with the freshness of youth and the goodness of the early days. "We are left, as the ancients would say, 'nearsighted and half blind by the dirt in our eyes.'"

Nell was busy trying to piece together what she meant by that when a thundering gong made her jump. Once, twice, it reverberated through the classroom and outside, in the gardens. Nell swiveled in her seat. Was it a fire alarm? She looked to Mistress Meva for answers and was surprised to see the expression on the woman's face. The Shepherdess had gone pale, her face contorted in a tight-lipped grimace. As Nell watched, tears sprang to the woman's eyes.

Five clangs of the gong, and then silence. But the noise of life did not resume.

"Girls," the Shepherdess whispered, "stand now, to mark the punishment and mourn the soul lost."

The girls rose to their feet. Nell stole a look at Wista, in the seat near hers, and saw the girl's hands trembling. She clutched her copper pendant so tightly, her fingers were red.

When they'd resumed their places, she looked to the Shepherdess for explanation, but the woman seemed undone. "Keep quiet as you return to your rooms" was all she said. Her voice caught.

The girls filed out silently. In the hall, beneath the weaving of an ivory sky over a dark land, full of the silhouettes of people moving through a river of shimmering blue thread, Nell caught up with Minna. "What was that all about?" she asked her. "Did somebody die?"

The redheaded girl looked sweaty and a little green. "They'd be better off if they did," she said, her voice low. "That was the signal of banishment. When the elders decide someone's broken the rules, they push him back through the mist. It's exile." She wiped a damp hand across her dress, then suddenly clenched the fabric into a tight ball.

"So they have to go back to the city?" Nell asked her, not understanding the look on the girl's face. At the other end of the corridor, the rest of the class was already dispersing, moving quietly toward the library to cross to their rooms.

"I don't know where they go," Minna said, casting a glance their way. "But that's not what's awful about it. When you're pushed out that way — when the mist takes you, it *takes* you. Understand?"

Nell shook her head. Down the hall, doors shut with small clicks and quiet puffs of air.

"It takes *you*. Your soul. Your mind. Everything. The banished ones change back, to the way they were before they came. But on the inside, they're not like they were. They go mad. They don't know their own names, or how to speak, or anything. They're like animals that once were human."

Nell didn't move. Into her mind had jumped the image of a wild creature the size of a man, baring its teeth at Susan. She could feel the hot breath of the slashers in the cave, the stench of them as they pressed her to the ground, tearing at the bag of food.

"The — the ones in the city, then? The wild men that attack the sleepers? Those come from here?"

Minna nodded, lips pressed tight together. "We don't speak of it," she whispered. "But I saw one when I first came. Some of the others did, too. Mistress Meva told me that it's the punishment for rebellion. If they'd known to do it in the ancient times, we would have been spared the Genius."

Minna took a half step away, looking again up the hall.

"What? How?" Nell asked.

"I can't explain it," Minna said, taking another step toward the door. Nervously, she rubbed her sunburned nose, shedding small flecks of dead skin onto the hallway floor. "We're not supposed to talk of the banished ones! Forget it, Nell! Pretend it didn't happen. It's better that way."

Minna turned and hurried down the hall; Nell watched her go. When the door had closed behind her, Nell ran down the stairs into the gardens. They were suddenly empty of people. A breeze cascaded through the curtain of the great willow, and the grass bent softly beneath it; all the doors were shut. Nell moved quickly to the first passageway, the great tunnel that had taken them into the sanctuary, and emerged into the valley as the breeze died. The stillness held her for a moment, made her stand and look at the orchards and the fields, desolate in the settling heat. Then, far to her left, along the outer wall, she saw a group of men clustered, standing at attention, faces turned toward the hills.

Nell squinted at them, trying to see what they were looking at. Suddenly, from up the slope, a wail shattered the afternoon. It was an animal cry, but something more — a nearly human sound of despair and terror, high-pitched, frantic. The sound echoed across the valley, so terrible she put her hands to her ears. In the distance the robed men turned and disappeared into the sanctuary wall.

Again and again the cry pierced the afternoon until Nell, unable to stand it any longer, fled inside.

*T*oo soon again, the sounds of terror and pain jangled the thickets and tore at the silence of afternoon. Newly lost, the outcast thrashed on the grassy clearing, wailing and scrambling, until all signs of those who had come before were gone. From a hidden place among the trees, the exile waited with the food wrapped in its blue bundle, but the newly wild lunged to its feet and lurched past, just as so many had fled past the small welcome of the cottage garden.

Years ago, when the first of the lost had come into the woods, pulling at its face and arms, tearing at its changing skin, the exile had tried to say a word of solace, to call the thing back from the abyss. It had not heard. None ever had.

Now the frightened creature ran on, only to fall bloodied and exhausted among the trees, eyes rolling in its head until sleep, merciful and powerful, took it.

Gently, the exile laid the bundle beside it. Outcasts were forever hungry, empty in a thousand ways.

Food could fill only one. And yet that, too, was a mending.

Chapter 49

Nell felt that the world was tilting and all the solid things, the up and down of gravity, the bulk of trees and rocks and houses, were poised to fall out of the light of day into the dark. Sober-faced men stood in groups turning people into monsters, nodding and consulting and ripping the mind from a man before walking sedately back to their studies. How could such a thing be? Worse, how could the old man not know about it?

He did know. He must know.

A cold terror wrapped around her bones when Nell understood this, and on shaking legs, she ran back to the room, to Susan, to Kate and Jean.

But it was Max she saw when she came panting through the door. He was sitting on her bed, hands pressed between his knees, rocking. The room was bright with the light of the afternoon sun streaming through the windows from over the mountain, and Nell thought suddenly, *It shouldn't be. It should be dark.*

Max jumped to his feet when he saw her.

"Where have you been? Didn't you hear what happened? We were starting to think it was you they put out!"

He was white faced and unsteady, as unsteady as she felt. *He must know. He must have seen*, she thought. He must understand, as she did. He'd been there, with the old man, with all of them. . . .

"We have to go!" she said, moving past him to the window. The valley spread out below her, still desolate, and silent now, after the terrible sounds from the hill. "We'll have to run for it while they're still inside —"

She was making plans, hastily trying to determine the safest route away. They wouldn't want to meet it, or the men who had made it. Did anyone follow the thing up the mountain when it fled?

"Nell, what are you talking about?"

Max was staring at her. For a second, he had looked relieved at the sight of her. Now he only looked confused. She glanced at the others. The fear she'd seen when she first rushed in was going. Kate and Jean had been huddled on the bed, Jean squeezing the air out of Barbie's plastic skull. Now she set the doll in her lap and looked to Susan, who had been slow to raise her head.

They didn't know. The look on Max's face, the upset and fear, that was on her account. They wouldn't look this way if they knew. They'd be worse.

"The sound from the mountain! Didn't you hear it?"

But they hadn't. The windows and doors were shut. Only she had followed. After the gong, they'd been sent upstairs, and Max had crossed the gardens to join them. No one else had been in the fields. She looked from one to the next and saw they'd only been waiting for her, half panicked at her absence.

Shakily, she told them what she'd seen, what she'd heard. Max abruptly sat down, and Susan looked sick.

"Slashers?" Max said. "From here?"

She nodded.

"No," he said. "No, they wouldn't."

Nell stared at him. He'd come to his senses in a second, if she'd only wait. She practiced her patience, though it was hard, with her legs shaking so, to sit still.

Again, Max said, "No."

Nell turned to Susan. Why was she so quiet?

"Susan, say something!"

Susan blinked, her hand pressed to the side of her face. A cloud crossed the sun outside, and the brightness faded from the room. Behind Susan, the image of the golden man emerging from the pool dulled.

"Max, you were with them," Susan said. Her voice sounded muffled, as if she'd just woken. "You would know. What did the old man say? Did he tell you anything?"

Worry had made Max's face look young. He shook his head. "He only said something about discipline, and the protection of the sanctuary, and the great gift we have to be grateful for. He means our minds! He'd never do that, Nell. Never! You're wrong!"

Nell bit her lip. She'd seen the men standing in a group! She'd heard that terrible cry!

But Max was talking fast now, words and words and words that battered her until she wasn't completely sure anymore. Could she have been mistaken? She remembered the old man's lovely voice, the warmth of it. Max asked if she'd seen him there, and she hadn't, or if she'd seen the man who cried out, and again, she hadn't. She tried to say something, but he kept talking, quicker than ever, rolling over her until she frowned and pressed her lips together, trying to think whether anything made sense.

She hadn't seen the old man. She hadn't seen the slasher. She'd only heard that terrible wail, that sound. That lost, broken sound.

"It's different here," Max was saying. "It's not like the city. Do you know that the whole place, all of it, is one big school? They saved the books, Nell, saved all that knowledge when the Genius tried to burn them! They want people to know things! Not like the Genius! They hid away and protected all the things that are important. Would people like that turn someone into an animal? How could they? Why would they?"

It was rare that Nell couldn't think of something to say, but the urgency in Max's voice, the mix of concern and certainty, pressed on her. And then there was the old man himself. She'd seen him in the sunlit room. She knew. . . .

"You don't know, Nell," Max was saying. "Really, you don't know what you saw. We have a chance to learn here. To find out things we couldn't ever dream of on our own. You do want to get home, don't you?"

Blankly, she nodded.

Max heaved a sigh and stopped talking at last. In the silence, Nell looked at Jean and Kate, who were regarding all of them with round eyes. She looked at Susan, who stared back at her, something desperate in her face. And finally at Max, who was breathing heavily, eyes fixed on her.

"Just don't break their rules," he said in a low voice. "Just for now. They're so strict about it. It would ruin everything."

She had thought they were afraid the way she was afraid —
of something real. But they were only afraid she would cause
trouble, mess things up, step over silly lines that someone had
drawn and pretended meant something.

The familiar urge to say no, she'd break whatever rules she
wanted, rose up in her, and she almost shook her head. But the
old man wasn't the Genius. And this wasn't the city. She really
didn't know. Slowly, she nodded.

"Good," Max breathed. "Good."

Nell sincerely hoped it was.

Chapter 50

A hush enveloped the sanctuary the rest of that day, and long after Max had returned to his own room, the silence gathered in the hallways, oppressing Nell. She was not used to questioning her own memory, to doubting the evidence of her senses. And yet maybe here, in Ganbihar, where buildings wavered and faces changed, what you saw, what you heard, was less solid than it was at home. Hadn't she herself said real was different here? Maybe in a place like this, you could be fooled into seeing things that weren't true.

She drove herself nearly mad with doubt after that. At last, when Susan and the younger girls had fallen asleep out of sheer boredom, she crept across the hall to the oak doors that led into the great library.

She looked down into the canyon of books and at the volumes that ran behind her on this level, the third. Max had said this place had saved knowledge, that here they wanted people to know things. She remembered the Guide's warm voice, his saying that all who came here brought with them a question. Mistress Meva had said these were the books gathered from all of Ganbihar, from ancient times before the Genius, before the change. Books were solid. Books would help her.

She walked among the stacks, wondering in which of the thick, weathered volumes she would find an answer. She pulled out one and then another, but their titles confounded her: *Seeding in Early Spring: A Planner*, *The Art and Mystery of the Tapestry*, *Foot Rot and Other Contagious Diseases in Goats*. Not one of them seemed to promise anything but hours of tedium.

"Looking for something in particular?"

She turned to find a thin silver-haired woman with close-set, kindly eyes, brown except for a fleck of yellow in one of them. Everything about her was thin — nose, eyebrows, lips, jaw. And yet she gave an impression of contented fullness when she smiled. She wore a loose rose-colored top that flowed over a long, narrow black skirt. It made her fair skin seem pink, too, and the flowing, bright fabric stood out against the brown and gray and black of faded books and polished wood, a vivid surprise.

"I've been watching you wander the shelves awhile now. Maybe I can help you. I'm Mistress Bianna. I tend the books."

Tender of books seemed a good name for her. She held one now, one long hand resting flat on its cover, like a person gentling a horse. Nell wished she'd given better thought to what she wanted. "I — I'm new here, and I wanted to understand . . ." She trailed off, not sure how to put it.

But the woman nodded brightly. "Ah. I see. You're newer than you look. I wondered who would be out of rooms on such a day. But don't worry." She winked. "I never tell on those who love to read."

Nell waited as the woman thought, her fingers running absently over the cover of her book. "So what to give you? Hmm." Nell watched her eyes sweep the wall. She turned to lean against the wooden railing, surveying the acres of books below.

"I think I know," she said after a moment. "It won't be in this section, with the technical books. These are mostly tips on gardening." She looked over her shoulder to grin at Nell and said, "The boring section, I call it."

Nell smiled back.

"What you want is a little bit of a walk from here. Come, I'll show you."

Nell followed her across one of the bridges. She looked overhead as they crossed, to the distant skylights, white in the afternoon sun, and then down over the railings, to the tiles illuminated in squares that mimicked the pattern above. Mistress Bianna reached the twisted staircase and jogged down it, nimble as a child. *She must not be too old*, Nell thought, following her. And then again, despite her speed, she moved silently, reaching the ground without clattering on the stairs or slapping the tile. Nell raced after her as she set off across the floor, following the wall. She tried to muffle her own steps and glide, as the woman seemed to, but she could hear the squeak of her sneakers as they hit the marble, a squeegee, irritating sound she wished she could mute.

At last they reached a set of thick volumes with well-worn spines that showed signs of having once been richly colored. Strands of green or blue or red stood out in the cloth, which was worn or rubbed away in places so they now mostly hinted of long-ago dye. Some of the books were leather, and on these, glimmers of gold marked the dark spines, tracing the faded imprint of letters that must have once been bright.

"This one," Mistress Bianna said, choosing a thin leather

volume. "Always a favorite. Take it along to your room. I think you'll find it explains things quite nicely."

Nell studied the title in her hands. *Legends of the Ancients.* Her heart sank. She'd been seeking more than fairy tales and bedtime stories. But the woman looked so pleased, she didn't want to disappoint her. She'd come back another day and keep looking.

"Thank you," she said to Mistress Bianna. "I appreciate it."

She slipped back into the girls' hall and was nearly at her own door when she heard her name.

Heart sinking, she turned to find Wista peeking from one of the rooms. The girl looked guiltily behind her, then quietly slipped out the door and joined her.

"Zirri said you were out. I didn't believe it. Where'd you go? Weren't you scared?"

Nell felt a tick of annoyance. Zirri certainly had sharp eyes, she thought. Wista glanced back at the door.

"Don't worry about Zirri," she said. "She doesn't mean too bad. It's just hard, you know, being halfway. Anyway, she's asleep now."

Nell looked up and down the hall. Nobody was in sight. She showed Wista the book. "Just went to try to see what this place is about," she said. "Mistress Bianna gave me this."

Wista looked at it and flushed. "I don't read as well as I should yet. What exactly does it say?"

Nell's face grew hot. Another mistake. She seemed to keep making them here. But Wista was nice about it.

"It's all right; I don't feel bad about it. My ma couldn't read, either. She said she'd have liked to. She'd have taught me if she could. I know those small words anyway — *of* and *the*. Right?

It takes a while, but I'm getting it!" She smiled, and Nell, still blushing, smiled back.

"Is your mother here?"

It hadn't occurred to her that whole families would come.

Wista's smile faded a little, and Nell saw her call it back with effort. Her hand had strayed to the copper pendant, and she fiddled with it. "Oh, no," she said. "She couldn't come. But she told me about this place. She'd have liked it. Especially all the stories. Here even the pictures are stories!"

She motioned to the nearest tapestry, a wide scene of an old man standing on a rock, hordes of people below him, raising their faces as he lifted his hands to a stormy sky of yellow and gray wool.

"They're probably more interesting than this one," Nell said, hefting the book. "It's called *Legends of the Ancients*, which I think is probably Mistress Bianna's way of telling me to go to bed."

Wista laughed at that, then caught herself and lowered her voice. "Well, if they're good, maybe you could tell me some," she said. "Maybe at lunch? I like stories. Every time I learn one, I feel like I fit here a little better."

She waved and then slipped back down the hall, to be in the room before Zirri woke up. Nell watched her go. She doubted the stories in this book would make her fit here any better, but that was okay. She didn't need them to help her feel better about staying. She needed them to help her get home.

Chapter 51

Back in the room, she found Jean and Kate awake again and playing with the weathered Barbie, which had lately been given a bath and a hair wash. Its feet were grass stained, its hair a knotty mess, but now Nell could see once more its bright painted eyes and the perpetual mild grin it wore. The girls glanced every so often at Susan, frowning. Their older sister had moved from the bed to the window. Bleary-eyed, she sat there looking out at the valley and the hill beyond as if she'd left something up among the trees. Nell had thought to keep the book to herself awhile, but she changed her mind abruptly and handed it to Susan.

"I went looking for something to explain this place," she said. "It's not the greatest, but here's what I found." She pressed the volume into Susan's hands.

Susan looked down at the worn leather, and Nell noted with pleasure the way her expression sharpened. The look of distraction evaporated, and Susan brought the book up near her face.

"Smells like an old library," she said. "Like everything here, but more."

Susan smiled, and some of the tightness that had gripped Nell's chest for hours seeped away. She watched her sister study the title.

"Legends," Susan said. "This was a good choice. You can tell a lot about a place from its stories. Let's see. . . ."

She flipped the book open on her lap. Jean and Kate left off their playing and came to join them.

"A book!" Jean exclaimed happily. She reached over Susan's shoulder, her Barbie a pointer now. She poked its blond head at the inscription on the first page. "Hey, that's the song they taught us today — in the class!"

Nell pushed the doll's hair out of the way and read the words: "'*Take hope, for the smallest candle will light a torch, to make the end, beginning.*'"

"It's a song?" she asked. "How does it go?"

Jean immediately launched into the tune, and Kate joined her, two high-pitched little-girl voices, giddily singing. Nell glanced over to make sure she'd closed the door.

"That was the way they started the day in my class, too," Kate said. "A girl told me it's her favorite."

As Nell had suspected, Mistress Bianna had seen a child and given her a child's book. Her smile had been as pleasant as the doll's, and as meaningless. She sighed and made a sound of disgust. But when she tried to turn away, Susan laid a hand on her arm.

"Wait," she said. "Let's see."

She turned the pages of the book. The late-afternoon light blushed through the window, and the west-falling sun sparked and reddened as it dropped toward the trees. The book's creamy old pages turned faintly pink, under-laced with gold.

Susan stopped at a title printed in large letters: "The Tragedy of Rebellion." Most of the gilt on the words had flaked away, but a few smudges of shine remained.

"Rebellion," she said. "That's something we might want to know more about, after today."

They began to read and didn't stop even as evening came, and the light from the window darkened to orange shafts that fell across the beds. A girl entered, holding a taper, and lit the lamps in the sconces. "If you want dinner, it's downstairs now," she said. "The hours of mourning are over."

But they didn't want dinner. The glow from the window darkened to purple and then a deep blue, and finally was gone, replaced by flickering yellow as they sat listening to Susan read aloud. The story told of a young farmer's boy who came to be a scholar. He was quick and clever and eager to win praise.

"'At first, he did,'" Susan read. The beat of the words was different from anything Nell knew, and Susan's voice embraced the rhythm of it. "'For cleverness is the first of skills, and the lowest, and there are many who can take in words and rules as a mirror does, reflecting back to perfection while absorbing nothing of the essence of a thing.'"

Susan laughed. "They have a way with insults, don't they?" She grinned over at Nell. "I think we're going to like this book."

Where Susan had been distracted, she was now focused, and Nell settled down, glad that the feeling of wrongness that had clung to Susan since they'd come into the valley was lifting.

Suddenly Nell felt less alone.

Chapter 52

G o on," Jean prompted. "Keep reading!" They sat close together on the bed, leaning over Susan's shoulder, eyes on the old pages. Susan took up the story again:

"Then the time came for depth, and the quiet, patient climb to wisdom. In this, the farmer's boy stumbled, and the seed of his arrogance and pride flowered to rage. He brought the elders demands instead of questions, called the old ways foolish, and among the weak willed and the bitter found his disciples. In time his mind grew twisted, and he said the only true genius was to be found in nature, in the unleashing of passions, in the strength of the body and the embrace of the wildness of the world. For he was passionate, and strong, and wild. But unleashed, passion turns to violence, and so he burnt the first house of learning and chased the scholars from its halls. War came."

Susan paused. The flames writhed in the lamps, making light leap here and there across the paper.

"Well," Nell said, "we knew there was a war. Even Liyla said something like that. Do you think the rest of it's true? Is that the Genius they're talking about?"

Susan shrugged. "Can't be this one, but maybe a long time ago. Maybe a great-great-grandfather or something."

"He looked like he was a thousand years old," Jean said. "Maybe it *was* him."

Nell rolled her eyes, but Susan let that pass. She turned the page and continued reading:

> "The rebel called instinct wisdom and made virtue of urges, and so with joy the vengeful and the sullied rallied to him and fought, seeking the mindless ease of the animal. And, having called to it, the animal came into them. With animal strength, they fought; with animal fury, they conquered. Unseen within them, the change had begun, and, blind, they called it boon and victory as, unaware and unprepared, the academies fell."

"They were stronger?" Kate asked.

Susan nodded. "Because they were so angry. At first it just made them strong."

Jean had moved to the head of her bed. Mention of the Genius had dampened them all a little, and Nell saw Jean look out at the dark fields. The light of the flickering lamps was softer than lights back home, yellow as old paper and smelling of warm oil. The flames behind the glass were reflected in Jean's eyes when she turned.

"But nobody wants to be angry, do they?" she asked. "That's no good."

Nell thought of Zirri, so quick to lash out, and then of the people in the square, turning on the sleepers as the

Genius spoke. She wasn't sure how to answer. But Susan said, "Sometimes they don't know any other way to be strong."

Talk like this made Nell jumpy. She tapped the book. "And then?" she prompted.

Susan read: "'Like sheep, the weak followed the powerful.'"

"You mean they *liked* the change?" Kate interrupted. Jean pulled her knees to her chest and took up her Barbie again. She half turned away from them, bending her head to the doll, her face hidden.

"No," Susan said. "Don't you see? They didn't know they were changing. It was all on the inside, like the story says."

She continued: "'And death emptied the great places, the sacred halls. The rebel had tasted blood; feasted on it; and he hungered for more. He was not sated until the thinkers lay torn on the mountains and the rivers ran red.'"

Jean lifted her head. She was frowning now, all her delight in the story gone.

"You mean he killed them?"

Susan nodded, barely pausing. It had happened a long time ago, after all. And still, they had seen the Genius — this one, anyway — and the story didn't feel easy, or far away.

Susan read: "'Then came the just wrath of the universe, when the beast within became the beast without, and the life of man was cursed on the face of the earth.'"

The beast without, Nell thought, shuddering. She moved up to the head of the bed, beside Jean and her doll, and lay back to stare at the ceiling.

"But what about this place?" she asked. "How did this place survive?"

She heard the sound of pages turning.

"That's another story," Susan said. "There's plenty here. I think I could spend all night reading this thing."

She very nearly did. Long past midnight, she roused Nell.

"I finished it," Susan said. "And it's all here. In stories, in legends, but here."

Nell sat up in bed. The room was dark but for one lamp, flickering near Susan's bed. Jean and Kate slept curled together in the bed by the window, fully clothed.

"You mean how to open the window? That's in there?" Nell's heart began to hammer in her chest.

"No," Susan said. "Sorry. I didn't mean that. I just meant that the history of this place — what made the people the way they are — it's in here."

"Oh."

Nell felt deflated, half drunk with sleep and the feeling that she had woken from a bad dream. But Susan was still wide awake, more alert than she'd been since they'd come down the mountain. So Nell asked, half-heartedly, what she'd learned.

"It's a great story, really," her sister said. "Even in the one book, not all the stories agree with each other exactly. Legends are like that. But in one of them, it said that when the change came, the Genius *really* went nuts. He thought the surviving scholars had done it to him — some sort of revenge. So he hunted them down. He wanted to kill every one."

"And did he?"

"No. A few of them understood the danger and took a group of scholars and their families into hiding in the mountains across the sea. They took with them all the books they could gather and set out — the last of the thinkers."

"The library? That's a lot of books!"

Susan smiled. "There were more, if you can believe it. These were only what they could save. Plenty burned in the wars; I can only dream of what *they* were like."

She'd almost lost the thread of the story as she speculated, but now she took it up again, describing the years the scholars spent in the empty spaces they could find in the far-off lands, Elsare and Ferent and Sayca. Most of them had been lost among the people there, but a few came back when the first Genius was long dead, when his son and then his grandsons and great-grandsons had taken his place. Those scholars — Susan guessed they were the ancestors of the ones today — built the sanctuary in secret and hid it in the mist.

Nell thought about this. "If they can do things like make the mist, why haven't they used it to destroy the Genius or take the city? What's stopping them?"

But Susan had no answer, and at talk of the mist she'd retreated into herself again, if only a little. She set the book down and rubbed her eyes.

"I'm tired now," she said. "And I don't know. Maybe tomorrow we'll find out more. We'll tell Max, too."

She reached up and snuffed the lamp, leaving the room in darkness. Nell blinked and turned her head to the window, now the only source of light. She heard Susan lie down, sighing. Outside, stars crowded the sky, dust and glitter and splintered radiance, as the faint glow of the half moon, nearly out of sight over the sanctuary, spread a milky sheen across the dark.

Chapter 53

The corn harvest took the first hours of the next day, and Nell found herself walking beside Minna and a frail-looking girl named Chim beneath the tasseled heads of the corn, peering into them to check if the silk that flowed from them had browned. She pulled a fat cob from the stalk and tossed it into the wide burlap sack the others carried between them. She had the urge to lag, but Minna and Chim kept her moving. The morning mistress, a stout, dark-skinned young woman called Leese, was up ahead, lecturing as she pulled corn on the wonders of crop rotation. Mistress Leese spoke in slow, perfectly articulated sentences, as if she were always reading aloud at the front of the class. Nell tried to imagine her in a hurry, anywhere, for anything, and failed.

The morning cool lingered in the fields, and the sweetness of the corn was in the air. All around Nell, the green stalks waved and whispered, and she thought that she could love this kind of school, despite the Shepherdess's persistent cheer, despite Mistress Leese, now expounding on the mysteries of winter rye and oats and the beneficial qualities of hairy vetch. She could love it for the cool of the morning air and the smell of corn and the blue eggshell sky overhead, and the sounds of the little girls singing.

But corn and sky and hairy vetch were nothing to do with windows. She wondered what Max was learning.

Later, when the girls had washed and turned the corn over for shucking to Susan's group, who waited to separate the cobs from the silk before passing it to the herbalist who would take the silk for his medicines, Nell met Susan in the hall.

"The older class, what do they learn?" she asked her.

Susan frowned in that way she had now, as if she were hard of hearing and trying to make words out.

"I don't know. Proper shucking techniques, this morning. And the uses of corn silk."

"Yes, but what else?"

Susan shrugged. "Geography. Some history. And we're analyzing a long poem called 'The March of Anam,' about one of their heroes. Why?"

Nell didn't understand Susan sometimes. Had she forgotten why they'd come? It wasn't to learn to heal bed-wetting with corn silk.

"I'm waiting to hear about windows, that's why! Aren't you?"

But Susan looked again like she hadn't heard.

"Susan!"

Susan jumped a little, but now she only seemed annoyed. "Of course! Of course I am," she said. "And when I find the right person to ask, I will. Maybe Max has had better luck."

She moved down the hall then, as if they'd finished the conversation. Nell looked at the girls passing in the hallway in their brightly colored dresses, laughing and talking. Between the doors hung needlework scenes of young men beside a fountain, listening to an old man expound; a hooded man emerging from a cave; and crowds of robed scholars standing in boats, crossing the sea. Waves of cerulean wool, stones the color of ashes, vines of green satin thread that spread like fingers across low walls, these Nell turned to, away from the throng of people who moved past like flowing water, with Nell alone an unmoving stone, a solitary rock battered by a sense that something was wrong.

She studied the weavings, standing there a long time, until the hall quieted and she was truly by herself.

"They're beautiful, aren't they?"

Mistress Meva stood behind her, smiling as always. Nell took a step away from her. She disliked the earnestness of the woman, the strident jolliness that seemed like some kind of obligation the woman performed, a perpetual, hard-to-do good deed. But she knew her own silence wasn't polite, so she said, "Who made them?"

In the unseen but very heavy chart she thought the mistress carried around in her head, Nell could tell she'd just gotten a gold star. The Shepherdess grinned widely. "Women!" she said, as if the fact ought to be a shocking surprise. "Women all through the ages. Of course, these aren't as old as that. Only a few of the very ancient ones were saved. They say some go back as far as the sage kings, which is quite ancient. But of course those would be in the heart now, along with the books of mystery."

"The heart?"

"Of the sanctuary — in the last garden. A very special place."

"Have you ever seen them?"

Nell watched her invisible gold star drop right to the floor with the look of consternation this question brought to the Shepherdess's face.

"Oh, no! No, of course not! Only the council members go there — the sacred elders. And even they only on the most important of occasions."

Her smile came right back, though, as she explained that the weavings and needlework in the other bands were the product of the past hundred years, and that among the artisans, there were several weavers now who were known to produce beautiful work.

"You could visit them, if you're interested. We always like to encourage our girls' interests."

Nell said she'd very much like to see them, and the Shepherdess, delighted, promised she would speak to the artisans. Nell thanked her and watched the woman walk off, bouncing. She thought she'd earned back her gold star and another besides.

But by that afternoon, she'd lost them again, without understanding how. Each day, the girls began after lunch by reciting the chant of order.

To the day the sun,
To the night the moon.
To each its realm,
Its bounty and boon.
In order created
And in order, life.
Thus banish longing
And banish strife.

Nell had only just begun to learn the words, and she

wasn't sure she understood them. What did longing have to do with order, anyway? She discovered the answer by accident not too long after when, responding to a question from the Shepherdess, she said idly that she'd rather emulate the sage king Plauth than his dutiful mother, who had risen daily before dawn to bring her small son to the great academy in Kiyakosa, the mountain city.

"Modesty," Mistress Meva admonished her, frowning slightly.

Nell, who hadn't much experience provoking people unintentionally, just stared at her, and the Shepherdess softened.

"In the city," she said gently, "there is confusion and disorder. But here we understand that there must be those who nurture and those who lead, those who open the first of doors and those who go through them, to others. Do you understand?"

Nell didn't. Or perhaps it was that she was afraid she did, a little. And she didn't like it. Behind her, she heard Zirri snicker.

Nell said nothing, and she turned to the windows when Mistress Meva went on with her lecture. The afternoon classroom was one of the few that sat not above the kitchens but beneath the dormitories, and looked also onto the valley. From this angle, Nell couldn't see the hill; the view was lost in the high fronds of corn. Outside, women and a few men moved through the rows a second time, filling their coarse-woven bags with any cobs the girls had missed. Nell watched them, slightly hunchbacked as they picked, making the lacy heads of the cornstalks shiver and bend. She wished she were outside again. She wondered if Max was hearing stories of the great mothers and their many exploits gathering firewood in the snow and making do with little so they could send their sons away to cities that sat on peaks, full of forbidden doors.

In the sky outside, a bright mountain of white clouds crossed the sun, casting shadows onto the valley. From the west, a lone dark cloud drifted their way until it moved among them, a gray stain on a white dress.

*T*he rain came down and wetted the trees on the mountain and the plants in the garden, and the crops in the valley, far below. It had been a harvest-weather morning — clear and breezy, bright and fair. Now the rain came and the old rhyme with it, the memory of children chanting at the windows:

> A blessed rain damps the ground
> And never touches day.
> For the ground must feed,
> But the ground is blind,
> So why disturb our play?

In the valley there were children still, even newcomers, to sing songs and chant rhymes. And yet despite the joy of harvest and song, the mist boiled and rolled, unstopping. Like an unhealed wound, pricked and bleeding, like an animal hurt and enraged, it growled just out of sight, muttering and dangerous. Its venom seeped into the day, fouling even the blessed rain. Fearsome it had always been, lying in wait. But the exile knew the power of the thing and yearned suddenly for the old fear, known and long endured. For the sound told its tale. The mist no longer crouched, waiting. It was rising to the hunt.

Chapter 54

Late that afternoon, Nell found Susan alone in the room. She sat facing the window, a new stack of books beside her on the bed. Nell's heart lifted a little. Despite the annoyances of the day, Susan was shaking off the weight that had been flattening her lately. Here she was again, with her books. Nell waited for her to go on about Mistress Bianna and the rows and rows of things to read.

But when she came around the bed, she saw that Susan sat rigid, staring blankly at the book that lay open on her lap. A tremor passed through Nell; she had the urge to raise a hand and check Susan for fever. And yet the color remained in Susan's cheeks. Only her eyes looked strange. She gazed out the window, at the rain pounding the green corn and the ruby-studded grapevines and the rows of peach trees with their soft-skinned fruit among the leaves. The plants crouched and bowed beneath the downpour. Susan didn't look as if she saw any of it.

"What's wrong?" Nell asked her.

Susan glanced up, startled. "Nothing," she said. She seemed to wake to her surroundings, and looked down at the stack of books. "The nice woman in the library gave me everything I asked for. It's just — I wish I could get some quiet."

"You mean from the rain?"

Susan shook her head. "Rain? No. I'm talking about that echo. Don't you hear it? That sound from the mountain? Doesn't it get to you?"

Nell hesitated. She strained for a minute, trying to hear something beneath the rain. Was it like the sound bats made, high and scratchy, in the dark? She tried, but there was nothing.

"What does it sound like?" she asked Susan.

Susan furrowed her brow and closed her eyes, listening. "Like — like the sound a pot makes, bubbling, or the sound of people talking in another room. Words you can almost hear the shape of. I can't really make it out, but it's there. It makes it hard to think."

Nell shifted uneasily. Never in her life had she seen her sister unable to disappear into a book, and now she had stacks of them but sat frowning over a single page.

"Those books say anything about order?" she asked, trying to pull Susan from her funk. "That's all I heard about today! If order were a fat old man, I think Mistress Meva would be married to him by now."

Susan looked up and laughed at that. The sound was almost enough to make Nell relax. "Well, you can see why," she said. "Order. That's tradition, really, and it holds this place together. They'll pretty much do anything to protect it."

Nell stopped smiling, and Susan again grew quiet. Nell watched her look around at the light-colored walls, the unlit lamps, the rain.

"It looks like home in some ways," Susan said quietly. "Only it isn't."

"No," Nell agreed. "It isn't. And no matter how much people look like us here, I want to get out."

But Susan sighed. "We can't, though, Nell. There's nowhere to go. We have to learn what they know here, or how will we ever get back?"

"Yes, well, when are we going to *do* things, then? And not just hear about other people doing them?"

Susan shook her head. "I don't know. But that's their way. It's the old way, and so for them, it's the only good one."

"Hmph."

"It's going to be that way here, Nell. Don't you see? It's because of the Genius. He wanted change, and that's what he got."

Nell rolled over and stood up. The window had two smaller panes, one on each side, and she pulled open one of these, then thrust her hand out to catch the rain. She wondered if this was the mist, breaking into pieces, falling cold and gray on the pretty valley. If it was, would it be gone then? Or would it seep into the roots of everything and spoil it?

She turned her face from the window. "I'm starting to *hate* tradition, the way they talk about it around here. If it *were* a fat old man, I think I'd kick him."

Susan laughed. "You probably would," she said. "But it wouldn't get you anywhere." She closed the book she'd been staring at and studied the cover of it, running her hands along the raised lettering.

"I don't know," she said. "Traditions are important. They're really just stories about what used to be. And stories are what keep you knowing who you are. If they hadn't had the stories, they couldn't have built this place and turned the change back. You have to admit, it's beautiful here."

Nell shut the window. Her hand had grown cold. Outside, the water ran in rivulets down the glass, turning the valley and the hill and the trees at the edge of the ridge into green paint. She'd spent most nights since they got here telling herself stories of home to keep from forgetting. Maybe the Shepherdess and the Master Watcher and all the rest of them felt the same way. Maybe they thought that if they didn't keep hold of the stories, they'd lose everything. But could a story be good and also bad? Could it reverse the change and make the mist at the same time?

She had no answers, and Susan, despite her pile of books, could be no help. For a while, Nell watched her struggling to read, but when she hadn't turned the page after ten long minutes, Nell felt as if she could almost see the mist pushing at her sister, wrapping itself around Susan's head, trying to smother her. It made her want to jump in and block it somehow, put her arms around Susan and bat it away. But then Susan would never let her do that. So she sat, helpless, as her sister squinted blindly at the book. When she couldn't stand it any longer, Nell got up and left the room.

Chapter 55

If rain kept everyone indoors, Nell had the urge to be out in it. No matter how high the ceilings or airy the rooms in the sanctuary, looking at Susan's strained face made her feel closed in. She walked down the corridor toward the hillside stairs and on impulse knocked at Wista's door.

Zirri opened it and eyed her coldly.

"Nell!" Wista called from behind. "Come to tell me stories?"

Nell slipped past Zirri, who pointedly had not moved to make space for her.

"I guess so," she said. She looked uncomfortably at Zirri, who was sneering.

"Want to go for a walk?"

Wista bobbed to her feet, her copper pendant swinging.

"Of course! Zirri, do you want to come?"

Nell smiled to herself. You couldn't not like Wista, with her persistent friendliness. Her face had grown pretty, these last few days, as the last of the change had receded from it. She had become a round-eyed girl with a square chin and a little gap between her bottom teeth. The fingers that played with her pendant were slim.

Zirri, too, had completed the change, but if it had sweetened her disposition, Nell hadn't noticed.

"Why would I want to walk in the rain?" Zirri said. She went and sat on her bed.

They left her there and made their way downstairs to borrow a walking canopy from Mistress Seta, who kept a store of them for rain harvests. An oilskin strung between poles, it let two walk side by side, each holding a pole, leaving a hand free to work. They took it out into the cornfield and walked beside the lines that had yet to be harvested.

"Wista, after you came down here, did you hear the mist? You know — sort of a hissing or anything?"

Wista shrugged, making rain spill off Nell's side of the canopy and slap wetly into the mud.

"Does the mist have a sound?" she asked.

Nell guessed that was as much an answer as any.

For a while they just walked, listening to the rain. Nell couldn't hear anything else.

"You're different," Wista said after a while. "You and those others you came with. Maybe that's why you ask the questions you do. I wish I could do what you can."

A little jangle of alarm rang in Nell's chest.

"What do you mean, do what we can?"

"You know, read. And write. I saw that little one, Jean, do it. Who taught her so young? Did you?"

Nell let out the breath she'd been holding. "Oh, that. No, I didn't teach her. She learned in school. Didn't they have school where you came from?"

Wista shrugged. "Not for me. I come from a little mining village, down in the southern plains. Most girls there go into the mines young, so the parents can try for a boy instead."

It was a warm rain, but Nell felt the sick cold she'd known in the city, among the sleepers' children.

"Did you have to go?" she asked.

Wista shook her head. "No, my ma had been, but she was so smart, she learned metalwork, so she didn't work all the time below. That's how she lived, she said. She made me this." She lifted the copper pendant to show Nell. "Clever hands, my ma had. Wish I were as clever."

Nell thought Wista was better than clever. She was nice.

"So she kept you out?" she asked.

The other girl nodded. "Said it wasn't worth what the Domain would pay to send me. Wouldn't listen to a word my da said about it." She sighed and squinted out at the rain collecting in the muddy field. "She'd have liked me to read, I know, but she didn't know how herself. She did know stories, though. Told me lots of them. Birth of the Genius, the banishing, the unchanged time. All those were good. She even knew stories they passed in the mines, about the powerful ones. That's how I got here. When she got sick, she told me to go looking."

Wista's free hand went to her necklace, and she was quiet so long that at last Nell broke the silence with one of the stories Susan had read, the one about the rebel who became the Genius.

Wista laughed. "Different from the one my ma told," she said. "She'd have liked this one better, I think."

They walked on beneath the rain as the corn bent and the sky faded, and Nell could only wonder if maybe she fit in here after all, in this place where all the children seemed, in one way or another, to be lost and alone.

Chapter 56

Susan had sent the little girls to supper on their own.

"They were noisy," she said by way of explanation when Nell found her still in the room, in exactly the same spot she'd been more than an hour before. "If I could just get a little quiet, I know I could find something in here."

Nell looked unhappily at the books.

"Maybe we should leave," she said. "Maybe it's just no good for us here. We can tell Max, and he'll come — I know he will! If he'd just take a look at you —"

"Don't you dare!" For a second, the color returned to Susan's face. "You think I'll be better sleeping in caves with monsters? We're here for a reason, and we need to stay. If that means following a million crazy rules, then that's what it means!" She shook her head, then softened a little. "I'm just tired. If I get some rest, I know I'll do better."

Nell grimaced. Susan sounded like somebody's mother, like she'd aged ten years all of a sudden and would soon be a hundred if somebody didn't stop her. She was tired, all right. But Nell worried sleep wouldn't be enough to fix it.

By the time Kate and Jean returned, holding a new letter from Max, Susan was fast asleep on the bed, still frowning. Jean went to wake her.

"Leave her!" Nell said. "Can't you see she needs her sleep?"

Now I'm sounding like somebody's mother, she thought bleakly.

"But this one's harder than the other," Jean said. "She'd want to read it, wouldn't she?"

"I'll read it," Nell said. "And we'll show Susan when she wakes up."

To her surprise, Jean handed the letter over. "Go on," she said. "It's even longer than the first one."

Nell's heart raced a little as she unfolded the letter. Maybe this time Max had found something worth writing about!

"'Dear Jean,'" she began as Jean and then Kate jumped up beside her on the bed. "'I'm sorry I haven't been able to visit as much as I wanted. I know waiting is hard, but great discoveries take patience — I've read that more than once. It's historically right there in all the books. As it is, I'm working as hard and as fast as I can.'"

Nell hoped it was true. She raced on:

"'Tur Kaysh says it's important not to break concentration, and I'm trying my best not to because concentration is so important here. Maybe it is always, but it's different here. I'm starting to understand some things. You know how at home there can be some big kids who just outweigh everybody and push them around because of that? Maybe you haven't seen that so much yet in your grade. I have. Scientifically, it's just body mass, right? Like this advantage they have with this body they got into, and they throw it around and make things happen (like getting people's lunches or whatever). Well, here it's different. Here it's how sharp you can think that makes things happen. That is, it's a gift to have good concentration, like the Guide says, but you have to work for it, no matter what. When I think of it like that, I think that Ganbihar is better than home in that way. Fairer, right? At home people are always saying things like it's what's on the inside that counts, but here it really does. The Guide says the city is like a pit that we fell into from forgetting. He means the people here, but I was thinking that it could apply back home, too. Anyway, so don't worry, I'm learning a lot and I'm going to figure things out and then we'll all be able to get back. Just, I'm thinking that maybe it would even be better if we could go back and forth. Maybe I'll figure that out, too.

    Your brother,

    Max"

Nell sat looking at the letter a second when she'd finished. She glanced over at Susan. If Max could see Susan now, would he still want to come back to this place? She wondered.

Chapter 57

Kate often wore a strange and penetrating look, full of yearning, as if she would readily shed her own skin and take on another's, take Nell's or Susan's, if she could. Nell disliked it and Susan humored it, and Kate, unaware, went on looking with eyes like garden spades meant for digging. She wore that look now, watching Susan. Susan had gotten up from sleep no better than when she lay down. To Nell, it looked almost as if she hadn't gotten up at all, only opened her eyes and moved to sit stiffly at the desk, still dozing. Above her, the weaving of the man emerging from the water jumped in the lamplight, but Susan, though her face was lifted to it, did not see. She had lost all pretense of busying herself, and not even a book sat open before her to hide her distraction.

"Susan? What are you looking at? Hey, Susan!"

She called two or three times and then went and nudged her sister. Only then did Susan turn, frown in Nell's direction, and pull a book from the pile. But she only pretended to read. Nell watched her with mounting panic.

This time, Nell took Jean with her when she left the room. Jean, though not as watchful as Kate, well understood the meaning of the tight silence that filled the room and was happy to escape it.

"We're going to get Max," Nell said to her, and Jean's face lit up.

It wasn't as straightforward as that, unfortunately. Nell realized that she didn't even know where Max slept, though she had heard that the boys were housed on one of the upper floors of the first band. Minna had told her that families inhabited the far side of the band, but this side, the side facing west, was home to all the children who had come parentless to the sanctuary. Nell could only think to knock at the door of the woman who oversaw the younger girls, Mistress Dendra.

"You knock," she said to Jean. "She'll expect you to ask a question."

Mistress Dendra wore her hair in a thick black braid. She had a habit of playing with it, and Nell had seen her, taking Jean's group through the first garden, tugging at the end of it as if leading herself around on a dark leash. Mistress Dendra was pretty, and young, and not nearly as annoying as the Shepherdess.

She opened the door, looking sleepy.

"Jean? Are you all right? Is there a problem?"

There was, but no amount of arguing would convince the young woman that she should call for Max, and certainly not the Master Watcher, whom Nell brought up reluctantly. Boys were not allowed to visit after hours, even brothers.

And so Nell and Jean trudged back to their room, to the taut silence and the worrisome look on Susan's face.

The next day, Nell found Mistress Meva and reminded her how much she'd like to see the weavers at work. The Shepherdess, delighted, gave her leave to go. If Max was spending all his time in the third band, Nell decided, she'd have to get closer to it.

She did not expect to be much interested in the weavers or the embroiderers or any of the other artisans, all women, who sat in the second garden, working their looms or bent over embroidery hoops in the sun. But on her way past them, she glanced at the half-made tapestries and stopped.

The image on the nearest loom standing upright in the garden was of a boat cresting the waves. It stood half revealed, the bottom of the picture vivid and alive. Keel up, the boat hung suspended over a stormy sea of blue and gray, waves that tossed ivory foam into an iron sky. The icy water and the ship's hull poised above it and the red, chafed hands of people clinging to the rails were richly colored; they stood out, bright and alive, disappearing halfway up into lines of unwoven thread, shoulders and faces and mast and sail as yet unmade. But what stopped Nell was the color of the yarn that hung from the side of the loom, waiting to be drawn into the tapestry. It was all gray.

She watched as the weaver lifted a thread and pulled it through. Her fingers ran over it, tugged, and fitted it into place. As she did so, it colored, twinkling a little as the gray blushed orange and the thread settled over the others, part of a streak of sun breaking through clouds.

"How did you do that?"

The woman looked up, and the thread she was about to weave, which had begun to brighten, dulled again in her hand. Nell watched it in dismay, but the woman was untroubled.

"Weave, you mean? Are you the girl Meva sent?"

Nell nodded, and the weaver, who introduced herself as Iana, offered her a chair.

"I'm sorry to ruin your thread," Nell said, pointing.

Iana smiled and shrugged. "Oh, that? That's nothing. It'll come back. Come, and I'll show you weaving."

She was a talkative woman tilting toward old age, with a hawkish nose and a wrinkled chin, though around her eyes a little youth remained. And in her hands there was speed and strength and nimbleness. Nell watched her work, pulling the weft back and forth over the pattern she had laid. Each time, as she consulted her paper and drew a new thread into the weave, Nell saw it bloom color.

"How do you do that?" she asked again.

The woman shrugged. Amid all her talk of the weaving, she seemed to see the colorless thread coming to life as an afterthought, a happy convenience.

"We weavers have little songs of color in our heads," she said, tapping hers for effect. "That's one of the first things you learn, weaving."

"And it tells the thread what color to be?"

"Oh, no. I see that. It just gives you a little rhythm to see it by: *Life is ours, and color and light, the child we form, the yarn make bright.* It's like the growing-garden song, or haven't you learned that one yet?"

"You mean the chant of seeds?" Nell asked. She hadn't thought of the poem as a song.

"Yes, that. Just a little help, an aid to the mind, to make the work light."

Nell watched her a while longer, fascinated. Nearby, an embroiderer named Neetri worked pearls into a glossy cloth stretched over a large hoop. These, too, shifted and deepened in color as she worked. Nell wanted to know how it was done, but Neetri told her what Iana had, quoting an old saying that woman's work was in her belly and hands, and remarking that the great dyers of old, all men, were known to make colors more vibrant than any others.

"But that art was lost, you know, with the flight across the sea. Perhaps in the third band they'll discover it again, and we'll have all the lost shades. There were colors among the ancients, that would dazzle the eyes. Not like today."

Nell looked around the garden, freshly washed from yesterday's rain. Drops clung to the blush-colored petals of some flowers Iana called open-palms, glinting like crystal. Shallow pools of white rain winked in the folds of the rainbow canvases the artisans used to keep the sun off. Nell looked again at the tapestry of the ship, and the embroidery that Neetri called "the birth of twins to Priya, mother of all," a radiant scene built of beads of polished brass and gems and brilliant silks, and wondered what colors could have outshone these. But she didn't say anything. She went back to the first band, trying to remember the words to the chant about growing, and for the moment forgetting all about Max, and even Susan.

◇ ◇ ◇

*S*ummer on the mountain was unlike summer in the valley, with its bright sunlight and brighter crops, the women bending to toil together in the mornings, the girls in their lines gathering the harvest in their canvas bags, skirts catching on the tall stalks to make them rustle and swing and wave beneath the cloudless sky. At the mountain cottage, the garden grew in its small glade, untouched by any but one set of hands, one patient farmer collecting the day's harvest alone.

The exile dug carrots and turnips and a hard-skinned yam from the soil and thought that perhaps silence would have been the better way, long ago. Perhaps obedience and acceptance and dampened hopes were not such a price to pay for the vivid life of the valley, full of the company of others.

Silence had been the choice then, and the exile had refused it.

Now there was neither company nor silence. The roiling mist had washed all away, and even in the empty garden on the hill there was no peace.

Chapter 58

To the soundless voice the seed,
To the silent singer the flower.
Rouse the fruit
And draw the sleeper to light.

Sitting on her bed the day after her visit with the weavers, Nell recited the poem in her head, trying to make the words stick:

Grayfleck stone to the tammery,
For open-palm hint of sea.
Silverwhite to the urlis,
Firesand for the redlace tree. . . .

She'd thought of it all day after the weaver had mentioned it, and because the woman had named the small pink-tinged flowers open-palm. Another long night with Susan's silence and no sign of Max had given her time to think again about the color blossoming in the weaver's hand, about the songs that had seemed to her, until then, to mean nothing. The next morning, when the girls chanted the seeds, Nell had listened to the poem with a different ear. To her surprise, she found she knew the words already, having said them often enough now without thinking. At dinner in the garden, she'd plucked an open-palm, and now she sat on the edge of her bed with the delicate thing cupped in her hands. Evening flamed outside, and clouds like red coals burned above the western mountain, but Nell kept her eyes on the flower, wondering what Iana had meant by "an aid to the mind."

For open-palm hint of sea.

She had never heard of silverwhite or firesand, but the sea she knew. She remembered the sky hard as polished brass over the water, the rush and slap of the surf, the hot sand gritty beneath her feet. And the air — there was that, too — the salt-and-sour tang the wind carried as it blew chilly against her wet skin.

Was all that hint of sea?

To the soundless voice the seed . . .

She'd gone over it so many times the song ran on its own inside her head tonight, a soothing rhythm, something like the sea itself, the long sibilant inhale and exhale of the tide.

She lifted the flower and examined it closely. Five flat rosy petals surrounded a creamy center attached to a long, firm green stalk. Unlike a rose or a tulip, the flower opened flat to the sky, which Nell guessed was the reason for its name. But what of the sea? She brought the flower to her face and breathed. Beneath the faint smell of vanilla was an even fainter edge, the brisk aroma of air blown from the ocean.

To the silent singer the flower. . . .

After Max had made peaches, and Susan had drawn water out of nothing, Nell had tried to think of something for long enough, and with enough concentration, to make it take shape in the air. Max said that Susan had the knack of thinking of things fully, without distraction. But if this was the key, it was one Nell could not seem to find. She noticed things. In the forest, she had often forced herself to sit and try to forget the sharp odor of the barren ground and the calls of hawks and the shadows cast by leaves in the dirt. She tried not to see Kate drawing with a stick and Jean swinging her filthy doll and the way Max's hair stood up in wild lumps after he ran his fingers through it. And yet she was drawn to it all, no matter how she tried to quiet herself and shut the door to the world so she could think of one thing alone.

Despair began to edge in on her as she sat on the bed, thinking all this. Hunched over, she stared unhappily at the flower. All her life the twins had run just ahead of her, telling her to keep quiet and keep to her place, reminding her of how much she didn't know. She'd never listened to them before. Remembering this, Nell shoved aside the dark, useless thoughts. *Forget Susan!* she said to herself fiercely. Susan was even now walking the library blindly, listening so hard to one thing that she couldn't think! And Max — where was he? So taken with the one thing that he had forgotten them these past two nights. She straightened in disgust. There were other ways — always other ways — and she would be better at them. The best!

Abruptly, she stopped pushing aside all the things she saw and let herself look at them, unworried. There was the golden tapestry above the desk, and there the window, ablaze. And here the pink-palmed flower, open in her hand and smelling of the sea. She gazed at it and thought, *I see all of it; I won't be blind. But I can see it like I do sitting on the front porch, letting the world go by. I can collect it and hold it, to think about later. Like I did with the chant of seeds, listening and not knowing I'd heard.*

She cupped the flower and thought of the sharp tang of the sea and hands open to the sky. Still on the wall was the golden tapestry, and outside she could hear a group of girls running in the high corn, and in the hall, the footsteps of people moving past the door. But shining in her hand was the flower, and she saw it like a candle's flame, burning bright in a room crowded with shadows. She felt a tug of heat that slipped down her arms and tingled in her fingertips. Beside the open-palm, the air wavered, like an image reflected in water. Her hand shook. There was weight in the air, and now texture. A moment more, and a second flower glimmered and took shape beside the first.

Nell nearly dropped it.

Two flowers, identical, sat in her cupped hands. Shakily, Nell ran a finger over the silky petals of the new one, then brought it close to her face. It smelled of vanilla and salt. She smiled.

Immediately, she sat back and opened her mind to flowers. The air sizzled faintly, and Nell jumped at the shock of heat flowing through her. She felt suddenly as if she had lived every moment until now as one lives in a dream, seeing only flashes of things, images and slices, but never the whole. Now she saw it. The air around her was heavy and listening, and everywhere were seeds, ready to bloom.

She made flower after flower until her bed was littered with pink blossoms and the room perfumed with the smell of vanilla and the sea.

Chapter 59

Max came back to visit at last, the next night. He was beaming when he arrived, but the only one who beamed back was Jean, who showed him the little pile she'd made of his letters. Though Nell had wanted him to come as much as anyone, seeing him irritated her because he had the look of someone almost too happy to talk, too full of having exactly what he wanted. She knew that feeling, because she'd felt it herself, the moment the flower had formed in her hand.

Of course, Max being Max, no amount of happiness could stop him from telling them about how great it was to learn with the old man, up there in the sunny room.

"He calls me son now. You know how old-fashioned people do that? But I think he means it, kind of. He says he'd teach his own son what he's teaching me, if he had one. He never got the chance before. . . ."

Listening to him somehow drained the joy from Nell. She felt a small hurt flare in her chest, small like the pin that punctures the balloon, or the tiny break that starts a slow leak in the bottom of a boat. She realized after a while that Max was too full of his own happiness to see them, really. He didn't see Kate sitting glumly by the window. He didn't see Jean slowly deflate, watching him, until she sagged on the bed, slapping her Barbie against her knee. He didn't see Nell nudge aside the pile of flowers at her feet. She'd been waiting to show them to him, but now she pushed them out of sight. Worst of all, he didn't see how the moment after she greeted him, Susan's face had glazed over again until she sat like a statue in the chair, moving only when she winced and jerked her head as if trying to shake something loose.

"You won't believe what we did today," he said. "Tur Kaysh said he's been waiting for a student like me. We barely stay inside anymore. He takes me out to the gardens, to show me things. He says before the blight came — that's what he calls the Genius — isn't that a perfect word for him? Before the blight came, the world was a lot healthier all around. He said people barely even got sick back then, and neither did plants or animals. And if they did, well, the scholars back then could heal them — that's how good they were."

Nell wanted to break in, and she had the urge to say something cutting. But there was nothing to say. She wished the old man had been waiting for her.

But Max eventually became aware that none of them were saying anything. He looked around, frowning.

"What's the matter?"

Jean slapped her Barbie against her knee, twice, three times.

"You've been gone almost a week," she said. "I thought you were coming to take us home."

Max colored. "I'm sorry, Jean, it's just — there's so much to learn. We work late, just the two of us. And I am working on getting us home. It takes a lot to make a window, you know?"

Kate brightened. "So you've asked him about it?"

"Well, not exactly, no —"

"Not exactly!" All of Nell's confused resentment shot like an arrow to that point. He hadn't asked about the window! What did he think he was doing there, anyway?

"What are you waiting for?" she shouted. "You think we *like* sitting around here? Look what it's doing to Susan! You're the one who said they knew things in this place. Well, do they or don't they?"

Even Susan looked up at that. Max glanced at both of them, abashed.

"It's not exactly the way you're thinking. Listen, I know it isn't easy for you guys to wait, but the window — there's nothing like that here. Tur Kaysh talks all the time about what I'm here to do. What do you think he'd say if I asked him how to leave?"

Nell glared at him. "Why don't you ask him and find out?"

But Max only shook his head. "It's not like that. I will. I mean — I'm going to figure it out, but I've got to learn more, don't you see? There's so much more here than we knew! And he treats me like his own son! Don't you see I won't learn anything if he thinks I'm crazy? Or just ready to run off the minute I get the chance?"

He stopped then, aware, maybe, of the way they were all looking at him. He thought they didn't understand. But Nell knew that feeling of wanting something terribly, wanting it more than you'd ever wanted anything before.

She understood it, but seeing it in Max now, this way, only made her angrier. And Max saw that anger, and Susan's silence, and Kate's disappointment and Jean's hurt, and he flushed.

"You don't understand," he said again. "Today he showed me this poem that —"

But Nell had heard enough.

"Do you think we care?" she snapped. "Because we don't, Max. We care about one thing: getting out of here. So are you going to help us or not?"

Max's face was deep red now, and his neck was, too.

"You don't get it at all," he said. "Susan, tell her!"

But Susan said nothing. Max shook his head and went to the door. Jean jumped off the bed and ran after him.

"Max!" she said. "I care about poems!"

He turned back briefly and tried to smile. "I'll write you a letter," he said. "And tell you all about it."

Jean and Kate followed him down the hall, and when they'd gone, Susan stood and said she needed to go to the library, where Nell knew by now she would walk the long hall, looking at nothing. She let her go without a word.

Alone in the room, Nell bent to retrieve the flowers and found that the first of them, the one she'd gotten from the garden, had begun to wilt. She threw it away. The glow of the day had been all erased, and nothing seemed easy or possible anymore.

Desolate, desolate, desolate
The ruined lands
Where children wail, unanswered,
And mothers cry alone
In the barren wood.
   — *Writings of Eyn, Age of Fire, Ganbihar*

*T*he seer of the age of fire had named the bleakest of sounds unanswered weeping. Often the exile thought of the great dispersal, for in that age, exile had come to all. Banishment was an old punishment, far older than the sanctuary. As old as the time of visions, or perhaps, if not so long ago as that, at least of the golden age of sage kings, when the disputes of thinkers sometimes flowed out of the halls of learning and threatened the places of power. But exile then was merely a brief turning away, a rebuke. No madness came with it, no endless term alone. For they lived in a fuller world then, where no one was lost for long, but only wandered a land rich enough to absorb the wayward until his time came to return, forgiven.

Then had come the age of fire, plague, and banishment. With it fear, and rage, and madness.

How was it, the exile thought, that this was the world familiar, that this was the known? Only in the old writings could one find that other, softer time. And what would those ancients have said, seeing the sanctuary and the mountain?

In the night, again, had come dreams. This time, they were no images of thwarted hope, but the sounds of fear and despair. A child lost in a gray dust, one voice calling to another, unheeded. The exile tore from sleep to escape it. But the broken silence of the mountain held in it no memory of the cities and farms of old, waiting to welcome the wanderer. There was nothing, waking or asleep, but desolation, three times over.

Chapter 60

With the brightness of that first flower had also gone Nell's appreciation for lessons. Even when Mistress Leeta brought in the extended stanzas of the chant of seeds, full of the names of ancient plants that had by now been lost, Nell could find no interest in it.

Worse, Max kept his promise, to Jean at least, and next day she came running in with the newest letter, delivered to her by Mistress Dendra herself. She broke the seal and handed it straight to Susan for reading. Nell was so glad to see Susan interested in something besides her long aimless walks that she didn't even protest. They all sat down on the bed to listen.

"Dear Jean,

I'm sorry about yesterday. You might just be the only one who gets how important it is for me to be here, even if it takes longer than we were hoping."

Nell snorted loudly at this, and Susan frowned at her. She cleared her throat pointedly and continued:

"It's not like school back home. That poem I mentioned? That was about a tree. When I read it the first time, I just thought it was a nice little rhyme, but the Guide told me it's not just words, like at home. It's instructions. Then he read it, and all of a sudden I could feel this buzz in the air, that wanting feeling I've noticed before, only much stronger this time. It's like the air's ready to change things, cook something up. I wish I knew what made that work, but I haven't figured it out yet. I will, though! Tur Kaysh says it's just in the nature of things, but of course he hasn't been back home, where it's different. Most days now are like that. We spend them outside in the garden on our own, and yesterday, after he taught me the poem, he held my hand out to the air, told me to close my eyes, and said I could bring the tree to life like that, layer by layer, just following the rhyme. I tried it, and you know, it worked! I felt the air go funny the way it does, and I wanted to open my eyes, but he covered them, said feel the essence of the thing, boy, which like I said is what he calls me. That and son. So I didn't use my eyes anymore, but my mind, and all of a sudden I *could* feel the essence of it, like I was inside it, instead of looking at it from outside. It was a red maple, and I could smell the sap coming as the bark wrapped over it. I could feel the color just under the green as the leaves unfolded. Soon those leaves were tickling my palm. Can you believe it? Remind me, Jean, and maybe I can take you to see my tree one of these days. Isn't it something here? In some ways, it makes more sense than home does. Tell everybody we'll figure it out soon and then we can maybe go back and forth through that window as much as we want. I wouldn't mind coming back for a visit, and you can come with me.

Your brother,
Max"

Susan folded the letter and handed it back to Jean. "Well, that's something, isn't it?" she said to Nell. "He's learning. If he can make a tree, a window can't be far behind, can it?"

But the letter lodged like a piece of dry bread in Nell's throat. For the rest of the day, she couldn't help picturing Max alone with the old man, and that tree rising to meet his waiting hand. Not a single one of the mistresses could do anything like that.

By the next day, she was so disenchanted with everything in the first band that it took her a moment to register that Mistress Meva came in the afternoon not to lecture but to announce a gardening day. Beside Nell, Wista let out a happy squeal, Minna grinned, and even Zirri smiled. They gathered their tools and stood in line waiting for the Shepherdess as she disappeared briefly and returned with a sack for Nell. Nell checked inside and found a spade, a small rake, and several packets of seeds. Annoyance flared. Max wasn't working with a spade.

"To each her own plot of food and of flowers," Mistress Meva said too cheerfully as Nell examined the bundles, wrapped in dried grass that had been woven into small pockets. "You'll have a chance to raise both, because sustenance is nothing without beauty. That's a quote from Tur Lanto, of the second age."

Nell resisted the urge to say something sarcastic. She only rubbed her fingers over the grass parcels. They crackled at her touch; the faint aroma of earth clung to them. She followed the others out across the library floor and into the first garden, ducking beneath the weeping willow on the way to the second ring. They emerged among the metalworkers, and Nell looked to see if she could spot Iana and Neetri in the weavers' booths along the wall. But she was too far away. They crossed the flower beds, full of open-palms and other blossoms she couldn't yet name, and reached the edge of the second garden, where the vegetable patches spread out below the windows on the outer wall of the third band.

There was a plot waiting for her, and despite her mood, it did look inviting, a green square full of promise. She couldn't help wondering if some of the seeds in her packets were open-palms, and what the Shepherdess would say if she told her she had no use for seeds. The thought gave her a brief flush of satisfaction, but she glanced up at the third band and thought of Max and the old man on the other side. The thought dampened her interest in sparring with the Shepherdess, who seemed a little pitiful suddenly.

Besides, the woman had begun the chant of seeds, and the girls were joining in. Its rhythm quieted Nell, and she bent to the earth to begin.

To the soundless voice the seed . . .

The heat rose as they worked, planting, watering, and weeding. Even Wista, who for a time talked happily about the progress of her flowers, soon grew too tired to say anything. Nell thought of the cool shadows of the third garden as the sun burned through her thin dress and drew lines of sweat down the side of her face. Out of the corner of her eye she saw the Shepherdess, red faced, standing in the limited shade of a dogwood, wringing out a small cloth she kept running across her forehead.

"Do you stay here all afternoon while we work?" Nell asked the woman.

"Certainly. Why?"

Nell wiped a mud-stained hand across the back of her neck. "No reason. You just look so hot. I think you ought to drink something."

Mistress Meva smiled. "I would enjoy some more shade."

Nell tugged at a dandelion root she'd just noticed at the edge of her square of land. "Well, we're big enough to come back on our own. Why don't you go in?"

Mistress Meva hesitated, looking from the row of girls up to the wall of the third band and back.

"I shouldn't," she began.

Nell said nothing. She waited, and sure enough, a moment later, the Shepherdess exhaled loudly, waved a tired hand in front of her face, and called, "Minna? You'll lead everyone back when they're done, won't you?"

Minna looked up from the small bush she was pruning. "Certainly, Mistress. Thank you!"

The Shepherdess had not been gone ten minutes when the girls began to rise and dust off. "It's awful hot today," Wista said. "I don't think Mistress Meva would mind if we stopped early. Do you, Minna?"

"Oh, no! She wouldn't want us to keep at it in this heat, I don't think."

One by one they drifted away, until only Nell remained. When they'd gone, she stood and made her way through the passage to the other side of the third band, thinking with some satisfaction that there was more than one way to use your mind to get things done.

Chapter 61

The heat had emptied the scholars' garden.

Across the width of it, Nell caught sight of the iron gate that led into the center, what the Master Watcher had called the heart of the sanctuary. A thick lock hung from it. She turned and peered down the length of the third wall. Here, on its inner face, a series of doors stretched away from her into the distance. She wondered in which thicket she'd find Max's tree. Moving silently along the path, she peered beneath willows and into mossy patches rimmed with bushes, keeping an eye all the while on the closed doors along the third band wall. She had half a mind to sneak in and peek through one of the classroom doors. The scholars in the old days could heal people, Max had said. Even now they could make trees grow from nothing and cloud the valley with mist. They knew about lots of things, none of them hinted at by the mistresses. But the thought of Max and the old man elbowed even that out, and she looked searchingly into the trees, wondering if they were there or in the airy room at the top of the stairs, full of old books and cool sunlight.

She came abreast of the door she'd gone through with the Master Watcher. To her left, a clump of hawthorn and dogwood made a thick screen across the garden. She paused, considering where to go, when she heard Max's voice. A question, though she couldn't quite catch the words.

The old man said something in response, but she could hear only the melody of him. She crept closer and peered into the shadows. There were tall trees past the dogwoods. A fat sycamore with scaly bark, a magnolia. And in a little patch of sunlight, a slim young maple, just about her own height. She stopped, suddenly breathless.

Just steps away, Max stood facing the old man, who sat on a bench with his back to Nell. Max bent toward him, nodding, intent. Nell's heart thumped, and she took a step closer, clinging to the low branches of a dogwood.

That song of a voice came more sharply now. "Concentrate," the old man was saying. "See the color. See the heat. What is its essential quality? It devours. Can you see that?"

Barely nodding, Max fixed his eyes on his own cupped hands. He looked sweaty and tired, but Nell had never seen him more completely absorbed. She could feel the weight of his will in the air, feel that undercurrent of hunger, that buzz of wanting he had written about tugging at her own skin. She almost stepped out to reach for him, the wanting was so strong. She wanted it, too, whatever it was! *Show me!* she thought. *Show me, too!*

She stopped herself just in time, by force of will alone, and hung on instead to the dogwood, her fingernails gouging the smooth bark.

Like a pool of still water suddenly disturbed, the space above Max's raised hands rippled and bent. A flare, a glow, and then, like a bud uncurling, a flame bloomed, throwing a wild spark into the shadows.

Max stared at it. His mouth fell open and then he was grinning, grinning and laughing. "I did it! Fire!"

Behind him the new maple rustled a little in a sudden breeze.

"Good boy! Fine boy!" the old man said in his musical voice. He was laughing, too.

Nell crept away then, her hand smarting where it had caught on a hawthorn twig, and something worse uncoiling in her chest. She slipped back through the thicket of low trees and out into the heat of the gardens, into the hot, uncharged air.

She hurried now, nearly running along the inner band back to the tunnel. She stopped only when she was back at the vegetable garden, staring down at her small sack, her rake, and spade.

They were nothing. Nothing. She could have had them at home. Ordinary metal things, and seeds, and dead earth that didn't listen, or maybe it was that she had nothing to say. She swallowed against the boulder lodged in her throat and held out her hands, thinking of fire, but her mind was too full of the old man, laughing, and the look of delight and wonder on Max's face.

Chapter 62

It was not until later that it occurred to her to puzzle over what she had seen. They could make fire. This was different from the mist, which wrapped itself around the sanctuary, waiting to ensnare unwanted visitors. Fire could do things. She wondered again why the Guide, who Max said hated the Genius so, didn't go after him. If Max could learn to make fire, what could the old man do?

She asked Susan about it after supper as they climbed the stairs and crossed the library footbridge to reach the dorm side of the first ring. Voices echoed in the great canyon of books, so she lowered hers.

"Did you know they could do things like make fire? Does it say that anywhere in any of those books?"

Susan didn't answer right away, which had become normal lately. She only ran her hands over the brass railings and kept walking. Yellow light poured down from the skylights and caught in her hair. Nell frowned and tried again.

"Did you know it, Susan?"

Her sister glanced her way, looking disconcertingly hazy. "Who told you that? The Shepherdess?"

Nell shrugged. "I just heard it."

"It's in the books," Susan said. She motioned to the stacks of them ahead. "But it's just a legend. Do you think they'd be hiding here if they could make fire?"

"It's not a legend!" Nell said, too quickly. Her words bounced back at her from the far wall, and her tone sharpened the look on Susan's face.

"What did you do, Nell?" she asked warningly.

Nell only shrugged again, but Susan kept pushing until she admitted that she might have seen something like it in the third band. "You know, through a window."

Unfortunately, Susan knew better.

"You snuck in there!" she fumed. "Don't try to lie!"

Lie, lie, lie echoed off the books.

"Shh!" Nell snapped.

Susan glared at her but said not another word until they reached their room. Jean and Kate were already there, playing their invented game of stones. They took one look at Susan and scurried into the hall. Nell watched them go with a sinking feeling. Susan had been growing more irritable by the day.

"Well?" she demanded. "Did you go in there or not?"

When Nell didn't answer, Susan's face turned colors.

"What were you doing?" she said. "I thought we agreed you weren't going to break the rules here!"

Nell lifted one shoulder in another half-hearted shrug. "I was just looking."

Her sister ground her teeth. "Just looking! Do you think this is some kind of game, Nell, like you play at home? It's not — I can promise you that. You get caught and what's out there is worse even than what we saw in the city!"

She seemed desperate in a way Nell had not seen before.

Looking at Susan made her wince, and suddenly fear crowded out all her anger at Max and her hunger to be in the third band as she searched her sister's face, trying to understand what was going wrong.

"What's happening to you, Susan?" she asked. "I can get Max if you need him. I can get anybody. Somebody here's going to know how to fix it!"

But Susan only shook her head. She pressed her lips together and shut her eyes, as if the light hurt them.

"There's nothing to fix," she said. "It's just a little ringing in my ears. People get that, you know. And don't change the subject!"

Nell wanted to change the subject. The subject was all wrong in her opinion. But Susan went on, talking more than she had in days, to tell her to leave well enough alone, to leave it to Max, to leave it to Susan herself, for she was sure to find the answer soon, in one of the many books.

Her parting shot was the worst. Putting her head in her hands, Susan tugged at her own hair as if she were trying to rip her skull open and make the sounds she heard stop. "Just *listen*, for once in your life, Nell!" she said.

Nell turned her face to the window. Outside, the mist was invisible, but it was there, up the hill, flowing through the window in the pink evening light like a germ, like a disease. She tried not to be angry. She told herself that Susan wasn't herself. But then, in some ways, she was. Even at home, Susan listened to Max and no one else. Leave it alone. Leave it to Susan and Max, even if Max barely came around anymore and Susan disappeared into herself more and more each day. Nell thought of telling Susan exactly what she thought, but she peeked at her sister's hollow face and kept silent.

Chapter 63

Nell tried to imagine what it was like inside Susan's head. She wondered if the sound that plagued Susan was like the slow *shhhh* of water in a kettle just before it broke into a whistle. Or maybe it was the *sssssss* of a snake. She'd heard that herself once, in a wooded patch near home. She liked to go exploring near the house in a thicket on the edge of the park, where a bed of heart-shaped leaves rose from a coil of woody stems. They were so pretty, those leaves, striped with lines of yellow and green, and she had liked to wade through them, up to her ankles in green and yellow, as the whole bed of them bounced and wiggled and tickled her legs. Walking along once, she'd heard a whisper and stopped. *Sssssss.* There it was, and then gone again, as if she'd imagined it. Curious, she'd separated the leaves with a stick. Among the scribble of stems, a spotted snake with eyes like a cat's lifted its head, hissed at her, and sped away. She'd run, too, the other way. Susan, hearing about it, had laughed and said the expression was true, then: *A snake in the grass.* But Nell said it wasn't. It was a snake beneath the beautiful leaves.

Where the chant of seeds soothed, Susan's words grated.

Tradition, obedience, patience.

Tradition had built the sanctuary. The orchards and the fields, the corn glazed with sunlight, the women singing at the harvest, the smooth-faced scholars, and the children playing in the gardens. Obedience had done that. Patience.

So Susan said.

But tradition kept her from the third band and from the joyful, lilting laughter of the old man. Worse, tradition had spread the mist vile across the valley, and obedience and patience had let it thicken. And now, when Susan spoke, her voice was too loud, as if she were straining to be heard over that hiss, the sound beneath the pleasant wind that swept down from the hills, beneath the happy laughter in the gardens, like a snake beneath pretty, pretty leaves.

"You can't always have your way, Nell. Don't you see that?" Susan pressed her over dinner.

Nell concentrated on chewing. She didn't answer.

"It's better than the city, isn't it?"

When Nell refused to speak, Susan turned to Kate and Jean. "Well, isn't it?"

"Anything's better than the city," Kate said helpfully.

Nell didn't even look up to glare at her.

That night, she tried again to see Max but was told that he was still busy in the third band, though Mistress Dendra had another one of his letters for Jean. Nell carried it back, a chunk of lead in her chest, and when she came into the room, Susan shouted at her and then said she wasn't shouting.

That night Nell lay beneath the window, staring into the moonless night and thinking of that slim maple trembling in the sun, and of the luminous flame dancing over Max's open hands. She rolled over and saw the folded page of Max's letter glowing dully in the starlight. She'd refused to listen when Susan read it to Jean tonight, but now it seemed irresistible. She slipped out of bed, retrieved it, and took it into the hall, where the lamps still lit the way to the bathrooms.

Max's cramped printing covered half the page, and Nell could see that he'd been churning with excitement as he wrote, because the letters slanted across the paper as if they were hurrying.

Dear Jean,

Remember when you asked me when we first got here if this was a dream? We were kind of hoping it was, so we could just wake up and be done. Now I've been thinking that if this is a dream, I hope I never wake up. Yesterday was the best day ever, maybe the best of my life. Most of our time is spent outside now, because Tur Kaysh says we have to hurry and learn with our feet near the roots of the world and our lungs drawing the open air. Today he took me out of the sanctuary, far out into the empty fields on the east end of the valley. It's all flat ground there, where he says the land is breathing, and he had me stand there in tall grass for a long time, not saying anything, until my own breathing slowed down and I could start to hear what he meant. There's a rhythm to everything outside, he said, a hum of life, and underneath it all there's this lightning buzz, like a live wire, sparking. You can only hear it if you stay still for the longest time. I didn't used to have patience for this much standing still, but it's different now. When the Guide's around, I can feel the weight of him, standing there near me. Sometimes, for just a second, it's almost like I've jumped from my own self into him, and I can feel this crush of thoughts and power vibrating there. I wish I could describe it. It's like standing near the heat of a fire and then suddenly being inside the fireball, all crackle and glow. The other thing I notice, lately, is this waiting. I get the idea he's waiting for something. I asked him about it, and he said he is waiting, he's always been waiting, but time is the one thing that can't be changed with will. He seemed very sad when he said that. I hate to see him sad. It's like feeling a fire go out.

Your brother,

Max

Susan had fallen asleep that night with her hands over her head, like someone in a crashing plane. When Nell finished reading, she felt like she was falling out of the sky right alongside her. She clutched the letter and thought about everything Max had said.

Maybe if she could teach Kate and Jean how to make the open-palm flowers, they could go to the old man together and show him, and he would want to teach them, too. Wouldn't someone with a fire inside him want to know about other people who could do things? And if he knew how it was hurting Susan, he'd do something about the mist, too. She was sure he would.

But when she stepped back into the room, she saw Jean asleep with her doll propped on one cheek, its plastic hand tangled in her hair. Kate and Jean were small, still playing with dolls and stones. What help could they be?

She guessed that was how Susan saw her, too. And so

Susan chanted her awful little song of tradition and obedience and patience, and expected Nell to wait the way the little
girls waited — for someone to figure it all out and take them
home.

Well, she was not going to wait. She was not small. Susan
couldn't see that. Max wouldn't. But the old man would, if she
could only show him. . . .

She had kept up her nightly ritual since their time in the
woods. In the dark, sometimes, she found herself reaching
for the blanket that was gone, longing for the smell of home.
She'd lie there with a crater open in her chest, and to fight it,
she'd close her eyes and walk herself through her house, always
starting at the front door and moving on through the rooms,
one by one, as if she'd just come home from a long trip.

But now the hollowed-out longing pushed her toward a
different door. She let her mind's eye wander over the halls
of the first band, out through the gardens, and past the artisan booths. She walked herself through the working gardens
and on, through the boys' school, on, toward the last garden.
She concentrated then, remembering hard. Did the gate have
a lock?

Yes.

She'd seen it, and could see it now, in her mind's eye. A
great iron lock, twice the size of her hand, and surely too heavy
to lift. Nothing she'd seen yet in the sanctuary had a lock, not
even a small one. Not the bedroom she shared with her sisters,
or the classrooms, or even the doors to the third band, where
she knew she'd been forbidden to go.

But the inner garden had a lock.

Max had said even the old man worked only in the third

band. Mistress Meva had said the inner garden held the great library, and the books of mystery.

And the council met there only once a year.

The next morning, she went to class as usual but told Mistress Leeta, halfway through the morning hour, that she hadn't slept well and needed to be excused. Leeta smiled sympathetically and wished her well.

Nell nodded weakly and made her way slowly out of the classroom and down the long hall.

Then she ran.

She skipped through the first garden in the summer sunshine, aware of the heat on her head as she circled to a far door, one she hadn't used before. Here she came out among the woodworkers. She breathed in the sweet sawdust and waved to a man who stood there, saw in hand.

"Checking on my garden!" she called to him, and he smiled and waved back.

She passed through the working gardens, slipped through the tunnel that cut through the third band, and dived into the thickest part of the scholars' garden until she reached the stone wall that ringed the heart of the sanctuary. Careful to keep out of sight behind trees and bushes, she circled the wall until she reached the iron gate.

Just as she'd seen it in her head, it was there: a thick iron lock. She tried to lift it and couldn't. She bent down to examine it, looking for a keyhole. There was none. The lock was a solid ring of metal, twice as wide as her hand.

Nell glanced behind her. The garden was empty in the light morning air.

She turned back to the lock.

Focus, she told herself. *Concentrate.*

She closed her eyes a moment and saw the metal ring again. Her mind wrapped around it, felt its weight, tested its density, measured the smooth warmth of it. This was not like making flowers. The lock existed. How could she change it?

She thought about what the Shepherdess had told the girls about their gardens. Everything, she'd said, was made of something else. Plants of water and soil, sun and seed.

It had seemed obvious when she said it, but now Nell reconsidered her words. The lock, too, was made up of things. What?

Nell remembered something Max had said once when he was trying to show her she knew nothing about science. He'd asked her if she thought he was full of holes. Of course not, she'd told him, imagining a person leaking like a balloon. But he'd said then that everything was full of holes, and hard things were just made up of tiny pieces packed a little closer. Even people, he'd said.

Now she thought: *Even iron.*

Instead of focusing on the metal, she thought about the holes. She pushed at them with her mind, so many pockets of air, empty as soap bubbles, expanding into space.

And they opened.

With a clang, a piece of metal fell to the ground. Her eyes jerked open, and she looked down to find the lock at her feet, dissolving like sand.

Chapter 64

The central garden was more densely planted than any of the others. Shade trees and thick bushes lined its narrow paths, shielding the domed structure at its center. Everything here had been laid out with elaborate care. Beneath a maple sat an iron bench with carved feet, its back a metal tapestry of winding vines and flowers. Another was engraved with faces, metallic silhouettes that sparkled in the morning light.

Nell hurried past them. Ahead of her, she could see the white stones of the building called the heart, the domed structure she'd seen as they walked through the mist.

When she reached it, she realized it was taller than she'd imagined. Its stones were the white of sun on cloud, its door overlaid with a frame of hammered gold set against rose-colored wood.

It had no knob, but a single gold ring, as big around as a young tree, hung from the center of the door. After a moment's hesitation, Nell reached up and pulled.

The door swung out with a whiff of cool air full of complicated smells: old books, dust, wood, wax, and other things she couldn't identify. Nell stepped in and dragged the door closed behind her. Despite the age of the place, and the puff of dust that rose when she closed the door, the wood swung silently on its hinges.

Nell blinked in the sudden shadows. She stood in a small foyer, where the white stones of the building gleamed coldly in the walls, reflecting dimly off the polished floor. Light seeped in around the doorframe and ahead, around the edges of another set of doors that ran from floor to ceiling. She pushed through these and blinked. Here, she stood beneath a rainbow, color pouring down on her from above. The dome she'd seen from a distance arched overhead, full of stained glass, skylights that tinted the sunlight striping the tiled floors and the table at the center of the room.

As the Shepherdess had said, the walls were full of tapestries. She stopped at a familiar scene — the man emerging from the pool. Where the needlework over the desk in her room showed only the man, the bright pool, a few trees, and the sky, this one had been rendered so that she saw the scene like someone standing on a hill. A rich, strange wood ran from one end of the piece to the other, layered with sunlit young trees thick with apple-green leaves and cedars woven with malachite and onyx. The primeval wood was full of glinting shadows, but above them, the weaver had laced the sky with sapphire and pearl and flecked silver. Shafts of yellow-silk sunlight streamed to meet the water and the joyful, vibrant figure rising from it with a glittering splash.

Nell thought she had never been in a room more beautiful. *So this*, she thought, *is what they meant by the heart.* A heart should look this way, lovely with color and tinted, falling light, with a thick oval table of polished red wood and embroidered chairs, with rose-wood doors and tapestries like these on the walls.

She moved around the table, looking from one scene to the

next: a broad-shouldered old man marching through defeated warriors toward a tent where a woman stood half concealed, her face etched with joy; people flowing from the gates of a gray city into an amber and green field, wheat bent on either side of them. She rested her hands on the backs of the chairs as she circled the table. Polished cherry, the color of the table and with needlework cushions, they stood five on one side and six on the other, with a larger chair at the head, its arms carved with images of corn and wheat and grapes and flowers.

The last chair, at the foot of the table, was out of place. It was pulled away and faced the wall. Absently, she ran a hand along it as she passed. She had come almost all the way around the room when a cold spot stopped her. There were no windows except the ones above, and she held still, clutching the back of the last chair a minute, in case the outer door had been opened. But it was closed. Still, she felt chilled.

Her heart pounded as she took a step forward. Now she felt like she'd swallowed ice, so that the cold reached down her throat into her belly. It was coming from the door nearest the foot of the table. Curious, she pushed it open. The cold worsened. It was not the brisk, sharp air of a winter's day but the dank, awful stillness of a cellar that had been shut up too long, full of scurrying sounds and without light.

The room on the other side was dim, lit from above with the edges of the stained-glass skylights that crossed over the threshold. Once she stepped through the door, the cold was bearable. There were warm spots here. Unlike the richly appointed center room, this one was empty except for a long narrow table resting along the side wall. Several objects sat on it, clustered there in the colored shadows.

A narrow, dangerous-looking ivory knife, etched from hilt to tip with strange figures, rested on a stone that dripped water steadily into a shallow dish and a drain that Nell saw led to the wall. Beside it a dirty canvas sack, and next to that a branch in full flower, a fragrant cutting from a tree. With a pang of alarm, she realized that Mistress Meva must not have known what she was talking about, saying no one came here. The branch was freshly cut!

Abruptly, she turned and hurried from the room, the cold intensifying as she moved away from it, like a dog snapping at her heels. She darted back to the center room and then to the next chamber in the circle.

The library.

As the other room had thrummed with cold, this one was warm and sweet with leather and old paper and the richness of oil lamps. So many of them stood in the corners and against the bookcases that she wondered how the room hadn't gone up in flames long ago.

She turned to shut the heavy door, anxious to put the thick wood between her and that crowded space next door full of the cold she had roused. But she realized she'd be in the dark if she did. No edge of skylight peeked over the doorframe above and no window broke the line of books on the walls. Nell searched for a match, a bit of flint, something to light the lamps.

There was nothing. If only she could make fire, as Max had!

But why not? Opening the lock had emboldened her. She could almost feel that sizzle of electricity Max said was in the air. Carefully, she sat down across from the largest lamp, a branched candelabra, oil and wicks ready for lighting. What had the old man said of fire? It devoured.

She'd known plenty of heat in the long walk in the mountains, too much of it in the tiled room. She remembered the feeling of being suffocated by it, heat taking the air she was meant to breathe. That was devouring, she thought. Heat swallowed the air. She was suddenly aware of it in the room, rising off her skin, warm in her breath. Could she use that? She imagined pulling it to her, a churning, gathering pressure. She'd seen a flower in her mind, and it had unfolded in her hand. Now she saw a bright, flickering spark, ready to ignite the lamp's golden oil, red blooming in the shadow.

A warm gust blew across her face, and the central lamp blazed up, bubbles surging in the oil as it fed the new fire.

The room was alight.

Chapter 65

A man is a thing unformed, edgeless as water,
Ever-changing as cloud,
Soft clay at the base of the creek
To be trod underfoot and remade.
Only with the armor of thought
Does the shaped join the shaper,
Sharing in the gifts of the making.
Rise, my sons, and become solid as the mountain,
Strong as the onward rushing sea
That pounds the sand
To remake the edge of the world.

Such says the mind that made all.
Such is our gift and our joyous call.

At last, the books satisfied Nell. She had pulled out a fragile old volume called *The Mind of the Universe* and turned its pages, silky with age. Words bounded from the page, and she felt like a person who had gone to sleep working at a problem and woken from a dream that made everything clear. But, like a dream, the meaning was as fragile as cobwebs, and she had to grasp it carefully, slowly, only half understanding.

As the newborn bird is blind,
As the fledgling falls from the nest,
So are we
Rising from the dark,
Untaught and unprotected.
But we, too, may soar into the light and above the wind
If we force open our eyes
And spread our arms to the sky.

Her heart leaped, reading it. But she couldn't understand exactly. At some points, the passages seemed like a conversation, one person to another, an argument.

And yet beware, for we are
But creatures of thought and change,
And we dance the line
Uneasily.

There was that. She wondered if it had been written when the change came. Then another:

The wise know a great secret:
We are no bird
But a fanged, wild thing,
Crouching,
Waiting
To return.

She guessed it had already returned. A few pages later, the passages spoke of the language of creation. Nell put her finger on that word. She looked up at the lamp, blazing before her.

What else could she create? she wondered.

"Barriers are small things to one who understands," she read. "Take care, seeker, for in this, there is danger as well as joy. In all things balance. Where there is illumination, there is also darkness."

Barriers, she thought. *Barriers are what keep us here.* Something held the window back. Could this book show her a way to break through?

She stifled a desire to flip the pages, searching. The book was old and fragile.

Then she heard something. A sound, in the center hall.

Someone was coming.

Chapter 66

Nell slammed the ancient book shut and hurried to the bookcase, where she wrestled it into place, sending up a cloud of old dust that made her long to cough.

But she swallowed against it. Someone was in the center hall. More than one person. Footsteps echoed across the floor. She had no time. Where could she hide?

There was no place to go. The table offered no shelter. The walls were all books.

And the lamp was lit.

Before she could move to snuff it out, they were there — the Master Watcher and the Guide.

She had meant to surprise the old man. She had hoped — she had expected — to see the look on his face, the look he had given to Max, given also to her. Her eyes darted again to the light, hoping he would understand what that meant, hoping to see the expression on his face change the way the books said things changed — from dark to light.

The change came, but it was only from surprise to horror. The Guide looked from the burning lamp to Nell, and she wondered how she had ever yearned to go to him.

He was terrifying.

He stood a step ahead of the Master Watcher, a tall old man with rigid posture and a great mass of white hair swept back from his forehead. Something radiated from him now, but it was not love or joy or welcome.

It was power, and anger. His fierce, bright eyes were alive in a way she had not seen before, or expected, in an old man, to see. They burned with rage.

Nell looked from the Guide to the Master Watcher. Lan looked smaller, suddenly, standing almost stooped in the doorway. His face was drawn, half furious and half afraid. Seeing that fear in the Master Watcher's face made Nell quake more than his anger would have. But she could not look at the Master Watcher long; the old man drew her so. His shoulders trembled with fury as he stared at her and then the lamp, his mouth twisted and his brows coming down over those frightening too-bright eyes.

"The exile sent you," he growled. "As I suspected. *Sent* you."

Nell took a step back, wiping her sweating hands on the sides of her dress. The music was all gone from his voice. It grated harsh in her ears.

"Who do you mean? What are you talking about?"

"No shame, even now? Sending children! Are we taken for fools, then?"

Nell didn't know what he wanted from her. Couldn't he see what she'd done? Where was his laughter? Where was his praise?

"No one sent me," she said, trying to keep her voice steady.

The old man took a step into the room, and Nell fell back

against the books. He approached the lamp, staring into its fire. "Rebel," he growled. "What did the exile teach you?"

Nell looked at him, not understanding. The man seethed, and Nell flinched, trying to be ready for the blow.

Behind him, the Master Watcher whispered, "It's only rumor, master. No one is certain the exile exists."

At the sound of his voice, hesitant, placating, Nell looked his way. Could he help her? Would he?

She couldn't tell. His face was strange — she saw fear there, but something else. Hope.

The Guide half turned, and the Master Watcher drew back as if slapped.

"Was it you alone? Or the others, too?" the old man demanded.

She shook her head, trying to think past the knocking of her own pulse in her ears.

"No one even knows I'm here! I came alone!"

At that, the hope disappeared from the Master Watcher's face like a light extinguished. Now Nell could see nothing but fear. The Master Watcher inched closer to the old man.

"The girl said it was this one only. Not the others. No need to take the innocent."

The Guide flinched. "If they *are* innocent."

The younger man nodded. "The boy —"

"Never mind the boy! I know the boy!"

Nell looked from one to the other.

"I only came because I wanted to study, too," she said. "That's all. I wasn't hurting anything. I can do things! I'll show you!"

A fresh wave of anger rippled across the old man's face, and even the Master Watcher glared at her.

"Ingrate!" the old man spat. "Did we welcome you here so you could spy on us? So you could sully this place with your shameful, grasping boldness? Here? Here in the very heart of the sanctuary?"

He stopped himself, narrowing his eyes. He turned to the Master Watcher, but when he spoke, it was as if no one else existed. "There's no need for anger," he said. And this time, his voice was cool. "Calm in all things. The punishment is clear."

Nell grew suddenly cold. Punishment?

The Master Watcher said nothing. Lips tight, he watched the old man.

"Child," the old man said, and his voice was gentle now, as seductive as when she'd first seen him in the round room. She felt the stir of that voice inside her and leaned forward. But the old man continued, "As Guide and Protector of this sanctuary, I pronounce the punishment upon you."

He looked at her out of his creased face, then raised a finger and pointed at her. She cringed.

"Exile," he said. "For now and always. Exile."

Chapter 67

They gave her no time to tell the others. When the old man made his pronouncement, the Master Watcher came for her, taking her by the arm and whisking her from the room. He dragged her out to stand beneath the rainbow of light in the center hall, while the old man stepped past them, disappearing briefly through the door where the strange cold had chilled and tugged at Nell. Now an icy blast barreled from it. Nell's legs nearly buckled and she trembled. The old man emerged, a grim smile on his face, and shut the door.

The Master Watcher dragged her from the domed building and the garden as a finger of cold — terrible, bone-freezing cold — followed her into the summer air.

She was too cold, too cold and confused and terrified even to struggle, too stunned to gather her thoughts enough to try to resist. And then they were beyond the walls of the first band, and he was dragging her up the hill, toward the invisible line. The old man walked behind them, the old man and the knife of ice that even now was whittling through Nell's skin, carving its way into her bones so that her teeth chattered and her hands shook uncontrollably.

For the first time, Nell could understand why Susan cringed at the mention of the mist, why the deep furrows had formed beneath her eyes, why she could no longer read or sleep. Through the terror and the cold, she could feel something more — a weight against her back, as if the power she'd felt drawing her to the old man and now pushing her away was gaining size and voice as it thrust her toward the mist. And she could hear now what Susan heard, hear the buzzing and the whispers. She could hear it from behind, as the old man advanced, and from ahead, in the quickly gathering vapor taking shape in the clear air of the hillside.

Abruptly, the Master Watcher stopped, and the old man was upon her. She looked swiftly at Lan and saw that despite his firm grip on her, he was pale, shaken. He looked once at the Guide, a pleading in his face. But the old man was implacable, and the Master Watcher fell back. The Guide seized her then and drew her toward him, piercing Nell with those terrible eyes.

You, she heard, *sought to break the patterns of the world. Desire drove you; now let it take you.*

Nell squirmed. The man's lips did not move. His voice penetrated her head, shouted inside her mind. It was then she began to fight. She tried to pull away from him, tried to summon enough focus to fling him off her, but he gripped her like a machine, his face set, his long legs propelling them both forward as his words drilled into her thoughts. *Push him away!* she screamed furiously to herself. *Run!* But she couldn't.

Desire, animal desire, she heard. The man's voice whirled in her head, clouding it, confusing her. *The passion of the beast, who respects nothing and knows nothing! Become, then, what you wished! Satisfy your passions; let desire, let the animal, take you back!*

No!

She shouted it in her mind, struggling, writhing against his voice. Visions of beasts, of the city, of the terrible, savage things she had seen rushed into her mind, and she fought against them, fought with thoughts of home, of her parents, of their voices, of — *All are animal. The beast lives in us. Listen to it. Let it claim you,* the voice commanded.

He was moving swiftly, on up toward the mist, faster than seemed possible, and a wind rushed past them, blowing in her ears. It made the terrible cold harder to bear. Her thoughts and vision blurred, and it seemed, as she struggled, that there were others now, behind the old man, a silent platoon, pushing her out with their very eyes.

Welcome it. You desired it, and now it reaches for you. It is you. Return. Return, rebel, to the beast.

They had reached the mist, thick now, as substantial as a white wall, loud with the echo of the old man's voice, and the voices of others — terrible voices, jeering, calling, magnetic.

The hillside rose abruptly beneath her, and the Guide threw her to the ground. Gasping, she looked up in time to see the mist gather like smoke.

"Wait!" she shouted.

There was no one. She staggered to her feet and tried to follow. *Susan!* she thought. *Max!*

But she couldn't be heard. Voices howled through the mist, taunting her.

Try! Try! she pleaded with herself, blindly groping, trying to get her bearings. Her hands were stiff now with the cold, her feet like clubs. She stumbled.

Susan had opened the mist. She could open it, too. She had to open it!

Nell pressed her numb hands to her eyes, then her ears. The roaring would not stop. It howled from all sides, jabbing at her, hurting. She swayed and staggered backward.

Animal! it screamed. *Exile!*

The sound seemed to crawl inside her. It echoed behind her eyes, a dizzying, hateful wail that she couldn't push away. It choked her, and she realized she was sobbing, gasping for air that wouldn't come. She fell to her knees, holding the earth for reassurance that something was real. Something was solid. But her fingers were frozen and useless, unfeeling. The world spun.

The mist swirled white around her. Now patches of darkness marred it, blotches in nothingness, holes and passages into more nothingness. It yawned before her, and she rolled, choking, gasping, beneath the terrible landscape of emptiness, a pit sucking at her from every direction.

Exile! it howled. *Ingrate! Beast! Beast!*

The black moved overhead, a blank wave, a hole, an abyss.

And then there was nothing.

◇ BOOK FOUR ◇

KATE

Chapter 68

There is a time, in the hour before dawn, when the heaviest darkness drains away, leaving merely gray. It is the effect, if not the coming, of the light. Kate, never before having spent many full nights awake, hadn't know this, but her time in the woods had taught her the night's various shades: its twilight blue, midnight black, and that final uncertain lack of tint as night makes way for day.

It was in this gray hour before first light, the air cool and smelling of wet, that she found herself outside the sanctuary walls, searching.

Panic had bloomed in her chest when Zirri brought news of Nell's disgrace. The girl was gloating; Kate could see the hateful joy she took in her news. She'd rushed to get to them, coming before Mistress Meva could, before any of the others.

"She broke the biggest rule," Zirri had smirked. "She went to the center."

Immediately, Kate had looked to Susan. Susan, who had grown sick these last days, her face blank in a way that made Kate feel hollow and jittery. But still, Susan would know what to do. It was an emergency.

And she did. She'd turned on the girl, her eyes suddenly focused, impatient. She had no time for Zirri. Even Zirri could see it.

"Where did they take her?" she demanded.

The girl pursed her lips and shrugged.

"How should I know? The old man said she was an exile now and that we shouldn't think of her anymore."

Susan frowned, and Kate's spirits lifted. Susan would fix everything!

"You *know*," she had said, moving closer to the girl. "You know because you told on her, and you'll tell me now or you'll be sorry." She said it so fiercely that Zirri backed up, knocking into Jean.

"Outside the walls," Zirri said. "That's all. I saw them take her outside the walls. But she isn't there anymore," she added. "I know that, too."

The Shepherdess hurried in, and Zirri made a swift exit.

Mistress Meva was tearful when she sat down, and Kate wanted to pull away when the woman took her hand. She acted as if someone had died. But she was talking about Nell!

"I'm sorry, children," she'd said. "Truly I am. But some are lost, you know. Some don't know how to accept the gift we have here. Your friend understood what was expected, I thought. Didn't she? I can't make sense of it. Why did she go?"

"Our sister," Kate had whispered.

But the woman didn't seem to hear. She wasn't really asking questions, after all. She was only trying to put Nell away, to finish with her. Kate saw it and looked to Susan.

And Susan did demand to know where Nell had been taken. She asked over and over as Kate winced at the uncomfortable feel of the Shepherdess's sweaty hand pressing hers. Mistress Meva had nothing to offer. Exile was the absolute punishment, she'd said. The end. Terrible. None had ever returned.

By the time the woman had gone, Kate's heart was smacking the inside of her chest so hard that her dress shivered with the force of it, and Susan, furious, set out to find Max. She told them to stay in the room, but Jean, sensibly, started bawling, and so Susan fumed and took them along, running up the stairs to the boys' section.

They'd just stepped into the thickly carpeted hall there, where the wall hangings were full of long-faced old men, when a group of young scholars came charging at them. The Master Watcher stormed behind them, his eyes bulging. Kate cringed and yanked Susan back a half step, sure he would raise his hand to strike her. But with a shudder, the man stopped himself and only told them acidly that Nell's fate was a warning to them — the last.

Jean had burst into fresh tears, and Kate had stood there, thinking that he'd confirmed something for her. People talked more with their faces than they did with their mouths; she'd always known it. Known also that the two said opposite things sometimes and that faces were by far the more reliable.

From the start, she'd worried about the Master Watcher. His smooth face had been a nice shock, and it had almost made her want to trust him, but he wore a tight expression, and his eyes were nervous, suspicious. He watched Max too much, and Susan even more, and he was afraid. All the time, afraid. It had made Kate afraid herself. Even at home, she'd noticed that frightened eyes too often came with angry voices. Adults who were so afraid were dangerous, and to be avoided.

And yet she had seen, too, how Max willingly followed

him. It had confused her, worried her, as Max had gone away with the nervous-eyed man and Susan had disappeared into herself. Now she knew that Max had been mistaken. It made her more afraid than ever.

"We want to see our brother," Susan had said to the man. "You can't keep him from us."

But he could.

"Your *brother!*" He nearly spat the words. "You'll see him when he's ready to see you. Now you'll leave. And don't try to come back this way. We'll be watching."

The boys had pushed them back then, and the man did nothing to stop them. They nearly tripped Susan, and she'd retreated at last, red faced, taking Kate's hand with such force that Kate nearly yelped.

"What will we do?" she asked Susan when they'd returned to the room. "Nell's outside alone! Do you think she's hurt?"

She didn't want to say the other thing, what Nell had told them about. She pressed her hands together to keep them from shaking and watched her older sister.

Susan slumped on the bed. "I don't know," she said quietly. "I don't know what they did to her." She put her hands to her eyes, then her forehead. "We're not the same as the people here. We don't change. And we walked through the mist. Maybe it's okay. I don't know."

I don't know! Maybe! The words hit Kate like a slap.

"But *you* hear the mist, don't you?" Jean asked. "Nell said it's hurting you!"

Nell had been right. Kate could see it. Kate could see it. . . .

Susan shook her head. "Just let me think. I have to think. If I could only let Max know — he understands how they do things in this place! Maybe I could send him a message, and then we'd go after her. . . ." Her voice trailed off and she began pacing. Kate started to ask another question, but Susan refused to talk further.

"Let me think!" was all she'd say. "I just need a minute to think!"

Kate watched Susan late into the night as she moved from window to door, restless, sleepless. Kate must have fallen asleep watching, because then the dream came. No matter how many times she had them, she could not get used to the nightmares. This one was terrible, and new. In it, Nell sat in a gray fog, calling their names, shivering and rocking as the cloud pressed in around her.

Kate woke with a start.

Susan had fallen asleep fully clothed. She lay on the end of Jean's bed, head on her hands, curled up like a much littler girl. Kate went and stood beside her, looking into her face. Even in sleep, it was creased with worry; she had the look of someone tired, someone forced to run with no more strength left to do it.

For as long as Kate could remember, Susan had been there, knowing everything, taking care, making it all better.

But now Kate stood in the dark room and saw that her sister didn't know. And Kate realized then that Susan would wait too long.

Chapter 69

She had crept from the room, from the building. Crept through the open gates and out, past the trees and up onto the hill. She didn't see the mist, but she knew it would be there if she tried to turn back. So she didn't. She climbed as the slim new moon set in a charcoal sky and the darkness seeped away, and the dawn came.

And she stood, finally, at the edge of the woods, in the light. Kate saw no sign of her sister.

It was then that the fear hit. The nightmare that had propelled her out of bed had long since faded, and the climb had been enough to keep her from thought, from worry. Now, as she looked into the vastness of trees — the forest she knew to go on much farther than the eye could see — she felt small, and alone. Nell could be anywhere, or nowhere. Kate might walk for days and miss her. She would be alone, just herself, in the endless woods. And then — Kate tried not to think it, but the thought came — Nell might not be Nell anymore. She might find — not Nell, but something else.

Kate clutched at a nearby trunk and tried to think. Susan would be calm. Max would have a plan. What did she have?

Nothing.

"Nell?" she called, her voice faint beneath the giant trees. "Nell?"

She took a step forward, into the woods. "Nell! I came for you!"

She couldn't think of anything to do but call, so she did, over and over, until her voice failed her. At last she sat down, slumped on a mossy root, and let the tears blur the image of the trees and the silent, great, answerless forest.

And she heard someone.

Surely it was not Nell.

A desperate, soft mewling came from the hillside. Kate stood, shaking, and walked toward it.

Almost hidden by the growth, yards from where she had passed, climbing, her sister lay sprawled in the tall grass. Kate ran to her and turned her over.

"Nell? Nell!" She shook her.

Nell's eyes were closed, her face tight and pasty. Mud stained her cheek, and Kate saw it in her nails, as if she'd been digging with her fingers, clawing at the earth. She whimpered — a strange, unfamiliar sound; Nell's voice but not Nell's voice, the familiar turned alien and awful, as if someone had lodged some pitiful animal in her throat.

"Nell! It's me; it's Kate! I've come to get you. It's okay, Nell! Wake up!"

But Nell would not wake up. She shivered and twisted, eyes shut tight, the strange, broken animal noise shuddering from behind her closed lips, a ragged sound, dry as autumn leaves.

Susan, Kate thought. *Help me! I can't! I need you!* She could not do it alone. *Could not. Could not.*

She took Nell by the shoulders, pulled at her, and Nell, limp, whimpered again. If she could only get her down the mountain, Kate thought, back to Susan, she would be all right. Susan would know how to fix her.

But as she pulled at Nell, dragging her a few feet down the slope, she felt the air change. Around her the mist gathered, and the breeze began to whisper words just on the edge of hearing, brushing past her like so many moths, weightless, repulsive.

Nell shrieked. Her body convulsed, jerking itself from Kate's grasp, rolling into the grass, writhing. Kate ran to help her, but Nell flailed, the awful, half-mute wail sounding from her. Then she stopped and was still.

"Nell!"

Her sister was not breathing. Kate rolled her onto her back and saw the faint tinge of blue on her lips, her damp skin going waxy. Air! She needed air! From some long-dormant place, she recalled her father telling her about breathing, about pushing air into empty lungs and saving, saving—

Kate jerked Nell's chin down and covered her sister's open mouth with her own, blowing with all her might. Air. Air. *Breathe!*

Nell coughed and gasped, drawing breath, and around her, Kate saw again the mist, the hideous cloud come to attack. Nell could not be near the mist. It was hurting her, killing her!

With all her might, Kate jerked her sister up the slope, scrambling to get away from the vapor, even as it pursued them. *Up! Up!* she screamed in her head, wishing she could send Nell flying backward, far, far from the awful thing, the haze, with its whispering, terrible sounds.

"Susan!" she cried aloud. "Help me!"

And then Nell did seem lighter. Kate pulled at her with renewed strength. She could see she was outrunning the cloud now, nearing the tree line above. *Susan!* Kate thought with sudden joy. *She's come! She's here! She's helping me!* She pulled Nell over the ridge of the mountain, reached the shadow of the trees, and looked back to see the mist disappearing over the edge, drawn back like a receding wave.

A tremor of relief shook her, and Kate looked around, trying to find Susan. Where was she?

"Susan?" she called. No one answered. She turned toward the woods, searching. "Susan!"

Nell whimpered and coughed on the ground.

"Susan!"

Someone answered then, but it was not Susan. It was a woman with coppery skin and straight dark hair pulled back in a braid, who emerged from behind a tree without a sound. She wore a patched and faded green dress with a large front pocket like the one Liyla had worn. The pocket bulged with rolls of papers, a spade, and a small rake. The woman looked from Kate to Nell, lying strangely there beside her on the moss.

"Child!" she said. Her voice shook. "You need help."

It was not a question. But the woman waited, keeping her distance, until Kate nodded.

Despite the shock in her voice, in her eyes, she had the look of someone used to waiting. She glanced at the spot where the mist had slipped backward into the valley, took a breath, and turned back to look searchingly at Kate a moment, before dropping her eyes to Nell.

"Can you help her?" Kate asked. The quiet face leaned

over her sister, and the woman rested the tips of her fingers on Nell's cheek, brushed hair from Nell's eyes. Nell no longer whimpered. She seemed asleep, but Kate feared she was more than that. Mutely, the woman nodded. She lifted Nell, stood, and turned to walk deeper into the wood as Kate ran to follow, hoping Susan was just out of sight behind them.

*D*reams had woken and emerged into the dawn. Children through the mist, children now! Devoured, hunted, exiled. Surely the sky should crumble and the mountain fall before this, but they didn't. They never changed, despite horror, despite heartbreak.

And yet the child lived, unchanged, and here was another, walking through the wood, the cloud of her hair catching the light. It was this she had seen in dreams. Laysia stumbled at the thought, nearly losing her grip on the other one, and the young girl took her arm.

"You okay? I know she's heavy. Susan helped me before."

Her words were unfamiliar, some of them, and the name Laysia did not know, but the sense of it came through. She found her voice.

"No, I'm all right. Forgive me. We're close now, and then I'll lay her down."

She had not asked the child's name. She could barely ask it now, lest the two evaporate with the audacity of the question. It was such a sweet dream, such a vivid one! If this was madness, how much better it was than she had imagined. And yet there was no help in pretending, now she'd thought of it.

"Child," she said, trying to keep the catch from her voice, "what do they call you?"

"Kate," she said in her pretty way. She walked along, solid as ever, a real flesh-and-blood child who had emerged from a dream. "And this is Nell."

Chapter 70

They walked through the forest together, Kate trying to keep track of the way. She memorized the direction of the rising sun over her shoulder, the tangled path, the place, somewhere below and to her left, where the sanctuary lay.

The woman cradled Nell like a baby. Kate could feel how careful she was, as if Nell were made of china and might break with a wrong step. She looked at Kate, too, strangely, and Kate worried that she had misunderstood something, done something wrong. She didn't hear people right sometimes. She didn't like to be with this stranger alone on the mountain, without Susan or Max or anyone to tell her what it all meant.

But Nell needed help. And Susan must have turned back, once she'd gotten them up the hill, to get Max and Jean, maybe. So she hurried beside the woman as the trees thickened and they moved away from the valley. The sun unfurled yellow ribbons through the branches and gathered in the leaves like white pearls.

After a time, the woman said quietly, "Who is she, to you, that you came for her?"

She had a smooth, narrow face, and her expression was hidden in the shadows and sudden glare of the morning forest.

"My sister," Kate whispered.

"Your sister."

She said it differently from the way the Master Watcher had. Not as if she disbelieved it, but as if it made her sad. Kate worried that maybe Nell wouldn't get better.

"What should I call you?" she asked the woman, trying to banish the thought.

"Laysia" came the answer. Then the woman shook her head and laughed a little.

"What?"

Laysia moved right, striking deeper into the wood.

"It's been a long time since I said that name. It feels strange to say it."

Everything she said was hard to understand. Did she have another name, then? If Susan would only come, she'd explain it. As it was, Kate said, "Do they call you something else?"

Again, that laugh that sounded too much like crying.

"Oh, yes, but that's not what I meant."

Kate sighed. Too often life felt this way, people full of puzzles. They talked too fast or in riddles, and by the time Kate had unwound all the knots of their speech, they'd gone on to something else and she'd missed the point. It was why she kept quiet in school most of the time. It was why she liked to stand next to Susan, or her mother, in crowds, because they would know to look at her and whisper what it meant.

Neither of them was here. Kate cleared her throat. "I don't think I understand."

The woman lifted her head and turned at that, and Kate saw that there was no meanness in her face. The laugh hadn't been at her expense.

"Forgive me," she said. "I've been a long time alone. I'm unused to conversation. I've lost the art of it."

"Oh."

"It's what happens in exile. But you gave this one a great gift, following her. You didn't let her be alone."

Exile. Now, that was a word Kate knew.

*I*t was as if she had stumbled into the wood where the first had emerged from the pool of life, from the waters of beginning, and seen the full expanse of it, that wood of dreams and legends, that place from which all the stories had come. It would be strange, yes, but familiar, as this child was familiar, as they both were. And yet strange — so strange! Not in look or manner, but in the very essence of them. Laysia studied the child as they walked along together through the brightening wood. She clasped the older one, the mist-hounded girl, to her chest and tried to puzzle out the meaning of such a mix of difference and sameness. What was it?

And then a memory came to her, of another day on the mountain, years past. Midmorning in a brilliant autumn it had been, and she, still new alone and hopeful, had heard the sound of the rising mist and followed it all the way back to the ridge overlooking the valley, so close she could feel the weight of the cloud in the air, so close she must cringe at the scream of the man it drove to the ground. So close she could see it as she'd not seen it when it came for her. Soft, it appeared, like the cotton that flew from the trees in spring. Soft even as the color dampened, and it was a vague, blurry, terrible thing, falling on him. Frozen, she watched it drop and sink into his skin, and covered her ears against wails that called back the sensation of the thing as it had reached through her, weaving itself around muscle and bone. She had thrown it off. He could not. Like water drawn into the soil, it found its way and took him.

She had never come so close again, until today, when the call of the child drew her. There again was the smothering cloud, there

*again the writhing victim. It descended upon her, but where in
time past the mist flowed unchecked, now it pounded at the child,
a wave against the jetty, an invader rattling an iron gate. It could
not enter. In the first, stunned moments on the ridge, she had not
marked what she did now. Pursued, hurt, near broken, the child
had not been taken.*

    *Reluctantly, Laysia opened her mind to the mist. She could
hear it, always, its ugly whispering, a noise beneath all the noise of
the wood, of the day and the night. But it was like a pain grown
dull, with the mind turned from it. Its sting had subsided to an
ache that could be set aside. Now she did not ignore it. She did
not push it away. She let the pain stab at her. She listened. And
through the miserable spasm came a strange, unfamiliar note:
outrage. Outrage, fury, and frustration.*

Chapter 71

When the sun had inched a fraction higher in the morning sky, they reached a clearing where a low stone wall kept a crowded garden from spreading into the forest. Like the hillside that ran into the valley, it was full of everything — plump yellow squash peeking beneath wide leaves, vines full of small tomatoes that tumbled over the wall, studded with red and green and orange fruit, a line of fringed corn, like a row of tall women standing along the back, even a few grapevines that leaned over the stones in the far corner. Behind it, half hidden by the corn, stood the house. It was a stout little cottage made of stone and wood with a chimney sprouting from one side of the roof. The rest of it was all topped with a fleecy curtain of moss that hung over the eaves. Even from the outside, Kate could tell it was a light-filled place, because every wall held an open window. Beneath each of these were flowers — delicate open-palms, like the ones Nell had filled their room with in the sanctuary, and others Mistress Elna had showed her in the first garden: the bell-like dangles in their many colors, the yellow-and-purple bee-sweet, the red-and-orange dawnbuds. As they neared the house, the morning air thickened with the smell of them — vanilla and mint and honey.

The woman used her hip to push open the front door of the house. Before Kate saw the inside of the cottage, she caught a whiff of books mixing with the scent of flowers, and so was disposed to like the place. Like Liyla's house, it had a large main room with a fireplace and a smooth old table with sturdy chairs, but unlike Liyla's, it was a sunny, airy space, brightened by a soft woven rug and crowded with books. Shelves of them stretched up into the rafters and had been hung above the windows made up of polished boards. Books sat in stacks beside several cushioned chairs and in a small basket near the woven rug; books rested on a side table beside covered dishes and stood on a cart beneath the plates and cutlery and an old varnished pitcher with a chipped handle. At the sanctuary, they'd said the books in the great library were only a fraction of the ones that had been before, in the old times. Kate guessed maybe the others were crammed into this small, sweet-smelling cottage.

There was not enough time for looking just then. The woman moved directly to the back wall, where three doors led to other rooms, and pushed at the right-most of them. Kate followed her into a small bedroom with a wide bed. She set Nell gently down upon it.

Nell sighed softly, and Kate felt her shoulders relax at the sound of it. In that small sound, she could hear again the sister she knew. Nell burrowed into the bedclothes, her face half in shadow. But Kate could see that the tension had gone from it. A crisscross of morning light, streaming through the window over the bed, fell across her still form.

She would have liked to sit down, even lie down near Nell, and wait for her to wake up, but the woman put a finger to her lips and motioned her out. When she'd closed the door behind them, she said, "She's away from it now and can rest. They can't reach her here."

Now that they were face-to-face, Kate felt shy. The woman stood awkwardly before her, saying nothing else, and Kate wondered what to do next. She looked around the room, seeking inspiration. The woman confused her: silent, uncomfortable, staring. Maybe she ought to go get Susan now. She suggested as much, but Laysia looked at her with alarm.

"Back through the mist? What if it goes after you?"

"But I didn't break any rules!"

The woman looked swiftly at the closed door of Nell's room. "What rule could she have broken? She's only a child!"

Kate shrugged. She didn't know. But the woman's mention of the mist worried her. What about Susan and Max and Jean?

"I need to go back and wait for the others. They're coming."

Before either of them could say anything more, her stomach said it for her, loudly. And for the first time, the woman's smile reached her eyes. Kate was surprised. Gone was all the timidity, all the holding back she had sensed on the ridgetop.

"And again, years alone have made me stupid," Laysia said. "A wise man once told me that, after all, the first of things is a good meal of bread and cheese. Sometimes I think now it's the best of them, too. Here, sit."

She motioned to the table, and Kate sat, watching her as she busied herself at a cupboard by the front door. She brought over the chipped pitcher and Kate saw now it was full of water. Kate fidgeted at the table, wondering how Susan would know where to come. What if she walked the other way into the woods? What if, even now, she was circling, calling for them?

"Mistress Laysia?"

The woman looked up, the last of the smile still on her face. "Laysia," she said. "Only. I'm no teacher."

Kate thought that a strange thing to say for someone with so many books. But adults were often strange.

"I can't stay here. Susan will be looking for us. I need to get back to the top of the hill."

Laysia set a mug and a plate in front of her.

"Rest easy. I'll know if someone comes up through the mist. The sound of it changes. If I hear that, we'll go."

"Hear it? But we're so far!"

The sad smile replaced the easy one. "If the mist has come for you, its voice lingers. Perhaps your sister will hear it when she wakes."

Kate said nothing. She was keenly aware of being behind, too slow to catch what others did. Maybe this was like that. She'd have to wait for Nell, now, to tell her what it all meant. She hated to, for two reasons — first, because Nell despised the job, and second, because she'd never let her forget it. Nell, even more than Susan, liked to remind Kate that she was younger and would never catch up. Every year older Kate got, Nell got, too — evidence, her mother had once confirmed, that the universe was not fair. She lived with it, but she didn't like it. Thinking that way sent a pang of guilt through her, and she looked furtively at the door behind which Nell slept.

"She'll be okay now, right?" she asked the woman.

Laysia nodded. She lifted the cloth off one of the covered dishes, sending a whiff of fresh bread into the air. Beside it she placed a plate of mild-smelling cheese.

"Soon she'll be thanking you for bringing her."

Kate doubted that.

"Is that what happened to you?" she asked, hoping to change the subject. "Someone pulled you away from it?"

The woman shook her head.

"Didn't you have any family, to come for you?" Kate asked.

At this, Laysia winced, and Kate flushed. Nell had once complained that she asked stupid questions, and too many of them. Now she kicked herself inside, thinking this must have been the stupidest of all. But after a moment, Laysia said. "I had family. A brother. But he couldn't come."

Kate thought of Max. She couldn't help herself.

"Why not?"

Laysia leaned back in her chair. "That's a story. A long one."

But Kate was familiar with stories, and she knew a statement like that was as much a beginning as *Once upon a time.*

*S*he did not like to tell the child unhappy stories, but this was one who had climbed through the mist and seen her sister nearly taken. This was the child who had walked in dreams. Still, grief clung to the words and made it hard to begin. Laysia glanced at the worn books and wished one of them could speak for her. But the stories in them belonged to the ancients, and this one, this small private tale of anguish and loss, had no place there. What mattered one exile, one woman alone? The visions of the orchard had been gifts of the infinite mind, the pattern maker. Even if born in bitterness, they were grand enough to reach through time. She had only herself—a voice unused to speech, and words unpolished and workmanlike, too narrow to fit the tale. Yet she had been asked, and the small one waited in silence, in this place where silence had gathered too long. So she began.

Chapter 72

I t was my brother who saved me first," the woman said, and Kate thought again of Max. "Like many others, I was unwanted, a girl child born unexpected, when only a boy would serve. They were farmers, my parents, and needed strong arms and a broad back, if they needed a second mouth to feed at all. Of course, I know this only from my brother, who told me later. I begged him so often for details of them, the memories almost seem my own, but they're not."

The woman laughed at herself. She had taken a seat at the table and was running her hands over a section where the good, dark, varnished wood had dulled. Kate wondered how many hours the woman had sat here, rubbing her fingers in that single spot.

"My brother was already half grown when I was born, and he was a great one for hearing things and spying them out. He heard my parents talk of putting me away. Do they still call it that, in the villages? I always thought it strange, as if a child is a thing to lock in a cupboard or set out in the woods with the trash."

She looked up at Kate, who could only shrug, and quickly looked away again. "Maybe they have different words for it now. But at any rate, he heard, and heard, too, word of the hooded ones, though these were just market tales. He thought to find one or, failing that, to raise me on his own in the ruins. He might have done it, too, he was so stubborn."

She laughed again, but a little dread crept into Kate, listening to the story. She had a feeling she knew what was coming. At home, she never liked stories like this, where the good people didn't make it to the end. She didn't even like to read about all the trouble people had on their way to happy endings. She'd beg Susan to tell her the end, to avoid the awful waiting for the bad thing that was coming. Now, though, she kept quiet, reminding herself that she needed to know things here, without the others to help her.

"As it happened, he found the fabled powerful ones, and they gave us sanctuary. My brother loved the life in the valley. We both did, when I grew old enough to know anything. He was much celebrated there, having come away on his own, a boy so young. And then, too, he was eager to be taught and had a quick and ready mind. So he learned, and moved up in rank, and came each night to tell me stories of his lessons. I doubt you've heard those yet, being so young, but they were wondrous. As time passed, I wanted nothing more than to be like him, to learn what he learned, to discover for myself whether the marvels of those stories were true."

Kate had spent enough nights hearing Nell argue with Susan to begin to understand.

"But they wouldn't let you."

The woman shook her head. Her hands had retreated into her lap, and now she glanced out the northern window, where the sun glossed the trees. The birds were making a racket in the branches, and suddenly a cloud of them rose at once, dark pebbles thrown into the sky. They swooped and played and then settled again to blacken the branches.

"It was not the way, for girls. So I sought answers in books. When that wasn't enough, I began to frequent the scholars' garden. Things were different in those years. The Guide had just been elevated, and the council was still of two minds."

Kate blinked, confused. She warned herself against asking. *No stupid questions.* Nell's voice rang in her head. But the woman noticed, and paused.

"I mean, they were not as set in their ways as they are now. My doing, I suppose. At that time, there was an old man, a great scholar, who thought that those like me, who sought learning, should have our chance with the mysteries. He was overruled many times, but he went his way and invited me to learn. So I did, coming at night to meet him outside the walls, among the crops. I came, and others, too, for a time."

Outside, the blackbirds had started their commotion again. Their hectoring voices tumbled from the trees and through the windows and made Kate feel that they were urging the story on to its bad end. She kept thinking of Laysia's brother, the smart, quick one, the brave one who had saved her. She wondered who had hurt him.

But the woman went on, ignoring the birds.

"How could I know the doings of the great ones? The council is full of intrigue and pride — that's what my teacher told me — and yet I heard those words as nothing more than the words in a story, to be set aside, to be moved past as if you understood them. I didn't understand them, didn't see the danger coming. But then, perhaps, neither did he. He was an old man, as I said, and had weathered so much. Perhaps he thought this, too, was only the bubbling jealousy of young men, which passes, in time. Only it didn't. Or perhaps it was that he didn't understand my impatience, my passion. I don't know."

Kate sat perfectly still, knowing she and the racket of blackbirds and the late-morning sun gilding the windows were forgotten. She was used to listening in silence to this kind of talk. Even at home, she'd learned that when people talked this way, if she stayed quiet enough, she'd learn the answers to questions she didn't know to ask.

"So we went on that way, for a while. And the fights of the great ones grew more heated, until to his surprise, I think, Tur Nurayim was turned out of the council and shunned. Exile was not the same then, you see. Still, it hurt him. His students left him, afraid of the taint of it. All but me. He built this place then and taught me in solitude. And perhaps I wasn't enough, for he died not long after. And then I — broken a little, too, I think — grew impatient. And bold. I thought I would show the elders the wrong they did. I would convince them. I decided to enter the heart, where the books of mystery are kept, and prove that I belonged among them."

Kate looked up sharply at that, but Laysia, her finger again circling the wood grain of the tabletop, didn't see.

"A great lock keeps the gate of the inner garden closed," she said. "It has no key. The legend is that only the worthy can open it, a scholar with the power of a trained mind. I found that to be true. It took me a long time, but I managed it. When I did — and I'd gotten inside — they found me."

She remembered Kate then, because she looked up with that sad smile of hers. "They saw that I had gotten in, but it meant nothing. Worse, it meant that I had betrayed them — broken their rules. And so they put me out. In exactly the way they put your sister out. I was the first exile."

Kate waited. She thought she must have lost the thread of the story now, because of the brother. She'd been listening for him. When Laysia failed to go on, she finally asked what happened to him.

The look on the woman's face at her question made Kate think at first it must be another stupid one, and that she'd failed to hear Laysia tell her about her brother's accident or sickness. She started to apologize, but the woman held up a hand.

"No, it's all right. I should have said. I have no knack for stories, do I?" She shook her head, trying to laugh, but no sound came with it. At last she sighed, like someone very old, or very tired.

"My brother. He'd become a great favorite of the council by then. A rising scholar, a great mind, a champion of the ancients and an upholder of the pattern. That's a great thing for a young man. For anyone, really. And he did protect them. He was still good at hearing things, even then. Still good at spying things out. It was he that saw me go to the garden that day. And it was he who told them I was there. My brother — Lan."

The arguments of sages could be heated, but they had never been hateful, until the end. Laysia had told herself often enough that she had been blind not to see what lay ahead, but then Tur Nurayim himself had been blind to it. He had seen things always in the pretty terms of debate — are we this or are we that? What road is best, what manner of thought? He did not understand until the end the dangerous nature of threats.

"Many have called the sanctuary the last flame," he told her once, so near the end that it seemed foolish now to have talked in calm voices amid the waving corn and wheat on a late-summer afternoon. "But is it the bit of warmth kindled in the window of the farmhouse so the traveler might see, and take of it for his own lamp and campfire, on his way? Or is it the devouring fire that burns the infected seed from the ground so the farmer might plant his own there? Or if it be like water, as others say, does it quench thirst or wash the mountain away in a great deluge? Some choose the gentler way, the warming lamp, the small cup of water. For others, there is only the devouring flame and the punishing wave."

So he spoke, even then, not of Kaysh and himself, but of some and of others. There were no enemies in Tur Nurayim's calculations. No calculation at all. Only the sometimes contentious debates of sages.

Tur Kaysh favored a harsher calculus. He had been a watcher in the city when the present Genius rose, a terrifying figure so ambitious and magnetic that he pushed his own father aside. The new Genius roused the city with promises of the change gone, of a coming era of power and glory. Witness to his ascent, the young Kaysh had returned with thoughts of a different future. Laysia remembered him in his later years, as he gained his seat on the council and rose. He had been charming, powerful, the kind of man that made other men fall in love with him. Lan had worshipped him from the start. She recalled her brother's talk of the man's brilliance, his depth, his wisdom, his warmth. "We need a leader," he had said. "Tur Kaysh says the end of times approaches, and leaderless, debating intricacies, the council dallies. He would lead them! He should!"

The early scholars had written approvingly of the thousand faces of truth, truth like a diamond, facet upon facet full of light. Tur Kaysh spoke of truth as the tip of an arrow, a single sharp point ready to pierce and destroy the evil that had overtaken the world.

Soon all the young watchers spoke as he did, and their elders followed, until at last the sages of the council turned their backs on the thousand faces in favor of the one. They grew impatient with quiet, impatient with gentleness, impatient with patience itself. Unlike Tur Nurayim, Tur Kaysh had no trouble speaking of enemies, and finding them. And the first of his enemies was Tur Nurayim himself, the kind old man who spoke quietly, who voiced doubts and urged a different view. For Kaysh, nothing but the devouring fire, the punishing wave, would do. And soon the council bowed to him and swept the gentle sage from their table, turning his chair to the wall.

Until they did it, Tur Nurayim, for all his farsight, had not seen what could come. Not to him, not to her, and not, as the fire burned and the wave rose, even to children.

Chapter 73

Nell woke that afternoon with a howl and her hands around her head, but it was only fear of the mist that made her cry out, not any real change. Kate tugged her arms down and whispered to her, and when she opened her eyes, miraculously it was Nell there, not something strange and fearsome on the soft pillows in the back bedroom. The light slanted through the window now and made the dust dance in its path. Nell turned her face to it, then sat up and looked out. Over the wood, the blackbirds swooped like daredevils in the windy sky.

"Where are we?"

Kate told her. As she did, she watched Nell grow sharp-eyed and alert again. She looked past Kate, trying to see into the big room.

"Where's Susan? Is everybody here?"

Kate didn't know how to explain that, so she said only, "She's getting Max. Then she'll come."

Nell's brow wrinkled. She seemed about to ask something else, when Laysia returned from a trip to the garden. She came straight to the door to welcome Nell and to tell her that she looked hungry, which she didn't, Kate thought. She looked full to bursting with questions, but Nell didn't ask them right away. She only thanked the woman and followed her out to the table.

"Jean?" she asked, looking over at Kate.

"She's with Susan."

Laysia took up the chipped pitcher and went to fill it. Nell watched her go.

"She's the one who helped us?"

Kate nodded. "The exile, they call her."

At the word, Nell turned her head sharply. "The exile," she said slowly. "I've heard of her."

After that, Nell moved around the room with interest, examining the books and peering out the window. She stepped outside and walked to the garden, and Kate followed her as she circled the house, looking. At one point, she stopped and squinted eastward through the trees.

"The valley's that way," she said. She frowned, shook her head, and went inside.

Laysia had again set out bread and cheese on the table, and Nell took the seat she offered.

"They told me about you," she said. "The old man. He thought you sent me."

One dark strand of hair had fallen from Laysia's braid, and she was in the process of tucking it back when Nell spoke. She let it drop again.

"I'm sorry," she said in a rough voice. "It's on my account they've done this." She shook her head, and another loose strand fell. The sun was in the western half of the sky now, and the front room sat in shadow, the windows full of cool light. Impatiently, Laysia brushed the loose hair from her face.

"Children, exiled! Was it for asking too many questions?

For wandering in the wrong garden? What could you have done, after all?"

Nell looked a little affronted at that, but she said nothing right away. She hadn't finished studying Laysia, and when Kate opened her mouth to speak, Nell shook her head briefly. She looked over at the cheese on the table and said suddenly, "Where did the cheese come from? I didn't see any animals in the yard."

Kate thought that a strange thing to say, especially in the accusing tone Nell used. Laysia raised an eyebrow at the question, and Kate flushed.

"She really likes cheese," she said.

Nell frowned at her and said to Laysia, "Where did it come from? There's nothing for miles here."

Again Laysia didn't answer, and Kate couldn't understand the guarded look that had come into her face. Maybe it was Nell's rudeness, she thought. Trying to smooth it over, she said to Nell, "Maybe she has a refrigerator, you know, under the rug, like at Liyla's house. Maybe she got it from someone."

Neither of these answers would serve, it seemed. Nell shook her head again, never taking her eyes from the woman. And Laysia dropped her gaze to the table. After a while, she said, ruefully, "I can see why you frightened them, down there."

Nell didn't say anything. She waited. Her bangs had grown down into her eyes in the time they'd been through the window, and she glared through them, unappeased.

Dismayed, Kate watched the two of them stare at each other. Nell was not as old as Susan, and yet she seemed suddenly very old, as if coming up the mountain had let her jump across the bridge that made her an equal to Laysia, or any of the others. She was full of the secret understanding adults always had, and she sat there, unafraid despite the brutal trip through the mist, challenging the woman. And Laysia, to Kate's surprise, neither brushed the question off nor turned away. Instead, she said, a little tentatively, "There are some things maybe you would not understand."

Nell's eyebrows came up, and Kate suddenly felt sorry for the woman, saying all the wrong things. She watched the two of them a second, each holding her secrets close in that funny, opaque game adults played, saying things by halves, making you guess and give your ignorance away.

After another second, Nell sniffed and looked sideways at Kate.

"She thinks we can't make peaches," she said.

Kate decided not to remind her that neither she nor Nell had, in fact, made peaches. And anyway, Nell was looking at her hand in the fierce way Max had looked at the ground when he made food for them in the woods. A little buzz tickled the air, and then, in Nell's cupped hand, a fine blur. A second later, one of the flowers, a pink open-palm, lay there.

Nell looked up at them, that challenging, half-angry expression bending into a grin.

"Better than cheese," she said.

Dreams and fragments of dreams
Are we,
A musing thought
In the mind of the maker of patterns,
Soft skinned, moldable as unglazed clay.
Such is the world
And such are we,
Yet we carry the shaper's tools,
Gouge and blade and wire in hand,
And thus unfinished,
Ever firming our own lines and edges,
We may yet reach out to remake
The very surface of the world.
— Vision of the Walking Sage, First Age of Sage Kings, Ganbihar

A child had opened her hand and made a flower. A child! How could it be? "Such is the world," the Walking Sage had written, "and such are we": "soft skinned. . . . ever firming our own lines and edges."

Years ago, Tur Nurayim had quoted the passage to bolster Laysia's patience. She had been a young student then, chafing with the work of learning. How tedious the tasks he set her, the endless fixing on a stone or a flower or a mound of sand. And for two hours' strain, she earned nothing more than the sand swirling in its bowl!

"Is it a simple thing for us to remake the surface of the world?" he had chided her. "Much of a man's mind is busy holding his own *self firm, though he may not know it. In this dark age of ours, we've learned even that might be lost, without some effort. So to do more, he must spend years sharpening his mind like the sculptor's blade. Only then can he turn outward."*

Hearing this with impatience, she had wondered aloud why man — jewel of the pattern and graced with the gift of shaping — couldn't simply be born hard boned and unchangeable. Why such a flimsy-edged thing? Why not stiff shelled and invulnerable?

A wistful look had come into Tur Nurayim's face when she said it, and he'd told her that, indeed, some spoke of other places, worlds like tapestries hung in the great hall of the pattern maker — a thousand of them, more.

"Among these, they say, there are iron-hard lands full of people edged in steel, impervious to change."

He sighed. "But not in this one. Here we are of the soft-skinned variety. Perhaps for fear of what we might do, unfettered by our own weakness. Maybe in those other lands, men are wiser."

The memory echoed in Laysia's head now as she stared at a child — a child! — whom the mist had battered and could not take.

What were these children of dreams? From what tapestry had they emerged?

"Why did they send you through the mist?" she asked the girl.

"For going to the center," Nell answered promptly. "For breaking their stupid lock and their stupider rules."

Another thought came to Laysia. The child had said "we." We

make peaches. She turned to the small one, the quiet cloudy-haired child whose face she had known in dreams.

"And can you, too, do this?"

The little one shook her head. "I don't think so. Only Susan and Max."

Her sister frowned at that. "You could learn. It's not that hard. You and Jean both."

Laysia sat and counted names. The small one, Kate. Her round-faced sister with the soft profile of a child and the sharp eyes of an adult, Nell. And these others: Susan, Max, Jean. Five. Five glazed and firm edged, unbending, unchanged and unchangeable. Five who walked in dreams.

"Tell me how you came here," she said.

But there was most certainly steel in this one. Nell refused.

"You'd think we were crazy," she said. She sat still and wary, watchful with those sharp eyes. But Kate patted her hand and leaned over to whisper in her ear, motioning Laysia's way.

Nell frowned and shook her head and at last gave in.

"It was wintertime," she said. "And the five of us were home from school. We weren't doing anything special. Then our window — we have a big window in that room — it changed. I don't know how, but it opened. And we came here."

At the word "window," Laysia froze. She thought again of worlds like tapestries in a great hall, of colors and designs and threads woven in patterns that had never been seen or imagined.

Nell glared at her across the table, defiant. "We're not crazy," she said. "Kate will tell you the same thing. We all would. It happened."

Shakily, Laysia stood and took from her shelf the worn copy of The Age of Anam Tur Nurayim had set there so long ago. She opened it to the most familiar of all the orchard visions.

Out of the longest night,
Into the age of wolves,
The five
Will come.
Strangers
Bringing hope of light.
Watch for them
When the time ripens
And the danger grows.
Wait then
For the opening
Of the window.

Nell whitened when she saw it.

"The age of wolves," she said. "That's now."

"Who wrote it?" asked Kate.

Laysia thought of the arguments of sages. Anam himself wrote it, though he was not named. Another, a disciple, a follower. Neither. It was the product of a different, earlier time; it came from the very dawn of life and passed from the first on. Which answer would she give to these, who were themselves an answer? Who and what the five would be had been debated for centuries. And the window? On that there had been unusual agreement — it meant not a window at all but a moment, an opportune time.

And now here stood two of the five, telling tales of windows, come into the age of wolves. So she said only, "An ancient. We don't know who."

"But they knew about the window!"

The small one, Kate, plucked worriedly at her dress, and Laysia reminded herself that after all, this was still a child, uncertain as children were uncertain, afraid as children were afraid.

"How are we supposed to fix things?" the girl asked. "We don't know anything about bringing light!"

"Perhaps you know more than you think," she said, not knowing another answer. "I would never have dreamed a child could resist the mist — or another save her from it."

Nell looked puzzled. "What do you mean? Wasn't it you who saved me?"

"Hardly. It was this little one here."

She watched surprise flower on Nell's small, soft, shrewd face. Kate colored.

"I think Susan helped me," she muttered.

"No," Laysia said. "There was no one else on the mountain. I would know."

Nell turned those keen eyes her way, and Laysia saw them flare with sudden pain. The girl knew the sound of the mist, too, now. Hard-shelled though she was, she could hear its acid whispering. Laysia watched her struggle to push it away.

"So these five," Nell said at last. "What are they supposed to do?"

Chapter 74

Laysia didn't seem to know, and that worried Kate. She didn't like expectations, and suddenly the woman seemed loaded with them. She had looked into her big book, face etched with disbelief and fear and surprise, and the words were like a shovelful of promises poured into a basket, heavy, heavy, and waiting to be carried. But Kate didn't know how to carry them.

"How can people see what's going to happen before it happens?" she asked, trying to find a way out of it. More, she wanted to know where the part about going home was in that big, knowing book. She wanted to read about windows opening to let you out as well as in.

"And this was written before the change?" Nell asked. She seemed unafraid of the book and its demands. Surprised, yes, but not terrified. Nell was never terrified, Kate thought with a mixture of relief and resentment that she couldn't have sorted out even if she had had the time to mark it.

Laysia explained that people often foretold things like that and wrote them down. Or at least they used to. In the old days, they'd known the change was coming. So when it came, they had hope — they waited.

"Well, what did they think they were waiting for?" Nell asked.

Laysia shrugged. The long, still light of afternoon fired the windows to her back and side, and it was not cool and white anymore, but buttery, a warm glaze that slipped through the glass at the edges. All the little cups and plates and the bindings of the books with their worn gilt lines twinkled and sparked with it.

"They debated," she said. "These things are never clear. Some thought the five would be warriors. Other said the five would come from the watchers, for after all, weren't they watching for signs that the end of the dark age was near? My brother, when he first became a watcher, used to imagine he would be one of them, one day."

Kate had whispered the name of Laysia's brother to Nell, and she received this news sourly. "I thought the watchers stayed away from the Genius. All we saw them do in the city was run when anyone came near."

Kate couldn't see Laysia's face when Nell said that. She had turned a little away at mention of her brother. After a moment, Laysia got up and set the chipped pitcher before them. She looked into it steadily, and suddenly Kate heard the lapping sound of water rising up from its round opening. Laysia set two cups before them.

"They run, but not out of fear anymore," she said as she poured. The afternoon light danced along the stream of water as it spilled from pitcher to cup. "Once, they did. When the sanctuary was new, and they were small in number. They were weak then. All they could do was watch. Later, their numbers increased as they began bringing in the unwanted, like me. So over time they grew strong. It would be folly to think them weak. They are part of the power that is the mist."

She looked up briefly at Nell, who flinched at the word.

"If they're so strong, what do they hide for?" Nell asked.

The woman sighed.

"Again to the cherished debate."

Kate looked at Nell for an explanation, but she only shrugged.

Laysia said, "It's an old saying. Argument sharpens the mind, and so the sages often do it. And though one side may not prevail, still their reasoning is treasured and kept for the lesson it offers. Or at least it used to be so, before Tur Nurayim was turned from the council. He argued that the time had come to show our faces, to offer proof that the change could be turned back. He lost that argument to Tur Kaysh and the followers he gathered around him, which after a time included the council itself. Kaysh insisted there is nothing to salvage in the city. It's evil, and the watchers must hide their faces until the time comes to punish it with the hand of justice."

"Hand of justice," Nell said quietly. "Is that something in your books, too?"

Laysia nodded and raised her hand, bending each finger in turn. The punishing hand of justice. Kate looked at her own five fingers and frowned.

$$\diamond \; \Diamond \; \diamond$$

*A*t dusk, as the sky bled and the trees gathered shadows round their ankles and knees, the howl of the mist rose, bending with a whistle at the newcomers who dared traverse it. She watched as the girl Nell turned that way, wincing.

Laysia promised to return with the others and then set out through the falling light, wading through fireflies that rose from the grass to meet the shadows. She returned to the fourth gate in time to find slim figures bent in the dusk. They had just emerged from the fog. Briefly, she glanced at it — a white haze that stained the dark. Then she turned to the children and found herself momentarily tongue-tied at sight of their half-remembered faces. She called the names she had been given: Susan, Max, Jean. But there were only two.

The older steered the younger toward her as they climbed the last of the rise, stumbling. The older girl raised her head so her eyes caught the faint light of the crescent moon.

"Do you have my sisters?"

The thin moon and white stars could not brighten the wood, and so Laysia led them back through such darkness that they were forced to follow like the smallest of children, clutching her skirts. The girl called Jean sniffed and broke into tears as they went, and Susan hushed her. Laysia thought of nothing to say. She had failed to grow wise in the way other women she'd known had grown wise, full of the deep-welled passions of age — passion for children and the future. Instead, she had gained the meek wisdom of solitude.

She wondered if Lan had become a father. She doubted it. They were lonely souls, she and her brother. He had been perhaps more lonely even than she, leaving home to give her life. If later he had pushed her away, sent her unknowing to a terrible fate, that did not erase the first gift. It never could.

Chapter 75

Kate strained to hear it. Whatever it was Laysia had heard, whatever Nell heard, she wanted to hear it, too. She stood at the window, chewing a knuckle and watching the fireflies twinkle as the dark erased the lines between the trees and crept over the garden and took the sky. For a long time, she could pick out nothing but the chirp of crickets outside and the sound of Nell behind her, kicking a chair leg as she turned the pages of *The Age of Anam*, which Laysia had left on the table.

But a million years seemed to pass, or maybe two million, while she stood there. After a while, she noticed a faint rumble beneath the crickets. It vibrated warningly from the woods, an animal roused from sleep. She glanced back at Nell and saw her hunched down, her shoulders pulled in as she frowned into the book.

Eventually it receded, and Kate was back to listening to the empty night. She had begun imagining she could pick out the soft, combustive hiss of the fireflies by the time footsteps sounded outside. Nell reached the door first, leaping from her chair and flinging it open.

"Nell! You're okay!"

Susan's voice, sharp with relief, not dazed, not faint, the way it had been the other night.

Laysia stepped through the door, and Susan rushed through behind her, grabbing a grinning Nell and swiveling to snatch Kate nearly off her feet. Susan was back! Now everything would be better! Laughter bubbled in Kate's chest, and she almost shouted. Susan sounded like Susan! Now they were all together. Now they'd —

"Where's Max?"

Nell wasn't grinning anymore.

The door had closed behind Jean. And Jean's eyes were red. Kate's rising laughter turned abruptly into a stomachache. She saw Susan flush.

"He didn't come with you?" Nell asked. "He stayed there?"

Susan started talking too fast.

"He doesn't know! They wouldn't let us tell him. We went again today, and they stopped us. And we had to come out to look for you and Kate!"

All Susan's happy relief had soured, and she scowled down at Kate. "You should have waited for me! Why didn't you wait?"

Kate cringed and glanced at Laysia, who had gone to sit in the chair by the fireplace. The woman looked from one to the other of them, a little bewildered. Couldn't she tell Susan how bad it had been? But Laysia said nothing, and Kate couldn't find the words, not in front of Nell, who looked now like she might hit somebody.

Jean burst into tears, and Nell reddened.

"How could he not know?" Nell said. "He'd know if he wanted to! He's too in love with his new teacher to know."

Laysia cleared her throat uncomfortably, and Susan shot a warning look at Nell. At home, they knew better than to fight in front of strangers. Nell glared at Susan and swung around.

"Teach us what he's learning," she said to Laysia. "Teach us everything."

But the fight wasn't over. Kate knew that much.

Chapter 76

The thundercloud had been hovering from the second Susan and Jean shut the door behind them without Max. It burst the moment Laysia went to bed and the four of them were finally alone together.

"You're nuts if you think he doesn't know," Nell said, turning on Susan. "How could he not know? Didn't he hear the gong?"

Susan grimaced. "It wasn't like before! They didn't sound it. Zirri came and told us and Mistress Meva. He's probably thinking we're still there, all okay."

Nell snorted. "Okay? We haven't been okay since we got there. He saw you! He saw all of it! Or he should have! Don't tell me he didn't know. He *should* have known!"

Susan looked pained. Kate slipped between them.

"He doesn't know," she said to Nell. "Otherwise he'd have come, like last time."

Jean made it worse by crying.

"Shh! You'll wake her! Max'll come looking for us when he sees we've gone!" Susan said. "I know he will!"

"If he even notices we're gone!" Nell cut in. "When was the last time he visited? Two days? Three? Maybe he'll find out next month. Where will we be then?"

"Don't exaggerate!" Susan snapped. "He'll come. I left him a note."

Nell rolled her eyes. "A note. Great."

Kate listened to them with mounting desperation.

"A note's good," she said. "Maybe they'll give it to him, like he sends those letters! He'll come!"

She looked over at Susan and saw the lines rumpling her forehead again. "Don't worry, Susan."

But Susan looked back in surprise, wincing a little.

And then Jean wailed, "You said he'd come!"

"He will!" Susan said in a frantic whisper. "I said it because he will!"

The fight went on like that, Susan repeating things, and Nell glaring, and Kate trying to stand between them until they were both angry at her, too, and told her to get into bed next to Jean, to keep quiet, to let them think.

So Kate lay beside Jean, who even in sleep shuddered from all the crying she'd done, and thought she'd never heard such loud thinking in her life.

W e had dreams at home, before we came," Susan said the
next morning.

The previous evening, in the temporary truce that had followed
Laysia's promise to teach them, Nell had showed her sister the passage of the orchard vision. Susan blanched when she read it, then
sat brooding over it until Laysia had gone to bed.

"At least Kate did," Susan went on now. "Max, too, I think.
Maybe someone was calling us. I didn't know that could happen."

Laysia saw Kate and Jean exchange a glance, and Kate looked
worried. At mention of their missing brother, the dark-haired girl,
Jean, blinked and drew the back of her hand across her eyes.

None of them looked steel edged. They seemed too soft to come
from the world of iron Tur Nurayim had described.

"What's it like, the place you come from?" Laysia asked Susan.
She tried to imagine a world of hard lines, of iron-skinned people
fenced off one from the next. So many walls! She wondered how
one moved in a place like that. And yet the window had opened.

"It's different," the child said. "It's so hard to describe how,
when we use the same words and don't mean the same things with
them. Nobody there can make water from nothing, or peaches, or
move the wind. We have tools—machines—to do things for us."

It did sound like a leaden place when the girl said that. On the
other side of that window, could one could stand on a mountain
and see the breadth of things, as she liked to do standing in the sea
clearing? Were there seas there?

The greatest of the sages were the seers who had walked the
orchard and seen, perhaps, more than this world alone. To learn to

take the clay of life and reshape it, one must see. But Tur Nurayim had also spoken of the heartbeat of the world, and the scholar's ear to hear it. Laysia wondered if in that other place, there were those with such eyes and ears.

Laysia had said she would teach them, but in the light of day, with the noise of the mist threatening and four faces out of dreams turned expectantly her way, she nearly lost her nerve, and so decided to lead them as far from the valley as she could, toward the clearing over the sea, where the voice of the mist would not harry them.

As they walked down toward the seaward path, Kate stayed close beside her, her honey hair lit with the cool sunlight that streamed through the morning wood.

Laysia had thought her a silent child until now, when she began to ask questions.

"Do you have to be almost grown to learn to do things?" she asked. "I mean, Nell can do them. Do you think I'll be able to?"

Laysia had no answer to that. She doubted it, but she didn't like to disappoint the child. And after all, what was doubt anymore, when she'd seen such wonders?

"What's that? Look at it! It flashes!"

They had emerged from the break in the trees that signaled the last clearing of the high land. Far off, a great blaze of light flared up.

"The crystal cliff," she told the girl. She looked toward the wave of glass that jutted from the mountain range to the south. The morning sun sparked on its facets and ridges to dazzle the southern sky.

"Is that natural?" asked Susan. "It just grew that way?"

"No, it was made during the last upheaval, as the scholars fled."

They stood and stared at it awhile, that glass wave like a flame, frozen in its leap toward the sky. And yet the water, still alive, flowed beneath that lucent crust. Laysia wondered if that was what the world on the other side of the window was like, beneath its rigid armor. Perhaps it was alive and warm, like these children.

Chapter 77

The wood smelled of moss and dirt and wild mint, and in it, the slight noise of that terrible cloud Kate was learning to hear made walking heavy. Or maybe it was that she herself had grown heavy, Kate thought. She considered that she must weigh at least a thousand pounds this morning. Max had told her once that if she ever took a walk on Jupiter, she'd weigh as much as a young gorilla. Maybe here she weighed as much as an old one. She was very tired after last night's fighting, and each step through that fuzz of noise made her heavier, heavier than Jupiter, maybe, and two or three grown-up gorillas. So she was surprised when they broke through the line of trees and the tang of the far-off sea washed the weight away.

Kate looked out toward the water. In the distance, the glass cliff sparked pink and white, a wave frozen as it crested. Below, she could see the blurred line of the beach and the blue haze of the moving sea.

Susan threw her head back and breathed deep. Kate glanced her way and was relieved to see that her face finally seemed clear of trouble and distraction.

Laysia, too, stood a little while looking out at the sea. Then she left them standing there and went around the edge of the wood, collecting sticks. She handed one to each of them and sat, cross-legged, in the clover. Kate took a seat next to her,

her back to the wood. Though they were well away from the place where the clover petered into bare dirt and the rock of the mountain ended in open air, she felt better keeping an eye on it.

The others sat, too, and waited for Laysia to say something, but she only stared at the stick she'd set on the ground in front of her. After a second, it drifted into the air and began to rise and fall in a pattern that mimicked the distant waves.

Jean laughed, startled. Laysia smiled, and Kate watched the woman's stick flip over, seem to bow, then settle slowly to earth with the motion of fluttering leaves.

"Now you," she said to them. "You try."

Kate's chest tightened. She was afraid to ask how to do it. Maybe she was supposed to know how. Nell and Susan didn't ask. Instead, Nell folded her arms carefully behind her back and fixed her eye on her own stick.

"You don't move the stick, right?" she asked. "You move the air."

Susan seemed to understand this strange statement, but the look on Jean's face told Kate that she didn't get it, either. Move the air? What did that mean?

Laysia said nothing, but Nell narrowed her eyes, no longer seeming to look at the stick at all.

In a moment, Nell's stick jumped, then floated up over her head, bouncing as if on an invisible current. Not to be outdone, Susan put her hands on her knees, gave the twig in the grass a sharp look, and hunched forward, her shoulders hovering over her folded legs. Her stick shot past her face as if it had been blown from the ground by a sudden geyser.

"How did you do that?" Kate asked her, astonished.

Susan was looking skyward. Her stick fell into her waiting hands.

"I pushed the air," she said. "And it lifted the stick."

This made no more sense to Kate than when Nell had said it, but Nell startled her by explaining.

"Think," she said. "You can't see the air, but it's there. You can feel it. You feel wind, don't you? It's all made up of tiny pieces of air — molecules, they're called. And they move together, and that's air. If you can see that, and if you push them together — lots of them — that's wind. And if you push wind underneath the stick, the stick flies. See?"

Laysia was nodding. For the first time in a long time, Nell seemed happy, letting her stick leap over invisible waves and dip to surf past her eyebrows. Kate tried to see.

She thought of air, and wood, and the line between them. She tried to see the tiny, invisible pieces Nell talked about. But she thought, too, of the clover and the birds gossiping in the trees, and the dazzle of the sun reflecting off the crystal cliff. Eventually the twig did flip and lurch, but it didn't rise.

She glanced at Jean. Jean's stick rolled over half-heartedly on the ground like a sick dog.

"It's *hard,*" Jean muttered. She had brought her Barbie in her waistband, and now she pulled it out to play, hunching her shoulders so maybe the older girls wouldn't see.

Jean was little. That's what Susan always said. Kate and Jean were little and had no patience. Kate would not be little that way.

She tried again. And again. On her sixth attempt at forcing herself to see nothing but pieces of twig and air, the stick rose, shakily, and held at eye level.

Laysia had been watching.

"Well done!" she said. "You've answered your own question, then."

She had, but not quite in the way she'd meant it. She couldn't do what the others could. She watched Nell's stick do a jig in the air, watched Susan graduate to making pebbles and even rocks move, and, by the end of the day, Kate had gotten her stick to rise steadily and move in any direction she wanted, even as Jean's still shook haltingly just beside her shoulders. So she was almost satisfied.

All day they practiced moving things without touching them, until Kate felt shaky with exhaustion. She wondered why she should be so tired, when they'd been sitting in the clearing all day. They walked back through the woods amid the late-afternoon clamor of birds, and she nearly stumbled. But Susan reached for her hand, to steady her.

Coming from the clearing back toward the cottage felt like walking into a rainstorm. Everyone drooped. To Kate, it was like taking off in a plane, her ears full and popping with a hateful rushing noise. After a while, it receded, like a bad smell that had grown familiar, but it was there just the same.

Moods turned, too. Susan's lips pressed into a thin line. Nell stomped. Jean was worst of all, maybe because she was loudest. That evening, she demanded to know how she'd get her letters when Max didn't know where to send them and ordered Susan to take her back down so she could get them.

Susan looked as if someone had punched her. Without a word, she took a book from Laysia's shelf, went into the bedroom, and shut the door. Nell had some words, none of which would have been allowed back home. Then she barged out to the garden, where Laysia was harvesting vegetables for supper, and yanked carrots from the ground as if she'd caught them doing something bad.

"Jean, he'll come. . . ." Kate tried.

But Jean shook her head and ran outside to sit behind the house, away from the others. Kate followed her. There was no garden in back, only clover and grass and tall trees crowding the edge of the clearing like children pushing to get out the door at the end of school.

Jean had unfolded one of Max's letters. She kept the ones she'd gotten all crumpled in her pocket, and the page she examined now was veined with creases and smudged with fingermarks.

"Which one is that?" Kate asked her, trying to make conversation.

"The one about teachers and trains," Jean said in a muffled voice. Her nose was stuffy from crying.

"Want to read it to me?" Jean had read them so many times that she knew all the hard words now.

Jean gave a one-shouldered shrug. "You can read it."

Kate took the letter and smoothed it as best she could. She remembered this one. Max's cramped, dark hand sloped across the page in the fading light.

"'Dear Jean,'" she read. Kate glanced at her sister, who made an effort to quiet herself so she could hear, despite the fact that she'd heard it twenty times before.

"'It's a good thing I've been spending my days here, even if Nell doesn't think so. You can tell her I said that.'"

Jean sniffed loudly, and Kate wondered again if Max knew what had happened to Nell. To all of them.

"Well, go on," Jean prodded. Her voice sounded a little better. Kate cleared her throat and read on:

"The reason is because what we learned on our own was just a percent of a fraction of what there is to learn. We were like somebody trying to figure out how to build a car by himself, just because he figured out how to make one wheel. Here, people have been studying how to do things, how to understand things, that is, since almost the beginning of time. They have books and books and books of people's thoughts and learning and discoveries, and Tur Kaysh says that in the old times, they knew even better than we do today, with us being so far from the beginning of everything. I've never met a teacher like him before. At home, questions aren't always so welcome. Teachers get impatient, and they want to move on. Don't you hate when they say that? It's like the class is a train and I'm holding everybody up in getting to the next station. It's not like that with the Guide at all. It's more like having a conversation. We talk and talk — that is, he talks and I listen, but he doesn't mind questions. He says questions are the lifeblood of thought. He says they're the mark of the true student. Wait till I tell them that at home. Maybe I can skip a grade and get to college faster. Even if I did, I don't think it would be as good as this. When I visit next, I'll show you some things you wouldn't believe. See you soon.

Your brother,

Max"

Neither of them said much when she'd finished. Jean wiped her nose with the back of her hand, then kicked at the clover until she'd gouged out a clump with her heel. Overhead, the sky had begun to fade gently into its long summer twilight. After a while, Kate folded the letter back into its wrinkled square and handed it to Jean.

"He'll come get us," Jean said, and Kate was glad to hear that she was done crying.

"Yeah, he will."

Jean retrieved her Barbie and made it walk back and forth across the clover, jumping the little ditch she'd made. After a while, Kate left her there and wandered around the house. Nell had left the garden, and she could see her through the window now, talking to Laysia at the table. The first of the fireflies were blinking in the shadows rising from the grass. She didn't feel like going inside just yet, to the scratchy feel of more upset and irritation.

Instead she sat down under the trees past the garden, where the wood took back the clearing, and watched the fireflies winking at her, appearing and disappearing in unexpected places. She thought about Max being a true student.

As hard as she could, she tried to put her mind to sticks flying up, and pieces of air, and peaches and water and all the things the others could do so much more easily than she could. She wished she understood things the way Max did. Then she could look in the big books and know all the answers and they could be home, away from the awful noise down in the valley. Maybe if she were better at things, she could help open the window, but right now all she could do was sit and listen to the mist grumble and mutter as the sky faded to denim, and after a while Susan called her in for dinner.

Chapter 78

By the end of that first week, even Jean could make her stick, or pebbles, or leaves, fly. Still, she'd lose interest rapidly, and whatever she'd sent up would rain down on them, sometimes knocking one of them on the head if they failed to pay attention.

"It's hard to keep thinking of it," Jean said by way of apology.

It didn't get easier for Kate, though she did learn to think a little more of the one thing and not the others, and could hold on to it longer, until one day she lifted Laysia a foot or so and sent her laughing, in a sudden flurry of waving arms, several paces across the clearing.

It was easy, during days like that, to forget that they were waiting. But at night they knew it. As they walked toward Laysia's house through the rose gold of evening, the light turning the leaves to silk and the tree trunks to velvet, they could hear the low static of the mist and feel the pressure of it like the weight of the sun on an August afternoon. And they remembered.

They were waiting for Max, and he didn't come.

After the first day, Susan and Nell had stopped arguing about it. But their silence bothered Kate more than the talk had. Some nights, when the others were sleeping, Kate saw Susan go to the window of the small bedroom that looked out into the black of the wood and peer through it. Or she'd go to the table in the big room, where Laysia sat bent over her books. Kate couldn't hear their whispered talk, but once she heard Susan's voice rise.

"Yes, he would ask for us!" she said. "He will."

Kate wanted to go and join them, to ask Susan how she could be sure. But she knew Susan wouldn't welcome the interruption. She'd only say not to worry, that Kate wouldn't understand, that she'd take care of it. Susan thought Kate was little. She wouldn't change her mind even if Kate could make sticks fly. Even if she could lift Laysia herself.

Halfway through the second week of lessons in the clearing, a drizzle cut the day short. The four of them had spent the morning making fire and dousing it, but the dull persistence of the rain sent them home. Nell asked why Laysia couldn't push it away, the way she did the wind, and she said that it would be wrong to deprive the ground of nourishment.

"Rain is part of the pattern, made by a far greater mind than mine," she said. So they went back. Kate lingered for one more look at the far-off ocean, an iron line in the faded landscape, before following the others. She hated to leave the wide-open space and retreat through the damp wood, slogging along as the trees closed in. The gray light and dingy sky reminded her of the mist, and she began to feel hopeless. The scholars were stronger than Susan, than Laysia, than anyone. They could shut the world down faster than rain.

Nell must have been thinking the same thing, because

when they'd gotten back, and all Kate could do was watch the rain pebble the windowpane, she heard Nell ask Laysia how the Genius had managed to beat the scholars in the first place.

"They could demolish him. Why didn't they?" she asked. "They could have pulled the guns right out of those red cloaks' hands! Light the air on fire around them! Why didn't they win?"

Laysia set lamps on the table in front of Nell and watched them a moment, until flames sparked and leaped behind the glass globes.

"So say all the young watchers when they begin. So said my brother when he first took the watcher's oath. To see and defend, they say. But if I can make fire in this room, or in the clearing, does it mean I can do the same when the threat comes? If one man runs at me, thinking his own violent thoughts, shouting them to make himself fierce and give himself courage, what about me? Don't I hear him? What does it do to me to hear him?"

Nell looked steadily at Laysia. Kate saw her open her mouth to say something, then decide against it.

Laysia saw. "You understand, I think. That's the secret of the mist. It seeps through all the cracks; it can outshout your own thoughts. You can be very strong and still hear. Maybe the strongest hear it most of all. And meanwhile, fear bewilders you. The scholars were not prepared for the violence of the Genius and his war. By the time they understood the danger, it was too late."

The lamp yellowed the room, and everything in it looked soft. Susan sat on the cushioned chair near the basket of books. She'd been leafing through one while Jean used the rest as a mountain for her Barbie to scale. Kate had thought maybe Susan wasn't listening, but now she looked up.

"Is that why we understand you, do you think?" she asked. "I've been wondering since we came about that. When we first got here — for a little bit — the people we talked to sounded strange, like they had a different accent. Then that all went away. Don't you have different languages here?"

Laysia seemed happy to have a question that didn't carry such pain in it. She shrugged. "That's a fascination — you mean that two people speak and don't understand each other? No, we don't have it. Only the old speech and the new, and there's not much difference in them. Just new ideas that need new words, or old ones, full of words for things we don't think anymore. What's it like where you come from? Two standing side by side can't speak to each other?" She shook her head wonderingly. "Even your words are walls!"

"Maybe they are," Susan said. "Where we come from, different countries have different languages, and people can't talk to each other across them unless they've learned to. But here you must hear thoughts, a little, at least enough to get the sense of a thing." She looked over at Nell. "I keep thinking this place is the same because it looks it. It isn't!"

"No," Nell said grimly. "It isn't." She turned to Laysia. "But anyway, one thing you said doesn't fit. We only found out what we could do here when we were half crazy with fear. Being afraid didn't stop it from happening. It made it happen!"

Some people, Kate had noticed, never really listened to questions. They were too quick with the answers. Laysia wasn't like that. She listened, thinking, without fear that she'd lose her chance to speak. Maybe that came from being by herself so long; Kate didn't know. So the question hung there for a while.

Finally, Laysia said, "Yes, and in that is the kernel of the unseen difference. Or perhaps I should say the half-seen, for I sense it sometimes, when I look to what it is you brought with you through that window from another place. What a strange land it must be! Here, thought brushes against us as the wind brushes skin, like the sun weighs upon the shoulders. For us, thoughts are like a song that moves us to dance before we know we've heard the tune. And here come you, unbent by the wind, unburnt by the sun! And yet you hear the song and sing it back from within the walls you each wear. How is that? Where we are permeable, you are solid."

Kate wondered if it was a trick of the lamplight that reddened Nell's face so. Laysia glanced at her, then out at the woods, where the drape of clouds erased the treetops and the sky was a blank.

"A song," Nell said sullenly. "Susan said that once. It doesn't seem much like a song to me."

Again, that long silence. Then in her quiet voice, Laysia said, "The mist is very hard. You do hear, as I said, and when it comes for you, even armored as you are, you may yet fall. And then, too, the mist is worst for those it has cause to know. It uses your very self against you, twisting first mind, then body. Always, though, there is some hope. The mist can, after all, be mistaken."

Susan's head came up at that. "Is that how you escaped it? It made a mistake?"

Laysia nodded. "I felt the change beginning, felt the wildness at the edges of my mind. And I would have let it come, but the Guide, Kaysh, misunderstood me, and it was his thoughts that flowed there, his anger and his misunderstanding. What I heard of them stopped me."

"What do you mean?" Nell asked her.

"I mean they were a lie. He called me beast, and one who desires the beastly. From beast we all rise, yes, but I didn't desire any return to it. I wanted learning — that was all."

"He called me that," Nell told her, forgetting suddenly that she'd been angry a moment before. "An animal, he said."

Laysia nodded. "Knowing you are no longer a beast is a great strength," she said. "And with all his knowledge and skill and power, it's one the Guide does not yet possess."

$\diamond \ \Diamond \ \diamond$

*I*n the whispering orchard, Laysia walked beneath a sky of polished copper and trees aflame. She had not known seasons to touch the orchard, and yet the wood burned red and yellow and orange, though no leaf had fallen.

Through the ruddy trees, she saw a clearing, and there a pool, tarnished silver in the yellow light. No bird sang, and no wind moved the leaves.

She was startled to see not a child, but an aged woman on her knees beside the water. The years had puckered the woman's cheeks and hands. When she turned, her grief-stricken eyes were the color of winter.

"Gone," she said. "All the children, gone. Even the last one."

Fear seized Laysia and she stopped walking.

"No," she said. "Don't say that."

"Should I not speak the truth here in this place?" the old woman said in her hollow voice. "The child is lost! Did I not plead for him?"

She turned to gaze into the water. The trees reflected red there.

"The pattern is laced with pain," she said. "Why must all the threads of life unravel in agony?"

Laysia had no words to give her.

"Look," the woman said. "The water is all blood."

Full of dread at her talk, Laysia wanted to turn and run. But the woman was as old as Tur Nurayim had been in the last years. Laysia thought of the mother she had never known, and the grandmother. She watched the woman bend toward the water, doubled *in her pain.* No one should be so alone, *Laysia thought.* Not even in dreams.

She knelt beside the stranger and pressed her own dark hand over the woman's fair one.

"Be healed, wise one," she said.

She looked to the water and saw that the clouds reflected there had turned to hills in a glade, and it was red, all of it, as the woman had said.

Again, the fear gripped her, but when she turned, looking for the woman, she saw that her hand rested only on the long flat grass that bent toward the water.

Chapter 79

Laysia seemed troubled in the morning, and when Kate asked her why, she said only that she had fallen behind, been slow and blind, and that now she must hurry. Kate wondered how she could fall behind. This was not like school, with its homework and tests. But she saw the look on the woman's face and kept quiet.

They were all dour that morning as they walked through the wood. An hour after the sun rose, the air was heavy. Wet beaded the leaves and clung to the weeds, weighing them down so they hung into the path. Even the tree bark sweated. Kate trudged beside Jean, who had started the walk ahead of the others but had dropped back to complain about the heat, the hike, and the long day ahead.

"I miss cars," Jean said. "Do you know what my dream come true would be? My dream come true would be if somebody would drive by and pick us up right now."

Jean had lots of dreams like that. At home she'd once said her biggest and best hope would be waffles for breakfast, and Mom had asked her where she'd learned such gaudy talk.

Now Susan, walking nearby, rolled her eyes.

"Dream bigger," she said.

Kate thought about dreams. Not the wishing kind but the other, the kind that came to you without being asked for. She had the sense, sometimes, that she'd dreamed of places she couldn't remember. She wondered if that was the only way home now.

"Do you know what my dream is, Jean?" Nell asked. "My dream is that my little sister would keep quiet for half an hour."

Jean eyed her. "Dream bigger," she said.

Laysia had moved on ahead. Now she called back to them to keep up. She still wore that strange look on her face, full of upset and worry and something else Kate didn't quite know how to name. Maybe anger.

"We have much to do today," she said.

In the clearing, she didn't sit but strode almost to the edge, to look out at the sea.

"The great forces," she said. "Light and air, fire and water. These are the tools the scholars of old used in battle."

"Battle!" Susan said. "Light and air? Really?"

"I thought she said kids didn't have to fight," Jean whispered to Kate. "I don't like the sound of this."

Kate shifted uncomfortably from one foot to the other. Below them, the sea pulsed out toward the horizon, fleeing the shore.

"Light and air," Laysia said again. "Misdirected light, air with the force of a mountain thrown. These were the tools with which the sage kings took the lands around them. With these tools, they defended their kingdom, and with these they built the golden age."

Susan was looking uneasily at Laysia.

"You said they couldn't keep it up," Susan said. "They lost to the Genius. How strong could they have been?"

Laysia glanced her way. That mix of fear and anger in her

face unsettled Kate more than anything she said. "They lost then, yes, for the reasons I told you. They were strong, and yet he found their weakness. That is a weakness you will not have, so let me give you their strength, too. Let that be our hope."

Kate agreed with Jean. She didn't like the sound of this.

But she did turn out to like the lessons of that day, and the next, and the next. They were lessons on the fragile nature of light, how it bounced against you, like a ball, and rebounded to the eyes of whoever was looking. If you were careful and still, and kept your mind fixed on it, you could push that light away before it got to you. And no one could see you.

Jean saw the possibilities right away.

"Wish I could do that," she said to Kate. "That would be a trick! Then Susan wouldn't be able to see when I'm not listening!"

It was like that with Jean, Kate thought. Tricks. Maybe because Jean knew how to listen without even trying to. Though she'd complained about *thinking thinking thinking* all the time, back at the cottage, when the others were busy, Jean had made her Barbie into a teacher like Laysia, and Kate had fashioned sticks and stones and a little girl tied out of grass to be Barbie's students. Jean had made the stones pop up and down when Barbie told them to, though she hadn't even known she'd done it. Kate wished she knew that trick.

But she'd never had that knack, of doing things easily. So it took her a long time to think of light as something she could see, but as she'd learned to with air, she got used to thinking of it there, all around her, able to be moved and used. She imagined light like grains of sand, like dust caught in the sun. Untouchable but there, movable.

Susan was first to do it. Kate watched her, sitting on her knees in the grass, facing the far-off water. Then she wavered, like water herself. Kate blinked. Susan was there, solid — the familiar shape of her sitting under the sharp blue sky — then she wasn't.

"Susan!"

Nell, who had been trying to make a rock disappear, with limited success, looked up. Her eyes widened. Jean, playing with her weathered Barbie, stared around, looking for Susan. Laysia smiled grimly.

"She's done it!"

Kate wondered why it didn't make her happier.

Master, at what age does a man attain wisdom?
So the young student asked.
Some say when he comes to manhood, for then flows his
strength.
Some say with the taking of a wife, for he is then complete.
Some say after ten years of study, for only then does he begin
to understand.
Some say more, and some say never.
For wisdom is a ladder of a thousand rungs, and what man
can climb them all?
And the first rung of that climb? the young man asked.
Play, said the sage. For without it, there is nothing.
—"The Ladder of Wisdom," Tur Rime, Second Golden Age, Ganbihar

There was little time for play. Only the smallest of them sat in the clearing with her strange doll and dreamed as children should dream. The others bent to the task, and Laysia led them like the ox too early in harness.

To make up for it, at night she told them stories. The tale of Tur Doli, first of the sage kings, who climbed the peak and conquered the mountain city with a riddle. The little one's favorite was the tale of Tur Gafen, who crossed the ocean to Elsare and learned that with a playful mind, he could banish walls and move the sea as easily as a single drop of water.

"See?" Jean told Nell, who had that day scolded her for her games in the clearing. "Even the old men play."

Laysia thought of Tur Nurayim, grown old but ever loving his riddles and games. His board of shells and boxes still sat on the shelf in the cottage, long abandoned, for it was meant for two. He was one who loved little tricks and cleverness, and lessons full of play. He had made the first rung of wisdom into a kind of song he would sing to her, teasingly, when she was too impatient with her lessons.

"You want the flower without its seed," he had said. "Can such a thing be?"

For the seed was the child-sight, seeing the possible without building the wall of impossible to stop it.

"To the greatest mind, the wave is but a water drop, and so is the sea. In dreams, there is no great and small, no time, no walls at all. This is the lesson of the orchard."

Such was his song.

He had many of them. Songs of play and teaching, songs of power and of healing. He sang them so often to her that she found herself humming them, sometimes, in sleep.

She had cause to think of his songs often in these last years, after she had become an exile. The old man, Kaysh, was ever certain of his impossibilities. And so, as a poor substitute for their time on the first rung, she sang the children Tur Nurayim's song, a water drop to a wave, the first rung also the last.

And the next day, on the cliff's face, the littlest one, Jean, sprayed them with water drawn from the sea. In her play, she had called a wave.

Chapter 80

Laysia told them often that they were doing well, but there was an unhappiness in her voice, behind the praise, and Kate thought it must be that she was disappointed, maybe not in Susan and Nell, but in her and Jean, who were smaller than she had expected. How could the five include them? They were little, and not good enough.

Jean was not interested in trying harder. Each day when Max failed to come, she grew more silent. And though she perked up a little when they sat by the ocean, at night when they walked back to the cottage, she shrank down into a flat line like a cake pulled too soon from the oven.

Sometimes she'd invite Kate to go out back with her to read over Max's letters, but though these pleased Jean, who in a brief flurry of hope would always find some new proof that Max was coming tomorrow, or even an hour from now, they made Kate feel smaller than ever. So when Jean had finished reading and gone in to eat or play, Kate would creep out to the line of trees past the garden and practice the day's lesson again, hoping for a head start on the morning.

But she was very tired, and so mostly what she did was sit and listen to the woods. One night, she sat as the dark gathered, trying not to hear the hissing of the mist, trying to shake the leaden press of it from her bones. Somewhere in the distance, a fox yipped, and instead of being afraid, she found that the noise comforted her. So many things lived out here that didn't care about the mist, or the valley, or any of it. She liked thinking about that.

She listened and found that the forest was full of comforting sounds, busy with its own concerns. A lonely night bird screeched, and the wind hushed it. Crickets ran files across the bars of their legs.

Fireflies sparked and caught in the trees with a sound like small puckering kisses.

Something jumpy thrilled a little nearby, then waited. What was it? A rabbit, she thought, getting a sudden sense of a quivering, glass-eyed presence, What was it listening for? she wondered. A second later, she knew. A sleepy, half-interested bear, not too far off. How had she known that? She couldn't tell, but its presence tickled at her, something like a whisper, half caught. She sat very still. What else was here?

A squirrel, busily dismantling a nut. Hungry, hungry, hungry. The rabbit, tensed. And then — something complicated and sad. She turned to see Laysia coming to find her. The woman stood at the edge of the garden, peering into the wood, looking for her in the gathering dark.

"Kate?"

"I'm here."

"Don't you want to eat with the others?"

"Not really."

Laysia sat down, scattering the fireflies. The squirrel, full of caution, stopped working at its nut. The rabbit took off.

"I see you sit here often," Laysia said. The question floated unsaid into Kate's head.

"I'm just listening," Kate told her.

"Ah. You hear it, too."

"Not only that."

Laysia's face was unreadable in the dark, and Kate didn't say anything. The woman's presence had driven out the sounds of the wood, and again there was nothing much but the mist. But in time, as they sat quietly, Kate relaxed, and her ears opened up again.

Together they sat watching the fireflies glitter in the crown of trees, and listening to the calm beneath the mist, the life of the wood going on.

Chapter 81

Clouds of birds rose from the wood and swept toward the sea as the sun drifted westward in late afternoon. Kate watched them swirl out over the water and curve back, chattering hordes of them that rose, and then settled in the trees at the edge of land. Again and again, they swept up and then down, cresting hills of air that rolled across the sky.

"I like that sound," Jean said, looking up from her spot in the grass. She had set her Barbie across from her and was playing a game of four stones with it. "It's a lot better than the other."

Kate had not realized Jean could hear the mist. She'd never said anything about it before.

"You're right," she said. "Much better."

It was also the signal to start back, and so they walked beneath the noisy trees, barely aware, at first, of the persistent hiss of the valley. But as they left the birds behind, they heard it. And then it changed, its pitch rising. Kate cringed.

"Someone's coming through," Laysia said.

Everyone's head came up.

"Let's go!" Susan said. "It'll be him — I know it!"

They began running, leaping roots and dodging branches, toward the growing sound. Relief made Kate fast. Now everything would be all right again. Now Max would be back.

She outstripped the others, running through the clearing where the cottage lay, running toward her brother. She had reached the edge of Laysia's garden when she saw the figure lurching through the wood.

Not Max.

She froze. The slasher still wore clothing, a dress of light fabric that extended past its knees. A girl, then, but one who had grown horrible, twisted and furred, with wild eyes swirling in her head, her mouth open to show dangerous teeth. At the sound of Kate running toward it, the thing swiveled and howled.

Kate's head rang with the sound. Too much was in that howl. A strange wildness, terror, hunger. Kate heaved, her chest bursting, and gaped at it. Without warning, it swung forward, something bright flashing in Kate's eye.

Her legs would not move fast enough. *Disappear!* she thought furiously at herself. *Evaporate!* The thing lurched toward her, terror blaring from it, and Kate scrambled to grab the light, light like dust, like the cloud of birds, pieces and pieces. She saw it; she pushed it. The light wavered and bent. She felt the crackle in the air, and the hair on her arms rose. It seemed suddenly as if she looked through water. On the other side of that rippling wall, the slasher paused, blinking. Kate clutched the light, fragile as blown glass, balancing, balancing . . . and then that flash of reflection came again, and Kate saw it for what it was — a copper pendant.

"Wista!" Nell screamed from behind.

The wall of light dissolved, and the thing that had been Wista — pretty, cheerful Wista — turned and growled low in its throat and leaped.

Gray. A gray wall fell between them so suddenly that the thing slammed into it, and Kate could hear it squeal in pain. She was too stunned to move. Frustration, rage, terror. On the other side of the barrier, the slasher howled. Blankly, Kate lifted her hand to touch the wall. This wasn't light. This was —

"Stone," Laysia said behind her. "It was the best I could think of. I hope I haven't hurt him." She took Kate's hand. "Come," she said. "Quickly."

"Her," Kate said blankly. "It's a — her."

Nell came running. She pounded on the wall. Behind the stones, the thing that had been Wista screamed. In horror, Kate closed her ears. She wouldn't hear — she wouldn't! Her own terror shoved the other out, and she could hear Nell again, shouting.

"Let her come. Let me talk to her!"

Laysia put a hand on Nell's shoulder, tried to pull her back. "She can't hear you now," she said. "Come away, child. There's nothing for her."

But Nell wouldn't come away.

"No! No! You can't just let her go with those others. I saw them! We saw them in that cave!"

They stood there, all of them, staring at the stones, Nell shouting and insisting, until Laysia finally agreed to catch the thing and keep it, at least for now, from running farther into the woods.

"Fetch me a basket from the cupboard by the door," she said. "And put whatever food is left in there. Quickly."

Kate turned and ran before the others could and found the basket. It was lined with blue cloth. She filled it with bread and cheese and new tomatoes just as Susan and Jean, both looking sick, stumbled inside.

"She says to wait here," Susan said. "But Nell won't go. Give me the basket. I'll take it."

There was no use arguing with Nell; Kate knew that. But Susan looked like she might pitch over.

"I'll take it," Kate said. "I'm not afraid." She ran out without waiting for an answer.

The gray wall loomed at the edge of the garden, prematurely darkening the day. Nell was shouting Wista's name through the stones.

Laysia took the basket, laid it in the grass, and pulled Nell from the wall. They stepped back, and Kate watched the stones crumble to dust. The slasher that had been Wista stood a moment, bewildered, her hands bloodied from slamming the wall. Then her head swiveled to the basket, and she pounced on it. As she did, the wall returned, growing to encircle her. It closed her in. For a moment, they heard only the sound of the basket being torn to bits. Then the thing screamed again, a piercing wail that made Kate want to run. Another moment, and a dull thud followed — the slasher throwing itself against the wall.

"She'll keep there," Laysia said. "But she won't like it. Let her go, Nell. She'll only hurt herself against the stones."

"Then make it softer" was all Nell said.

Nell would not leave the wall, and so Kate stayed with her, even after Laysia went to see Susan and Jean. For an hour or more, the slasher screamed behind the stones. Nell peered through the chinks, talking to her.

"You're not a beast, Wista. You're a person. Your mother gave you that necklace, remember? You were going to learn to read. Remember? Wista? Wista!"

The thing growled and wailed and at last fell to whimpering as the dark came on. All the time, Kate tried to hear the girl's voice in it, nice Wista, happy Wista, who had come to their room asking for Nell. She couldn't.

Chapter 82

Now even in the wood at twilight, there was no peace, nothing but fear everywhere, fear blaring from the raving thing behind the wall, fear unsettling all the small creatures Kate had learned to listen for in the underbrush. Even the bear stopped its placid lumbering and knocked jaggedly against the trees out of sight in the woods.

Kate wanted to shut it out, all that noise of fear, but she didn't know how. It invaded her head like a bad dream, clung to her like humid air, like fine rain.

At dawn, Nell was back at the wall, but the sound of her voice only infuriated the thing behind it, and at last, after lowering a basket of food into the small fortress Laysia had made, she agreed to come away for a while, to the clearing.

Laysia said they needed air, but Kate thought there would never be enough air anymore, ever. Susan had barely spoken since the slasher's arrival. Jean, too, was silent. Now, as they walked together through the trees, Jean said, "Max wouldn't change like that, would he? He couldn't, right? Like you didn't, Nell, right?"

Kate saw a muscle jump in Nell's jaw. "It's all in your head," she said. "It's not even real."

"We're different," Susan said firmly. "She said so, didn't she?"

But they didn't seem so different anymore. Not so different from Wista.

Susan must have seen the look on her face then, because she at least took her hand as they went on, and the firm grip of it eased the walk a little.

In the end, though, none of it was enough. Not that day, and not in the days that followed, as Nell stayed most of the time by the wall, talking to the wailing beast behind it, and Susan grew as distracted as she had been in the valley.

There were moments, though.

One day that week, Laysia told them that of all the tools of the warrior, one was not learned, but remembered.

"We all dream of flying," she said when they stood away from the trees, facing the ocean. The glass cliff blinked like a beacon over their shoulders. "We are born knowing that we should rise. Only Loam holds us to her with her iron grip. We need simply convince her to loosen it a little."

As she spoke, she grew suddenly taller, and Kate saw that her feet were not on the ground.

"Try to remember," she said. "You've flown in dreams."

Finally, Kate thought, *something that makes sense.* In dreams, she had floated out of her own house and swooped in great dips, like the blackbirds. But here she was awake. Could a person dream standing up?

She didn't know how, so she did what she always did, and listened hard. She understood now that there was more to listen to than just voices. Beneath Laysia's talk, she found the wind hurrying the waves to shore, the ecstatic birds leaping up to meet the tide of air, the pop and crash as it tossed them toward the sun.

The birds are dreaming, she thought. *I can hear them doing it.* She reached for their shrill voices, those delirious, wheeling sounds, and for a dizzying second, they filled her up until nothing existed but wind and sun and the distant, unimportant lines of land and sea. Then a giddy lightness took her, the kind of loosening that came with floating in water. She could feel the wind breathe through her. The faint pressure of the ground against her feet disappeared.

Somebody called her name, but it was far away, and she barely heard. The sound of the wind was in her ears and the sky was all around and Kate was part of it, like the clouds, like the sun. The ground had nothing to do with her; she had forgotten it. Weightless, she felt the soft breeze ripple through her skin, sharp, like the splash of cold water. And again there was that sensation of rising, floating upward like a tuft of dandelion seed, so much fluff, riding the current.

She bobbed along and looked to the sea, and suddenly she was there — drawn to the pulsing, moving mass. She drifted down and settled on the sand. She had never seen such an untouched beach. It went on in both directions. She turned and looked. The cliff was far behind her, the people on it only specks. The sand she could feel was as soft, almost, as the sky.

"Sky child," Laysia said from behind her. She had followed and was standing a little way away on the sand. "Loam barely has a hold on you."

"It does feel like a dream," Kate said. This close, the sea was loud as hands clapping; it foamed at the hard sand along the edge of land. "Why didn't the others come?"

Laysia laughed. "Perhaps you live more in dreams than the rest of them," she said.

Kate didn't want to return to the cliff, to leave the bubbling welcome of the water, the sand that glittered in the summer afternoon, the cool salt breeze that washed the heat away into the mountain. But at last she let herself hear the birds again, and this time it was easier to fall into the dream and float up to follow Laysia back to the others. She settled to the ground in the clearing with the feeling of waking from a good sleep.

"You weren't afraid!" Jean said to her, astonished. The others told her they'd fallen down almost as quickly as they'd risen, but for Kate, for once, something had been easy. Susan and Nell looked at her with approval, and Kate felt for a moment as if she were still flying, as if she might keep rising forever, through the roof of the world, out into another universe, out toward home. Maybe, if the window didn't open, that was the way.

Smiling, Laysia said that Kate had begun to sense the parts of things; like the ancients, she could pick out the single voice in the group at song. Kate felt full of giddy possibility. Everything was there before her, and she could touch it, move it, remake it if she pleased. She could sense the bits that made up the steamy wood, and the garden, and the clearing overlooking the sea. She laughed then, forgetting everything as joy popped inside her chest like fizz. The others laughed with her.

But in the end, when they were back at the cottage, the joy ran out, and they ceased to laugh at all. Again, Kate found herself watching Susan as her sister watched the woods, waiting, listening, impatience carved into her forehead and around her mouth.

Despite the dream of flight, each night as they returned to the cottage and Nell went to the wall with her basket of food, calling Wista's name, and Max did not come, the world grew heavier, and Kate felt that it had been that way ever since she'd fallen through the window. Even Laysia seemed slower, weighed down by that sense of something needed, someone who wasn't there and should be.

Missing had become such a familiar feeling that it almost didn't surprise Kate when she woke to find Susan gone. It didn't surprise her, but it frightened her so badly that she nearly couldn't move.

She stood in the yard, trying to hear over the screams behind the wall, eyes scanning the empty woods. She tried to outshout Wista.

"Susan? Susan!"

But she knew Susan wouldn't answer. She heard the door behind her and Nell's voice.

"I can't find her anywhere."

Behind the wall, Wista wailed and then subsided into a whimper.

"She's gone to the mist," Nell said in the sudden quiet. "She's gone to get Max."

Laysia ran past her, toward the woods. Jean and Nell followed, and suddenly they were all sprinting toward the heavy place where the world seemed to tilt, where all the good feeling ran out like water down a drain.

Nell got there first, but they were all right behind her, breathless even though they were strong and the summer sun did not burn hot in the morning forest.

Susan lay on the mountainside, eyes open, tears tracing lines down the side of her face, her lips quivering.

Laysia dropped to her knees beside her, stared into her face, shook her, talked quickly. Kate saw Susan raise a hand, cover her eyes, and look away.

"She's all right," Laysia said when Kate crept closer. "She withstood it. But she couldn't get in."

Susan said nothing as they led her back through the woods. She walked like an old woman, hunched, slow. And when Kate tried to take her hand, it was limp. Kate squeezed, but Susan did not squeeze back.

◇ ◇ ◇

*L*aysia understood now why she had never been given a child. She would have failed it, as she had failed these she had been given to watch over, so briefly. She could not even overcome the objections of one half-grown girl, and so she had caged the pitiful remains of another child, its wits all gone, behind stone, so it could torment the rest day and night.

Tur Nurayim had been wrong to have faith in her, wrong to teach her. She had done nothing with his gift but harm.

She thought these dark thoughts all morning after she'd led Susan back from the edge of the valley. Now the girl sat alone and wept, head resting on her arm, she whom the others said did not weep, this child she'd seen conquer the powers of the warrior — air and light and fire.

It was all nothing, for she whom they had trusted had no answer to give.

She tried to think what Tur Nurayim would say, but it was hard, now, to imagine. He had not known this world, this place that had become empty without him. The world had changed, with the loss of him, and though he had known strife, he had never known this aloneness, this place where children were devoured. What would he have made of it?

At last, undone, she could do only the simplest of things and soothe the child with quiet talk, with tea and cinnamon, as Lan had done when she was small.

"The mist is terrible," she said. "We all know it."

But the child did not raise her head, and from outside, the lost one wailed and wept and threw herself against the stones.

Chapter 83

They set it against me," Susan said that night when she had finished crying and become furious instead. "You know what that means, don't you? They're holding him! They know we'll try to come for him, and they won't let us. It wasn't me who broke their stupid rules!"

Kate saw Nell's shoulders go up. They had spent the afternoon baking bread in the small brick oven behind the house. It was the first time they'd used it since they'd come. Laysia said that like the garden, work done by hand was soothing. Now Nell, who had just returned from lowering a loaf over the wall to Wista, narrowed her eyes.

"You think this is about breaking rules?" she said slowly. "Still? What rule did Wista break, do you think?"

Kate looked over at Laysia, but the woman didn't know how bad the two of them could get. Weeks of upset seemed to wind themselves into Susan's face when she answered.

"Maybe the rule about associating with us," Susan said. "Why couldn't you have just listened when I told you not to make waves there?"

Nell looked like someone had punched her. Kate cringed. Outside, the bread had quieted Wista, and only the crickets were loud now.

"Listened?" Nell said. "If I'd listened, you'd be the one we had to drag out of there. You were losing your mind, or don't you remember? But why would you? You were waiting for Max to do something."

The shaky sound of cicadas buzzed through the window, and Susan turned her back.

"Maybe they're not holding him," Nell persisted. "Did you ever think of that? Maybe he's just forgotten about us!"

"No!" Jean shouted. "He wouldn't!" She had begun to pull at her doll's hair in her agitation, and blond strands of it glittered on the floor.

Susan said he wouldn't too many times after that, and Laysia, caught between them, would only say that yes, it was possible they were holding him. She couldn't tell anymore what they would do. And Nell, furious and near tears, went out to the wall.

The next day, no one went to the clearing. Nell stayed with Wista, talking in that low voice she used, while the slasher moaned and shrieked. The rabbits and the squirrels had long since fled the sound of her, leaving the wood too empty in the circle around the house. Kate felt sick with the emptiness and with the noise. She watched Jean leave the house to draw figures in the dirt beneath the trees. And Susan sat on her bed, sullen and silent.

"Max will come," Kate said to her. "And then we can take him to see the ocean. He'll love that."

Susan nodded distractedly.

"Don't you think so?"

"Hmm?"

"Don't you think Max will love to go to the ocean?"

Susan wouldn't really look at her. She wasn't listening.

That night, Kate woke abruptly in the dark, her heart thundering in her chest. She thought she must have dreamed something terrible, but she couldn't remember it. All she could think of was the mist. Susan and Nell had both pricked it, and now she could hear it muttering in the dark, restless and hungry. Like some hideous beast, it would soon climb the mountain, jaws wide, to swallow them, just as it had swallowed Wista.

She slipped out of bed, into the main room, and then, without even finding her shoes, out the front door. The crickets trilled, and in her walled prison, the slasher moaned and grumbled in sleep. There was no moon.

The stars shimmered overhead, sandy grains of light that barely separated tree from air. But the mist whispered at her, and she felt the persistent weight of it beneath the breeze. She turned and made her way toward it.

The forest floor hurt her feet, and she picked her way through it, trying to step lightly. After a while, the sudden jab of a twig or the pull of a thorn didn't bother her. The mist was louder, and the thickness of it swam around her, blotting out other things.

It won't notice, she thought. *Like Susan doesn't, like Nell doesn't. It will think I'm too young to worry about.*

Her pulse beat in her throat and up around her ears, until it was nearly as loud as the murmuring air. *It doesn't know my name,* she told herself.

She reached the edge of the forest and stepped out. The

land dipped. Below her, she could feel the valley, and its foggy boundary, stretching up to meet her.

I'm little, she thought. *It will leave me alone.*

She stood for a second, listening to the steady roar of it, the hiss of a hundred angry voices. But it didn't change. Though she stood close to it, she could hear no question, no warning.

She stepped down into it.

The mist closed around her, and the muttering rose — strange, unintelligible words, a grimy whiteness that she wanted to drag from her eyes. She shut them against it.

It wanted to come inside her. It wanted to seep in behind her eyes, worm its way there, push into her head. She had lost, all of a sudden, her sense of direction. Which way was down? She needed to walk down, but now she stumbled, thinking that she could go on forever and always be standing right here. She was lost, lost like Nell had been lost, lost like Wista was lost!

Panic clanged in her brain and she nearly fell.

No! Laysia said we're not like them! We're different; we have a shell. My skin is all hard lines, and it can't take me!

She thought it as loudly as she could, keeping her eyes closed. Voices whined in her ear, sinister words in some other language she didn't recognize.

It didn't call her name. It didn't shout at her. It didn't know her.

She breathed in and out, listening to the sound of her own breath.

What had Susan done, that first time?

Don't open your eyes, she told herself. *Don't make it more real than it is. It's like the light, there but not there. Bend it, like the light.*

The mist, too, was only pieces. She'd been thinking of it as a fog, but it was a sandstorm. A million individual drops, able to be nudged apart.

She pushed at them and felt the weight pressing on her give a little.

Tentatively, she opened her eyes. There was the valley below, glinting dimly in the starlight.

Kate ran through the tunnel in the mist.

Chapter 84

No one stopped her this time as she made her way alone onto the boys' floor. She didn't know which room was Max's, had no idea where exactly to find him, and so she moved from door to door, barefoot and silent, looking in on the sleeping boys.

She found him at last in a room alone, asleep beneath a window that was open to the night. She stepped inside, closed the door behind her, and shook him.

"Max! Max! It's Kate!"

He bolted to a sitting position even before he was fully awake. When his eyes had focused, he looked at her, confused.

"Kate? Kate!"

He grabbed her then, hugging her so tightly she lost her breath. "You came back! I'm so glad!"

Kate nodded, trying to get the words out. She told him of the mountain, and Laysia, and the others.

"You don't have to stay here!" she said. "You can come with us!"

But as Max listened, he dropped his arms and pulled away. He was watching her now, eyes shrouded in the darkness.

"Kate," he said, "who sent you here?"

Startled, she shrugged. "No one sent me. I came because I wanted to!"

He was sitting back now, regarding her in a way she didn't understand. "Alone? I don't think so," he said. "They said you'd gone to that woman they told me about. Did she send you? The exile?"

"Her name's Laysia."

"*Laysia,* then. Did she send you?"

"I told you, no!"

"Kate, stay here. I'll make sure they take care of you. Jean, too."

She stared at him. "What about Susan and Nell?"

Max dropped his eyes. "Them, too — just not right away. I've tried to talk to the Guide about that. Explain that things are different where we come from. He doesn't understand just yet. But he'll come around. I know I can make him understand. He'll let them back soon."

Kate's stomach twisted. "Who can you make understand?"

"Tur Kaysh. The Guide. And the Master Watcher. He's almost as big. Did you know that? And he came for us himself!"

She shook her head.

Max leaned forward, eyes alight. In the next room, a boy mumbled in his sleep and a bed behind the wall creaked. Max glanced that way and lowered his voice.

"Listen, Kate. What I'm doing here is important! Jean knows — I wrote her about it! We're different from the people here — did you know that? We can do things even they can't do — at least not as easily, not as naturally. Do you know, when

I showed Tur Kaysh what I'd learned to do in the woods, he said it was a sign that the time is coming? Do you realize what that means? Do you see?"

But she didn't see. She only understood that Max was not being held. Max wanted to stay. Nell had been right.

Chapter 85

Kate sat across from Max in the dark room, trying to make him see.

"But they pushed Nell out! And Susan, too! They *hurt* people, Max. They make the mist! Do you know what it does to people? What Nell told us is true! Don't listen to them, Max! Come back with me."

Max thrust his lip forward, and his eyebrows came down.

"It's not true," Max said. "The Guide is a great man! He knows what he's doing. It's all for the good, Kate. You'll see!"

She pulled away from him, stunned. *All for the good?* What was he saying?

"How can it be, Max? Hurting Susan? Hurting Nell?"

"Kate, you don't get it."

But she did get it. She did.

Max reached across the bed and took her arm, shook it lightly. "Kate, I know it's hard for you to understand. You're not big enough. But trust me. Trust me! You wouldn't believe the things I'm learning here — things we'd never have dreamed of in the woods! Things we couldn't do on our own! And it's not for nothing, Kate. It's not just for fun!"

She pulled herself from his grip, folded her arms across her chest.

"Can you fly, then? Can you push the light away so you can't be seen?"

His mouth opened, then closed. He regarded her a moment.

"Where did you hear about that? The exile? Did she tell you?"

Kate set her jaw. "You don't have to learn here, Max. You can be with us."

But he wasn't listening. His eyes were gleaming.

"Kate, listen. Something big is happening. Here. Not out there. Most of them here don't even know about it. But the Guide told me, because I'm part of it, don't you see? My coming is part of it!"

Outside, an owl hooted in the moonless night.

"Part of what?" she asked him.

"The end of the Genius. You saw how terrible it was there. What they do to people! Remember what they'd have done to us! But it's almost over now. The Guide's been preparing for years, and it's almost time. We're going after him now. We're strong enough!"

"We? You, too? You're going back there?"

He leaned forward, so focused on what he was trying to express that he nearly stood up.

"I have to, don't you see? I'm stronger than I was before! Different! I know things. We all do. The Guide's been teaching us, and we can do what they never could do when the Genius took over. It's time to end it. To finish them in the city. And I'm here for that."

"No! Max, the Genius is dangerous!"

He laughed, so suddenly it made her jump.

"Kate, *we're* dangerous. To him, anyway. More than he's ready for. And I'm part of that. Do you think we came here by accident? Do you think we just *fell* through that window?"

She shook her head. "Why are you saying this? Did they tell you about the five?"

He sat back, surprised. "So she told you that, too. They're right that she's dangerous, spilling secrets like that. But yes — the five. I'm one of them! The Guide knew it from the first! I'm here because I'm meant to be, Kate. I'm going to help them get him. Finish him."

Kate felt a heat rise behind her eyes, and her throat tightened.

"But what about us?" she whispered. "What about the five of us?"

He barely seemed to hear her.

"Max! Laysia says it's the five of us who are here for a reason!"

That got his attention. He frowned and shook his head.

"Kate, she *is* crazy, telling you that. You're a little kid! Don't be ridiculous. Can't you see how dangerous she is?"

Kate understood suddenly that nothing she said would matter. He wouldn't listen.

"Max," she said, "what about getting home?"

"Later," he assured her. "There'll be time for all of that. After the Genius is gone, I'll come back. And then we'll go. I promise."

He reached for her hand, but she drew back.

Max was different now. More different, even, than Susan.

◇ BOOK FIVE ◇

JEAN

Chapter 86

Jean had had enough of the waiting. Max had said this wasn't a dream, and at last Jean had come to believe him. There wasn't so much waiting around in dreams. Not even in nightmares. Until now, she'd been patient, she thought. More than patient.

She liked to remind herself that she was small. She wasn't like Kate — the suggestion didn't make her mad. Who wanted to be big, anyway? She preferred to play, which was what small people did. She didn't like all the fuss and effort and upset of big people. Nell in the sanctuary, for example. Jean hadn't understood that. The people there were nice, and her teachers had been cheerful, and she liked the songs.

Most people were nice, in the end. Even Liyla, who Jean hadn't liked at all, turned out not to be too bad. Like Jean, she had a mother and a father who cared about her. They were strange, true, but then lots of people's parents were strange. Not like the Genius. Of all the people Jean had seen here he, he and that pinch-faced lady in the red dress, were unrecognizable. Jean was pretty sure neither of them had a mother or father.

Thinking of mothers and fathers made Jean feel bad, and she tried not to think of her own, waiting for her back home. Countless times over the past two months, she'd pushed such unhappy thoughts away, and she did it again now, reminding herself that Max would have to be here sometime, and at least the Genius and Ker were far away now, and put away, like a bad dream after you woke up. And since that bad time in the city she'd played wonderful games here, even Susan and Nell and Kate had played. She'd seen Susan flicker out like a candle, only her voice left. Kate had surprised her by swooping off the cliff without shrieking in terror. And Nell had sent a fire-cracker of flame shooting from her hand into the sky. That had been worth being here for. Here, she could bounce her Barbie on the air or sing a little *come here* song to the sea and feel the splash of the wave, even up high.

But that was all gone now. For days, there had been only the awful thing behind the wall, and the waiting. It was time to go.

Max had said he would get her home, and she believed him. But he was taking too much time coming. Small people shouldn't have to wait so long, she thought. Wasn't that the use of being small?

She sighed. This morning, even Kate would not wake. She slept beside Susan, her dirty feet poking from under the covers. There would be no games of stones, no Barbie school or party, nothing at all to help fill the long hours while Susan and Laysia talked or looked into the worn books on the shelves. As usual, Nell was crouched at the stone wall near the garden, her face pressed to the cracks, talking steadily at the wailing thing on the other side. Laysia worked nearby digging carrots, look-ing strained as the beast shrieked and pounded.

"Come away from it," Jean said to Nell.

Thud, squeal, thud, squeal, went the beast behind the wall. Jean flinched. "Do something with me."

"Not now," Nell said.

She called the thing by name, and Jean ran away, hating to hear that. It was not a person behind the stones. No matter what Nell said, it was *not*.

A nightmare would be better, she thought. A nightmare would end with waking up, with Mom slipping into her room in the dark, with her head pressed against her mother's chest, the steady *thump thump* of it slowing her own heart to match. Here there was only *thud* and *squeal* and the hateful hissing of the cloud that kept Max on its other side.

She wandered behind the cottage to the mossy place beneath the tall trees, wondering when Max would come. She pulled out the wad of his letters and selected one. She could tell which was which now, even without unfolding them. This particular letter had grown furry, she'd handled the paper so much.

Dear Jean,

I'm sorry I didn't get to come over yesterday. Please don't be sad about it. I'm just trying to get us home, and to do that, I have to learn as much as I can. Every day is filled up with so much stuff, I can barely sleep. Yesterday I asked Tur Kaysh why the air crackles when we change things. Remember how it does that? I don't know if you felt it, and half the time I didn't notice it in the beginning, but now that I do, I can feel that shiver in the air. He was surprised I felt that, and he called me a bright light. No one ever called me that at school back home, I can promise you that! He said that I need to see how the pattern of the world is at our fingertips, and if we understand the order of it, we can change things. That's how rebellion ripped a hole in the world to begin with, he said. After that all the learning leaked out, and everything went dark. He pointed west when he said it, and I knew he meant the Domain. It's only the sanctuary that's still trying to fix the problem. I asked him if it wasn't too big a job, just for the few of us here. He said no, anything can be done if you understand the order of things. I think it's like that probably at home, too, but here the pattern isn't locked, like it is there. So you see, Jean, anything can be done, even opening up windows. I'll get to that any day now, I just know it. You can tell the others what I said, and maybe they'll be a little better about the waiting.

See you soon,

Your brother,

Max

She sighed and folded the letter and put it away. She hadn't seen him soon, and she wanted to know when she would. How much learning could a person do? Wasn't he done yet? She retrieved her Barbie from the grass and held her up to the light. The doll's smooth plastic features smelled faintly of home. Thorns had ripped her pink dress, and one of her tiny arched feet was stained green, but she was still beautiful. She was a birthday Barbie, though she hadn't been given on a birthday. Jean remembered the day her father had brought her home, in a box of glossy cardboard, Barbie standing elegantly behind clear plastic, smiling out as if from a store window.

She wanted to go *home*.

"Jean?"

The girl's voice surprised Jean. She looked up. The clearing on which the cottage sat didn't go very far, and a little way from where she played with her back to the house, the long-necked trees stood in the warm morning, the leaves waving now and then with the humid breeze. The gray and black trunks made lines that kept the shadows in, and she couldn't see into them. Who was it? It couldn't be one of her sisters.

"Who's there?"

She stood, swinging her doll by its legs, and ventured to the edge of the trees. Again, the voice came from the shadows.

"It's me, remember? You came to my house. I got lost — I — I need help."

Jean took a step beneath the trees and blinked. Not far off, standing shyly beside an elm tree and picking at its bark, stood Liyla.

"Hi!" the girl said. "Remember?"

Jean raised her hand to wave back wonderingly. Where had *Liyla* come from? Maybe she'd brought her here by thinking about her.

"C'mere," the girl said. "You know me. Remember?"

Jean glanced back at the house. No one moved there. Laysia was on the other side, in the garden. But Jean did know Liyla. She moved toward her.

"How'd you get here?"

Liyla smiled, her lips spreading to reveal those sharp teeth.

"I didn't like the city anymore. I left. I heard there were places to go here, in the woods. Is it true?"

Jean nodded.

"Can you show me?"

Jean looked back again, over her shoulder. A small cloud of insects buzzed in the sunlight near Laysia's house.

"I don't know," she said. "I don't think I should go alone."

Liyla's smile widened. Her eyes were very round. "I'll be with you, though, right? And we know each other."

Still Jean hesitated.

"Maybe I should get Susan. She'll want to know you're here."

Liyla grinned and nodded. But as Jean turned to go, the girl caught her hand. "Wait," she said. "We don't have to bother her yet. I'm tired. I thought I'd rest awhile. I've been walking so long. You want to stay with me? Just right here?"

Jean didn't like the feel of Liyla's hand. Those sharp, clawed fingers. And despite the heat of the day, Liyla's touch was cold.

"Okay," she said, pulling her hand gently back. "Just for a little while, I guess."

Liyla sat down among the tree roots that jutted up from the ground like bent fingers.

"Come on," she said. "Sit down, why don't you?"

Jean sat. But she inched backward when Liyla tried to move closer to her. There was something odd about the girl, different from before. She fidgeted too much. Her eyes darted out into the forest, then back to Jean.

"Does your mother know you're gone?" Jean asked her.

"What?" Liyla jumped a little and reddened beneath the roughness of her strange face. She brought her hand up to smooth her wild hair.

Jean stared. The girl's collar had dipped, revealing a wide, ugly scab that ran down into her chest. All around it, the hair that had coated Liyla's skin was gone. Liyla saw her looking and jerked her shirt back in place.

"I got splashed with some tea," she said.

"Oh."

Jean wanted to leave. But it wouldn't be nice, she thought, to simply run from the girl. She was alone, too, after all.

Liyla kicked at the knotty side of a root, trying to worm a toe under it. She looked again into the forest.

"Hey," she said, smiling suddenly. "Want to play something? A game I know?"

Jean shrugged. "What game?"

"It's a follow game. You know, I'll do something, and you see if you can match it. We play it all the time back home. Want to?"

Jean tilted her head. She hadn't noticed Liyla being much interested in playing before. But maybe it was being alone like this and far from home. Jean understood that.

"Just right here?"

"Sure. We won't go far."

"Okay."

Liyla stood and stretched her arms. "I'm first," she said. She hopped on one foot over the roots, making a bouncy circle around the tree. "Now you."

Jean did the same. When it was her turn, she hopped backward over the roots. Liyla tried to follow and lost her balance. But she only laughed when she fell, an unsettling, fluttery sound.

"My turn," Liyla said. She wound her way, skipping, around several trees. Jean followed. Then Jean climbed to a low branch, and Liyla did the same.

"You're a good climber," she said. "But can you run?"

She took off at a sprint then — and Jean followed, Barbie's yellow hair flying. When she caught up to Liyla, the girl was panting, bent over double.

"You're good," she said, trying to catch her breath. "Little, but fast."

Jean smiled. She turned, but she couldn't see the house.

"We'd better go back," she said.

"Okay."

Liyla was still smiling when someone grabbed Jean from behind.

Chapter 87

Jean kicked and squirmed and tried to scream, but a hand was over her mouth, a thick, gnarled hand that smelled like wet dog. And then she was moving, so quickly she could not wriggle away. One minute Liyla was smiling, and the next the smile was a grimace as Jean flew past her, fighting, pinned to someone large and swift moving.

"This way!" she heard a man growl, and the trees whipped by as she was jostled and bounced, her captor's ragged, moist breath against her neck.

They didn't go for long. Over another hill, and she saw them, hundreds of soldiers of the Genius, their red cloaks garish and out of place in the muted, sunlit wood.

"We've got one!" the guttural voice called. Jean could feel the scratch of his whiskered face against the back of her head. The soldiers lounging against the trees looked up. One nodded briskly, turned, and ran off.

The man carrying her slowed to a walk. He marched past the others, who peered at her and laughed when she thrashed and tried to wrench free. She kicked and fought as they hurried up another rise and down a small hill, to where the forest thinned into a wide, low clearing. Tents like red spiders crouched in the dirt there, and felled trees, their stumps wet

and yellow as skinned knees, sat beneath a haze of new sawdust. The man carrying Jean breathed hard, jogging again
toward the largest of the tents. A soldier stood at attention
there, holding a flagpole in his rough hand. Jean stopped
squirming. At the tip of the pole, lashed with a red wire, hung
Kate's Barbie.

Ker emerged from the tent, dressed in a long red tunic,
leggings, and a half skirt that flowed behind her so the back
brushed the ground just enough to have picked up a crust of
sawdust around the hem. She saw Jean and smiled.

"Well done," she said. "I knew you would become a good,
obedient girl yet. Come here."

Her shoulders slumped, Liyla slipped past Jean and moved
toward the woman. She didn't turn to look in Jean's direction.

Ker smiled her ghastly blunted smile and blinked with eyes
like slits at the girl. "The Genius always keeps his promises,"
she said to her. "And he remembers his friends."

Liyla nodded faintly, head down.

But Ker had already moved past her, and she was beckon-
ing in Jean's direction.

"This way," she said, indicating the tent behind her. "Here.
And put her down. She is our guest, after all."

Jean found herself slung to the ground. Immediately, she
turned and slammed her doll across the knees of the red-
uniformed man behind her. He wrenched it away and handed
it over her head to Ker, whose smile widened.

"The mate. He'll be pleased. What cunning things
these are."

She reached down and snatched Jean roughly by the wrist.

"Careful, now," the woman hissed. "You'll want to be on

your best behavior here. The Genius does not abide disobedience. Even from *guests*." She dug her fingers into Jean's skin for emphasis.

Jean didn't want to go into the tent. Her breath came in rasping gasps and she drew back, trying to force her heels into the dirt, to keep Ker from pulling her forward. But the woman was strong, and she leaned down to Jean's ear.

"You're not with the others now, child," she whispered. "No strange wind will save you this time. Obey me, or you'll see what comes of those who don't."

She yanked Jean upright, hard, and thrust her forward into the tent.

The air was sticky inside, and the light came red through the canvas. Toward the back, the Genius sat in a stiff jacket of ruby brocade, too heavy for the weather, his raw, unnatural face flushing with the heat, and his knobby hands clenching wetly at the arms of his chair. His black dog lay beside him, but as Jean stumbled in, it raised its head.

The Genius leaned forward and rubbed his perspiring palms on his legs.

"Well," he said, "so the girl did it after all."

"She did," Ker said. "This is the smallest one. And I'd dare say the weakest."

The Genius grinned, and his ugly, too-large teeth made Jean shudder. "Oh, I remember her," he said. "This one especially. We know each other, don't we, child?"

"You don't know me," Jean said, and she blushed to hear her voice shaking.

The Genius only grinned wider, his square teeth like stones in his mouth. "Oh, but I do. You've lived here so long."

He tapped his head when he said it. The man was crazy, just like Nell had said.

"I'd thought you were bigger, older. But our memories play tricks on us, don't they?"

She found nothing to say to that, and the man looked at her a little longer with those wet eyes of his, pale as shells. His face was hairless as a worm; he had no brows or even lashes. Only the bony edges of his forehead and cheeks, too sharp, framed those hollow eyes.

At last he turned to Ker.

"Will they come for her, then?"

Ker shoved Jean closer so she nearly fell; she caught herself several feet from the Genius.

"Such a pretty thing?" Ker said. "I believe they will."

"Let me see her," he said. And Ker jabbed her again, so she'd go close. The ugly hand came up to her cheek, and the Genius ran a finger along it. His touch was gritty as sandpaper.

"So perfect," he said. "Just like the miniature. And this time, really mine."

Ker leaned over and took Jean's hand, forcing her palm flat. "Everywhere. Look here, at the fingers. See how straight they are? And the nails?"

Jean struggled, but the woman's grip was heavy as cement, and Jean felt the Genius's humid breath across her knuckles. He took her hand in his, cupping it in his gnarled palms, and laughed.

"And the others so near. If it's as our mysterious friend says, this will be a most rewarding trip. Soon, now, I'll have them all."

He touched Jean's face again, wetting his lips with his tongue as he swept those pale eyes from her forehead to her chin. "Leave her with me," he said to Ker. "She's a wonder to see. And send for the girl. I want to hear again what she was told."

Chapter 88

Jean didn't wait to hear what Liyla had to say. The minute Ker loosened her grip and turned to go, she ran, not even thinking of the soldiers outside or, worse, the black dog. But it pounced before she'd taken three steps, knocking her into the dirt and holding her there, its feet on her back and its teeth at her collar. Jean squirmed as it pressed its wet nose into her neck, growling, until the soldiers pulled the beast off her. When they dragged her back to the Genius, he at least no longer wore his sickening smile.

"Bind her," he said to the soldiers, and they tied her so tightly to a chair that her arms stung and her back, forced straight, ached with stiffness.

For the first hour, she tried to free herself, concentrating on the ropes and trying to pull them to pieces, strand by strand. When that didn't work, she hoped she could at least make the wind blow, as Susan had, and knock the ugly Genius from his chair. But she managed none of it. Her heart pounded too insistently in her chest, and the shaded area around her seemed to fracture into a hundred jagged pieces. In the end, she was too small, too frightened.

The morning wore on, and old men in fancy uniforms came to the tent, to peer at her and examine her Barbie, which rested now on a table beside the Genius's seat, next to a long blade with a red enameled grip. They leaned over Jean with their terrible, ferocious faces until her breath caught in her throat, and she closed her eyes against the sight of them.

"See! See!" the Genius told them as they pressed closer, rancid with sweat and sour breath, touching her face and hands. Nausea engulfed her and her head swam. Her heartbeat pounded in her ears, muffling sound, but not enough to block the Genius's awful voice.

"Take a look at our answer," he said. "Take a look at the face of the future!"

Jean whimpered and felt as if she were choking. At last the awful men were gone, and Liyla came back, head down, walking in an odd, tight way as she entered the tent. She answered the Genius in a quavering voice. Yes, she had seen the house, just where they said it would be. There were several more like this there. All girls. They would come for her. Yes. Definitely. Soon.

He nodded, and she crept aside to stand silent and hunched in a corner near Jean's seat.

"Look your fill, girl," the Genius said, noticing. "Soon you, too, will have a face like that. All of us will." And he smiled without showing his teeth.

Jean's belly had turned to water. Terror was a jackhammer pounding in her stomach and throat. She would have liked to scream or cry, but her throat closed against it. Not even a sound could make its way up through that tight space. The heat rose, the tent baked, and sweat crept from the roots of Jean's hair and trickled down her cheek. For all that, her body was a block of ice.

At last the Genius took his dog and went out into the air.

"Jean."

Liyla's voice cracked on the name.

"Jean, I'm sorry."

Jean pretended she didn't hear.

"I couldn't help it. They made me. I couldn't — I couldn't do anything else. You don't know them; you don't know what they do. I *couldn't*, Jean. Don't you see?"

Jean's voice had come back to her, but she wouldn't use it. She clenched her teeth. She hated Liyla. Hated her. Wished she were dead, ripped into a thousand pieces like shredded paper. She hated her "couldn't" and "Don't you see?" She didn't see. She wouldn't. She turned her face away. It was the one thing she could move.

Chapter 89

The hours wore on and Jean was alone with Liyla. No one brought food. Not for Jean, and not for the girl, whose stomach growled so loudly it made Jean jump, setting her arms throbbing against the ropes.

"You hungry?" Liyla asked.

No, no, no, Jean thought. She remembered Liyla in the orchard, dropping plums into her basket and stuffing them into her skirt. Remembered her bargaining with the fruit seller. She'd never asked if Jean was hungry then.

Liyla went out and returned quickly with bread. "I can't untie you," she said, still not meeting Jean's eye. "But if you want, I can feed it to you."

Jean just looked at her. The inside of her mouth tasted sour, and her tongue stuck to the backs of her teeth. No, she wouldn't eat.

But Liyla tried to push the bread to her lips. "Eat," she whispered. "Eat, or you'll be sick!"

At this, Jean finally spoke. "Sick! Since when do you care who gets sick?"

The tiled room, with its straps and needles and knives, flashed before her eyes. Jean shivered, remembering the cold.

Liyla flushed, and she dropped her hands to her sides. She left the tent, and Jean was happy, furiously happy, that she had gone, but the girl returned and forced a cup of water to Jean's lips.

"Drink," she whispered. "You have to! I don't want you to be sick."

At last, Jean drank. Her throat had begun to stick to itself. She could feel it closing, making it hard to breathe. Panic darted through her again.

Liyla watched her, nodding anxiously. She drew the cup back and let Jean swallow, then offered it again. Jean shook her head and closed her eyes.

"You sold us," she said. "You sold us for money. You gave them Kate's Barbie and helped them find us!"

"No!" Liyla croaked. "No, they came and found me! They made me come!"

Jean only shook her head.

"It was a fanatic," Liyla said, quick, low. "One came to my house, looking for you. He told them about this place."

"I don't believe you," Jean said, turning her face away.

"Would I know how to get here by myself?" Liyla asked her. "A week's walk from home, in the mountains? Why would I know?"

Jean looked at her. She had to be telling a lie.

❖ ❖ ❖

Fear:
The great bird of prey
Come to rip our throats.
Madness:
Our house
A heap of bricks.
Salt and ashes,
Salt and ashes.
We choke on the food of despair.
— *Poem of the Wanderings in Elsare, Author Unknown, Ganbihar*

*F*rantic, the children called and searched. The broken one screamed in her wall of stones. The smallest of them was gone. Kate had bolted from sleep near midday, shouting of wrong on the mountain, and Jean, the playful child, was nowhere in the house or garden.

Salt and ashes.

Salt and ashes.

The house would topple to a heap of bricks, and birds of prey circling.

The mist was rising.

Laysia ran breathless through the garden. She could feel the mist climbing the mountain, a smothering cloud rolling up to take the wood. No single broken soul stumbling, this, but the smoke rushing before a devouring fire. The air shuddered, and the children cringed and bent at the sound of it, a shout where a whisper had been.

"It's taken her!" Susan cried. "Not Jean, too!"

She ran toward the coming wave.

"No!" Kate shouted. "This way!"

Behind the wall, the lost one's wail choked and fell silent, and Laysia scattered the stones and released her. The maddened child fled before the onrush as the others turned to meet the tidal force, calling for their sister.

Chapter 90

The smell of dirt and sawdust and baking leather clogged the tent as the hours wore away. Heat wrapped around Jean's body, muffled her breath, slipped into her head to dull the edge of her thoughts. At last even the fear grew distant, an ache that throbbed behind a red curtain.

She hung listless against the ropes as the sun seeped orange across the canvas. Then a flash of white made her jerk upright.

A soldier had lifted the tent flap. From the corner of her eye, Jean saw the little mound curled beside her come to life. It was Liyla, wet with perspiration. The black dog bounded in, followed by the Genius and two soldiers. Looming figures in the reddened light, they were too big for the tent, pungent with animal musk and wool gone sour with damp.

"Ready the banner," the Genius said. A soldier lifted Jean's Barbie from the table and lashed it to a pole. The Genius took the red-handled knife and slipped it into his embroidered belt.

"Good. Bring them."

Before Jean could protest, they jerked the chair from the ground and hoisted her between them. The ropes tore at her skin.

"Wait!" Where are you taking me? Stop! It hurts!"

No one answered. Over her shoulder, she could see a soldier yank Liyla, startled and blinking, to her feet.

Tears blurred Jean's eyes in the sudden glare, but when they cleared, there stood Ker with a company of soldiers, the strange bald angle of her face twisting as she smiled.

"At last we begin. Hurry now. They've been sighted. A force of some size."

The Genius's voice came from behind Jean. "How many?"

Ker seemed uncertain. "The scout said he couldn't tell. Something obscures his vision."

The Genius only laughed. "Excellent. I would have expected nothing less." Satisfaction curled from him like smoke.

From her place on the raised chair, Jean looked out at the hollow with its stumps and tents and red cloaks. Fewer than a hundred soldiers remained in the bowl of land. She turned her head, trying to see the others, and couldn't.

"Come now," the Genius said.

"Hiyup!" one of the soldiers called, and the men carrying Jean took off at a trot, heading west.

Chapter 91

The soldiers climbed toward a half dozen tall trees that clung to the land overlooking the camp. The dog galloped ahead, turning when it reached the ridge. Another tent sat there, blocking Jean's view of the forest, but she could see the trees sloping down to the west, dark lines in the breathless wood.

They set the chair down and released the ropes.

"Get up," the Genius said. "Walk with me." He spoke as if Jean really were his guest; he was as gleeful as he'd been when she'd entered the tent.

A soldier jerked Jean to her feet, and she stumbled on rubbery legs.

"Spark enjoys the woods," the Genius went on, nodding in the dog's direction. "So much less crowded than the city."

He'd begun to stroll past the tent, and the soldier dragged her along. When they'd passed it, Jean turned to see the wood, rolling out from the camp, and nearly fell down again. In the near distance, waiting among the trees, were thousands of red cloaks, so thick on the mountain that she could no longer spy any of the bushes or vines and knots she'd waded through with the others. Silent, the mass seethed, waiting beneath the leaves, and though she craned her neck to find it, Jean couldn't make out its end.

"Of course," the Genius went on blithely, "too many people discover a pleasant spot like this, and it quickly becomes crowded."

From the corner of her eye, Jean saw Liyla, shoved forward by another soldier to keep pace with them. They came to a second structure, a low barn with two wide doors and no windows, a flat roof, and walls of mud-plastered slats. To its left, a corral of sawed-off branches sat on a raised bit of land with a good view of the hollow. Inside it, four men and one woman sat hunched on the grass, their wrists manacled, attached by long chains to cuffs at their ankles. They sat strangely still, and with a start, Jean saw that the woman with her head resting against the splintery fence was Liyla's mother. The girl's father sat with his eyes half closed beside her.

The Genius saw her looking. "People pay for their visitors here," he told her, and laughed. "Though some were confused on that point and thought perhaps I should be the one paying."

As she stared, he went on. "I suspect you know these others. Perhaps you recall my warning that other smooth-faced girl what happens when people tell me lies." He tilted his head, amused. "So often people forget the meaning of true genius."

The wind blew hot on the hill, but as Jean peered into the corral, she shivered. There on the grass sat the fruit seller Liyla had spoken to that first day. Beside him, the soldier who had asked Max to bless him and the younger one, who'd been knocked out by the branch. Each sat as if made of stone, barely flinching as the soldiers dragged Jean and Liyla among them and unrolled two metal chains with cuffs at either end.

"Tie them to each other," the Genius said to the guards,

and they snapped an iron cuff on each of Jean's wrists, then fastened her to Liyla so she was forced to face the girl. When they were finished, the soldier who'd done the fastening jerked the chain down and the girls fell to their knees. Jean lunged back up, flailing, trying to pull away.

"Please," Liyla gasped. "Hold still!" Jean's thrashing had pulled her forward, and, trying to balance herself, she'd fallen the other way, almost into her mother's lap.

"Girl! Hold still!" Liyla's mother wailed. "Please!"

But she didn't lean down or reach to help Liyla sit up. Surprised, Jean stopped moving and looked at her again. A crust of dried blood ringed her neck, and despite the ragged clothes she wore, she had on a necklace, a bright silver ball the size of a fist that dangled from a black ribbon at her neck. Behind Liyla's mother, Jean spied a basket full of the pendants, coiled in a nest of black ribbons.

Jean wondered why she hadn't seen them before. The men, too, wore the necklaces. She looked up at the Genius and saw that, grinning, he was watching her. Without a word, he pulled the red-handled knife from his belt and leaned over Liyla's mother. Jean flinched, but the woman didn't move. With a laugh, the Genius snagged the necklace with the flat side of his blade and the pendant swung free, flashing in the sunlight.

"My lady Ker tells me you are small, and weaker than the others," he said to Jean. "She says alone, you'd never be able to loose a strange wind." He lifted the pendant higher, so it hung just before the woman's eyes. "And yet even the graceful Ker can be mistaken."

Liyla's mother held perfectly still, and now the others had turned. All the dull eyes had brightened suddenly.

"It would be a shame to lose you a second time," the Genius went on. "So let me demonstrate something for you." With a flip of his knife, he let the pendant fall. *Pop!* It hit the woman's chest and erupted. Fire leaped to her shirt and raced across the fabric. The woman shrieked and tried to raise her arms to throw the pendant off, but the fetters jerked her hands down, and all she could do was slap wildly at her chest and then throw herself onto the grass. The flames snuffed, she lay there heaving, the smell of charred skin in the air. No one moved to help her. Her husband trembled beside her but didn't reach a hand. Jean burst into tears.

"As you can see, my little gifts of jewelry are sensitive to being jostled," the Genius said. He motioned to a nearby soldier, who came and slipped a fresh necklace over the woman's head, then put one on Liyla.

The man smiled down at her, then turned to Jean.

"Gifts for all your friends, you see? And they do look to you, don't they? Such a good girl. They're relying on you to care for them. So I expect you understand, now, how dangerous it would be if anyone were to loose another strange wind here."

Chapter 92

J ean."

It was Liyla, whispering to her. The Genius had taken his dog and moved off to stand beside Ker at the edge of the ridge beneath the emblem he had made of Jean's Barbie. At the corral, the captives were circled by a trio of guards, who gazed indifferently at the motionless group.

Jean tried to catch her breath. Liyla's mother whimpered in the grass. The fruit seller had been sick, and Jean gagged on the smell of it. Everywhere she looked, there was something awful to see. On her right, the misery of Liyla's mother and the wood behind her, clogged with waiting soldiers, on the left the hollow and its hundred men standing in grim silence.

"Jean!"

She'd tried hard not to look at Liyla, waiting there across from her, not with Liyla's mother lying in the dirt and the awful pendant hanging round the girl's neck. Now she was forced to raise her eyes.

"Jean, you can do things. They kept asking about it after they took us. Asking us if you did anything like make a wind blow. Can you do anything else?"

Jean shook her head. "No."

"But they said —"

"I can't. Susan can. Even Kate. But I was too little to learn all of it."

"But something!" Liyla pleaded. "Anything. Let us loose!"

Jean didn't know what to do. She glanced over at the ruddy-faced soldier who'd let them go on the mountain. There were tears in his eyes.

"The boy blessed me," he whispered. "I thought he meant it."

Liyla's father moaned and shifted gently, gingerly plucking at his shirt with a shaking hand. The cloth peeled away to reveal a weeping section of raw skin. The second captive soldier nudged Liyla and pressed a torn piece of his cloak into her hand. "Give him this," he said. "Slowly."

Jean watched Liyla pass her father the rag. Careful not to move too quickly, he dipped forward and slipped it between the wound and his shirt.

"Needs more padding, in case it happens again," the younger soldier said. "His have cracked more than once."

Jean's eyes went to the Genius.

"He likes to test them," Liyla whispered. "A sharp tug can make them go, or a hard knock. And then, too, the wind blows on its own sometimes."

Liyla's breath was warm in her face, and it was as hot here in the open as it had been in the tent. Jean eyed the silver pendants. What would happen now if the others came? They wouldn't know; they might do something bad. She closed her eyes and wished the ribbons away, wished the terrible silver balls would float up into the air and go. But wishing never did anything, at least not for her. She'd played once and brought the sea splashing skyward. But Laysia had said that was the way for the very young, who needed to play. This was no time for playing, and so she could only sit shivering across from Liyla, thinking that, after all, she was sorry for how mean she'd been to the girl in the tent.

$\diamond \ \diamond \ \diamond$

*I*n a thousand nightmares, the mist had risen to pursue her, to seek the exile it had relinquished. Now it did so. But rising, the mist touched neither Laysia nor the children. It hunted greater game. Uncoiling through the wood, a beast of the deep with a hundred arms, it rushed past through the trees, its whispered voice full of terrible promises.

Long ago, Tur Nurayim had spoken of the sanctuary — the council's sanctuary — as wave and fire. Laysia remembered now that final debate of sages. Shall we nourish or destroy? And here was the final word in that debate — the sanctuary roaring it to the sky.

Behind the mist, Laysia could just make out the line of dim figures driving the wave. Full they were with fury and joy. Was the Master Watcher among them?

The thought made her stumble, and she half turned to search for him, shrouded there in the haze, when Kate's cry stopped her.

"Jean!"

"Where?" Susan shouted. "Where? Do you see her?"

Kate had stopped abruptly near a ridge where the trees gave way to a low clearing that created a hollow to the west.

"No — no — he has her. He took her. . . ."

"The mist? She's in the mist?" Susan gasped.

But Laysia knew the valley had not gone mad to rise up thus against one small child.

"No! She's there —" Kate pointed straight ahead, to where the mist broke free of the empty wood and slipped down into the clearing like water.

"Who has her?" Nell snapped. "Tell us!"

Kate was shaking. "The Genius," she cried. "He took her. He's here."

"No!" Nell shouted.

Kate shuddered violently and bent nearly double, hands pressed to her ears. Laysia ran to her, grabbed her hand—and reeled.

Voices crashed over her, the howling madness of the mist—but beyond it, more. She could feel the creatures in the wood scattering in terror, and the children, the battering of their fear and guilt, their hope and their anger. Startled, she dropped the child's hand, and the sensations evaporated. In shock, she stared down at Kate. At the child's touch, all the boundary between Laysia and the world had fallen away. The turbulent babble of life had poured into her ears, unfiltered.

"Kate! What did you do?"

Guilt, fear, worry. She did not need to hold the child's hand to see it on her face.

"Nothing! Please! Can you get Jean?"

"Yes!"

She said it, but for a moment, though Susan and Nell charged ahead, Laysia stood rooted, caught by the memory of the sound rushing at her. So this was what the child heard! Laysia had read of such things and thought them only legends, but here was the world blaring its passionate intention into her ears. She looked back at the child and took her hand again, as the sea of emotion pulsed at her, vivid as the mist.

Chapter 93

The mist slid into the hollow, a woolly fog crackling with static. The sound swelled and the haze rose as Jean shook and tried not to shake, tried not to disturb the terrible pendant around Liyla's neck. And yet it was hard to be still when below the soldiers in the clearing faltered and bent, dropping weapons and putting hands to their ears. Already the men were changing, the hair on their faces thickening. Jean gasped, and the rancid air choked her, made her head swim. In the hollow, soldiers buckled and sank beneath the cloud, shrill wails of terror and pain shouted to the sky.

"Slashers!" the younger soldier croaked. "They're making slashers!"

Despite the fire pendants, the captives cringed and bunched together.

"What is that?" Liyla's mother cried. She'd struggled to sit upright, and Jean caught sight of the raw spot below her neck where the hair had been burned away. "Will it come here?"

From his place on the ridge, the Genius laughed out loud.

"As you expected!" he said to Ker. "Exactly!"

In the corral, the captives watched in horror.

"But they're his own troops!" the ruddy soldier whispered. "What's he done?"

"He's mad," the younger one said. "Gone mad, and feeding his own men to the beast."

Jean stared into the hollow, watching the men twist and fall beneath the mist, then rise again, horrible and malformed. Howling, they ran in all directions, scrambling for the rise and falling back, and even running farther into the mist, blinded and wild.

*T*he Listener of old had first heard the world speak and described the sound as a voice, ever singing. He had been mistaken. It was ever weeping, ever screaming, ever frightened and pleading. For that was the sound that rushed at Laysia now as she clung to Kate's hand and heard the terror and pain that vibrated from the mist and the hollow. How had Kate withstood this voice of terror and fury? Was this what she'd heard all along?

Chapter 94

G o!" the Genius shouted, and Jean watched Ker hoist her banner. The first line of red cloaks pounded from the wood, sweeping past the corral to ring the ridge.

"Now!" Ker called. With a roar, the soldiers charged into the hollow, firing. The fog thinned. Jean could see a line of smooth-faced men appear, stopped suddenly halfway across the field. The gunfire had hit several of the slashers, but it had reached the scholars, too, and as they fell, the new-made slashers sowed chaos, leaping for the scholars' throats and throwing bewildered men to the ground.

The last of the mist evaporated. The afternoon sun glittered on the melee in the camp, the edges of the fallen sharp as if cut from paper.

"That's all?" the ruddy soldier cried from his place beside Jean in the corral. "That's all the power of the great ones? We're lost!"

But before anyone could answer him, a hammer of wind slammed from the opposing wood, sweeping a line of red cloaks into the sky. The ground shook. Gasping, the captives grabbed hold of the fire pendants, trying to keep them still, and Jean looked to the clearing, hoping. Max had to be there! Max would come for her!

If he was, she couldn't find him in the chaos. Gusts of wind roared through the camp, and she saw a tent buckle, walls bending, curving inward. A peg popped, and then another. Canvas flapped in the wind. The tent burst into flame, and another exploded from the dirt, its poles whirling to mow down a group of charging soldiers.

Still the red cloaks kept coming, fresh lines advancing from the wood, and now a whole platoon followed Ker as she plunged into the clearing. The wind knocked some down, and others came behind, pounding past the corral, shaking the ground. As they descended, a whirlwind leaped from the center of the hollow, spraying dirt and blowing tents skyward.

"It's coming!" Liyla shouted.

The captives threw themselves down, pressing the fire pendants into the dirt. *Pop!* The ruddy soldier screamed and rolled in the grass, madly slapping at his flaming shirt.

"Stop!" Jean screamed. Was it Max sending it? Dust flew from the grass, the trees thrashed, stones shot up, and clouds swirled overhead. Daylight blinked out and then returned, once, twice, again.

"Save us!" Liyla cried. "Do something! Jean, please!"

But Jean could only cringe from her and cry out to the scholars in the hollow, though her voice was too small to carry.

*E*verywhere, confusion. Sound, sound, sound, and Laysia tried
to understand the meaning of it. But the child already knew.
A dart of rage, and Kate jerked her backward as a soldier bounded
their way, gun raised.

"How —?" Laysia began, but the girl only pulled her back
again, as a red cloak snatched at the place they'd been.

Laysia hurled the man away with a blast of wind. Where were
the others? Kate pointed upward, and they took to the air, swooping over the tents toward the needle of focus that said . . . Susan!
They dropped to the ground behind her. But where had Nell gone?

Boulders exploded from the ground and snapped muskets from
men's hands, crushing them into the dirt. Fire leaped out of the
grass and caught red cloaks from behind; wind snatched the guns
from the soldiers' hands. Then Nell appeared, a whirlwind whistling behind a cluster of tents.

Hatred, terror, pain . . . and then, all unexpected, surprise and
joy lanced through the air.

"Max!" Kate shouted.

A boy had appeared beside the girls, bulky and dark haired
and pulsing alarm and confusion.

"What are you doing here? Susan? Nell's too small to be here!"

He swiveled, glanced behind Laysia, and blanched.

"You brought Kate?"

"The Genius has Jean!" Nell told him. "She's with him now!"

Panic rolled from the boy.

"The Genius!"

He whirled and ran toward the other end of the clearing, flickering in and out of sight.

"Max!" Susan screamed, following. They gave chase, Laysia half blind with the wild confusion that rang in her ears. Lost ones, soldiers, watchers, their passion poured in on her, their madness, their frenzy of anger and fear. She lost her way, once, twice, bombarded by so much noise. But the child pulled her on, following the others as they darted in and out of sight. And then Kate stopped short.

"Oh, no."

Laysia sensed the iron contour of the man's mind a moment before he burst into sight before the boy. Tur Kaysh, age heavy in his face, and blasting rage.

"You've left your place!"

"My sister's been taken! And I have to get the rest of them to safety!" Max shouted over the noise. "They can't stay here!"

Tur Kaysh's eyes followed the boy's waving hand to Kate and locked on Laysia. In an instant, all the violence of his outrage, the staggering force of his fury narrowed and shot toward her like an arrow.

"Exile!" he screamed. He turned on Max. "What have you done?"

"Nothing, I — They're my sisters! I have to get them out!"

But the man had gone white with anger, and his hands trembled as he reached into the pouch that hung from his robes.

"Is all I've taught you nothing? Look at her! She thinks me weak, coming here! And you stand beside her!"

"No! No, I —"

But the boy stopped when the old man drew a small ash-coated stone, a bone-handled knife, and a leafy twig from the pouch. A chill sliced through the heat.

"Chaos from all sides," the old man growled. "And my students too weak to resist it. But I don't suffer from such weakness."

Then he touched knife to twig and stone, and mist, dark and potent, poured forth to engulf Laysia. *Beast, unclean beast who sullies, who grasps, filth, filth . . .* The thoughts swarmed in, and with them the throb of hunger, of wanting, of the desire for release. *So many years lost!* Anger bubbled in her, yes, rage, not only outside but her own now! Fear and despair were heavy, and she had carried them so long! Fury washed through her, a cleansing wave, and she reveled in the strength of her arms, her hands, *beast, beast* —

"Laysia!"

Fear shot through the mist, and worry, and . . . trust. The image of the dream child came to her, the cloud of hair, and the dark-haired boy, and the smell of green. Kate was shaking her. Laysia found herself on the ground, trembling, the mist a cloud simmering in the dirt. But the touch of the child's hand had called her back. She shook her head, trying to free it from the weight of the fog, and saw the old man stare at her with loathing.

Then another voice caught her attention. Nell, shouting.

"We're wasting time! The Genius has Jean! Laysia, get up!"

Rage clotted the air and a cyclone whirled from Tur Kaysh, knocking Nell to the ground. Laysia tried to rise, to help her, but weakness had leadened her limbs, and she felt the terrible wind press her down. She couldn't reach the child! The wind drove Nell down with its smothering force, and Laysia could do nothing but hear it, cringe at the screaming fury of the man and the riveting power of the wind, pounding, pounding.

And then the sound broke. The boy had bounded into the face of the wind and stood over his sister. His clothes billowed and he staggered, trying to keep his feet. The old man's head came up. Confusion pricked the air, surprise.

The mist that still clung to Laysia echoed with outrage.

"Your first loyalty is to me!" Tur Kaysh shouted.

But the boy would not move.

Hurt, fury, guilt whirled between them, and then knife gnashed on stone again and the mist thickened and rose to engulf the boy. He hunched down, his hands flying to his ears. Vaguely, Laysia felt Kate clinging to her hand, but shadows marred her vision, and from her knees, she fell to the ground again, the mist grinding her into the dust. She saw Susan fall, and the boy tottered, head in hands.

Chapter 95

A tarry cloud billowed in the hollow, more dense than any mist Jean had seen before. It shot through the lines of running men, swallowing them and spewing out slashers to stampede blindly among the opposing sides.

And still thick as pitch, it climbed toward the ridge.

"It's coming for us!" Liyla breathed.

Jean saw it engulf the soldiers who were in its path. On the ridge, the troops paused, but the Genius only stood watching for a moment before returning to the corral, his dog at his heels.

"Send the men," he said to the guards. "And the woman, too."

The guards moved into the corral, lifting the deadly pendants from the captives' necks and hustling them to their feet.

"Perhaps the girl, too?" the Genius mused to Spark. "It might be interesting to see."

For the first time, Liyla's father spoke. "Please!" he cried. "My girl's a useful one; she's shown you, hasn't she? Don't let it take her! Who will keep hold of the stranger?"

The Genius stopped and seemed to consider.

"Perhaps you're right," he said. "But of course, if she remains, she'll have to shoulder the burden the rest of you have dropped. As you say, who will keep our guest quiet if she doesn't?"

He motioned to the pendants the soldiers had removed, hanging now on the fence.

"Put them on her," he said. "Carefully."

One by one, the soldier slipped the orbs over Liyla's head as she sat wide-eyed. They plucked even more from the basket, until her chest bristled with pendants. Liyla looked as if she wanted to cry out, but only a squeak came.

Then, as if they were in on a joke together, the Genius grinned at Jean. "You think me mad, don't you? Have those old men in the valley convinced you that I can be beaten by their tricks?"

She wanted to tell him that he would be, that his own soldiers were even now falling beneath the mist, but like Liyla's, her throat had snapped shut; she had no voice.

He laughed outright this time. "No need to say it. I know what you're thinking. Didn't I say we know each other well? Yes, so you doubt me. But small children make poor strategists, even if they do have lovely faces." He winked. "It's true that my friends in the valley have become expert at turning out beasts, but beasts, too, have their use." He patted his dog's sleek head. "Watch, I'll show you."

Then he waved the guards on, and they herded the captives from the corral, pushing them to the ridge and onto the slope of the hollow. Liyla's mother turned back, and Spark came running, driving her down toward the mist.

The darkness reached their feet first, then wound around

their legs. The ruddy soldier screamed, and the fruit seller collapsed. They were changing, all of them. The skin rippled on their faces, and they bent and writhed, their screams changing to howls as Jean and Liyla watched.

"Da!" Liyla cried.

For a moment, her father's rippling features turned her way, and his eyes seemed to focus. Then, behind him, the dog snapped, and he fell, overcome.

*D*arkness, the noise all gone, light snuffed out, and despair yawning for her, madness coming, bleak, empty.

In the end, it had defeated her, and Laysia felt the mist take the last of memory, the last of joy, the last of hope.

A breeze riffled the darkness. The breath of life. Green promise stirred her, and light returned. Laysia blinked at the clearing mist, and the world tilted and righted itself, and she could see, now, Nell, on her knees behind her brother, her hands cupped round a sapling. One slim maple leaf unfolded, and another. It was a frail thing, this small tree between the child's hands. And yet it breathed life.

The boy had fallen to his knees, pressed his head to the ground, but now he looked up and around. Laysia rose to a crouch, and again she could feel Kate's hand on her. Nell took hold of the newborn tree. It shot up another foot, flowering, and the mist melted away. Sound returned to the world.

Kate screamed.

The Guide had raised a hand, and before Laysia could stand, a bolt of electricity sizzled through the air. A streak of fire shot from him up and over the children and across an open space, through the tents to where a woman, running along the border of the receding mist, was charging toward them, waving a tall pole, soldiers behind her. It hit with a flash, and the woman screamed, her clothes aflame.

"Attend!" the man shouted at the boy. "This is what you were made for!"

Chapter 96

With a shriek, Ker hurtled over the hollow, aflame. *Don't look!* Jean told herself. Then the scream broke. She glanced up. Twisted at odd angles, her clothes smoldering, the woman dangled from the high branch of a tree, arms flapping in the wind.

Cringing, Jean looked to the Genius. What vengeance would he take now? But the man barely glanced in Ker's direction. Below him, the mist was suddenly retreating, leaving behind the bent figures of the soldiers and the captives it had swallowed. As it left, they reared up, screeching. Wild, changed, they turned on the soldiers who had driven them into the darkness, and attacked.

"What use is it?" Liyla sobbed, watching. "What use?"

The Genius never lost his vicious smile. "Yes, they've become like savage dogs, haven't they?" He tilted his head toward the girls. "But I know something of savage dogs. They respond to power." He watched the new-made slashers tear at the soldiers another moment before he added, "And they can smell fear."

He nodded to the guards behind the corral, and they heaved open the barn doors. Huddled in the dim space were more than two dozen children, who blinked now in the sudden light. Fire pendants glittered in heaps beside them, and every neck was adorned with a deadly orb.

Jean could not at first drag her eyes from the fire orbs. Mountains of them glinted among the unfortunate children, taller than some of the smallest of them. And seeing this, she at last looked at their faces. A dark-haired girl with a bald spot at her chin stared out at her, the collar of her shirt blackened and burned.

"Omet!"

The girl said nothing. Stomach churning, Jean looked from face to face. There was Sefi, the girl who'd sung songs about the useless to put the others to sleep at night. Nearby sat Yali, who'd been so gentle with Kate. She saw the boy from the sleeper shed, Espin, sitting with hands shielding his chest, and Modo, who'd helped hide them under the floor. Child after child, all were there, and many more.

"Go! Go!" the soldiers shouted, rousting the dazed children from the barn. Chained wrist to ankle, the children couldn't lift their arms above their shoulders, but they grabbed the pendants and held them away from their chests as they staggered out into the sunlight, trying not to fall.

"Wait! Please don't!" Jean saw Yali stumble and catch herself, the fire pendant still in her hand.

"Omet!" Jean cried again. And as if she'd been speaking to him, the Genius nodded.

"Resourceful girl," he said as he watched Omet stumble toward the ridge. "She'd built quite a nest there, infesting the buildings. Pity she was useless." He gazed for another second at Omet, running toward the battle, driven by the soldiers and their dogs.

"Of course, I've found a use for her now."

And as the children descended into the hollow, the wild-eyed slashers raised their heads, turning, and leaped to pursue them like wolves to the hunt.

◇ ◇ ◇

*T*he old man shook the ground. Gentle, the scholars had been once, but not now! All the rage Laysia could feel in the air flowed into the wind and fire that raced from him out toward the red cloaks. And still the far wood poured forth the enemy, a hemorrhage that would not end. They came and came, red as a gash in the mountain, and even the shaking of the foundation could not stanch it.

Then from the east, soft at first, a new wind came whistling. Shadows striped the ground, and Laysia saw a mass of watchers soar overhead and alight in the clearing. The first of them turned, and she saw a familiar profile, a well-remembered face.

Lan.

There was pain, very sharp, very sudden. All the loss that had been dulled with the years, the joy and sadness put away, came shattering now the barriers built of patience and time. And yet there was no space to feel it. This new company of watchers looked skyward, and branches snapped from the trees to rain down upon the coming warriors, knocking the weapons from their hands.

Then, from Kate, a jolt of panic, and the boy yelled, "Stop!"

"Look!" Kate shouted. "Look at the children!"

Children poured over the western ridge, propelled by red cloaks and dogs. Hobbled by chains, they lurched down the slope while, like jackals roused by the scent of blood, the lost ones bounded after them.

Stumbling, awkward, the children made easy prey. A maddened slasher snatched at the neck of a redheaded girl; a dog yanked a boy to the ground. To Laysia's shock, fire spat from the first child, throwing the slasher off. Around the boy, the grass flared. Laysia had almost reached them when she stopped. What was happening?

Nell charged past her. "Make a path for them!" she yelled. And stones jumped from the grass to knock the dog from the boy; dust flew up to blind a soldier hurrying their way. His shirt in flaming tatters, the boy rolled to his feet and ran, the girl at his heels, their wild fear blaring in Laysia's ears.

But if she could hear the children, the old man had gone deaf. He paid no heed to the small figures running amid the chaos. He raised a hand, and lightning slammed into the ground, throwing soldiers to the dirt and heaving a curly-haired girl down beside them. A shower of sparks shot from her, and as she rolled there, the old man roared, "Charge! Now! This is your moment!"

And Lan — even Lan! — ran forward.

The fleeing children swerved and turned back, caught between the troops pouring from the hill and the watchers who ran to meet them.

Laysia spun around. "Stop!" she screamed at Lan. "They're children!"

But she could see the watchers changing. The skin of her brother's face rippled and bent.

Madness! Its poison was everywhere; it choked the air. Laysia and the children hurled wind and stone and threw the dust from the ground into the faces of the attackers, into the fires, but no one stopped and no one heard beneath the shattering noise of flame and wind.

Fear sliced knife-like through her chest. Kate! The girl let go of her hand and darted after her brother, who'd bolted past the fleeing children toward the oncoming soldiers.

Madness in the children, too! Laysia chased after them, calling — when a light sparked and shimmered, and the sunlight ignited. The noise of the coming stampede abated. Laysia froze.

A wall of thick glass shimmered between the panicked children and the red cloaks.

Behind her, she heard Nell laugh.

"A window!" the girl said. "Max made a window that doesn't open!"

Shielded now by the glass, the fleeing children stopped. Behind Laysia, the watchers did the same. But the old man shouted, "No!" and hurled a wind to batter the wall. The bewildered children ducked beneath the blast of air and tried to run, but they were bound, and more — they each held their hands out, stiff, as if running with a gift to show.

Laysia could make them out now: silver balls that hung around their necks, pulled out and held in their cupped hands. What was this?

Then a small boy tugged at his neck, tearing the orb away. A flare, and his sleeve caught fire.

"It's on them! They're wearing it!" Nell shouted. "Max! Stay back!"

The boy stopped short, but Susan didn't. She ran past Laysia toward the child trying to douse his arm in the grass.

"Espin!" she shouted back at them. "It's Espin!" Horror poured

from the others as the boy writhed. Max and Nell snatched up a fallen cloak, torn from one of the attackers, and beat at the fire. Kate and Laysia ran to do the same.

Still the watchers sent the wind, trying to shatter the wall and reach the enemies on the other side. The children cried out, the orbs glinting in their hands.

"Get them off! Get them off!" Nell shouted. And Laysia and Kate, Max and Nell ran from child to child, lifting the orbs from their necks. But the wind blew too sharply, and one after the other, the orbs popped. Stung, the children dropped them to the grass, which lit, flames shooting up into the heat.

Then Susan stopped moving. For a moment, Laysia again feared madness, but no dark terror pulsed from her now, only that needle of focus, the hungry shout to the listening world. The air shuddered. Beneath Susan's feet, the soil buckled.

"Get back!" Nell screamed at her sister, but as the ground churned, Susan shot into the air. A sheet of water tore the grass in two. The geyser ripped upward, throwing the rest of them to the ground amid a shower of dirt and grass and foam. It arched overhead and then splashed to earth, drenching the children and dousing the burning swath before the glass wall that shimmered and glittered now with spray. Once, twice, the water shot heavenward, until the fire had been pounded from hair and skin and clothes and grass.

Chapter 97

Suddenly, silence. Jean looked up and saw the wall of glass, glittering in the spray, and the Genius, his hand raised. The troops had paused on the ridge. As it had in the tiled room, the man's face shifted before her eyes, its already rough edges going jagged, the hair thickening, the eyes receding further into the bony skull.

"Coward!" he shouted, and his voice echoed strangely across the now quiet hollow. "How long will you hide your face from me behind pretty walls? The time has come, old man! Show yourself!"

For a beat, nothing moved on either side of the wall. And then two figures rose from behind it to land on the glass ledge.

"Yes! See my face!" the old man called back. "Look at the face of a man before you feel the weight of his hand!"

Muttering anger from the troops on the ridge, but the Genius only laughed.

"Oh, I will! I'll look at your face and your outstretched hand. It offered me five smooth-faced children, after all. Who wouldn't come for such a gift? But, old man, did you think that was all I'd take?" He flicked his head at Jean and said to his guard, "Bring me the girl!"

They dragged her from the corral, Liyla tripping after her, and the Genius grabbed Jean by the shoulder and pulled her against him to face the hollow. Liyla hunched before her, clutching the gathered pendants.

On the glass wall, the second man called out, "Who are you to speak of courage, dog? You hide behind a child!"

Jean gave a start. It was the voice of the Master Watcher!

"Ah, but I don't hide my gifts," the Genius countered. "I make use of them. Look how I adorn this one you sent me!" And then the basket was beside them, and as Jean struggled to pull away, he slipped a necklace over her head. She recoiled as the weight of the metal pressed through the thinness of her dress.

"Do you think you can deter me now? With this?" the old man shouted at him. "When so much is at stake?"

The Genius's laugh shook them both, and Jean cringed. "Deter you? Never! We are the same, you and I, aren't we? We always have been."

"You're a dog who barks at men!" the Master Watcher roared. "This great man is nothing like you!"

Again, the Genius laughed. "Really? Look at him! Better, look at yourself!"

The Master Watcher turned and looked at Tur Kaysh. Jean looked, too. The Guide's features were shifting. Anger seemed to swell him, curdle his high brow and the sharp line of his jaw. The Master Watcher staggered and raised a hand to his own face.

"Tricks!" the old man roared. He pulled his lips back and bared his teeth. "Conjuring!"

"Tricks!" the Genius repeated. "Oh, yes. But not the one

you think. Is all your storied power, too, only sleight of hand? Old man, you're as easily fooled as a child! You've been looking the wrong way all along!"

He half turned, taking Jean with him. The soldiers on the ridge had drawn aside to reveal a row of cannons that had been hidden beneath the mass of red cloaks.

"Fire!" the Genius called to them. "Now!"

And with a thundering boom, the guns let fly. The wall buckled and cracked, then shattered, as the old man leaped to the sky. But the Master Watcher, still staring at his own hands, tumbled earthward, falling amid a shower of broken glass.

*T*he world crumbled and fell to nothing. Only a single point of light remained — Lan among the shards, wet with blood and a gray cast shadowing his changing skin. Too late, she had seen him drop, too late to catch him with the wind or soften the fall.

Salt and ashes, Laysia thought bitterly. Salt and ashes.

Chapter 98

F inish them!" the Genius called, and with a whoop, the soldiers charged past the smoking cannons, a red tide swallowing the land.

Jean spotted the others in the ruins of the wall. Her heart contracted. Max had come, but he couldn't save her. There were too many of them. It was over. The Genius must have seen it, too, because he let go of her shoulder and came around to look into her face. His teeth had gotten sharp in his mouth, his lips were black, but his voice was velvet again, as if the battle in the hollow had disappeared when he turned his back on it, as if they were alone together in the tent once more.

"Is this illusion, too?" he asked, squatting to touch her cheek. "Pity. I would have liked it to be otherwise, but there's no use fooling myself. I should have guessed you were too small to be useful." He made as if to get up but stopped himself, smiling.

"Perhaps we can salvage something from you after all, though. Such a pretty thing. Like the doll you brought, only softer. That was made of sturdy stuff. Tell me, are you the same? Can this pretty illusion survive the heat?"

And he shoved her backward. She toppled, taking Liyla with her.

Jean grabbed her pendant as they fell, holding it as she hit the dirt, while two, three, four of the orbs on Liyla's neck burst, vomiting fire. Flames ripped across Liyla's shirt and caught the grass. The heat sent Jean reeling, and the chains still holding her to the girl bit through her skin, but she held her own pendant, arm shaking.

Small, small, small echoed, hateful, in Jean's ears as Liyla flailed, violently jerking Jean's arm. Jean slapped at the flames and fought to hold still and felt the hot tears pour down her face as she forced her arm out, desperate to keep the orb away.

No one should be this small! She scrambled in the dirt. Was it her imagination, or was the thing turning hot in her hand? If only it were covered in glass, like the wall in the hollow! Or, better, ice — something to soothe the burns, something to heal the terrible pain racing up her arm!

But wishing was nothing — that's what Max had said. It wasn't wishing she needed. It was seeing. Was she too small to see? Was she?

The fire had raced across Liyla's sleeve now, and Jean felt it sear her wrist. Liyla cried out and the Genius laughed and the silver orb burned against Jean's palm.

With all her might, she tried to see ice. Hadn't she known cold aplenty here, even in this terrible summer? Hadn't she shivered in the tiled room? Awful, awful cold it had been, cold so it hurt.

The screams from the hollow dimmed. The Genius's laughter, too. In her ears, there was a rushing now that blocked the rest, blotted out the clang of metal, the boom of explosions, the wrenching, terrible sound of Liyla sobbing.

Then suddenly her hand burned, but not with fire.

She opened her palm and stared. The silver orb glittered there, encased in ice, sparkling in the sunlight.

"What's happening?" Liyla's voice was thick, but she'd stopped crying. She lay gasping in the dirt, her chest adazzle with ice that had doused the fire and glassed the pendants. "You took them away!" she whispered.

But they were still here, simmering beneath the ice, waiting. Jean could not stomach it. The orb hung at her neck, and with her mind's eye she flung it away.

The chain at her wrists snapped, and the cord at her neck. From Liyla the cluster of icy silver jerked skyward, the ribbons frayed and shredding.

Away, Jean thought, and a chill shot across her arms. The glassy fire pendants shot out, knocking the Genius onto his back, shot over the lines of soldiers rushing from the wood— so many! Too many to stop! But there had been a song—what had Laysia told her? A water drop and a wave, not different at all, really, because there was no small, there was no big, there was only the song, and seeing . . . The air bit at her skin, and this time a sharp pain shot through her. Shadows filled the sky, pebbling the light on the grass. Jean looked up. The handful of orbs had multiplied into a thousand, and the new-made fire pendants hung overhead, all glittering and slicked with ice. She didn't wish it this time; she saw it. *Away!*

The wind whipped overhead, the trees thrashed, and the pendants shot away, across the streaming line of soldiers, out and out, falling and flaring in a hailstorm of fire and ice.

$$\diamond \; \diamondsuit \; \diamond$$

*O*n a bed of mud and broken glass, the scholars and soldiers fought, the difference gone from their faces. Laysia braced herself among them, holding the space where her brother lay. Pain and terror and fury curdled the air, but she no longer heard it, for Kate had run ahead with the others, racing to find their sister.

Moving shadows blotted the sun; Loam rumbled beneath her feet, the air snapping and alive. Laysia looked up at the stippled sky.

A hailstorm had spun upward from the ridge. It hung there a moment, frozen stones in a summer sky, before it whipped across the horizon. Ice fell and turned to fire, and the wood flamed. Beside her, even the fighting men stopped to watch it, agape.

Then two small figures appeared on the ridge and raced down into the hollow, the sky glittering behind them. Jean!

She watched the children run to meet their sister, shouting with joy and relief. With dread, Laysia had remembered the old woman's words, a child lost, a child gone, but perhaps even dreams could be mistaken!

Then, to her horror, another figure topped the rise, a man in heavy brocade, teetering, aflame. Before she could call out, he dived toward Jean, swinging a fistful of the deadly pendants over his head like a slingshot.

Chapter 99

A shadow fell across the hill, and Jean spun in time to see the silver orbs flash against the sky. Then a squall shot across the hollow and knocked her aside. She fell into the grass as it plowed past, sweeping the man from the hill and heaving the pendants against him. *Pop! Pop! Pop!* They exploded, igniting his hair and clothes. Flaming, he shot backward, through the barn doors and into the pile of orbs heaped there. For a beat, the barn seemed to glow, then it withered, buckling. With a volcanic roar, it exploded skyward in a shower of fire that lurched to heaven before falling in a mass of flaming pieces, a thousand shooting stars snuffed to ash.

❖ ◆ ❖

Hungry dark,
Devouring.
It will come
And teach you
To know fear,
And you will lose
Your very selves
Amid a blood tide
That pierces to your heart.
But take hope,
For the smallest candle
Will light a torch,
To make the end,
Beginning.
　　— Orchard Vision, Age of Anam, Ganbihar

*F*rom the smallest of them, the child at play, had come the end of all things, and the beginning. Laysia had watched the old tale unfold all unexpected. She should have been joyous. But in the shattered hollow, she sank back to her knees beside her brother. Lan lay torn beneath the empty sky, and unlike the ancients, she had no healing.

"I remembered your song," the little one said, coming to her with trepidation. Glass crunched underfoot, and Jean kept her eyes from the fallen man. "The water drop and the wave."

✦ 536 ✦

Tur Nurayim's song, Laysia thought as she praised the child. *She heard her own voice from a distance. Not mine. Tur Nurayim's song. He had so many. Songs of play, and teaching, and power, and healing. He had so many that she had hummed them, sometimes, in her sleep.*

She watched the life seep from her brother, his face so changed, and thought, This, at least, I can give him. A remembrance of lost power as he goes, a song of comfort, of mending. *So she sang of fibers rejoined, of wholeness, of health.*

Beneath her hands, the wounds closed, and Lan breathed easy.

◇ Book Six ◇

SUSAN

Chapter 100

The age of wolves had ended.

Or at least that's what Laysia said, when a day had passed. Susan was happy for her, happy for all of them who acted like they had woken from a bad dream.

In Susan's opinion, though, the age of wolves had given way to the age of awkward silences. For a full day after they'd returned from the clearing, Max had been quiet. If she looked at him, his eyes slid away and he would find some work to do, helping guide people down to the valley, now that even some of the red cloaks came looking. The hours that had followed the battle had been full of confusion. Some of the watchers had disappeared, and the old man — the Guide — could not be found. But then red cloaks approached, this time seeking entrance, and help, and already their faces had begun to shift as they streamed down into the valley, where the sanctuary stood out in the summer sunlight, the mist all gone.

She'd been waiting for Max for so long, she thought they'd have lots to talk about.

But the absent old man still stood between them. Max mumbled an apology there among the red cloaks and the watchers, but it was not enough, and he couldn't seem to find the words for what would be. Uncharacteristically, he had run out of things to say.

And Susan, who'd longed for quiet ever since she'd heard the first hissing of the mist, now found that the sudden silence just made the gaping hole between them seem bigger. She'd wanted quiet, but not this kind.

It was Nell who finally put a stop to it. She and Susan found Max on the hill after he'd shown a knot of newcomers to the outer wall.

"Max . . ." Susan said.

He looked briefly at her and then found the wheat stalks mesmerizing.

"Oh, for goodness' sake!" Nell burst out. "How hard is it to just say you were wrong? W-R-O-N-G. Wrong! For once, the great brain made a mistake!"

Max looked up at that, color in his face. After a second, he seemed to come to some kind of decision. He laughed a little.

"Okay, fine. I was wrong. W-R-O-N-G. And you — you were right, Nell. You tried to tell me."

Nell, who had been fully prepared to elaborate, looked stunned.

"I was right?"

"R-I-G-H-T. Yes, I admit it."

Nell looked over at Susan.

"This *is* a magical place."

Susan thought it would be even more magical if it had been Nell who'd admitted she was W-R-O-N-G, but she kept her mouth shut. The three of them stood looking at one another a minute more, and then Nell shrugged.

"Well, the old man did have a nice voice," she said.

Max smiled a little painfully.

"Yeah," he agreed. "He did."

A warm breeze made the wheat stalks flap and brought the smell of smoke down the hill. The forest had burned for half a day, until the scholars who remained had been able to douse it. But with the odor of charred wood there was also the smell of late summer in the air, and wildflowers growing in the clearing above the valley. Finally, the quiet was the good kind. They went together down the hill to look for Kate and Jean.

*O*nce before, Laysia had stood in the heart, on the day years ago when she had been made exile. There she had seen Tur Nurayim's chair, turned to the wall. There she had seen her brother's face gone hard. The thought of it brought the shadow of old pain, and yet here now was Lan, abashed, his face almost his own again, come to summon her back.

Few words had passed between them, but they had been enough. *Lonely souls still,* she thought, *both of us.* And yet he walked beside her and led her through the iron gate to the center garden, open and waiting.

"Who sits there now?" she asked him as they made their way along the path, thick with its summer beauty. Tur Kaysh had vanished from the battlefield along with many of the watchers when the last change took them. If any had expected them to join the red cloaks and those of the city who streamed down to the valley now, returned, they had been disappointed. And so amid the joy at victory, there was also shock and horror at the Guide's betrayal. Like people reviving from too long a trance, the scholars shook their heads and exclaimed at what they saw now, though it had been before them all along. *Children used as bait for the madman! So many years of waste and anger!* Some spoke of punishment, but the old man was beyond retribution. *He was dead,* some said. *Mad,* said others, *taken by the mist he himself had made.*

Laysia did not know, and not knowing, she had feared to approach the inner garden, even as the bewildered scholars read the old visions anew and spoke to one another of exiles and children, even as the remaining watchers sought her out.

"Tur Sarom," Lan said.

She paused at the gilded door and nodded. Tur Sarom had been the last of the council to abandon Tur Nurayim near the end. Laysia remembered seeing them walk together, even when the others had shunned him. She recalled the old man's praise of him. Thoughtful. Wise beyond his years. Perhaps that thoughtfulness had saved him. Alone among the council, he had withstood that final, withering change.

"Come," Lan said. "Don't keep them waiting."

She smiled. Again the teacher. Ever the elder brother.

Beneath the prism of sunlight, the council table was mostly empty. Tur Sarom sat on one side; four watchers had taken seats nearby. Like Lan, they had nearly regained their smooth faces. At the wall, Tur Nurayim's chair still stood out of place.

Tur Sarom thanked her for coming. He had grown into his years now and was gray headed and vigorous. She nodded but said nothing. The weight of that room pressed on her, and she could feel the cold that still flowed out of its side chamber.

"As your brother explained, we are leaderless," Tur Sarom said to her. "The returned flow in from the city, and we must teach them, guide them, even as many of our number are gone. They call for us, and we must respond. So we have convened a new council, small as it is, and turn to you to lead us."

"Me?" She stared at him.

Lan had said nothing. All she knew was the commotion of the returned, so many of whom had come that they were camped now beneath the fruit trees in the valley.

The gray head nodded. "You withstood the mist. You nurtured four of the five. Who else would better serve?"

She glanced toward the side room. "I would not be accepted, I think, among the mass of watchers and scholars. Perhaps you, Tur Sarom, should rise to be Guide."

The man shook his head. "A new time is upon us. We must step forward to meet it. None of the old will serve. You are the new, and you will guide us to embrace it, as your teacher counseled long ago." He indicated the watchers seated near him and nodded in Lan's direction. "These are the senior watchers that remain to us. We are all of the same mind. Once, we failed to listen. We are not so hardheaded that we will be deaf to the counsel of the wise again."

She longed to catch Lan's eye, but he stood behind her now. She looked around the room. This was what she had desired. Long ago, she had wanted the door open. Now it was.

"Finally," Tur Sarom said, "at last, let us change for good."

Laysia thought of Tur Nurayim, hopeful to the end.

"Very well," she said.

She walked over to the old man's chair and turned it from the wall.

Chapter 101

A nd still they could not get home.

Susan had been half sure that just the end of the Genius would bring the window, as if some silent bell had been rung.

Time to go home! it would tell the universe. And then, like a machine with the right button pressed, Ganbihar would produce the window, *snap*, and they'd climb through.

But Ganbihar turned out not to work like that. So she made her way, with Laysia, to the center garden, where all the books of mystery were kept. The place had no lock now, and the five of them went through the gate, Nell hesitating only an instant, to see if in all that vast library, all those pages full of visions and predictions and secrets, there was one that explained about windows.

The days passed as they searched, and summer ended and the trees began to turn, brushing color across the mountains. The sanctuary in those weeks turned into a bustling, noisy place, with people streaming out for the cities, and others streaming in. One morning, she saw Mistress Dendra, a watcher now, lead a ragged, bewildered group down into the valley. Nell gave a shout. Wista was among them — Wista, found in the woods, filthy, scratched, hungry, but free of the mist now, and back to herself. On another day, Susan saw Omet standing by the tall corn, talking to Liyla, and she almost passed them by, they were so different. Liyla now was the same mild-faced girl she'd seen for an instant when they'd met — narrow jawed, light haired. She'd recovered from the battle sufficiently to be negotiating with Omet, who'd organized the sleepers' children as guides between city and valley.

"I know shortcuts," Liyla was saying. "Give me maybe two ven, and I'll take twice as many as those others."

Susan recognized Omet more by her voice than her face. She was still dark haired and dark eyed, but the rough hollows of her cheeks had filled and smoothed, and now she was a tall, serious girl with a square face and black brows that arched over bright, intelligent eyes.

She sighed. "I told you, they don't use that currency here. And we're not doing this for a fee. You'll get food and lodging, like the rest. No more . . ."

Susan laughed to herself. Things changed, and things stayed the same. She wished she could figure out what made the one or the other. Maybe that was the key to opening the window.

She returned to the inner garden and found Laysia standing beside the strange little museum room. Something about it made Susan feel at home there, as if her family were all gathered around her. Laysia said it was because they belonged here, in Ganbihar.

"You're part of this place," Laysla said to the children as they returned to the books in the inner library. "No matter where you began. Perhaps you were meant to stay here."

Susan worried that she might be right. She did feel tied

to this place. But she was tied to home, too, and she couldn't believe they'd never go back. There were people waiting for them on the other side.

Jean and Kate sat playing four stones on the floor of the center hall, where the stained glass cast squares of color. The outer door opened, and the Master Watcher came in, Max at his side, bringing oil for the lamps.

Nell, who had been peering into a book, looked up.

"It's all riddles." She sighed. "And poetry. I like poems, but really, it would have been nice if one of these visions gave someone a straight answer once or twice."

"No luck, then, I guess," Susan said.

"Nothing about windows, doors, or even buildings at all," Nell said.

The Master Watcher came in and set the oil on the table. Laysia began filling the lamps. Susan thought the two of them ought to have enough awkward silence between them to fill the Grand Canyon, but to her surprise, there didn't seem to be much of that.

"The books of mystery are not a construction manual," the man said astringently, and Nell made a face into her book. The Master Watcher still looked half outraged at the sight of them in the heart of the sanctuary, but Max had assured her that he was getting used to it.

"We need to figure out how the window opened the first time," Max said. "I've been wondering that since the beginning."

"Isn't it enough to know that you were needed, and a way was made?" the Master Watcher asked him. "Do you always have to know how?"

"Yes," Max said simply. "I do."

Laysia stood back from the lamps and watched them flare up. The page Susan had opened brightened. For the hundredth time, she repeated the words aloud. Was there something she had not seen there?

"*'Out of the longest night, into the age of wolves . . .'*"

Max's head came up. "Wait a minute," he said. "Say that again."

She did.

He tugged at a piece of hair that had lately grown into his eyes. "I never thought of that before. The longest night. That wasn't here. It was summer here. How did whoever wrote that know what it was like back home?"

It was true. The vision had described more than the window. Whoever had written it had seen the other side.

"Perhaps opening a window between two worlds requires more than a window," Laysia said. "Perhaps you need to be able to see through the glass as well."

"But we can do that!" Nell protested. "We know what home is like!"

"And yet you can't open the window," Laysia said. She pulled a thick old book from the shelf and set it softly on the table. "So what don't we know?"

They all bent to the books then, all but Susan. She sat thinking about it awhile. Kate had abandoned the game in the hall and come to see what they had found. She wandered in beside Susan, looked curiously at the book she had open, and then, unconsciously, began to hum to herself.

Nell shot her an annoyed look. "We're trying to read here!" she said, and Kate stopped abruptly.

It was so like home that Susan felt something flare inside

her. They did need to see through the glass, as Laysia and Nell said. But what were they looking at, exactly?

She glanced over at Max, who sat pulling at his rumpled hair.

"When you think of home," she said suddenly to him, "what is it?"

He looked up, startled, then shrugged. "I don't know. Everything. A lot of things, I guess."

"What about you?" she asked Nell.

"Riddles," Nell said promptly.

"Riddles?" the Master Watcher cut in. "How are riddles anybody's home?"

Nell grinned at him, which, Susan noted, must have been a first. Maybe that was a good sign.

"We like them. We tell riddles at dinner sometimes."

"And jokes," Max added. "Sometimes even funny ones."

"Kate sings at night — loudly," Nell said, grimacing at her little sister.

Susan felt as she sometimes did when she walked into the back door of a house after she'd only ever come in through the front — disoriented by the new angle. Things did look different that way.

The Master Watcher was looking at Laysia with an expression that told Susan he was not used to lots of people talking at once, especially if those people were under the age of thirty.

"What do riddles and songs have to do with opening windows?" he asked her.

Laysia patted his shoulder, and the familiar act seemed to startle him and then loosen him up a little. He smiled faintly.

"I don't know," she said. "But perhaps a world full of walls is made of such things. Perhaps ours is, too."

And Susan thought: Riddles and songs and jokes at the table — all of that had plenty to do with windows.

She laughed to herself. She had thought that another world was a thing like a chair, or a peach, or water, or fire. But she'd had it wrong. It wasn't one thing at all, but a thousand of them. What did home look like, after all? A satiny dip in the couch, where she could read and catch a glimpse of the sky. Kate humming without knowing it. Jean giving her Barbie a bad haircut. Nell telling riddles at the table, and Max reciting letters to Jean.

Not all the books of mystery, not anything in the sanctuary, or any one of the scholars, could open the window. She knew that now. How could they? Maybe they could see a house on the other side, but they could never see home.

"What does that mean, a world full of walls?" Kate whispered to her. "Does that mean we can't ever get back there?"

"I don't think so," Susan told her. "Even walls can be opened. You can make a door, after all. Or a window."

Susan marveled that she could pull fire from the air and make water flow from nothing, but she had not been able to see this simple fact until now.

They gathered outside, in the garden, cool and smelling of fallen leaves. The sun had long set, and a pearl of a moon glossed the air. Laysia and her brother stood behind them, watching.

This time, Susan didn't think of windows. She thought of her parents' faces, her room, the book she had left open, even Mrs. Grady, waving, as she sometimes did, from her kitchen.

It occurred to her suddenly that if she could see that, then maybe, like the people who visited the dream orchard that Laysia had spoken of, she could step outside time, too — or into it. Maybe the moment they had left waited there for them, like a bubble caught in glass.

"Think about home as we left it," she told the others. "Think about that winter night."

The air crackled a little and buzzed. In the darkness, the moonlight seemed to smoke and wrinkle, then fracture. A stuttering, broken image shook a second in the glimmering space and resolved. The window. And on the other side, a familiar maroon couch, a book, a wall full of pictures.

*L*aysia had dreamed of the orchard, and walked there in a wood outside time, but that could not compare to this moment, when she stood at the heart of the world and watched the moonlight cleave the night to reveal a land beyond.

Tur Nurayim had spoken of a thousand worlds, tapestries in a great hall. It had been a half-meant tale, a flight the mind must take to understand what cannot be.

And yet it was.

Beside her, Lan gasped. She looked to him, and saw at last the joy that had been so long absent. Together, they peered at the place beyond the glass, that world of walls and hard edges. It was softer than she would have guessed — a room like others, with its cushions and its portraits and its mess of scholar's papers. Like the children, she thought, its differences were not at first easily perceived.

Susan reached out to the glass, and this, too, was unexpectedly soft.

"Come on!" the little one said, pulling at her sister's hand. "Before it goes away!"

But the older one hesitated a moment.

"Will we see you again?"

How could she answer? They were children of dreams. They had come to her first outside of time. This gulf seemed greater still.

She would have liked to give the child the gift of ancient words, some bit of wisdom passed on. But she could not think of any just then. So she gave her the only truth she knew — her own.

"Always and often," she said. "In dreams."

Chapter 102

Susan felt herself sink into the warmth of the window, its glass pliable as honey. She could still smell the fading greenery of the fall garden, the rich half-sweet aroma of turning leaves, when the honeyed glass dissolved and she found herself stepping down into her own house, her own well-remembered thinking spot.

The scent of paper, wood, and the worn maroon couch replaced the scent of the garden, and she sucked in the first breath of home.

"It's the same!" Nell marveled. "All the same!"

Max touched the sofa, the notebook on the table. "It's like we never left. Like we weren't away a second!" He looked at Susan. "Do you think we can do any of it here? Is it all gone now?"

"I don't know," she said. "But I feel different. Don't you?"

He nodded.

"Me, too," Kate said. "Better, because we're home."

Better, Susan thought. But not the same.

From the hall came the sound of familiar voices. Jean was first through the door. In an instant, the others followed, running.

But for a moment, as her siblings flew on ahead, Susan paused. It *wouldn't* be quite the same, she thought. Theirs was a world of walls, but doors could be made. And windows.

She turned back and touched the window, wondering. It was hard again, and cold. On the other side, Mrs. Grady's kitchen light filtered out, through her colored glass, into the deepening blue.

❖ Epilogue ❖

B ut it wasn't so easy to go home, after all.

They had been gone more than two months or a moment, depending on which side of the window you stood on. And it was strange, stepping back that way into life. When they'd been home four days, the children met, as they had daily, in the school yard at recess. Before their trip through the window, school had been a time to separate, and Nell in particular had not liked to acknowledge that she had younger sisters. But it was different now. Now they sat together in their winter coats on the bench at the side of the yard, watching the others from a distance. Beside them a pile of discarded parkas made a small dark hill where the fourth-graders had dropped them when they'd begun playing tag. To their right, some girls from Kate's class jumped rope, chanting a jumble of rhymes and numbers that came out in little puffs of vapor in the cold air. And far to the left, in the field that connected the elementary and middle schools, Max's friends played kickball. After three days, they'd given up asking if he wanted to play.

Susan sighed and rubbed the end of her cold nose. "It's not the same," she said. "It all seems so — I don't know. Small. Was it that way before, do you think? And I'm forgetting?"

At a nearby bench, Lucy Driscoll held court before an

audience of younger children, doing a dramatic reading. She was dressed in a nylon coat so puffy it sounded like someone crumpling paper each time she moved. She looked up pointedly at Susan and flounced over to the bench. *Crumple. Crumple. Crumple.*

"You can stop moping," she said, folding her arms to the tune of newspapers being mashed. "I've had enough of your sitting here like someone's done something to you. And you and your little posse can stop spying on me, too, because it won't do you a bit of good!"

Nell squinted at her. "New coat, Lucy?"

Lucy ignored her, trying to pin Susan with her eyes.

Susan just looked back at her, puzzled. "What are you talking about, Lucy? Nobody was even looking at you."

The other girl raised an eyebrow. "Oh, weren't you? All of you five getting together now for four days just to talk? I know you're watching me practice, hoping I'll mess up! Don't try to deny it!"

Nell cocked her head. "You're practicing for what, again?"

Lucy looked mortally offended.

"My part in the play, of course!"

"Oh!" Susan said, her face clearing. "I'd forgotten all about that!"

Lucy turned red, pressed her lips together, and stalked off, crushing paper all the way. The children watched her go.

"That part. I could care less about it now," Susan said. "It all seems so long ago, doesn't it?"

"It sure does," Max said. "I can't get my head around the time change. No time here, and so much there. I've got to figure out how that worked."

Susan's eyes swept across the school yard again. "Doesn't it bother you, though? I'm happy to be home — you know I am — but it just seems so — I don't know — limited. Filled with Lucy Driscolls, I mean."

Max shrugged. He was sitting on the back of the bench, teetering there, and enjoying the crisp air.

"It's not, though," he said, looking up into the winter sky. "She's silly, but the world in general's not. There's plenty going on! After science today, Mr. Shire showed me a list of the greatest new inventions and discoveries of the decade. Did you know they've got windmills that can fly now, to get energy from the jet stream? And they've found a sugar molecule that might have started life on Earth! People are inventing new things all the time! It's huge!"

"He's right," Nell said. "It's different here, but that doesn't make it smaller."

Max got up. "You know, we were kind of moping."

He ran off to join the kickball game. Jean was right behind him, making a beeline for her friends near the jungle gym.

Nell shook her head. "It's no use wanting to go back, Susan. We'd only be missing home again, like we did before. It's one or the other, and if I have to choose, I choose home." She, too, trotted away to join her friends.

Susan said nothing for a minute. She glanced at Kate, who sat swinging her legs and thinking.

"What do you say, Kate? Do you miss it?"

"A little," she said. "But I missed home, too. Nell's right."

"Even school?" Susan asked. "Did you miss that?"

Kate laughed. "Not that, no."

They watched Lucy Driscoll another moment, pondering.

From near the jungle gym, some of Kate's friends ran up, calling to Kate to join them in a game of soccer.

"Go on," Susan said when she saw Kate hesitate.

"You should go, too, Susan."

"I will," Susan told her. "In a bit."

Kate went off, and Susan sat another second, letting her eyes sweep across the school yard. Max had it right — the world was big. She didn't want to see it the way Lucy Driscoll did, thinking this was all of it. She got up and went to find her friends.

And so it ended, in its way.

But Susan would say that once told, a story is never really ended.

Jean asked her about it for a long time after they returned, when blue window time came around each night. She wanted to know if the window, of its own accord, would ever open again.

Listening, Nell reminded her that a closed door could always be opened if someone wanted it enough.

And Max said that windows, anyway, were not like doors. Even when tight shut, windows let in the light.

Like many things Max said, this confused Jean for a long time. He talked of resonance and circles that vibrated, one affecting the other, even when they never touched. Jean thought that Max was being difficult, and she wondered what any of it had to do with windows, and falling through them.

But Kate thought that it was like something Susan had told her not long ago. If you lived in a world of walls, still, doors could be made.

And windows.